Praise for

THE PRISONER IN THE CASTLE

"The colonel sums it up best on page ten: 'If you take a pretty girl and teach her how to kill, it can cause problems.' Not just problems—*electrifying* action and nonstop surprises. I loved this book!"

—R. L. STINE, *New York Times* bestselling author of
the Goosebumps and Fear Street series

"Perfectly paced and brimming with intrigue and rich historical detail, *The Prisoner in the Castle* is an extraordinarily satisfying novel. Susan Elia MacNeal proves once again that she is a master, both at crafting characters and creating suspense."

—TASHA ALEXANDER, *New York Times* bestselling
author of the Lady Emily series

"*The Prisoner in the Castle* had me at 'new Maggie Hope mystery.' But once you add *And Then There Were None* and a Scottish castle, how could any mystery reader resist? Darkly atmospheric, enchantingly macabre, and as beautifully woven as a clan tartan."

—LAUREN WILLIG, *New York Times* bestselling
author of *The English Wife*

"*The Prisoner in the Castle* is a double agent of a novel! At the outset, it appears like a clever riff on Agatha Christie, but a few quick turns prove it to be an utterly modern, gripping thriller. Maggie Hope is smarter than ever, and Susan Elia MacNeal is truly at the height of her powers."

—SUJATA MASSEY, author of
The Widows of Malabar Hill

"MacNeal uses Christie's *And Then There Were None* as a framework for a character-driven mystery/thriller that successfully emulates the original."

—*Kirkus Reviews*

"Another literary tour de force . . . From the book's perfectly calibrated plot to its incisively etched characters, everything is handled with perfect finesse by the author."

—*The Poisoned Pen Newsletter*

Praise for Susan Elia MacNeal's

NEW YORK TIMES AND USA TODAY BESTSELLING MAGGIE HOPE MYSTERIES

Susan Elia MacNeal was awarded the Barry Award for
Mr. Churchill's Secretary.

Her Maggie Hope novels have been nominated for:

The Edgar Award · The Dilys Award · The Sue Feder Historical Memorial Award ·
The Bruce Alexander Memorial Historical Mystery Award · The Macavity Award ·
The Agatha Award · The Lefty Award · The Goodreads Choice Award ·
The International Thriller Writers Award

"I can't wait for the next . . . Susan Elia MacNeal."

—BILL CLINTON, "By the Book,"
The New York Times Book Review

"Delightful . . . as sweet as it is intriguing."

—*USA Today*

"Enthralling."

—*Mystery Scene*

"MacNeal layers the story with plenty of atmospheric, Blitz-era details and an appealing working-girl frame story as Maggie and her roommates juggle the demands of rationing and air raids with more mundane worries about boyfriends. . . . The period ambience will win the day for fans."

—*Booklist*

"With a smart, code-breaking mathematician heroine, abundant World War II spy intrigue, and a whiff of romance, this series has real luster. The author leaves readers with a mind-boggling conclusion that hints at Maggie's next assignment."

—*Library Journal* (starred review)

"Highly recommended . . . This is a series that gets stronger and more interesting with each book."

—*Deadly Pleasures*

BY SUSAN ELIA MacNEAL

Mr. Churchill's Secretary

Princess Elizabeth's Spy

His Majesty's Hope

The Prime Minister's Secret Agent

Mrs. Roosevelt's Confidante

The Queen's Accomplice

The Paris Spy

The Prisoner in the Castle

THE PRISONER IN THE CASTLE

The Prisoner in the Castle

A Maggie Hope Mystery

SUSAN ELIA MacNEAL

BANTAM BOOKS

NEW YORK

2019 Bantam Books Trade Paperback Edition

Copyright © 2018 by Susan Elia
Excerpt from *The King's Justice* by Susan Elia MacNeal
copyright © 2019 by Susan Elia

Published in the United States by Bantam Books, an imprint of Random House, a division of Penguin Random House LLC, New York.

BANTAM BOOKS and the HOUSE colophon are registered trademarks of Penguin Random House LLC.

Originally published in hardcover in the United States by Bantam Books, an imprint of Random House, a division of Penguin Random House LLC, in 2018.

This book contains an excerpt from the forthcoming book *The King's Justice* by Susan Elia MacNeal. This excerpt has been set for this edition only and may not reflect the final content of the forthcoming edition.

LIBRARY OF CONGRESS CATALOGING-IN-PUBLICATION DATA
Names: MacNeal, Susan Elia, author.
Title: The prisoner in the castle: a Maggie Hope mystery / Susan Elia MacNeal.
Description: New York: Bantam Books, [2018] | Series: Maggie Hope; 8
Identifiers: LCCN 2018024610 | ISBN 9780525621096 (paperback) |
ISBN 9780399593833 (Ebook)
Subjects: LCSH: Women spies—Fiction. | World War, 1939–1945—Great Britain—
Fiction. | BISAC: FICTION / Mystery & Detective / Women Sleuths. |
FICTION / Mystery & Detective | Traditional British. | FICTION / Historical. |
GSAFD: Spy stories. | Historical fiction.
Classification: LCC PS3613.A2774 P75 2018 | DDC 813/.6—dc23
LC record available at https://lccn.loc.gov/2018024610

Printed in the United States of America on acid-free paper

randomhousebooks.com

2 4 6 8 9 7 5 3 1

Title-page image: © iStockphoto.com

Book design by Dana Leigh Blanchette

To the brave women and men of Britain's Special Operations
Executive, who trained and taught at Arisaig House
in Lochaber, Inverness-shire, on the west coast
of the Scottish Highlands.

Thank you to Sarah Winnington-Ingram, Kitty Rose
Winnington-Ingram, Magnus Winnington-Ingram, and the
entire family and staff of Arisaig House, who honor
the memory of the SOE agents who trained there
and who helped me research this book.

There is a passion for hunting something deeply implanted in the human breast.

—CHARLES DICKENS,
Oliver Twist

There is no hunting like the hunting of man, and those who have hunted armed men long enough and liked it, never care for anything else thereafter.

—ERNEST HEMINGWAY,
"On the Blue Water"

Am fear bhitheas trocaireach ri anam, cha bhi e mi-throcaireach ri bhruid.

[He who is merciful to his soul will not be unmerciful to a beast.]

—GAELIC SAYING

THE PRISONER IN THE CASTLE

Prologue

Always remember, when you're on the run, instinct will take over—and if you're not careful, you'll become nothing more than an animal. The words echoed in her memory. *But you must never stop thinking, reasoning, applying your mind. Only then will you be able to complete your mission. And escape.*

Camilla Oddell, code-named Nadine, was part of the Special Operations Executive or SOE, the hush-hush organization created by Winston Churchill to "set Europe ablaze" and conduct espionage, sabotage, and reconnaissance behind enemy lines in occupied countries. She'd been trained by Captain Eric Sykes, a former officer in the Shanghai Municipal Police, who specialized in silent killing in close quarters, at a paramilitary training camp on the western coast of Scotland. And now his words resounded in her head as she prepared to make her escape.

It was just past midnight, the moon distorted behind a smear of clouds, the sky bigger than imagining. Camilla was navigating a brooding late-autumn terrain of pine forests, mist-swathed mountains, and cold rushing streams. The velvety darkness—thick, almost substantial—blanketed the landscape, rendering it in shades of violet, black, and blue. The moonlight gave the night a peculiar texture and wild intimacy, the knife-edged winds fragrant with salty sea air.

She looked like a shadow, wearing coveralls and leather gloves, her pale face and swan-like neck blackened with coal, her glossy golden hair tucked up and covered by a navy knit cap. She'd studied a map of the woods before setting out; she knew the landscape and where the safe house stood. What she didn't know was how she was supposed to get there—and who was out there lying in wait for her. Did they have a head start? Or were they somewhere behind her?

Camilla picked her way through the maze of conifers, sped on by adrenaline and raw nerves. Her breathing was ragged; her heartbeat pounded in her ears. She saw a rock-edged pool overhung with birch trees glowing white in the moonlight. She stepped on brittle bones in the grass, then stiffened as the cracking rang out like gunshots in the darkness.

She waited, frozen, her senses straining, heart thudding. *Breathe,* she told herself. *Think.* She took silent gulps of frigid air. Overhead, gnarled tree limbs spread naked against the star-studded expanse of the sky. Pine trees creaked back and forth in the wind and she heard a far-off shriek of an owl.

As the refrain of "Run, Rabbit, Run" wound through her head, Camilla broke into a sprint, following the faint deer path. It constantly changed direction, uphill and down, obstructed by rocks and roots, treacherous with frost. It led her to a stream, the peaty water splashing over stones and pebbles, glittering silver. Her foot slipped on a lichen-covered rock. She stumbled, one heavy boot sucked into the freezing mud. There was a swirl of shadow and a sharp bark as some startled animals escaped from the underbrush, leaping into the water and diving under. Camilla pressed her lips together as she pulled her leg out of the black ooze.

She crept over a wooden bridge, then ran through a tangle of bare willow branches. Deeper and deeper she wended her way through the woods, the fragrance of evergreen enveloping her, the pine needles cushioning her footfalls.

At the edge of a clearing, she stopped, listening. But beyond the rush of the stream and a sudden flap of bat wings, there was no sound, no hint of anyone on her trail. As she leaned against an ancient oak, taking a moment to gather her strength, she caught a flicker of movement from the corner of her eye. She froze, willing herself to turn to stone, like a beast trapped in the crosshairs of a gun.

And then she caught a glimpse of it—a shadowy, spectral shape, where there hadn't been a shape before. Someone. Someone tracking her. Hunting her.

She watched, shrinking into the gloom, as the man stood motionless, as if undecided. Finally, he took off into the wood away from her, his pace silent and steady.

If only he knew how close he'd come to finding her! The thrill of escape coursed through her veins and she felt strong, confident. She would make it. In the distance, she could hear the faint sound of a train's whistle and waves lapping the shore. Relief flooded her. She was almost there.

Camilla ducked through the thick undergrowth until she could see a flagstone house across a field in the gauzy moonlight—the agreed-upon pickup spot. With a last check of her surroundings, she left the relative protection of the forest and made her way over the frosted ground.

Then something lunged at her.

She spun. A figure loomed before her, a pair of eyes visible in a blacked-out face. Camilla panicked and tried to rush past, but gloved hands grabbed for her. She swung round, hitting and kicking.

"Stop it," the man ordered through clenched teeth. "You've been caught. The game's over."

Camilla stilled and then, without warning, kneed him in the

groin. When he sagged, she kicked him with her steel-toed boot, knocking him to the ground. Still, he held on to her. They struggled, rolling on the rough grass. Amid the panting, grasping, and the harsh breathing, she remembered Captain Sykes's words: *Kill if you have to.* She grasped the man's right arm and twisted.

He made an unholy cry as the bone cracked, but Camilla didn't let go. Her animal instincts had kicked in. She wanted to hurt him. She wanted to destroy him.

Biting her lip in anticipation, Camilla tightened her hold on his arm. She grabbed his head with her right hand and braced his chest with her left. She didn't hear the cries for help, for mercy—all she knew was she had him in her thrall. She held absolute power over life and death in that moment. The realization led to a frisson of terror combined with wonder and then sinful pride.

Camilla took his skull and twisted. His neck cracked and he went limp. A sinister, intoxicating joy flowed through her. She knelt over him, panting, triumphant, completed.

"Are you mad?" shouted a voice in her ear as a man yanked her up. There were more voices approaching, and someone switched on a flashlight, the shuttered beams piercing the darkness. The man Camilla had attacked lay on the ground, his legs and arms akimbo, his head at a strange angle.

"Judas!" the stranger exclaimed. "Eddie? Eddie?" He dropped to his knees and pressed his ear to the man's chest. Finally, he rocked back on his heels and looked up at Camilla. "You killed him," he said. "You killed Eddie."

Too late, reality thundered back. Camilla realized the body in black was Eddie Dove, a wisp of a man in her training unit, always with a joke at the ready and the smile of a sad clown. He was a few years younger than she, with impeccable French he'd learned from his Norman-born mother, and a talent for setting people at ease thanks to his pub-owning English father. Funny, gangly, awkward, skinny Eddie Dove. And now he was dead.

Captain Michael Lewis—*now* she recognized him, *now* she knew him—scrambled to his feet, hands clenched. "Are you insane? You killed a man! One of our own, for Christ's sake!"

"I didn't know it was Eddie, sir," she gasped. "He—he tried to stop me."

"He was *supposed* to stop you! It's a training mission! And you were brought down, fair and square. You were supposed to give in, to surrender, dammit! It was a bloody"—Lewis shook his head in disbelief, unable to find the right word—"*exercise*!" Around him, the other trainees shuffled their feet.

"I'm . . . sorry," Camilla managed.

"You lot." Lewis pointed to the others. "Carry Eddie's body to the infirmary. You—" He stabbed a finger at Camilla. "Come with me."

They walked in silence through the fields to the main house, the odor of woodsmoke from the chimneys carrying on the wind. "Why the hell did you do that?" asked Lewis finally. His voice was subdued, thickened by his Shetland brogue.

"I'm sorry," she repeated. "I can still go to France, though—yes?" she asked, her voice high and reedy. "I can still go?"

Lewis didn't answer.

Colonel Alistair Rogers sat at his desk in his office, a wood-paneled room reeking of leather, damp, and stale cigarette smoke. It had once been the library of Arisaig House, a Scottish shooting lodge on the west coast, commandeered by the British government to train SOE agents after war was declared against Germany in 1939. Rogers was in his sixties, with spiky brown hair dusted with white, narrow shoulders, and sunken cheeks. A fire crackled behind the grate, the flames dancing blue, and from the field outside came the muted *baa*s of grazing sheep. The colonel squinted through his glasses, reading over Captain Lewis's report of the previous night's events.

There was a knock at the open door. Rogers glanced up from his paperwork, removed his spectacles, and pushed back his narrow wooden wheelchair. "Ah, Captain Lewis—come in. Just the person I wanted to speak to. Finished your report about Oddell and Dove. Terrible. Simply terrible. We're getting word to the lad's parents."

"I spoke with them myself earlier, sir," replied Lewis, stepping inside. He was wiry, broad-shouldered, and sunburned, a man who'd lived his nearly forty years out of doors, his eyes shadowed from lack of sleep. He glanced around the room—the bookshelves were empty, the brocade curtains were dusty and moth-eaten, and a water stain marred the high ceiling. Out the mullioned windows, a reddish light was seeping above the horizon. Sunrise came late in the Scottish autumn.

"In your report, you say Miss Oddell broke the young man's neck with her bare hands?" Rogers asked.

Lewis made his way to the fireplace, where an official photograph of the King hung next to one of a glaring Winston Churchill over the mantel. He looked up at the image of the Prime Minister. "Gloved hands, sir. But yes."

Rogers rolled his chair out from behind the desk. "She's well trained."

"Indeed—Sykes said she was one of his most promising students," Lewis replied, staring, unseeing, up at King George. "I've overseen her training myself."

"From your notes—" The colonel stopped his chair close to the captain. "I take it Miss Camilla Oddell likes killing."

"I'm afraid so."

"What's her background?"

"She's a society girl. A debutante, from Kent. Father in the House of Lords. Posh." He glanced down at Rogers. "You know the type, sir."

Rogers turned up the corners of his lips in a ghost of a smile. "I've always suspected debutantes' hidden capacity for violence."

Lewis didn't laugh. "Sir, a man is dead. Eddie—Edwin—Dove, a promising young agent. This was the final training exercise. When this girl came up against resistance, her violent tendencies emerged. And she couldn't control them."

"In our line of work, I'm not sure that's a bad thing." Rogers rolled his chair to the windows, where he gazed out over a victory garden, down to what had once been a croquet lawn, now being used by agents in coveralls practicing jujitsu. Beyond the grass, a thick forest of rowan, alder, and evergreens led down to the silvery waters of Loch nan Ceall. "She has the looks, she speaks French beautifully, and she's athletic. This killer instinct might just serve her well in the field."

"But what if this 'killer instinct' jeopardizes a mission? Endangers our own people?" The captain cleared his throat. "Sir, I don't trust this girl is safe. Under the stress of operational conditions, she might turn on anybody." He cracked his knuckles. "One of us."

"We need bodies in France desperately, Captain. I've just spoken with Colonel Gaskell in London. F-Section needs more agents. Now we've lost—" He gestured to the file on his desk. "What's his name again?"

"Dove. Eddie Dove."

"Dove, yes." He pivoted his chair from the window to face the captain. "So we can't afford to cut another. We've been training Camilla Oddell for months. It would be a damn shame to lose her now."

"Sir, with all due respect, I must disagree. I've worked with her. She's young. Maybe too young for all this. And she relishes violence—delights in it. I'm not a psychiatrist, but I think she has all the makings of a sadist. She should be invalided out." He turned back to the fire, adding under his breath, "Beasts should be kept in cages."

"I suppose if you take a pretty girl and teach her how to kill, it can cause problems," the colonel mused. "Thank heavens women in civilian life have no idea what they're capable of."

Lewis looked back at Rogers, unsmiling. "Sir, I recommend she be sent to the cooler."

Rogers narrowed his eyes. "That's not a recommendation to be made lightly, Captain."

"I'm aware, sir."

"You're certain?"

"I am."

Rogers sighed in disappointment. "Well, since you've spent the most time with her, I defer to your judgment. Prepare the orders, then. 'Special training,' and all that."

Lewis nodded. "Very good, sir." Some of the tension in his shoulders loosened. "Thank you, sir."

"It's not good at all, Captain Lewis," snapped Rogers, rolling back around to his desk. "The Baker Street Boys in charge of F-Section will be apoplectic—*two* agents lost on our end, and when they're needed the most. And you're sure we don't have a choice, now do we?"

"No, sir. I don't believe we do."

Rogers picked up a heavy red telephone receiver. "Have Miss Camilla Oddell come to my office," he barked to his secretary. "Soon as possible."

"It's *Lady* Camilla, sir," Lewis offered.

"No titles here. Let's get this nasty piece of business wrapped up and done, Lewis. And then I must think of something to say in order to placate Colonel Gaskell."

Camilla Oddell was summoned from the women's dormitory to the main house and then let through to Colonel Rogers's office. In the daylight, even dressed in denim coveralls and plimsoles, she appeared slender and graceful as a Lalique figure. And although sub-dued, she radiated an almost rude good health and vigor.

"Please sit, Miss Oddell," said Rogers in a tight voice. Lewis nodded. The petite blonde glanced from one officer to the other, but did as she was bid, crossing one trim ankle behind the other, folding her hands in her lap.

Lewis avoided her glance. "Last night—didn't go quite as we'd hoped." Outside the windows, a ragged skein of geese flew in V-formation under the brightening sky, crying out in syncopation.

"I know." She dropped her gaze. "Eddie is dead. Again, I'm so, so very sorry."

Rogers gazed across his desk to the girl. "Cigarette?" He pulled out a silver case from his jacket pocket and offered it to her.

"No. No, thank you, sir." There was a strained silence. "I expect you will—" Her voice quavered. "Bring charges?"

"No, no," Rogers answered, plucking a cigarette out, then tucking the case back. "Nobody wants any trouble. In fact—" He gave a tight smile as he flicked his lighter. "We have marching orders for you—you'll be leaving this afternoon." He took a long pull, exhaling blue smoke.

She blinked long lashes. "Sir?"

"You'll be leaving for a special training establishment," Lewis said. "We call it Forbidden Island. You'll be briefed upon arrival."

" 'Forbidden Island'?" echoed the young woman.

"It's a specialized training camp, in a remote location," explained Lewis, his voice reassuring. "Has to be—essential work happening there. Vital to the war effort, of course."

"But—but I thought I'd be sent to France!" Camilla protested, staring openmouthed at the colonel. "Sir."

"At some point . . ." Rogers began. "But in the meantime, you're assigned to Forbidden Island. A car will take you to Mallaig, and then a boat to the isle from there."

"And this Forbidden Island, sir—what sort of thing goes on there?"

"Ah, Miss Oddell—that's top-secret. But don't worry—" He exhaled another stream of smoke. "You'll learn everything when you arrive."

Chapter One

"It's dark so early these days," said Maggie Hope, staring out locked windows at the lengthening shadows.

It wasn't yet four o'clock, but daylight in the highlands of Scotland was only grudgingly cast out before it was reeled back in again. The November sun was setting, touching the black and bulky hills of the island with glimmers of gold. Outside the oriel windows, Maggie could see past brittle old apple trees to a flock of geese that had settled in an empty field. Beyond lay the ocean. "Six hours of daylight's a meager ration. But then, we're used to rationing now."

From across a mahogany desk the size of a small boat, Dr. Charles Jaeger permitted himself a smile. He pressed his palms together, his long fingers tapered and elegant. Maggie had met many, many pale older British men since she'd moved from Boston to London in 1937, but Jaeger was colorless almost to the point of being invisible—his hair and eyebrows white, his face ashen, his eyes bleached blue. The doctor looked more like an ascetic saint carved from marble than a flesh-and-blood man. "You're always gazing outside, Miss Hope," he remarked in a low, sonorous voice, sounding amused.

In the late afternoon light, the sea was a glittering spearmint green. It stretched to the horizon, no land visible, an endless expanse of rippling water, tipped by white-capped waves. "Looking for an escape, I suppose." Maggie was a slim twenty-seven-year-old woman with thick coppery hair pulled back neatly into a low bun. She put down her knitting needles and the navy sock she was working on— socks for soldiers, each with Morse code V for Victory knit in.

"Watching the play of light on the water has been one of my comforts here—I wish I could draw or paint it. The ocean's huge, deep, and powerful, but we only see the surface. The secret is what lies beneath, isn't it?"

"And what do you think lurks below the surface, Miss Hope?" The doctor was backlit by the setting sun, a dark silhouette against citrine.

Foreboding crept over her, making the hairs on the back of her neck rise. *We're at war. The enemy always might be closer than we think.* "U-boats, most likely. Wolf packs of them."

"I don't mean literally."

"Well then, who knows?" Maggie turned her gaze back to him. "Salmon, before they make their way back up the rivers and streams to spawn? Sunken pirate ships? Monsters, mermaids—they call them 'selkies' here, don't they? The Blue Men of the Minch?" Maggie had learned from the castle's housekeeper that the Blue Men, also called 'storm kelpies,' were a race of sea devils believed to live in the waters of the Hebrides. "The sea's always a mystery, isn't it?"

She sat across the desk from him in a red-leather club chair, noting a shadow box of pinned butterflies hanging on the opposite wall. "And what would your Freud say about the ocean, Doctor?"

Dr. Jaeger was a psychologist who visited Forbidden Island once a month. A fisherman named Broden MacLean brought him on his small boat, along with food, supplies, and fresh laundry. The doctor's job was to monitor the physical and mental health of the prisoners—"the trainees," as they were euphemistically called. He was always immaculate, his Jermyn Street suits well pressed, his crisp white shirts giving the impression he could perform surgery at any moment. Dr. Jaeger met with each prisoner in the castle's library, a chilly, wood-paneled space redolent of beeswax polish, cigarette smoke, and dry rot, with glass-fronted bookcases and dark mahogany panels that stretched up to a plaster-medallioned ceiling. A reproduction of the English artist Sir Edwin Landseer's *The Sanctuary* hung over the fireplace's mantel—a painting of a wounded deer who had swum to an island, a momentary place of refuge from the violence of the hunt. In profile, the animal's large dark eye looked both accusing and sad.

Even though it was a library, the books looked to have been bought for display purposes only. The few tooled-leather–bound tomes that looked read were on hunting and fishing: James Watson Lyall's *Sportsman's and Tourist's Guide to the Rivers, Lochs, Moors and Deer Forests of Scotland*, Izaak Walton's *The Compleat Angler*, and the like. They were flanked by a selection of Sir Walter Scott novels, while H. G. Wells's *The Island of Doctor Moreau* kept company next to a set of Agatha Christie mysteries.

The blood-curdling howl of a passing Manx shearwater startled them both. The black and white birds were everywhere on the island, living on top of the rocky peaks of the eroded volcano, their loud screams wild and eerie. As the bird dove, like a Spitfire attacking a U-boat, the doctor scribbled something in his notebook, then glanced up. "I'm more of a Jung disciple myself," he told her, "and he had quite a bit to say regarding the ocean and the unconscious."

"I'm sure." Maggie gazed through a sunbeam thick with dust motes to the calendar on the desk—the date was November 12, 1942. Her last memory of being in London was June 22. One hundred and forty-three days had passed since she'd been brought, against her will, to Forbidden Island. For more than twenty weeks, nearly five months, she'd been held prisoner in the island's castle, unable to help the war effort, prohibited from letting her friends and family know she was safe. The inmates were completely sequestered. No phone calls were allowed. No letters could be sent or received. No radio communication was permitted. Beyond the castle, there was nowhere to go on the island—no town, no village, only uninhabited woods and lochs.

Forbidden Island, really the Isle of Scarra, located just off the western coast of Scotland, was a remote overgrown wilderness of three square miles, with moors, forests, craggy inlets, and shining sands. Golden eagles soared overhead and red deer wandered under the pines. There were no boats, of course—beyond the one that visited once a month—but even if there were, the island was surrounded by whirlpools, rendering passage treacherous at best.

Maggie and her fellow prisoners were housed in what had once been a shooting lodge, an improbably ugly structure called Killoch Castle, with long, unconvincing battlements and graceless corner turrets. The "castle" was a lumbering reification of Victorian and Edwardian excess, a florid fantasy of a medieval manse built as a private residence in 1900 for Sir Marcus Killoch, a textile tycoon from Lancashire. Sir Marcus had designed the structure in a castellated Tudor style, using blood-red sandstone shipped over from Annan at great expense. It had its own electricity supply, as well as modern plumbing and heating.

In its day, the castle had been infamous for luxury and excess. It boasted a Japanese garden, a maze, a bowling green, and a golf course—all created using topsoil imported from Ayrshire. A glass greenhouse had once housed tropical plants and flowers, as well as hummingbirds, turtles, and alligators, while the hunting hounds slept in a heated kennel. There was even a small stone cottage on the side of the mountain, a hermitage for a resident hermit, who would dispense wisdom to any inquiring guests. When Marcus Killoch died in 1922, he'd left no heirs. And when the war had broken out, the abandoned castle was taken over by the British government.

Maggie hated Killoch Castle. She thought it one of the most loathsome buildings she'd ever seen, a monument to colossal ego, bad taste, and greed. In her opinion, Marcus Killoch was the worst kind of nouveau riche Englishman, who played at being an island laird with his toy castle, rifles, and hunting trophies.

Dr. Jaeger remained silent, pen poised over paper. Maggie understood what he was doing; his prolonged silence was a technique, designed to make her talk. She recognized it from her spy training with the SOE. Still, she knew she could outlast him; he had nothing on the Gestapo interrogator she'd encountered in Paris.

Without compromising his ramrod posture, Dr. Jaeger tilted his head, face blank as a Lewis stone. "This is your fifth session, Miss Hope. And you haven't revealed anything yet. Anything of real import, that is."

"I like the peace in the library, Doctor. It's an excellent place to think." She picked up her half-finished sock. "And to knit. Since I can't be an SOE agent anymore—or do anything to help the war effort, really—the least I can do is help keep our soldiers' feet warm."

"You're not alone, Miss Hope. Most agents brought to the island rankle at even the idea of mandated therapy."

"Well, not me. I know you're just doing your job. So, let's make this simple. When you realize I really and truly won't talk—at least not about what those in the British Intelligence fear I might let slip—you'll release me. And I'll go back to regular life." She smiled. "And since I'll never talk, you might as well let me go now."

"Ah, Miss Hope." He raised his eyebrows. "I'm afraid it's not that easy. And even if it were, I don't have the authority to release you, or anyone."

Maggie's needles stopped midpurl. "Tell me what I need to do. To get out of this place. To leave this moldering castle and get off this island. Who can you talk to? Colonel Martens? Tell him I won't say anything. And I never will. I signed the Official Secrets Act."

She had once been part of a mission greater than herself, and now she missed it desperately. There was a war going on, a global war determining if people lived in freedom or died in slavery, and she wanted to do her bit. Something. *Anything*. Because without victory there would be no survival, for her or anyone she loved. "I'm no good to anyone locked away here. All the trouble His Majesty's government went through to train me, just wasted."

Maggie had been brought to Forbidden Island because she'd been asked by Colonel Martens to participate in a lie she'd felt was reprehensible. It wasn't lost on her that she'd been asked, and refused, only days after escaping from Gestapo custody in Nazi-occupied Paris, a costly disaster both professionally and personally. *And yet . . .*

The question still tormented Maggie, even after time on the island to think. *How desperate must a situation be for a certain action to be acceptable in war? How heinous must a course of action become before people decide a line has been crossed? And was it forgivable in the fight against an evil as pernicious as Nazism? Does the end ever justify the tainted means?*

"Miss Hope, when you were first here, you didn't speak for weeks."

"I—I had nothing to say."

"You stayed in bed."

"I was tired. That mission to Paris was exhausting."

"You threw things at the nurse. A vase of flowers, if I recall."

"I threw the vase at the wall, not the nurse," she clarified, resuming her knitting. "The flowers annoyed me. So very . . . cheerful. I loathe marigolds."

"So you *do* remember the first weeks you were here."

"Some of it," Maggie admitted.

"Do you remember we had to sedate you? And, one night, strait-jacket you?"

"No!" Maggie had recollections of slipping through the cracks of sanity and going under, but she wasn't about to discuss them. Then, calmer: "No, I don't recall."

"Do you remember why you were brought here?"

Yes, I do—but you're daft if you think I'll tell you.

"You were in F-Section," Dr. Jaeger prodded. "What went wrong in Paris?"

Maggie wasn't about to take the bait. "It's cold today, isn't it?" She set down the sock and buttoned up her heavy wool cardigan.

"You're changing the subject."

"As you well know, Doctor, I never discuss war-related information—with anyone."

Dr. Jaeger gave a wry smile. "I can see you're still suspicious. And I understand why."

"I'm under house arrest. Whatever I say to you, you'll undoubtedly relay to them."

"And who is *them*?"

"Colonel Henrik Martens, Churchill's so-called Master of Deception. Colonel Bishop with MI-Six. And whoever else they're working with. The people in charge of . . ."

"Of what, Maggie?"

F-Section. Agents going missing in France. A compromised network in Paris. A double, maybe triple agent. The secret of Pas-de-Calais and Normandy and the invasion of occupied Europe. "You know I can't say. And how much longer will I be imprisoned here?"

"And I can't tell you that, I'm afraid."

"Look," she stated, "I'll talk about myself, but not my work for SOE. Is that a worthy compromise?" She raised an eyebrow. "Besides, have you read my file?"

The doctor leaned back in his chair. "It's a page-turner."

Maggie gave a single sharp laugh. "Tell me about it—I lived it. And whatever they want you to know about me is in there. You don't need me to share anything more."

"I want to help you, Miss Hope. Will you let me?"

"I'm fine, Doctor. Just not sleeping. It's been months and months and I can't sleep."

"Since when?"

"Since I was drugged and kidnapped and imprisoned here," she replied tartly.

"I can prescribe you Veronal—sleeping tablets."

"I'd rather not." Maggie swallowed and picked up her knitting again, needles clicking at a furious pace.

"Why don't we discuss your childhood?"

Why don't you stuff it in your ear?

"You mentioned your father died last winter. Perhaps we should talk about that?"

"My father, my mother, my Aunt Edith, who raised me in Boston . . . It's all in my files, I assume."

"At least you must have had a stable childhood."

Maggie thought about growing up on the campus of Wellesley College in Massachusetts, taken in by her aunt, who had no real affinity for young children, doing her best and heating meals over the Bunsen burner in her lab. About falling in love with mathematics and attending the college as a scholarship student, graduating Phi Beta Kappa and planning to do graduate work at the Massachusetts Institute of Technology—one of the few universities to accept women—before her English grandmother died and left her the family house in London. *Which led to my working for Mr. Churchill during the Blitz . . .*

"Yes, I'm certainly grateful to my aunt."

"But how do you feel?"

"How do I *feel*?" Maggie took a deep breath. "Broken. Powerless. Trapped." She looked him in the eyes, hands tangled in yarn. "Dying by inches every day, unable to fight this war." She thought of friends she'd lost. "I just want to do my bit."

"What about creating a family of your own?" the doctor asked. "You're still a young woman—you could get married, have children . . ."

She made a dismissive sound. "With someone on this island? It's not as if I'm spoiled for choice." There were nine other prisoners on the island, as well as Captain Bernard Evans, their portly, benevolent jailer—"the zookeeper," they called him. In addition, there was a Scottish family of three native to Scarra, the McNaughtons, who kept up the castle, and did the cleaning and cooking.

"True." His voice remained bland. "Is there anyone back home?"

The man Maggie had once believed was the love of her life was now working in Hollywood on wartime propaganda. And as for Detective Chief Inspector Durgin—well, she had no illusions he was still waiting for her back in London, not after her leaving with barely a word in the spring and never contacting him again. "No," she said. "There's no one back home."

"And you're sure there's no one here? There *are* a few single men your age."

When she'd begun to socialize with her fellow prisoners, she'd spent some time with a man named Sayid Inayat Khan, playing chess and card games. He was handsome, certainly, with broad shoulders, shiny jet-black hair, and dark eyes glinting with humor. There was a slight gap between his front teeth that gave his smile a disarming aspect. But the young medical doctor had let her know early on that he was engaged—his parents had arranged for him to marry a Sufi Muslim woman. It made things easier, in a way. Even considering the possibility of a relationship with him was taboo, given their religious and cultural differences. Still, she enjoyed their time together; the two met regularly to see who could memorize the most poetry in the shortest period of time.

"No, no one here."

"Miss Hope, if I were you—"

She arched an eyebrow. "Yes?"

"Well, I'd make the best of it. Most people would give their right arm to be in a place like this in wartime—plenty of good food, warm fires, fine whiskey." He paused to choose the correct word: "*Interesting* company." He put down his fountain pen and straightened his papers.

Down the long corridor came the faint sound of someone picking out the tune of "Three Blind Mice" on the piano in the great room.

"I suppose," Maggie said, "a bunch of quarantined SOE agents all trained to kill silently and at close range—without any work to keep them busy—are indeed 'interesting.'"

"Miss Hope, I'm available, if and when you want to talk," Jaeger said as he locked his notes in the desk's top drawer. "Perhaps next month you'll be more loquacious. And take heart—your stay is only until this beastly war is over."

"And then?"

He glanced up. "I beg your pardon?"

"And then—what? We're all allowed to return to civilian life? Knowing what we can do? We'll sprinkle ourselves with pixie dust and fly back to London from Neverland?" *Will they really ever just let us go?* She had no faith in SOE or any of the intelligence services now. Their agents' lives were disposable to them, as she had learned all too well.

"Until next month, Miss Hope."

Sod that, Maggie thought. *I refuse to be locked away like a criminal, when I've done absolutely nothing wrong—nothing but serve my country. One way or another, I'm getting off this godforsaken island.*

When Camilla arrived on the Isle of Scarra, Captain Evans did his best to make her feel welcome. Although he was an ugly man, with the face of a gargoyle and clothing that strained at the buttons, his smile was kind, his voice soothing, and his manner cordial. After she'd been shown to her room and had a chance to rest, he knocked.

"I hope you're settling in, Miss Oddell," he said when she opened the door, wearing her drab brown FANY uniform.

"Thank you, sir. It's all very nice." She saluted, and he returned the gesture. "But I'd like to report to my commanding officer."

"That is I," Evans replied. "Although we're rather informal here, as you'll learn. . . ."

When she appeared confused, he smiled. "Why don't you get your coat and I'll give you the ha'penny tour?"

They made their way over the castle's paths, their feet on the soil releasing a dank, mushroomy smell. "In the castle and on the grounds, you have complete liberty," he said as they entered the orangerie, the air significantly warmer than the outdoors. "The whole island, in fact, is yours to explore." Through the curved glass roof, the sun's rays were slanting. "Although I'm afraid there aren't any neighbors. If you need to borrow a cup of something, you'll have to wait for the next supply boat."

"And how often does it come?"

"Once a month. But we make sure you're sufficiently stocked, and as you can see, we grow plenty of fresh food." The captain warmed to his prepared lecture as they walked through the greenhouse, past beds of broad beans, lettuce, and carrots. "You have every sort of opportunity here—there's hunting and fishing, a wireless and a phonograph. There are books and newspapers, as well as table tennis and billiards—that room even boasts the first air-conditioning in Scotland to remove tobacco smoke, so it never becomes too hazy.

"We also have a Steinway grand piano. One of our trainees plays quite beautifully and a few others sing, or at least try. Of course I'd never criticize—they could kill me in my sleep!" He laughed. When Camilla didn't join in, he continued. "The food is first-rate and we even have films once a week, on Saturday evenings. The last one was *Bambi*, I believe. Oh, and there's an orchestrion!"

"What on earth is that?"

"It's an elaborate contraption said to emulate the sound of a forty-piece orchestra. It's run on electricity and operated by means of a large pinned music roll. The sound is produced by pipes."

"That's hardly relevant to our work as agents."

"No," he relented, "but I do find it interesting."

"This all sounds very nice, Captain Evans," Camilla said, stopping next to trays of onions left to ripen, "but when do I leave? When is my mission?"

"I'm sorry, Miss Oddell," the captain answered, "but your mission has been put on indefinite hold."

She frowned. "Sir, I don't understand. On hold?"

The captain folded his arms across his chest and leaned against a table crowded with strawberry pots brought in for the winter. "There's no easy way to put this, but you've been compromised. Because of the sensitive nature of our work in SOE, it's a security situation."

She shook her head, bewildered. "I've only just completed my training. I haven't been abroad. I don't know anything—I couldn't possibly know anything!"

The captain shrugged. "Sometimes the Germans find out things. And so entire missions must be scrapped. It's not your fault. There are close to a dozen other people here in the same circumstances. Everyone here has had special training. Everyone knows something. Everyone is a risk."

"You think I would compromise a mission?"

"Of course not. Not intentionally, at least. But when situations like this arise, we keep people here in 'the cooler.' On ice, if you will. Until the danger's passed."

"This is because of Eddie Dove, isn't it?" Camilla looked crestfallen, blinking back tears. "I just . . . I just wanted to do my job. Do something for the war effort."

"I know."

"So . . . I'm to stay here for a while?"

"Yes, but as I mentioned, there are plenty of things to keep you occupied. And I'm sure you'll find friends among the other guests."

"Colonel Rogers at Arisaig House talked about special training . . ."

"Well, you can't expect Colonel Rogers to tell you everything outright. There is a war on, you know."

She managed half a smile at the sentiment. "Will there be time before the boat leaves for me to write to my mother to let her know where I am? The last time we spoke I told her I was training at Arisaig. She doesn't know I've been moved."

Evans shook his head. "I'm sorry, Miss Oddell. There's no communication with the mainland from here. No phone calls can be made. No letters sent or received. Whatever you told your mother the last time you spoke will be what she believes you're doing now."

She made a frustrated sound. "You said I have to stay here 'until the danger's passed.' How long is that?"

"There's no way to know right now. Could be quite some time, I'm afraid."

She gasped. "But—but I'm ready! I want to go to France! I don't want to be cooped up here!"

"I know it's hard, but you'll come around—the guests always do." The captain gave her a patient smile, then clapped his hands. "We usually have cocktails in the great room at six-thirty. Would you care to join? After you've freshened up, of course." He stood and made for the door of the greenhouse.

"I don't—I—This—I can't—" Camilla flailed her arms—at the house, the island, everything. "This isn't *fair*!"

"Fair?" Evans nearly laughed. "We're at *war*, Miss Oddell. Fair has nothing to do with it."

"I'm ready!" she insisted. "I'm ready. I'm trained. I want to *go*." She stamped a small foot. The captain raised one eyebrow. "I shouldn't be here. You can't keep me here."

"As I said, you're free to go anywhere on the island." He opened the door and gestured to the tree line, wreathed in garlands of mist, lit by the red setting sun. "Perhaps you might like to go for a walk instead? The grounds are really quite lovely."

She stared at him through narrowed eyes for a long moment, and then her expression cleared. "You're absolutely right, Captain Evans. This is all just—a lot to take in. A walk sounds ideal. Time in nature always helps me clear my head."

"I concur." He held the door open and waited for her to precede him. "But do watch your step," he cautioned. "There are some un-expected dips and drops, even on the paths. Cocktails are at six-thirty. I will see you then."

Camilla smiled, but didn't reply.

Chapter Two

After her session with Dr. Jaeger, Maggie changed into a blue woolen dress with a soft bow on one shoulder and her pearl stud earrings, fixing her red hair in rolls secured by a tortoiseshell barrette. As she walked down the worm-infested wooden grand staircase and into the castle's great room, she was struck anew by its aggressive ugliness.

The agents of SOE joked its initials weren't actually for Special Operations Executive, but instead for Stately 'Omes of England. Maggie had trained and taught in enough old manor houses across Britain to get the joke; however, she'd never been in one so intact, so untouched as this one. At Killoch Castle there was no government-issue furniture, no maps with pushpins, no metal desks. It appeared as if Marcus Killoch himself had walked out mere minutes before, leaving the doors open. It certainly was the oddest country house in Britain that Maggie had been in—a mad and ill-proportioned fantasy of a castle with what could only be charitably called "eclectic" décor.

It had the usual great house elements: the elaborate scrolled ceiling, the scarred paneling, the heavy dark velvet curtains. The one unique element of Killoch Castle was the dizzying collection of taxidermied wild animals. The entire place had a particular odor as well;

the castle's red sandstone acted like sponge, soaking up but never releasing the queer smell of age, mildew, animal pelts, and secrets.

Maggie walked through the enormous two-storied space, her footfalls muffled by vast Persian carpets. She sidestepped a lion-skin rug complete with an open mouth and yellow fangs. *A cruel room,* she had decided when she'd first seen it, with its red-and-gold flecked wallpaper and scarlet moreen curtains. Outside the massive deep-set mullioned windows, taped for protection, wispy clouds scudded across the indigo sky. In the distance, the water of the bay appeared inky in the fading light.

"Miss Hope!"

Maggie started. "Oh, Mr. Crane—you scared me!"

Sitting on a brocade sofa of repellent design in the rough-stone recessed inglenook was Theodore "Teddy" Crane, one of her fellow prisoners. An avid fisherman, he was busy with a needle and bobbin, tying fur, feathers, bits of tinsel, and a hook into a lure for fly-fishing.

Above him, on the marble mantel, was a clock. It was an example of the ugliest Victorian bric-a-brac Maggie had ever set eyes on: a gray china elephant with a gold-encrusted timepiece set in its side, and a little painted man in gilt turban whipping the beast as if to force it to strike the hours. Like all of the clocks in the castle, it was still, its hands frozen at 8:15.

"All hail!" Teddy called. "You look like a woman who could use a drink. Shall I make your usual?" His face creased into a smile around his briar pipe, the sweet blue smoke hovering in the alcove. He was a slightly hunched man, with a comfortable belly. The cuffs of his black dinner jacket were a little too short, and his bow tie was already slipping out of its knot. Beside him rested his hazel walking stick, the ivory handle carved into the shape of a grizzly bear.

"I think you have your hands full right now, making that lure, Mr. Crane," she responded, her voice ringing off the high ceiling. "May I make you a drink instead?" The bar was under a recess with three mounted stag heads—Maggie had mentally assigned them the code names of Curly, Larry, and Moe.

"Thank you, Miss Hope. An old-fashioned, if there's a spare sugar cube. Just whiskey, if not."

"The first time I met you, I knew you'd drink that," she teased him. "You're probably not all that much older than I am, Mr. Crane, but you're the walking definition of old-fashioned."

"You're kind—quite a bit older, I think. A bit of a relic," Teddy admitted.

"Aha, Mr. Crane! There *is* sugar today—Captain MacLean must have brought it from Mallaig with the rest of the supplies." Maggie made the cocktail for him, poured a glass of sherry for herself, and then picked her way over the animal hides to the alcove. Above Teddy, on one wall, hung a monstrous stuffed sea trout in a glass case. The fish was cut in half—according to the attached plaque, a shark had bitten it in half before Marcus Killoch could reel it in. Underneath was a vintage harpoon, presumably used to kill the shark. "He also brought more whiskey. Don't you think it's curious how there's never any lack?"

Teddy smiled as he accepted the drink. "They want to keep us sedated, I assume. We won't make any problems if we're tipsy or sleeping it off."

"Speaking of sleep," Maggie continued, turning on a fringed lamp and taking a seat next to him. "Dr. Jaeger encouraged me to try Veronal."

"And?"

"I said no thank you."

"Good. In my experience, it's far too easy to overdose on those powders."

She realized they weren't alone in the shadowy recess. "Oh, Mr. Novak! So sorry—didn't see you there. Would you like a drink, too?"

Ramsey Novak was silent, as always, sitting in a bobbin-turned chair in the corner, his gaze never shifting from the dancing flames behind the andirons. Ramsey was just past twenty, tall, gawky, and awkward, with dark hair and eyes ringed with thick black lashes. Upon hearing her voice, he looked up, then returned to the fire. His fingers plucked restlessly at a golden tassel hanging from a pillow embroidered with two intersecting green snakes. He was mute, although Maggie didn't know if he physically couldn't reply or if he chose not to.

Since she'd arrived, Ramsey had always been unresponsive; she had never heard him speak. *He's seen something, witnessed something, done something,* Maggie mused. *But then again, we all have. That's why we're here.* Maggie was glad to see Ramsey and Teddy had formed a companionship, as the others could sometimes be cliquish and unwelcoming.

"*Sláinte mhath,*" she said to both of them, raising her glass.

"Cheers," Teddy responded, taking a sip. "How's the Gaelic coming?"

"It's hard—really, really hard. Nothing like French or German." Maggie was trying, with the help of Mrs. McNaughton, the cook and housekeeper, to learn the ancient language. She glanced out the windows at the encroaching darkness. "It was lovely out today, wasn't it?"

Teddy grimaced. "Tell that to my arthritic knees, Miss Hope. The weather's about to change and for the worse, I'm afraid. I hope we can get in our fishing excursion tomorrow. But, as they say, 'There's no bad weather in Scotland, only the wrong clothing.' And our fish won't mind the rain, of course."

"I can't believe Killoch built his castle here of all places. I mean, *we* don't have a choice—but he did."

All three of them looked up at the full-length oil painting of Sir Marcus Killoch above the fireplace. He was bearded, with black hair, vampiric-looking dark eyes, and a high-bridged nose. In one hand, he gripped a riding crop; the silver handle appeared heavy enough to be used as a weapon. His expression seemed equally arrogant and brutish—as though he were ready to thrash a horse, a servant, or even a lover, depending on who was in his way. And although Killoch was an Englishman, he wore a self-created Scottish-style tartan with jewel-encrusted badges, a powder horn slung over one shoulder, a gold-inlaid dirk and sword at his waist, and a tasseled goatskin sporran fastened with gems. His leather boots were a shiny violet-black.

"Now, it would have been fitting if Killoch had been gored by a deer," she continued, glancing around at all the antlers. "A proper end to a bloodthirsty hunter. And I'm relieved there's only a painting. It wouldn't surprise me at all if he'd insisted on having his own body taxidermied, glass eyes glaring."

Teddy's lips twitched in amusement. "That lot would probably all stuff and display themselves after death, if given the option."

"The tartan's ironic, isn't it?" Maggie sipped her sherry. "Killoch created his own—rather rich, particularly after the English government's former ban on wearing them."

"Nothing the rich do shocks me," Teddy replied. "If you're poor, they call you crazy. But if you're rich, you're 'eccentric.' " He picked up his drink. "They say he's a ghost here on the island, you know."

Maggie was a trained mathematician and an agnostic. She wasn't one to indulge in fantasies about ghosts. "Where did you hear that?"

"Mrs. McNaughton," he confided. "She's worked in the castle since she was a girl. Knew Killoch. She says his ghost lives on."

Ramsey's eyes were locked on the fire again, but Maggie was certain he was listening.

"Like Herne the Hunter?" she asked, tone light, twirling her sherry glass. In British folklore, Herne the Hunter was a ghost associated with Windsor Castle's Forest and Great Park. He was said to wear a crown of antlers, ride a horse, torment cattle, and rattle chains. "Well, it wouldn't be Scotland without rumors of a ghost, now, would it?"

"In more recent news, we also have the paper." Teddy indicated a copy of *The Oban Times* on a side table. "Dr. Jaeger brought it for us, bless him."

Maggie put down her drink and grabbed at the paper, not caring about the ink staining her hands, or that it was backdated November 9. Desperate for information, they listened to the news on the BBC on the wireless as much as they could. But the printed word was always special and contained more details. This headline read, ALLIED FORCES CLOSING IN ON KEY DEFENSES OF NORTH AFRICA: ALGIERS ALREADY OCCUPIED.

Good, she thought with satisfaction. *We're getting a bit of our own back. So much has happened—and yet we've so far to go.*

She scanned the rest of the front page. SPY EXECUTED reported a small article. *A German spy named Jakob Meier, age thirty-two, was executed by firing squad at the Tower of London yesterday. He was sentenced after a weeklong trial held at the Royal Courts of Justice last month.*

The Royal Courts of Justice? The Old Bailey must have been bombed, Maggie realized. She wondered how they'd captured Meier—had he been caught sending a Morse message from a rented room? Spotted on a forbidden beach, taking photographs of ships? Or had censors observed his writing chess moves in German, which were really code for troop buildups?

She didn't know, of course. And she hated not knowing, not being part of the world of espionage. She couldn't bear being imprisoned on the island—not just because of the loss of her personal freedom but because captivity rendered her powerless to do anything to *help*. She was highly trained and experienced. To have to sit out the remainder of the war in a virtual penalty box—well, it hurt. She felt guilty, angry, impotent.

And on top of that, lonely. She was isolated, away from home, without her family—a family of friends, but family nonetheless.

Life was passing her by. It was passing them all by, all of them on this wretched island, as they waited out the war.

She knew beyond the castle walls, beyond the island, terrible things were happening. She remembered Hitler's thuggish Brownshirts swarming the streets of Berlin, killing with impunity. She'd seen several off-duty German soldiers in spring in Paris, drunk and disorderly, and when a Frenchman on a bicycle accidentally knocked one of them over, they shot him dead in the street in broad daylight. What countless other atrocities were happening? And still, she was unable to do anything. It was infuriating.

A voice from the staircase interrupted her thoughts. "By the pricking of my thumbs, something wicked this way comes!"

It was Quentin Asquith, the group's self-professed dandy: tall, slender, and elegant, fair hair plastered back with brilliantine. This evening, he was dressed for dinner in a dark blue double-breasted jacket, a boutonniere of red holly berries and glossy leaves pinned to his lapel. Under his left arm, he carried a russet taxidermic fox he'd found and named Monsieur Reynard; they were inseparable.

Maggie liked Quentin. He was odd, to be sure, but in a witty way. He eschewed any and all physical activity except fencing and instead spent his time indoors, reading novels, playing chess, and drinking. "I like the outdoors," he was known to declare, "but I don't think it returns the favor."

Quentin went to the wireless, turning it on and twisting the dial until he found music. The Glenn Miller Orchestra played "Don't Sit Under the Apple Tree."

"I was afraid Monsieur Reynard and I would be early for cocktails," he remarked as he walked to the bar.

"Not at all," Teddy replied.

"Welcome, both of you," Maggie added, smiling at the stuffed fox. Ramsey glanced at Quentin but said nothing.

"Well, thank heavens there's more liquor," Quentin commented, turning on a few more lamps, then mixing gin with bitters in a heavy crystal glass. "Never any lack of alcohol here, at least. They're keeping us drunk and happy so we won't complain or cause any problems."

He was right. Not only were intoxicants plentiful but personal relationships were almost encouraged. Early on, Maggie had become aware that a number of her fellow prisoners didn't meet only over a meal or cocktails in the great room. Sometimes footsteps echoed in the corridors at night and there were the faint but unmistakable sounds of doors being opened and shut.

"Have *you* caused problems today, Mr. Asquith?" Maggie deadpanned. "Or has Monsieur Reynard?"

"Neither of us, alas," Quentin replied, picking up his tumbler. "This life—it's not bad, really. I rather enjoy the solitude, especially the comfort of a warm lodge, ugly though it may be. It could be a club in St. James's, you know," he continued, "with hunting and fishing as topics of conversation instead of politics and business. Even if the décor is Elsie de Wolfe on cocaine." He winced up at a shrunken head in a glass case. The label beneath read: "TSANTSA, FROM THE AGUARUNA TRIBE, PERU."

"Yes, we seem to have found ourselves in a club with *very* exclusive membership. And far too many antlers." Maggie's gaze rested on the tall, cold windowpanes. "I don't understand why, with such a gorgeous view, anyone would want to use so much stained glass. You can't see out very well at all."

Teddy was refilling his pipe with sweet-smelling tobacco from a suede pouch. "Perhaps it wasn't about seeing out, but having others not see in. Have you seen those marks on the lid of the grand piano? Damage from ladies' high-heeled shoes, I believe."

"Someone could still peek in through the clear parts." Quentin smirked. "I heard when old Killoch was building this monstrosity, he paid his workers extra to wear kilts."

Maggie raised one eyebrow. But before she could respond, she noticed a flicker of movement. "Anna!" she called.

Anna O'Malley was dressed in a plain gray frock with a lace collar, her thin hands twisting around each other. She was slight and birdlike, with wiry brown hair obscuring darting eyes. Her face was narrow, ending in a sharply pointed chin. She gave the impression of fragility, but the word that always popped into Maggie's mind when she saw Anna was *scrappy*.

"Miss Hope—may—may I speak with you?" The younger woman looked to Quentin, Teddy, and Ramsey. "In *private*?"

"Of course." Maggie rose and walked over. "Why don't we put up the blackout curtains?"

Anna sidestepped a dead palm in a brass pot. She and Maggie both pulled on the heavy black draperies to block the light and protect against the spiking cold. "I keep thinking of Andrew," she whispered. The night before, Anna had confided in Maggie that she'd become pregnant during training, by a fellow agent who had been sent to France but hadn't been heard from since. She'd had the baby, a boy she named Andrew, and given him to her mother to raise in London. She hadn't seen her parents or sisters in over a year.

"I know, Miss O'Malley." The two women moved to the next set of windows. "But it's not good to dwell—" Another curtain closed, making the room confined and dim.

"I'm not dwelling! But I want you to know that since our conversation last night, I've made a decision."

"Yes?"

They pulled shut the final blackout curtains; the room was now a veritable bell jar. "I've decided I'm not going home—when this"— Anna waved a hand, indicating the hall, the castle, the island—"is over. I'm taking Andrew and running away. I'll pretend to be a widow. No one will ever know I had him"—she lowered her voice—"out of wedlock." She put a finger in her mouth absently and began chewing on the nail.

"I think that's an excellent idea." Maggie took a window seat and patted the dusty velvet cushion next to her. "If that's what you want. A fresh start for both of you."

"You don't think it's sinful to lie?" Anna sat.

"It's one of the least sinful lies I've ever heard."

"If Andrew even remembers me . . ."

"You're his mother. Of course he'll remember you."

"At least the Blitz stopped last year—although I know the bombings will most likely resume. The only thing I keep turning around and around in my head, though, is where will we live? I don't have any money. Everything I've made I've sent home for Andrew. I know my mother hasn't saved any of it for me. Not that I'd want her to, of course . . ." Maggie nodded. "I can sew," Anna declared resolutely. "It's what I did before SOE—I made ladies' hats. Pretty hats, too, with hummingbirds and flowers and ribbons and things."

"They sound beautiful."

"It's like a record skipping—I just can't think of how I'll be able to support us when I get out of here. If I get out of here."

"First," Maggie said, "you *will* get out. We all will. And second, if you and Andrew need a place to stay, I have a house in Marylebone—that's far enough from the East End, isn't it? At any time, any number of my friends live there. Sarah is a ballet dancer." Maggie swallowed. Sarah *had* been a dancer. And then a spy. What she was now, Maggie didn't know. She plunged on. "My friend Chuck—really Charlotte—has a darling little boy named Griffin. They're staying with me because their flat was bombed. Griffin and Andrew could play together!"

She took the younger woman's hand. "Why don't you both come live with us, until you get on your feet? There's plenty of space for hatmaking. And I can only imagine when this war's over, women will want new hats to celebrate. Come, live with me! It will be fun!"

"Are you—are you certain? I can cook and clean, earn my way . . ." Anna's face was hopeful but unsure.

"We all take turns with the chores, don't worry. And you'll be doing me the favor. I don't like living in such a big place alone, especially with so many in London without homes. Seems only right to share."

"Are you serious?" Anna straightened, eyes glowing. "Cross your heart and hope to die?"

Maggie made an X over her chest. "Cross my heart and hope to live, but yes."

"Miss Hope, you don't know what this means to me. I can't tell you how much better I feel."

"Well, good!" Maggie exclaimed. "Now, why don't you think of new hat designs, instead of fretting? I can't wait to see what you come up with. I happen to know a woman who started out as a hat designer in Paris"—*Well, that's one way to describe Coco Chanel*—"who became *quite* successful."

"Thank you, Miss Hope. Thank you so much. I'll start sketching . . ."

Maggie looked over to the alcove. Quentin and Teddy were deep in an intense discussion of anglers and writers, while Ramsey sat staring at Anna, his eyes unblinking. "Don't look now," she told Anna, "but I think you have an admirer."

"Ugh, Mr. Novak." Anna made a face. "He's always watching me. Don't you think he's a bit, well, *creepy*? He never says a word."

"Well, maybe he needs someone to talk to. You could help him. Perhaps he'd start talking again, with a little encouragement."

"Mr. Crane talks to him a lot, but it hasn't seemed to help." Anna frowned. "Do you think there's something . . . funny going on with Mr. Crane and Mr. Novak?"

"I think Mr. Crane is simply being kind."

"I don't know. There's something wrong with Ramsey Novak, I can feel it." Anna shivered.

Maggie was on alert. "Has he done anything to make you feel uncomfortable?" After a disastrous outing with a man from Mr. Churchill's office had nearly ended in her rape, Maggie had vowed she'd always trust her intuition. If Anna's gut was telling her something, it was worth Maggie's attention. "Did anything happen?"

"No—nothing, really." Anna brightened. "Did you hear about the new girl?"

Anna didn't appear to be concerned about Ramsey, so Maggie dropped it. "There's a new prisoner?" Maggie was intrigued. This latest arrival was the first since she'd come to the island. "Did you meet her? What's she like?"

"I just caught a glimpse," Anna said. "She was going off by herself at sunset, into the woods—isn't that odd? But she's young. Posh. Quite beautiful."

"Who's beautiful?" purred a voice from the doorway. It belonged to Helene Poole-Smythe. A statuesque woman with a raven bob, she made a grand entrance in a scarlet high-necked dress with a gold-beaded dragon around her neck, a cigarette in a long ivory holder pinched between two fingers, both hands loaded with heavy rings. The air shimmered with her sandalwood perfume. Helene had once been a showgirl but married a rich gin distiller, and loved to put on airs. Maggie found her pretentious and disliked the way she flirted with the men.

Leonard Kingsley, one of Helene's admirers, trailed at her heels. "*You* are, of course, darling. The most beautiful woman on the island."

"More gin—thank goodness. Make me a martini, Mr. Kingsley, won't you? Wet. I do so love vermouth."

Leo obliged, handing a coupe to Helene, who stretched, catlike, to reach it. "Anyone else for martinis?" he called to the room. Maggie didn't know Leo well. Tall and athletic, with a thick brown mustache and raffish beard, he played the piano and sang beautifully, which was a wonderful after-dinner diversion, and spoke with a slight Belgian accent. He was charming, but slippery, and hard to read. What was obvious was his infatuation for Helene, despite her ongoing affair with another prisoner, Ian Lansbury.

"Where's Mr. Lansbury?" Anna responded, ignoring Leo's question. Maggie had a sneaking suspicion Anna had a crush on Ian and was jealous of his relationship with Helene. Ian, originally from the streets of Manchester, had enthusiastically embraced the blood sports of the island, often being gone all day to hunt, fish, and trap. While the inmates were not allowed guns, Ian had carved a bow from an oak branch and whittled arrows, which he'd used to bring down any number of deer.

Helene responded with a graceful wave of her cigarette in its holder. "Ian took off early this morning. Hunting, of course. That man's insatiable."

So I understand, Maggie thought. She shared a bedroom wall with Helene and often overheard her and Ian together in the night.

"And he's not back yet?" Maggie asked.

Helene shrugged narrow shoulders. "How should I know?"

"You're thick as thieves," Anna retorted. "Although they always told us marriages made in the field never work out."

"Who said anything about *marriage,* Miss O'Malley?" Helene retorted with a wink, then turned to Leo. "Darling, do turn off the wireless and play a little something for us, won't you?" Before the war, Helene had been a chorus girl in Noël Coward's *Operette* in the West End, and she loved to sing and dance after a few cocktails, as well as regale them all with intimate tales of the theater. Maggie wondered how many of her stories were true.

Quentin turned off the radio, and Leo sat down at the piano. Lifting long, elegant fingers to the ivory keys, he played a familiar melody. Helene, recognizing the tune, came up behind him, and began to sing, her voice loud and brassy:

A-hunting we will go, a-hunting we will go
Heigh-ho, the derry-o, a-hunting we will go!
A-hunting we will go, a-hunting we will go
We'll catch a fox and put him in a box
And never let him go . . .

Quentin got to his feet, the stuffed fox cradled in his arms. He had gone pale. "Monsieur Reynard doesn't find that sort of thing at all amusing!"

Leo stopped, his hands hovering over the keys. Helene opened her mouth to retort when the gong sounded from the front hall. The metallic echo reverberated through the great room.

Teddy rose. "Ladies and gentlemen," he announced. "Time for dinner."

Chapter Three

As they entered the dining room, Maggie overheard Leo saying to Quentin, "We meant no offense to the fox, old thing. None of those ancient nursery rhymes are about pudding and plums and pretty maids, really—if you read them closely, you'll notice the plague and the murder."

"I'm well aware." Quentin reached to stroke the fox's ruddy muzzle. "Those mice with their tails cut off symbolized the Protestant bishops during the reign of Bloody Mary, who had their heads removed."

Dinner at Killoch Castle was held in the formal dining room, at the bottom of the western turret, round and red and always slightly damp. Sir Marcus had commissioned an artist to paint the walls and ceiling with depictions of grotesque primates clothed as humans—shooting, fishing, smoking, living the life of the Highland gentleman. The room was furnished with claw-foot Chippendale mahogany swivel chairs from Killoch's steamship; the table lights evoked Japanese incense burners. In the back of the room was a huge black marble fireplace. A dusty waterfall chandelier, dripping with prisms and ropes of cut-crystal beads, glowed overhead, cutting through the shadows.

As Leo pulled out a chair for Helene, he added, "And I read

somewhere that 'Eeny, meeny, miny, moe' and all those counting rhymes actually derive from ancient methods of choosing human sacrifices." Quentin was not at all comforted; he clutched Monsieur Reynard closer.

"Really, darling," Helene chided as Leo sat beside her. "Not appropriate dinner conversation."

Castle dinners were generally odd, a blend of the formal and casual, a ritual for individuals who under normal circumstances would never have broken bread together. *The conversation of prisoners,* Maggie thought. She found the meals tiresome, but unavoidable.

"We're talking about nursery rhymes?" asked Sayid as he entered the room. He smiled, his teeth white against his skin, and sat next to Maggie. The space between them felt small and charged. Her cheeks turned pink, but she forced herself not to look away. "They're rather grim aren't they?"

"And political, too, Dr. Khan," Maggie replied. "'Baa, Baa, Black Sheep' was protesting taxation. And 'Sing a Song of Sixpence' was about Henry the Eighth and his break from the Catholic Church."

"Perhaps we should add nursery rhyme study to our poetry-reciting afternoons, Miss Hope?"

If he only knew how much I look forward to our once-a-week poetry meetings in the library. "Perhaps."

Teddy glanced up. "Oh, one in particular used to give me the chills—*Ding dong bell, pussy's in the well. Who put her in? Little Johnny Flynn.*" He chuckled. "And, as we all know, cats can't swim." Next to him, Ramsey remained silent, his eyes fixed on the flickering candles.

"All of Mother Goose gave me nightmares," Helene added. "I remember them vividly—*Here comes a candle to light you to bed. Here comes a chopper to chop off your head. . . .*" She shuddered. "Ghastly."

Anna took a seat next to Teddy, and soon they were joined by

Torvald Hagan. Only four feet tall, he had straight white-blond hair, saucer-shaped blue eyes, short limbs, and a long torso. Torvald scrambled up onto his chair, cleared his throat, and quoted in deep plummy tones: *"On looking up, on looking down, She saw a dead man on the ground; And from his nose unto his chin, The worms crawl'd out, the worms crawl'd in."*

"Good evening to you, too, Mr. Hagan," said Teddy drily.

Nine of the ten prisoners were present. There was an empty place at the table, the one usually occupied by Ian. "Shouldn't we wait for Mr. Lansbury?" Anna asked.

"He's undoubtedly still out hunting," Helene replied. "Fancies himself a bit of a Hemingway. We should start without him." She glanced to Leo. "I'm famished."

"I hate to think of him eating and sleeping outside," Anna said as she spread her linen napkin in her lap, "like an animal."

"He likes it that way," Helene replied with a smirk. "Trust me." Anna scowled, but didn't respond.

The castle's gamekeeper, Angus McNaughton, entered carrying an enormous porcelain tureen. McNaughton was tall and thick, like an ancient oak. His hair and eyebrows were sprigs of frosted lichen, his face serious as a gravestone. He, his wife, and their son lived in the ghillie's cottage not far from the castle and had been kept on to maintain the prison. With massive scarred hands, McNaughton served the first course, nettle and wild garlic soup.

His son, Murdo, poured the wine. Murdo was somewhere in his late teens or early twenties, his face twisted with a sour expression he didn't bother to conceal. He was taller than his father, his long dark brown hair falling over a high forehead.

"Nursery rhymes," Maggie pointed out as McNaughton ladled steaming soup into her bowl, "are all rather ominous, aren't they? 'Jack and Jill went up a hill to fetch a pail of water,' for instance. Jack falls down and breaks his crown, and Jill comes tumbling after—but is there any chance they were pushed?" She looked up to the older man. "Thank you. It smells delicious." McNaughton grunted something in reply and moved to the next bowl.

"Sounds like an Agatha Christie novel," Teddy interjected. "I finished one today—*Ten Little Niggers*."

Maggie drew in a sharp breath on hearing that particular word, especially after her experiences in Washington, D.C., with Mrs. Roosevelt and the attempted execution of a colored man in Virginia.

"Was it any good?" Quentin inquired. "I *adore* murder mysteries."

"Perfection. That Christie is a national treasure."

"Speaking of national treasures, I propose a toast!" Leo exclaimed, picking up his wineglass. "To dear old Captain Eric Sykes, that bespectacled, gray-haired gentleman who taught us all how to kill silently, blow up bridges, and live off the land. Although stags are the biggest beasts to hunt on this island, with Sykes's training, they don't stand a chance. To Captain Sykes!"

"To Captain Sykes!" those around the table chorused, while Ramsey merely lifted his glass.

"He taught us to shoot .22 and .45 caliber handguns without using the sights," Hagan recalled.

"Knifes and garrotes, too," Helene added, almost wistfully.

Quentin nodded. "Explained the musculature of the human body and its most vulnerable points."

"*Fight with your hands open—and always use your fingers. And then knee him in the crotch!*" Maggie said in a broad Manchester accent. "Remember?"

"He was a good soul," pronounced Anna. Then she crossed herself. "Despite all the men he must have murdered."

"Remember when that trainee from Aberdeen wanted salmon and didn't have any luck catching any?" asked Maggie.

Teddy leaned in. "Do tell, Miss Hope."

She blotted her lips with her napkin. "He took some dynamite to the loch and blew it up, scattering fish everywhere. Scores of them floated on the surface and he just scooped them up with a net."

"As a self-proclaimed piscator," said Teddy, shaking his head in dismay, "I die a thousand deaths upon hearing that story. There's no elegance, no finesse in what he did. It's absolutely horrifying."

"Sykes thought it showed great ingenuity, if I recall correctly," Sayid pointed out. "*Don't copy the way they do things in Hollywood*, he'd always say."

Their reminiscences were interrupted by the entrance of their current commanding officer, Captain Evans. "Ladies and gentlemen—" he began. Everyone at the table quieted and turned their candlelit faces to him. "I'd like to introduce you to the newest member of our little club." A young blond woman stepped out from behind him. "Please allow me to present Miss Camilla Oddell."

"Oh, I didn't realize we were in mufti," she told them in a silvery, high-pitched voice. She was still wearing her brown FANY uniform and looked as if she were barely out of her teens.

There was a chorus of *How do you do*s from those assembled at the table, and the men all rose as Camilla nodded, smiling shyly.

"Please join us, Miss Oddell." Maggie indicated the empty chair to her right, set for Ian. The blonde did, smiling at Maggie, who did not find it at all sincere. *Miss Oddell is new here,* she reminded herself. *And nervous. Give her a chance.*

As Murdo cleared the soup bowls, the senior McNaughton served the main course: venison, charred on the outside, red and bloody on the inside, dark juices pooling on the platter.

"I'll leave you to your dinner then," the Captain said and walked out.

They all turned to their meal, silverware scraping against the plates and glasses clinking. "I'm concerned about Mr. Lansbury," Anna said again, after a moment. "Shouldn't he be back by now?"

"Well, he can't get lost." Teddy picked up his glass. "It's an island, after all."

Anna frowned. "He's always back by supper."

Leo rolled his eyes. "Dinner," he corrected. "And Ian has always been one of those rustic chaps—good with guns and crossbows and the like. We trained together. He excelled in all of that outdoorsman lore—snares for rabbits and such."

"Ugh, I hated the wilderness survival part of the training." Anna shivered. "The poor little bunnies."

"Best to call them 'hares,'" Leo replied. "It's not as if they're characters in a Beatrix Potter tale. And, if push comes to shove, it's better to kill a rabbit—or a fish, or a deer, for that matter—than starve."

"I was a vegetarian at school," Torvald offered. "For nine years, can you believe?"

"What happened?" Maggie asked, noting the gristle on his plate.

"I became very, very hungry." Those around the table laughed. "But," he continued, "if I was to eat meat, I realized I had to do the whole business—be accountable. I needed not just to hunt, but also to be able to skin, gut, and quarter the beasts I brought down."

"*You* can hunt?" Leo said, eyebrows rising in amazement that someone of Torvald's slight stature could do such a thing.

"I might need a ladder to reach a high shelf," Torvald retorted, "but I'm every bit as capable a hunter as you!"

"I hunt with my camera," Sayid intervened. He'd brought a Leica to the island, Maggie knew, with a thirty-six-frame roll of 35-millimeter film. He was careful to take just a photograph or two each time he went out to shoot, as film was so dear.

"You've never hunted markhor? Or ibex, with those beautiful curved horns?" Leo cried in mock horror. "Isn't that what you lot hunt in India?"

Sayid didn't take the bait. "I grew up in London—Bloomsbury, actually," he countered. "It's my father who came from India. But I find taking photographs is just as satisfying—and with far less blood."

"Still, doesn't stop you from eating your venison, now, does it?" Leo persisted.

"Not at all," Sayid replied amicably, taking another bite.

Helene picked up her wineglass. "No talk of blood at the table, if you please!"

"I—" Camilla cleared her throat and wiped a thin trickle of pink-ish juice from her chin with her napkin. "I was wondering just what sort of camp this is—"

There was an awkward silence as the group exchanged looks. *Is it possible she doesn't know?* Maggie wondered.

"It's a rather ragtag group, I'm afraid—" Teddy began.

Maggie cut in. "I used to be an instructor at Arisaig House, get-ting the trainees in shape. If you'd like to go swimming," she told the newcomer, "I'm up and out every morning at first light. You're welcome to join me."

"Swimming?" Camilla exclaimed. "In winter?"

"Just take it slowly if you're not used to it. You'll need to build up tolerance to the cold. And then, at a certain point you enjoy it, be-lieve it or not," Maggie assured her.

"I've seen you swimming in the bay," Torvald told Maggie, "like a mermaid."

"From the windows," Anna added, "your head like a bobbin, cutting the fabric of the water. Most impressive crawl."

Maggie smiled her thanks. "I started in Arisaig, but I kept it up in London, at the Ladies' Pond in Hampstead Heath."

"But what about training?" Camilla appeared confused. "For our eventual missions? When the danger's passed?"

The table was silent.

"Ladies and gentlemen—" Quentin put Monsieur Reynard down as he pulled a slip of paper from the breast pocket of his dinner jacket. "I found something interesting today . . ."

"Doing your own 'hunting' in the castle's attic?" Helene asked. "I don't know why you'd want to wear a dead man's clothes."

"*He* can't wear them anymore. Might as well make use of them."
Quentin looked down at the fox, whose glass eyes seemed to twinkle
in the candlelight. "Monsieur Reynard agrees. And, yes, I do like to
go through Killoch's old clothes—all that gorgeous Harris tweed
and Jermyn Street tailoring. However, this is something a bit different."

"What is it?" Teddy asked, as Quentin unfolded a yellow newspaper clipping.

"We were all told Marcus Killoch died on this island," Quentin
continued. "But what we *weren't* told was that he murdered his invited guests. And then he shot himself."

Someone cursed softly. Anna gasped, and Torvald dropped his
fork. "May I see?" Maggie asked.

Quentin handed her the scrap of paper. "Ten guests plus Killoch
died—the police ruled it a murder-suicide." He looked around the
table. "Just like us—we are also ten." He gestured to each in turn:
"Miss Hope, Dr. Khan, Miss Oddell, Mr. Novak, Miss O'Malley,
Mr. Hagan, Mrs. Poole-Smythe, Mr. Kingsley, and Mr. Crane.
And I."

Anna added, "And Mr. Lansbury, of course."

"Of course. Although that makes eleven." Quentin shook his
head. "Less like Miss Christie."

Maggie scanned the article. "It says one of the victims was
Killoch's wife. I had no idea he was married."

"I believe the portrait of the woman on the staircase is his wife,"
Leo said.

"*La Dame de Poisson-Tête?*" Helene quipped. "Now *there's* a
woman who must have been the embodiment of patience, what with
all her husband's stalking and the taxidermy."

"This—this house is the scene of a mass murder?" Anna
squeaked. "Jesus, Mary, and Joseph!"

"The island," said Quentin, retrieving the clipping. "It doesn't
say exactly where anyone was killed."

As Murdo cleared the plates and McNaughton brought in a tart apple jelly, Quentin asked him, "Weren't you around at the time the murders would have taken place, McNaughton? When Marcus Killoch murdered everyone and then killed himself?"

"Aye," McNaughton replied, not looking up from his duties. "I grew up on this island, one of a long line of crofters. Became the ghillie and boatman when Sir Marcus's father bought the island. Helped out with the hunts and fishing expeditions."

"Well?" Quentin insisted. "What happened?"

"Don't know," McNaughton replied.

"How could you not know?"

The older man shrugged. "I was living in the ghillie's cottage. We didn't have much to do with Sir Marcus and his set, just used the horses to cart their dead beasts back to the castle. Kept separate we were, although he'd always say hello or ask after the family if we crossed paths."

"So he was a *polite* murderer," Quentin quipped. "But surely there must have been people working at the castle, who witnessed what happened? There must have been talk . . ."

"Long time ago, sir," McNaughton mumbled. "Best not to speak of such things."

"Is—is Sir Marcus buried here? On the island?" Anna ventured. "In the graveyard behind the church?"

"No, lass." McNaughton's steely eyes met hers. "He wasn't buried on consecrated ground—had a tomb built near the western cliffs."

"I've seen that crypt," Maggie remembered, "on one of my walks. It's beautiful, in a desolate sort of way."

"Any . . . ghosts on this island?" Anna asked McNaughton in a tight voice.

"This is Scotland, miss. The whole blasted country's haunted."

———

After dinner, Maggie, Anna, Helene, and Camilla gathered in the drawing room as the men retired to play billiards, drink port, and smoke cigars. The room was one of the few places in the castle without animal heads, although Maggie had never liked it. It was chock-full of gilt mirrors, dusty chandeliers, and twisting ormolu candelabra; the hands of the grandfather clock, intricately painted in cerulean and gold, had long been still. The murky-green wallpaper had a repeating trellis pattern on it that always reminded her of the bars of a cage.

Instead of hunt paintings, the drawing room was hung with moody seascapes—ships caught in the wrath of storms, threatened by terrifying high waves and lightning. At least there was a warming blaze in the fireplace behind a long brass fender. The four women sat in brocade chairs, upholstered in patterns of emerald and oxblood red, drawn close to the hearth, and watched as the flames caught and grew. On the dusty marble mantel, a frozen clock face stared uselessly back at them.

"I caught a peek at one of the films brought for this month's viewing," Camilla offered. "Something called *Next of Kin*."

Helene stifled a yawn. "Oh, *Next of Kin*, again?"

It wasn't Maggie's favorite either. In it, a gossipy housewife is overheard by a Nazi spy while talking about what her son is doing, the slogan *Loose lips sink ships* taking on new meaning.

"Agreed," Maggie replied, picking up a paperweight from the side table; a scarab beetle trapped in amber. "It's more likely viewers will swear off attending the cinema rather than gossip." She put the weight back.

"It *is* a little frightening, though," Anna countered. "Don't you think? The idea that somebody's always listening, always picking up scraps of information. Really brings home how dangerous careless talk can be." She giggled. "Not to sound paranoid, but—"

"I thought we'd come have coffee with you ladies," Quentin said, entering with the fox tucked under his arm.

"Of course," Maggie replied, smiling. "Delighted to have you. I've always hated the convention of separating the sexes after dinner." Quentin sat next to the women on another plush chair as Mrs. McNaughton entered with a tarnished silver tray.

"Convention keeps us from becoming savages, I suppose," Anna offered.

Helene snorted. "We are savages, my dear. We *kill* people for a living, after all. Or at least, we used to."

As Mrs. McNaughton, Angus's wife and Murdo's mother, poured the chicory coffee into chipped demitasse cups, Maggie offered: "*Leigibh dhomh*—please, let me. You have enough to do."

"It's no trouble, Miss Hope," the housekeeper answered, continuing to pour and hand each person a fragile cup. She was a thin woman, with brown hair streaked with silver drawn back under a white cap. Her dress was plain and black, and a small gold crucifix hung around her neck. Her cheeks were flushed from the heat of the kitchen and she had scars and burns on her calloused hands.

Maggie had learned from their talks after her Gaelic lessons that Mrs. McNaughton's Christian name was Fiona, her maiden name was Morrison, and she was originally from Tolsta, a town on the Isle of Lewis. As a young girl, she'd gutted and packed herring in Stornoway before she'd come to Scarra to work as a maid in the castle.

"I must agree with you, Miss Hope, on not separating the sexes. I quite like an after-dinner brandy in the company of handsome young men myself," Helene purred, lounging back and fitting a cigarette into her ivory holder. "As well as the occasional cigar."

I'm sure you do, Maggie thought. Quentin caught Maggie's expression and snorted, then pretended to cough.

Helene allowed him to light her cigarette and blew out a stream of smoke. "Mrs. McNaughton, were you on the island when the Marcus Killoch murders occurred?"

Maggie thought the cook might spill the coffee, but she did not.

Instead, she looked up and asked, "H-how do you know about the murders, ma'am?"

Quentin volunteered, "I found a newspaper clipping up in the attic today."

Mrs. McNaughton muttered something under her breath. Maggie thought it was one of her often-used Gaelic sayings: *"Chuir sin an clamhan gobhlach am measg nan cearc,"* which translated loosely to "That sets the cat among the pigeons."

Quentin placed his cup into its saucer. "Where were you when the murders occurred? Were you on the island?" His thin face glowed with curiosity.

Mrs. McNaughton inhaled. "Aye, I was working here, sir, in the castle. I was a scullery maid back in the day. But I lived in the village."

"I thought everyone died?" Helene pursed her crimson lips to blow a ripple of smoke rings. "How did you manage to survive?" Her tone was casual, but Maggie detected an edge in the older woman's question.

"It was . . . just the guests, ma'am. And Sir Marcus and Lady Beatrix. None of the staff."

"You didn't hear anything?" Helene pressed.

The Scotswoman continued to serve coffee. But Maggie noted her hands were shaking. "No, ma'am."

"Before it happened—did you suspect anything?" Quentin wanted to know. "Did anything seem off?"

"No, sir. And now, if that will be all—"

"Do you think Killoch's ghost haunts the island?" Anna's voice wobbled. "I swear by all that's holy I've seen a figure in the woods—"

"The most logical explanation is that it's your imagination," Maggie assured her. "The madness of living in nearly constant darkness at this time of year, coupled with not enough to do, would make anyone imagine things that aren't there."

"Darkness is wicked!" Mrs. McNaughton rejoined. Her sudden vehemence made everyone jump.

"Darkness is just a natural phenomenon," Maggie said gently. "Due to the revolution of the earth around the sun and the tilt of its axis."

As the cook left the room, Maggie heard her mutter under her breath: "The people that walked in darkness have seen a great light: they that dwell in the land of the shadow of death, upon them hath the light shined."

Maggie looked to Anna, whose face was bloodless. "The dark is nothing to fear," Maggie continued, trying to reassure her. "Equating dark with evil is superstition. Besides, we're coming up on the solstice." She rose and went to one of the windows, pulling back the blackout curtain. The sky was wild with stars that looked close enough to touch.

"Darkness *is* death," Anna countered with unusual vehemence. "And in the midwinter, light is the birth of Christ—the coming resurrection."

"Oh, girls—you're *not* going to talk religion, are you?" Helene sipped at her coffee.

Camilla nodded. "No religion or politics, please."

Maggie replaced the curtain and returned to her chair. "Well, what should we talk about then?" She was in no mood for Helene's airs.

"We're British—we should talk about the weather, of course," ventured Camilla with a smile. "For example, it was a beautiful day today. Good sailing from Mallaig, with clear skies."

"Did you have a nice walk?" Anna asked the newcomer.

"Walk?"

"I saw you from the window this afternoon—going off alone, into the woods."

"Oh, yes." Camilla tossed her hair. "I just wanted some fresh air and time to think."

"Well, you'll have plenty of both here." Helene appraised the younger blonde from head to toe. "You really have no idea what you're in for here, do you? Poor thing."

"It's a . . . a prison," Camilla answered, her face crumpling. "That's what Captain Evans told me."

"Something like that." Quentin clutched the fox close.

From down the hallway, there was the bang of something heavy falling, the shatter of glass, and then a shout: "Oh my God!"

Everyone in the drawing room jumped up and ran to investigate. At the entrance to the billiards room stood two enormous elephant-carved doors, studded with ornate brass spikes. Maggie pushed them open. Inside, Captain Evans was lying on his back on the green baize table; his uniform was covered in vomit and his face was contorted and red. At his feet was a broken glass. The sickly-sweet jammy smell of port filled the air. Torvald, Leo, Teddy, and Ramsey stood frozen in a circle around the captain.

"Holy Mary, Mother of God," Anna breathed.

Sayid was examining Evans, his fingers on the captain's neck, trying to find a pulse. Maggie wanted to look away, but her eyes were locked on the unfocused, unseeing ones in front of her.

Finally, the doctor pulled his hand back. "He's dead."

Camilla gasped. "God in heaven," whispered Anna. Helene stood frozen in the doorway, eyes glittering.

Sayid bowed, murmuring, *"Inna lillahi was anna ilayhi raji'un."*

"What the hell does that mean?" Leo exclaimed.

"It's an ayat—a verse—from the Koran, recited upon hearing of a death. 'We are from Allah and to Him are we returning.'"

"What happened?" Helene managed.

Teddy gestured to the fallen man. "He was watching as I lined up my shot. And then he began gagging and—"

"He appeared fine at dinner, but was he feeling all right earlier?" Maggie asked, forcing herself to speak despite the icy sensation flooding her. "Does anyone know? Was anyone with him today?"

"I was," Camilla ventured. "I don't know him, of course, but he didn't seem at all ill . . ."

"It looks like he choked," said Torvald, getting up on a tufted brocade chair to appraise the body.

"What was he drinking?" Maggie asked.

"Port—we all were," Torvald told her.

"It could be a heart attack," Sayid suggested. "Captain Evans is—was—the right age, plus he's overweight, drank, smoked . . ."

Maggie walked to the captain; she closed his eyelids gently. "We must get in touch with SOE. Let them know what's happened."

"My goodness!" exclaimed Quentin. "Now no one is in charge. The animals are running the zoo." He hugged the fox in his arms.

"We're civilized people," Maggie reassured him. "It's just a terrible accident."

Teddy pulled his pipe from his mouth. "Indeed."

"Let's move him to the game larder for now," Sayid suggested. "I'd like to examine the body more closely." He glanced to Teddy, Leo, Torvald, and Quentin. "The men can help me carry the body. The rest of you, please go to bed. We'll figure things out tomorrow."

"Wait," said Maggie. "I know it's horrible but . . . I need to check his pockets for the keys."

"I'll do it," Sayid told her, but he came up with nothing.

"I'll find Mrs. McNaughton," Maggie said. "She must have a spare key to the Captain's office and the telegraph. I know we're not supposed to have access, but this is an emergency, after all. With any luck, we can get someone here by tomorrow. We'll all meet up again in the morning." Her hair had come loose from its roll and she pushed the straggling curls back into place with trembling hands. "Surely we'll have a response from the mainland by then."

The kitchen was Maggie's favorite part of the castle—big, but oddly homey, its walls a peeling buttery yellow, dented copper pots hanging from the ceiling, coconut matting covering the cold stone floor. "Hello, Sooty," she said to Mrs. McNaughton's black cat, a champion mouser. As she passed through, she heard a voice, singing.

Did you see the modest maiden
Whom young Neil ravished
On the top of a mountain on a sunny day . . .
Alas, O King! That I was not his
I would not shout out
Or cry out loud
Though the bosom of my dress were torn . . .

She waited for the song to end, then knocked at the door of the housekeeper's parlor. "Mrs. McNaughton?"

"Come in, Miss Hope—"

Maggie entered. This room was cozy and comfortable, with hand-knit afghans covering furniture in proportion to a normal human's body, paintings of wildflowers on the walls, a small framed photograph of a dark-eyed boy who had to be Murdo in the place of honor on the mantel—a world away from the grotesque Victoriana upstairs. "I'm so sorry to disturb you . . ."

The housekeeper was sitting in front of a popping fire; she was tatting, her rough hands nimble with the needle, thread, and shuttle. She looked up.

"I'm sorry to have to tell you this, Mrs. McNaughton," Maggie said. "But Captain Evans is, well—I'm afraid he's dead."

The older woman gasped. "How—what happened? How did he die?"

"We don't know," Maggie told her. "But probably a heart attack. Dr. Khan is moving his body to the game larder; he'll examine him there."

"My word," Mrs. McNaughton breathed, standing. The lace dropped to the floor.

"I'll need to use the radio to contact SOE on the mainland. Do you have the key to his office?"

The professional mask slipped back over Mrs. McNaughton's features. "Of course. Please come this way, Miss Hope. I'll unlock the Captain's office for you—then I'll make us tea. I think we can both use it."

Tea, the universal solution to any problem, Maggie thought in bleak amusement.

Mrs. McNaughton led the way to what had once been the butler's sitting room and pulled out a heavy key ring from her pocket. She found a shiny new key and unlocked the door. "Just let me know when you're done, miss, and I'll lock up. Those are the rules."

"Of course." She could pick the lock, as could any of them, but there was a certain honor among thieves.

In Captain Evans's office, everything was neat and tidy. Maggie focused on the radio on his desk, a complex-looking construction of wires and dials and knobs. She flipped on several switches, and the device hummed to life, red and yellow lights blinking as it warmed up. She experimented with the dials, trying to pick up a signal. It buzzed for a moment, then crackled.

She found the microphone and flipped the switch to Transmit. "Come in, Arisaig, come in. Over." Nothing. "Arisaig, this is Scarra. We have an emergency. Over."

There was more hissing. Finally, a woman's voice, strong and reassuring. *Come in, Scarra. Receiving you loud and clear. Over.*

Maggie took a deep breath. "Captain Evans is dead. Over."

Static crackled.

Maggie tried again. "Captain Evans is dead. We think he may have had a heart attack. We're requesting a boat to bring him back to the mainland tomorrow. Over."

There was a hiss over the airwaves. *What was that, Scarra? We didn't copy. Over.*

Maggie forced herself to say the words again. "Captain Evans is dead. Repeat—Captain Evans is dead. Over."

The woman in Arisaig couldn't help herself. *My God, that's terrible! I trained with Captain Evans. We all adored him.* Then *Er, over.*

"We'll all miss him, too. We will need a team to take Captain Evans back to the mainland. You'll need to call his family and the coroner. As soon as possible. Over."

The black cat jumped up on the desk and padded over to Maggie, rubbing against her face. "Not now, Sooty!" He flopped down and she absently stroked his head.

Of course, said the woman. *We'll send a boat at first light tomorrow to pick up Captain Evans. May he rest in peace. Arisaig out.*

Chapter Four

The next morning, Maggie woke and opened her red damask bedroom curtains. She looked out: it was a clear, blackish blue dawn, the sky still encrusted with stars. Maggie perched on the sill, watching as the sun rose, staining the horizon yellow. Outside was a windy world, the sea thick with foam and the trees coated in frost. The geese had returned from their breeding ground in the far north; she watched them as they rose and fell in the sky in unison, like a piece of cloth lifted by the breeze.

A note had been slipped under her door.

Dear Miss Hope,

I pray last night's unfortunate events won't keep you from your first fly-fishing lesson. My view on fishing is that it is necessary for the soul in normal times, but absolutely vital in challenging ones. I will be at Loch Scresort with two rods. I hope to see you there, at your earliest convenience.

Yours sincerely,
Theodore Crane

———

Deciding to forgo her usual morning swim, Maggie endured a harsh cold splashing in rust-hued water. She dressed hurriedly—layers of wool, rough Donegal tweed, an oilcloth, and boots—and ran her fingers through her hair, pulling it back into a ponytail.

Finally, she escaped, shivering as she left the castle, taking a moment to turn and look at it in the morning light, a red fortress of elephantine proportions with incongruous crenellations, fake battlements, and bartizaned towers. It appeared more like a factory or a Victorian train station than an ancient stronghold, a fortification sketched by a child who had no idea of actual war. Still, the power of the looming, improbable architecture in the light of dawn was considerable.

She couldn't help but grin when she remembered how Quentin had named the fortress Ivanhoe's Nightmare. It was classic Blood Sport Baronial architecture: intimidatingly ugly, inspired by Queen Victoria and Prince Albert's Scottish hunting lodge Balmoral. Killoch Castle had been built as a playground for the rich, a wild living park created by sport-loving romantics and tweedy buffoons—a salute to a golden age that never was, idealized and reinvented. Along with it came the slaughter of animals for entertainment, not food; needless hunting was the ultimate gentleman's pastime.

To Maggie, the Isle of Scarra was isolated, but savagely beautiful—a severed landmass, besieged on all sides by a hostile sea. Sometimes she felt as if she'd reached the end of the world. The harsh, mesmerizing landscape didn't seem to have changed much over thousands, even millions of years. Until the nineteenth century, the Highlands and Western Isles were seen by many as a mysterious, intimidating, dangerous area, populated, if at all, by barbarians, descendants of the terrifying Picts, tribes so ferocious that the Romans decided to build a wall rather than fight them.

She alternated walking and running through the dense forest of bracken, her legs burning and breath coming quickly. Away from the castle, she found a connection with an ancient world that hadn't entirely vanished, the tissue separating the past and present translucent and fragile. History was remarkably present in the landscape's ability to retain marks of previous lives: Viking burial grounds, remains of crofters' cottages, a one-room schoolhouse, and a tiny chapel were unchanged by the present.

The Isle of Scarra was small enough to be explored in a day. On a map of the Hebrides, the tip of a pinkie finger could blot it out. The terrain was rough, with steep hills, the serrated backbone of an ancient volcanic peak at the center resembling the curve of some sleeping monster. The lower parts were covered in narrow glens and bleak peat bogs, and dotted with tiny lochs. There were remains of straggling crofting and fishing communities that had thrived on the isle until the Clearances, the forced eviction of the crofters to Canada in the nineteenth century to make room for sheep grazing. Even more of the residents had been expelled when the island became a private hunting estate.

Wind whipped at Maggie's hair, loosening strands from her ponytail. She picked her way over lichen-slick rocks past a line of apple trees, then through a tangle of green rhododendron. Ravens conked, Manx shearwaters screeched, and in the distance, she could hear the crash of waves. Following an abandoned road to a narrow footpath, she wended over peat hollows and sour grass under interlocked canopies of sycamores and pines.

She stopped, her breathing ragged, ears stinging from the cold. The chilly, humid air was rank with salt and decaying seaweed. Something moved in the shadows—and for a moment, Maggie thought the shape was human. Her mind flashed to Marcus Killoch before dismissing the thought as utter nonsense.

Still, she could hear noises. *Something* was there, through the trees, thrashing brush and branches. She inched closer to investigate.

It was a stag, his winter coat coarse and thick, wearing his antlers like a crown. *Fiadh ruadh,* she remembered. Among the first things Mrs. McNaughton had taught her were the Gaelic words for "red feet" or deer. Maggie froze; the island's antlered bucks were large, powerful, and rightly threatening, even when it wasn't mating season.

Stepping forward, Maggie could see the problem: the creature's antlers were tangled in a mess of moss, bracken, and dead leaves. It had fallen over his eyes, blinding him. And now he had backed himself into the underbrush, frustrated and frantic.

Slowly, she crept closer to the majestic, entrapped beast. "Shhhh . . . It's all right." Maggie could make out the white flash of an eye rolling in fear. "I'm going to help," she murmured. "I'll help you so you can see again. Then you'll be on your way."

The deer started and strained but stayed in place, ensnared by the thick bushes, as Maggie inched through the shrubbery. But before she could reach the animal, a shadow sprang up behind her, quick as a mountain cat. A hand clapped over her mouth, muffling her scream. She heard a voice in her ear: "Hush." She obeyed, caught by surprise and terror.

An arrow whizzed past her head, burying itself in an ancient oak, flushing a flock of wrens. The stag, startled, violently shook off the bracken and crashed out of the brush, disappearing into the dark forest.

"You ruined my kill!" Maggie heard as she struggled to free herself. Leo was striding toward her, scowling. A vein throbbed on his temple. "I nearly had him!"

The hand that held her relented, and she pulled back to turn and see Sayid, his face apologetic, the feel of his body still burning into her. "Sorry," he said, their eyes locking. "Just didn't want to see you get hurt."

Both Leo and Sayid were in Harris tweed, their feet clad in heavy boots studded with nails and dull with dubbin. Leo carried a bow, one of Ian's. Sayid had his May Fair folding camera on a strap slung over one shoulder.

"That wasn't a fair shot! The poor thing couldn't see!" Maggie was still shaky and breathless. "It's ungentlemanly to shoot an animal when he's blind!"

"Nature red in tooth and claw, tenderfoot," declared Leo, gesturing with the bow. "And I've never seen you refuse venison for dinner."

"Mr. Kingsley," Sayid began, warning in his tone.

"I have no issue with hunting or eating animals," Maggie told Leo. "I'm not a hypocrite—I know meat doesn't start out wrapped in brown paper at the butcher's. But I don't think it's fair to kill when the beast can't even see!"

"Do you really believe Nature is 'fair'?" Leo challenged.

"No, but we humans should know better," she retorted hotly. "And it's not as if we're starving."

He grinned. "We're all just animals, when it comes down to it."

"Miss Hope, the deer on this island have nowhere to migrate to," Sayid explained. "They need to be culled. If they're not, they'll starve."

Leo shook his head. "Don't bother. She won't understand."

Maggie felt her temper blaze. "Well, it's not my fault if you can't hit a moving target and have to take down a stag at a disadvantage."

"And you can't just run into the middle of our hunt and start self-righteous lecturing. Not until you've picked up a weapon yourself."

She'd shot before. And killed. But a man, not a beast. "I know all too well how to shoot. And I prefer not to."

Sayid began:

"She leaves these objects to a slow decay,
That what we are, and have been, may be known;
But at the coming of the milder day,
These monuments shall all be overgrown."

"'Hart-Leap Well,'" Maggie said, recognizing the poem. And she finished:

> *"One lesson, Shepherd, let us two divide,*
> *Taught both by what she shows, and what conceals;*
> *Never to blend our pleasure or our pride*
> *With sorrow of the meanest thing that feels."*

"I always did love Wordsworth. I think that was one of the first we committed to memory when you arrived, wasn't it?" Sayid asked.

Maggie nodded, remembering their first time in the library in front of a roaring fire when he'd discovered her reading poetry, their early mistakes, and then the easy and frequent laughter as they memorized more poems and became acquainted.

"It's all right," Leo interrupted. The three began to wade through the rough grass. "You're scaring the beast away. In case you were feeling hungry, I shot another stag earlier."

"Could this one *see*?"

Leo bristled. "He could."

"Good then. And how did it feel?" she asked.

"Momentous, actually." He chose his words with care. "I felt impossibly powerful—but also profoundly sad." He shook his head. "It happens every time I kill. Death is always like that."

Death. Not only stags are dying on Forbidden Island. "Captain Evans . . ." Maggie began.

"That was something last night, wasn't it?" Leo said. "I never had much respect for his military skills, but Evans did seem a good chap."

Sayid nodded. "He helped us make the best of a bad situation."

"He'll be missed," Maggie added.

Sayid turned to her. "By the way, did you manage to make contact with the mainland?"

"Yes, I spoke with a woman at Arisaig House. She promised they would send a boat here to collect Captain Evans. If they left at first light, they should arrive by noon or so. Were you able to determine the cause of death?"

"Unclear," he stated. "The poor man. And to think he ended his life with us mangy lot—present company excluded, of course. Any news on Mr. Lansbury?"

"No," Maggie replied, remembering the figure she saw—or at least thought she saw—in the woods earlier. "You didn't see him at breakfast? Or run into him in the woods?"

"No," Leo replied. "Haven't seen him at all. Can't blame the man for wanting to get away, though. Same old faces all the time. Enough to make anyone go mad. And as for the widow Poole-Smythe—well, I don't think things have been smooth sailing between them."

Really, Maggie thought, remembering how close Leo and Helene had seemed at last night's dinner. *And while the cat's away, will the mouse play?*

"What are you doing this far into the woods?" Sayid asked Maggie. "Usually you stick to the shore—all of that swimming. Don't know how you force yourself to do it in this cold."

Well, there's not much else to do here and it helps me keep a hold on my sanity. "Actually, I'm meeting Mr. Crane. He's teaching me to fly-fish at Loch Scresort."

Sayid stepped closer, his eyes dark and sincere. "Miss Hope, I'm sorry about grabbing you. I apologize for giving you a fright. I just didn't want to see you hurt."

"I understand, Doctor. And I appreciate the gesture."

"Why don't I walk you to your fishing lesson with Mr. Crane?"

"Go ahead, Dr. Khan—I'm done here." Leo gave a halfhearted salute and turned to make his way back into the woods alone.

"I'm perfectly capable of getting there myself, Dr. Khan," Maggie told him, but her heart leapt at the chance of spending time alone

with him, away from the curious eyes and ears of the other prisoners.

He smiled. "Yes, I know you are, Miss Hope—but why would
you deny me the pleasure of your company?"

Scarra's fast-running river, the Tobermory, cut the island in two. It
had long, shallow rapids, punctuated by rock-edged pools overhung
with slender birch trees. As the morning progressed, the sun's rays
were becoming stronger and warmer; Maggie could nearly feel the
land sighing in the light, the earth warming in the sun, living things
reaching out from their wintry retreat. Above her and Sayid, the sky
was the pale blue of an eighteenth-century drawing room's ceiling.

Together, they followed the path, their footsteps cushioned by
moss and needles. Eventually, they came to a bridge, made of wood
with double railings. Maggie snuck a glance at Sayid's silent profile.
"I don't know if this little bridge has a name," she said as they approached, "but I've always called it Poohsticks Bridge."

"What under heaven are Poohsticks?"

"Winnie-the-Pooh is a bear, of course, and Poohsticks is a sport
named in his honor. He played with his friend, a tiny pig named, er,
Piglet."

The corners of Sayid's mouth turned up in amusement. "I see."

"All you need is a bridge over running water. Each player drops
a stick on the upstream side, and the one whose stick first appears
downstream is the winner."

"Well, then, since we're here—" Sayid responded, scooping up
a few twigs. "Shall we?"

Both their sticks hit the liquid glass of the stream at the same instant; they turned to the other side to see whose had gone the fastest.
"A. A. Milne's stories are for children, but there's one quote I always liked: *Some people talk to animals. Not many listen though.
That's the problem.*"

Sayid nodded. "That *is* the problem, isn't it?"

Maggie won the first round, Sayid the second, and then both their sticks crossed the finish line at the same time. "That was great fun, thank you," Sayid offered. "*Much* better than hunting with Leo."

They picked their way over the path, now on the opposite side of the stream. "You don't like hunting?" Maggie asked.

"I'd rather shoot photographs of deer than literally shoot the animals." Maggie was aware she was staring. She tore her gaze away. "A lot of the deer and game birds were imported here by Killoch, for his hunting parties," he mentioned as they passed a cluster of abandoned crofts. Silverweed coated the derelict gardens. A tiny whitewashed church stood at one end. "Do you know why it was called the Forbidden Island? Because anyone trying to come to the island who wasn't expressly invited by Sir Marcus was met by servants carrying loaded guns. He rid himself of the people who lived here, who worked here for generations, and then kept it all to himself. You wouldn't believe what was done. It makes my blood run cold. But no one man can own this land, no individual, certainly."

Maggie gazed at the deserted village, which now lay in desolation. What had happened to all the people who had once inhabited it, the ones Sir Marcus drove from their homes? The forsaken buildings looked raw and cold and empty, the windows like the eye sockets of a skull. "The crofters probably went to Glasgow—"

"And then Canada. Or the United States. And not willingly. They had no choice."

"Most of Scotland's and England's great houses—the estates— are fast becoming anachronisms," Maggie said. "Taken over by the government. Who knows what will happen to them after the war?"

Sayid didn't reply.

They had arrived at the lake, Loch Scresort, surrounded by dense holly bushes and fed by a roaring waterfall. Maggie spotted Teddy in waders, thigh-deep in cold, peaty water, chewing on his unlit pipe. With his bristly hair and protruding stomach, he really did seem bearish, almost like Pooh. She watched him for a moment as he reeled in his fly and then cast again, the line making a graceful arc.

"I'll say goodbye here, then." Sayid stopped and she did as well. Maggie tried for nonchalance. "Why don't you stay? Fish with us?"

He smiled and leaned closer. "Another time, perhaps." Maggie didn't know if she should shake his hand, embrace him, or kiss him.

At that moment, Teddy caught sight of them on the shore. "Miss Hope! Dr. Khan! How long have you been here?" He smiled, his homely face lighting up.

Sayid waved to the fisherman, then stuffed his hands hastily into his jacket pockets. "Enjoy." He smiled at Maggie, before turning and sauntering off.

Maggie forced herself not to watch Sayid walk away and instead focused her attention on Teddy. "Hello, Mr. Crane!" she called, trying not to sound disappointed Sayid had left. "And how long have *you* been here?"

"Well before sunrise—although that's not saying much in the Scottish winter." He waded back to reach her, splashing through the shallows. He used his walking stick. "There are apples and oatcakes in the sack, if you're hungry."

"I'm fine, thanks." Unlike the river, the lake was calm, dark and somber, reflecting the pine trees and purple-black hills. "Although Mr. Kingsley set his sights on a deer blinded by bracken—and I'm afraid I ruined his shot."

"Accidentally?" He grinned. "Or on purpose?"

"Accidentally—but I can't say I'm sorry. I don't have any issues with hunting per se, just want it to be a fair fight."

"A funny way to feel in the spy trade, isn't it? There's no such thing as a fair fight, is there really? However, fly-fishing's quite a different sport from stalking. Angling's a humble pursuit. There's nothing exclusive, nothing class-conscious about it. It's pastoral and democratic. Which is why, when the foxes are finally reprieved, fish will still be squirming on hooks."

As dead birch leaves spun down into the ghostly green water, she spotted a dappled, fat, brown shadow. "Mr. Crane, there's a fish!"

He chortled. "It's a brown trout, a 'broonie,' as they're called here. I've heard stories of the American Indians being able to reach into the waters and tickle the trout's belly to catch it, but I prefer the rod myself."

Maggie caught a falling dead leaf and twirled it between her fingers. "I don't suppose you've seen Mr. Lansbury?"

"He didn't show up at breakfast?"

"I left without having any—but Mr. Kingsley and Dr. Khan said they haven't seen him either."

"I'm sure he just wanted some fresh air and time to think," he assured her. "I take it you made contact with the 'Powers That Be' on the mainland last evening? About poor Captain Evans? What an awful night."

"It really was. And, yes, I was able to reach Arisaig House. They're sending a team of men by boat today. Most likely they'll send another commanding officer as well."

"Someone pulling the short straw, I'm sure." He scowled into the water.

"Considering our training, we're a fairly well-behaved lot." As she took off her own boots and drew on the extra pair of waders Teddy had brought for her, Maggie caught a glimpse of a flash of white in the mud. It was the porcelain head of a doll, the hair long gone, the paint faded by weather and water. She shuddered. Next to it were the broken pieces of a Dundee marmalade jar. *Long-ago picnics from ages past,* Maggie mused. What had happened to the little girl who'd brought the doll? Was she in Canada now? Did she ever think of her lost doll?

"Here." Teddy held out a rod. "Let's get you started."

Maggie took the rod and gingerly followed him into the water. Even through her rubber waders and layers of wool socks, she could feel the cold.

"Now, there's a quiet elegance to fly-fishing," Teddy explained. "It's dignified. Precise. A perfect balance between man and nature. Just watch me and do what I do."

Maggie observed him cast and then tried herself.

She failed.

"Keep practicing," he encouraged her as she reeled the fly back in.

She cast again. This time the lure flew out farther.

"That's it—you're getting there."

And again.

"That was better, you're getting the rhythm of it now," Teddy said. "It's all in the arm. Just hold it up for a bit," he told her. "Hold it like this, then pull up, flick, punch." He demonstrated: "Up, stop, throw the line out."

The next time, Maggie managed to throw the fly in an awkward arc.

"You're getting it!" Teddy exclaimed, chewing happily on the end of his pipe. "Although it's a good thing dinner doesn't depend on your fishing skills."

"Gosh, thanks."

"Don't think too much. And yet, you need to be entirely conscious of what you are doing and why you're doing it."

They fished in silence for a long moment, listening to the music of the waterfall. "I was reading about lures . . ." Maggie began.

"Please, Miss Hope—less talking, more fishing."

"You're no fun."

"Hush."

The moments turned into minutes and those accumulated. Maggie's feet were freezing. "So . . . where are the fish?"

"You're scaring them all away with your chatter."

Maggie wasn't so sure. "Maybe we should try another loch? Or a stream? The bay?"

"You must be quiet, Miss Hope."

Maggie couldn't help herself. "The ocean?"

Teddy ignored her. Maggie, bored and cold, said, "There's math in fishing, you know."

"Shhhh . . ."

Maggie distracted herself from her freezing toes by silently contemplating the mathematics of fishing—casting dynamics and rod static. *Propelling a line and attached lure such a great distance requires deft control of the body's ability to impart momentum—the product of an object's mass and velocity—to the rod and line. Following the moment of peak energy, the arm's snapping force passes through the rod to the flexible tip, which then wiggles back and forth. This motion translates the force from the arm to the speed of the line and fly.*

Nothing. No nibble on the line. Maggie sighed.

Because momentum—created by the arm, absorbed by the rod, and passed into the thin fishing line—must be conserved, the tiny mass of the line achieves tremendous velocity, especially at the end.

She almost giggled out loud. *Who cares about finding a unified theory of the universe, when I can be working on a unified theory of fly-fishing? Although . . . You'll still need to factor in how to outsmart the not inconsiderable intellect of a fish.*

Finally, she couldn't take it anymore. "Nothing's happening! I'm going to freeze solid just standing here."

"Fishing, Miss Hope. Not 'just standing.' *Never* 'just standing.'" Teddy heaved a defeated sigh. "Still, let's have some breakfast now, shall we?" They splashed their way back to the shore. Teddy lay down his walking stick, then spread an oilcloth and pulled out a few oatcakes. Maggie realized she was ravenous.

She took a bite. The oatcake was hard and flavorless, as she knew it would be. "As God is my witness," she declared, raising her fist like Scarlett O'Hara in *Gone with the Wind*, "when this war is over,

I shall never eat oatcakes again!" Oats were plentiful and Mrs. McNaughton made good use of the grain, in biscuits, scones, and bannocks. But they were hardly tasty.

She munched, flicking crumbs from the front of her coat. "We're getting older, accomplishing nothing. People are fighting—dying—for freedom all around the world, and we're stuck here."

"Your first assumption, relating to time, is incorrect," Teddy informed her. "The amount of time spent fishing is not deducted from the span of your life." He grimaced. "It merely increases the likelihood of your staying single or getting a divorce. As I should know."

"We're all stuck on this island while the war is being fought. I hate it—feeling so useless. I need to do my bit!"

Teddy reached for another oatcake. "Thank heavens I never had children. I'd never get any fishing done. But if I did, I'd want a daughter like you."

"Hmph," she managed, embarrassed but pleased.

"Miss Hope," he said, "you're a smart, strong woman, and you will do great things in this world." Maggie opened her mouth to protest, but he cut her off. "For whatever reason—perhaps because you're a woman—people will undervalue you." He gestured with his oatcake. "They will try to make you smaller, so they can feel bigger. Don't let them. You have the potential for greatness. One day, you will be called to make an important choice and I know you'll do the right thing." He waggled the pipe at her. "Don't disappoint me."

"And, in the meantime?"

"Fish."

"Fish?"

"If not literal fishing, find *your* fishing—whatever it is that calms you, restores you, makes the time fly."

Like Mr. Churchill and painting, Maggie remembered. "I'm sorry, Mr. Crane, but I don't think fishing's for me."

"Fair enough." Teddy tilted his head, studying her face. "It's not

for everyone. But you'll find it. Your passion. And your purpose."
He smiled. "You might even change the course of this war—you
never know."

"I highly doubt that," she said. Then she changed the subject.
"Dinner was interesting." Maggie watched a peregrine on a nearby
boulder examining his black feet, lifting one, then the other, as if he
were a dandy in patent-leather opera pumps who'd stepped in chewing gum. "Finding out Killoch was a mass murderer."

"I'd heard it from one of the boatmen when I was brought over."

"Really?"

"Yes. Apparently," he began, leaning back on his elbows, "Sir
Marcus had found out his wife was having an affair with one of his
competitors and a few business deals had gone sour. He invited his
wife, her lover, and everyone who'd ever crossed him to the island.
Then he shot them, one by one. He hunted them around the island,
like animals."

"Good God," Maggie breathed. "He must have been mad."

"Oh, absolutely barking."

"And the McNaughtons were here, on the island, when it happened?"

"Yes. Though old Killoch was quite insane, he did manage to
spare the servants. Of course, most of them moved away after the
incident, but the McNaughtons stayed on."

"I wonder why?"

"Young Murdo is a bit off, if you haven't noticed."

"I have." It wasn't the clubfoot, either—there was something
resentful, even malevolent, in his interactions with the prisoners.

"Might be easier for him here, rather than on the mainland. No
one to mock him or pity him. Who knows?" They both finished eating and brushed crumbs from their laps. "Shall we give it another
go?" he suggested, anticipation in his voice.

Maggie exhaled. "If we must . . ."

"I insist. You might yet catch a fish."

"A cold, most likely." She remembered words her friend David had once said: *My idea of a trip into nature is a suite at the Ritz and a book of Audubon prints.* She could see his point now.

As they waded out and cast their lines, a golden eagle circled overhead. Something caught on the rocks at the top of the waterfall, blocking the rays of the wintry sun. Maggie looked over, watching the object as it finally broke loose. It fell with a noisy splash.

Teddy frowned. "What's that? A log?"

Something was floating toward them. Maggie's stomach flip-flopped. "That's no log." She moved farther out into the loch, heedless of the icy water now filling her waders. "I need a stick!" she called.

Teddy made his way to the shore and found a piece of driftwood. He splashed back and handed it to her. She used the stick to pull whatever it was closer.

She was right: it was no log. It was a man, dressed in soggy tweeds, a long, ugly gash on the back of his skull. She and Teddy exchanged a look, and then together they worked to get him onto the shore. On the pebbles, she turned the body over, then gasped.

It was Ian Lansbury, his face pale and bloated, his lips blue. "My God," Maggie murmured. She and Ian hadn't been close, but still— they'd lived together on the island for months. He was a quiet man, handsome in a rugged way, always in the outdoors or reading about it. He'd allowed himself to be seduced by Helene, although whether from passion or just because he was tired of putting up a defense against her constant flirtation, Maggie never knew. Now she never would.

"This is bad business." Teddy rubbed the back of his neck, staring down at the corpse. "He must have taken a fall—hit his head upstream, then washed down here."

"Maybe." Maggie closed Ian's eyes. Beneath her fingers, his skin was clammy and cold. "Poor Mr. Lansbury." She shivered. They were alone in the middle of nowhere with a dead man, the second in as many days, their only contact with the outside world a single radio. *What are the odds? Two deaths in less than twenty-four hours?* Maggie shook off her fears. *Captain Evans's was a heart attack. Mr. Lansbury's an unfortunate accident.*

Right?

Finally, she stood. "Mr. Crane," she said, doing her best to keep her voice under control. "Let's get Mr. Lansbury back to the castle, shall we?"

Chapter Five

Detective Chief Inspector James Durgin straightened the tie of his dress uniform in the driver's mirror of the taxi as it neared the Royal Courts of Justice. Commonly called the Law Courts, it was a looming gray stone structure in the Victorian Gothic style, complete with pointed arches, detailed finials, and long lancet windows.

The driver stopped at the curb at the main gates on the Strand. "I'm used to taking you lot to the Old Bailey," he observed, touching his cap. The Old Bailey, half a mile to the east, had been bombed in 1941, and criminal trials had been moved to the Law Courts. "But whoever the blighter is, I hope you give 'im 'ell."

"We could be at the Old Vic for all I care, as long as we get the job done," Durgin responded, searching his pockets for a few coins.

"Right you are, sir. I hear this is where they're trying that monster—you know—the Blackout Beast. Hey—you're him, aren't you?" The cabbie sounded delighted. "The copper? The one who arrested the Beast? What's his name . . . Reitter?" Durgin didn't reply, but the driver was undeterred. "You *are*, aren't you! Whatever happened to that young chit—ah, my memory's not what it used to be—Mary? Margaret? Margaret—that's it. She was working with you? I'd like to shake her hand, I would."

Durgin's countenance was impassive as he handed coins to the driver. "Keep the change."

The sidewalks were filled with protesters, shouting, "Hang the blighter!" and "An eye for an eye!" On the opposite side, others proclaimed, "No capital punishment!" while waving cardboard signs with crude drawings of a noose and the writing NOT DO THEY DESERVE TO DIE? BUT DO WE DESERVE TO KILL THEM? In 1938, the issue of the abolition of capital punishment had been brought before Parliament and an experimental five-year suspension of the death penalty was declared. However, when war broke out in 1939, the bill had been postponed—and hanging was still a legal option in cases of murder and treason.

Durgin let himself out of the cab. He was tall and lean, like a distance runner, and his blue eyes burned with an intense, almost maniacal energy. His brown hair was touched with white at the temples and clipped short, his eyebrows bushy, and the diagonals of his widow's peak emphasized sharp cheekbones.

He spotted Peter Frain waiting for him near a sycamore and loped over to him. The tree's branches were nearly bare, the pavement littered with broken leaves. Frain was even taller than Durgin, with slicked-back dark hair sporting silver and cold gray eyes. He was broad-shouldered and trim, and stood with perfect posture.

"I thought you were a colonel," Durgin remarked, taking in the details of Frain's dress uniform. As head of the Imperial Security Intelligence Service, better known by the designation MI-5, Frain was in charge of catching spies. A spy himself during the Great War and a professor of Egyptology at Cambridge after that, Frain had become head of MI-5 when Winston Churchill became Prime Minister in May 1940. He and Durgin had been friends for years. Frain was also the man who had arranged for Maggie Hope to assist Durgin on the notorious Blackout Beast case.

"Honorary promotion last year," Frain admitted.

"And I'm sure you're the very model of a modern major general. The uniform's an improvement on your usual dandified threads."

"I dress like a gentleman," Frain corrected. "And you, old thing, usually resemble an undertaker."

Durgin shrugged. "I like wearing black. Keeps me focused on the important things in life."

"Such as friends and family?"

The DCI gave a crooked smile. "Solving crimes, of course."

Frain checked his watch. "Shall we?" Together, the men made their way through the crowd of noisy protesters, past barristers and judges in robes and wigs, more men in uniform, and women—stenographers or secretaries, presumably—in dark wool coats and hats.

As they approached the arched doors, Durgin flinched when a throng of journalists turned toward them. "I hate this," he muttered.

"Steady on, old thing."

The journalists, men in somber suits and bowler hats, swarmed the pair. Bulbs flashed and popped as the shouting began. "DCI Durgin, you must be looking forward to this day with relief!"

"It's just a plea. Once it's entered, Mr. Reitter will go back into custody before he's sentenced. Wheels of justice and all that."

"But the Blackout Beast's *guilty*!"

"Yes, based on evidence," Durgin said, "we believe Nicholas Reitter is guilty of murder. A team of dedicated officers has conducted a thorough investigation."

A short, stocky man with a pen and notebook pressed, "How will it make you feel to see him again?"

Durgin looked away. "Today is about the law."

"He's an animal, a monster—surely you must have some reaction?"

"I'm thinking of the victims and their families. As should you."

The two men walked on. Another reporter shouted, "Miss Margaret Hope brought the bastard down—shot him square in the face. Will she be here to witness the plea?"

At this, Durgin exchanged a look with Frain. A flashbulb exploded, temporarily blinding them both. "Right then, we're finished," Durgin managed. "Good day."

The two men walked past elaborately carved arches. At the highest point of the upper arch was a figure of Jesus; to the left and right at a lower level were those of Solomon and Alfred the Great. Inside the grand hall, with its ornate marble floor and soaring ceiling, the air smelled of wax and hair tonic.

Frain said conversationally, "Did you know the personification of justice balancing the scales dates back to the goddess Maat, and later Isis, of ancient Egypt?"

"Show-off," Durgin muttered. "We're in courtroom number thirteen."

"Lucky us." They walked down a long corridor until they found the chamber, marked with a sign in block lettering reading R V REITTER.

The high-ceilinged room was crowded but preternaturally quiet. Frain and Durgin slipped into one of the few empty leather-upholstered benches in the back.

"No blindfold," Frain murmured, gazing up at a statue of Lady Justice. "They say her 'maidenly form' is supposed to guarantee her impartiality, which renders the blindfold redundant."

Durgin was studying the people dressed in black. The families of the victims.

"I'm trying to distract you, old thing," Frain said by way of explanation as two barristers in robes and white horsehair wigs passed.

Durgin turned back to Frain. "Where *is* Miss Hope, by the way? I've left messages, but she's always 'away.' "

"Some hush-hush mission, no doubt."

"She should know what's happening with the trial—"

But he was cut short. "The court is in session, Mr. Justice Langstaff presiding. All rise!"

In unison, all stood—the families, the visitors, the barristers, the court clerk, the stenographer, the usher, and members of the press.

The judge entered, a tall, gaunt man, his white wig and red official robes relieved only by a lace jabot at his throat. The tippet over his shoulder indicated it was a criminal court. "Ah, Langstaff," Durgin whispered, recognizing him from other cases.

"What's he like?"

"Strict. But fair."

The judge mounted the stairs to reach his seat, at the highest level, just below a carved wooden Royal Coat of Arms.

"The case of *The Crown versus Nicholas Reitter*," droned the same voice. The stenographer, a woman with lavender-white hair and thick glasses, began typing. The clack of the keys pierced the atmosphere of hushed anticipation.

"Bring him up," intoned the judge.

There was a moment of rustling and whispering, and then the accused man emerged from a staircase underneath the courtroom. He'd been hospitalized and looked thin and weak, but was nonetheless escorted by two burly guards to the elevated dock, with metal railings. The lower right half of his face was swathed in bandages and his hands were cuffed in front of him. He fixed his eyes on the judge, the sentinels keeping watch behind him.

Despite the fact that the plea was a formality, the atmosphere of the courtroom was intense.

"Are you Nicholas Reitter?" The judge's query boomed in the silence.

"I am, my lord," the bandaged man answered quietly.

"Nicholas Reitter, you are charged with eleven counts of murder contrary to common law. How do you plead? Guilty or not guilty?"

The accused man mumbled something.

"Speak up!"

He swallowed. "Not guilty, my lord."

His words were greeted by a long silence, then a collective gasp. Then a little girl in black clapped both gloved hands over her mouth and her mother began to weep. There was a soft "No!" Then, increasingly louder, a chorus of "Oh my God!" "What's happening?" "He can't do that, can he?" As the courtroom's disbelief turned to outrage, a high-pitched scream rent the air and a young woman in a dark blue WREN uniform fainted.

Facing the judge, both lawyers appeared shocked. The lawyer for the defense, Tobias Skynner, was slim and elegant, a pince-nez on a gold chain falling from his face. He stood unblinking. On the other side of the courtroom, Aloysius Fullford, short and stout, poured a glass of water and gulped it down.

The judge glowered at the crowd. "I must ask for silence!" The crowd quieted.

"My lord," Skynner asked, "may I confer with my client?"

Judge Langstaff quirked one bushy gray eyebrow. "The Crown was not informed of the plea, I take it?"

"No." He added hastily, "My lord."

The judge turned to the accused. "Mr. Reitter, would you confirm your plea?"

This time, the prisoner didn't hesitate. "Not guilty, my lord."

"Well, then." The judge gazed at the lawyer. "I suggest you have a nice long chat with your client in the Tower, as we will now be going to trial."

The tall frame of the barrister swayed. "Yes, my lord."

The judge glanced down at his papers, then rose. "We shall convene Monday at ten," he announced as the stenographer's keys clicked, "when I shall hear opening statements. Good day."

All scrambled to their feet as he exited the courtroom. As the guards led Reitter down the stairs to his holding cell, Durgin exhaled. "Well, that was . . ."

"Unexpected?" suggested Frain.

"His victims—save one—are all dead! The devil could blame his fiancée or shift the culpability for the crimes with no witnesses. Miss Hope's our only living eyewitness—the only one to have survived. We need to bring her back to give evidence, or else there's a possibility this monster could walk!"

"Well." Frain scowled. "This changes things."

"It most certainly does!" Durgin's eyes blazed with frustration.

Together, the two men left the courtroom. "I don't suppose *you* know where Maggie is—"

"The honest truth is, I don't," Frain stated. "She's with SOE now, not MI-Five. They keep their secrets under the hat, just as we do." Then, "I'm not sure if you noticed in the papers—"

"About the execution of the German spy? Jakob Meier? Of course I did."

"Well, we took care of that one, but I'm sorry to say Home Security's been reporting a significant increase in illicit Morse signals in the U.K. My boys are on it, of course—but there will always be one or two agents we overlook. And we can't always pinpoint where the signals are coming from."

"These illegal radio transmissions—any patterns emerging?" Durgin asked.

"Sorry, old thing—can't tell you."

Durgin rolled his eyes. "Of course."

"Just tell your own boys to be on the alert, without giving any specifics. With any crime, have them check for a radio or any evidence of coding. What's that awful propaganda film they're pushing now? *Next of Kin?*" He quoted: "*This is the story of how you are unwittingly working for the enemy.*"

"Unfortunately, I've seen it," Durgin said. "*Be like Dad, keep Mum.* Two hours of my life I'll never get back."

———

Prosecuting Council Fullford summoned Durgin to his office, which was lined with gold-tooled leather-bound law tomes.

"Thank you for coming," Fullford said as he eased his plump frame into his tufted desk chair. He looked different without his robes and wig, the top of his head bald and shiny, a pair of half-moon glasses perched on his nose. Above him hung a gold-framed reproduction of Abraham Solomon's *Waiting for the Verdict*.

"Of course," Durgin replied, taking the seat opposite. His eyes strayed to the picture. It showed a shadowy courthouse waiting room and a hopeless family—the man with his head in his hands and the woman with her face full of pain. Another woman peered over her shoulder as the courtroom door opened. "The plea was quite . . . something."

"Changing his plea in the dock!" Fullford moved a brass justice scales out of the way, so he could see the chief inspector better. "It's insanity is what it is! You know he's guilty as sin."

"And yet his plea makes the whole thing seem as if a clean conviction's not a sure thing anymore."

"DCI Durgin, you must see how this puts us in a bind. All we have is circumstantial evidence. Of course they'll try to pin it on the fiancée. She'll deny it, but will it sow enough seeds of doubt to sway our case?"

"I can't say, Mr. Fullford."

"Then there's the issue with Miss Hope—she's our only living witness."

"I know." Durgin's voice was tight. He and his men had come upon Maggie after she'd shot Reitter in self-defense. After he'd lost six of his own.

"I know you were there, Detective Chief Inspector," Fullford continued, his tones gentler. "Don't mean to dredge up bad memories. But where is she? We need to get her on the stand!"

"She does very sensitive and special government work . . ."

"No one is *that* special." Fullford took off his glasses to clean them with an immaculate monogrammed handkerchief. "Besides, she was working with you and the Metropolitan Police at the time. I read the file—Peter Frain of MI-Five assigned her to the case, because of her connection with SOE."

"The thing is, she might not even be in the country."

Fullford put down his spectacles. "Well, even if she's on the dark side of the moon, you'd better damn well find her and bring her back."

"I know, sir, but—"

"Otherwise, the Blackout Beast has a damn good chance of going free."

Chapter Six

As morning turned to afternoon, dark, swollen clouds edged toward the island, throwing shadows over the woods and hills. Maggie and Teddy, with the help of McNaughton and one of the castle's ponies, brought Ian Lansbury's body back to the game larder.

The larder was an octagon-shaped sandstone outbuilding near the castle's kitchen. Here dead animals were hung until the meat matured. The tiled floor was decorated in circles with deer vertebrae, and had a drain in the center. Racks with hooks were bolted to the high ceiling, while axes, knives, and saws hung from brackets mounted on the wall. A headless stag, Leo's kill from the morning, was already on one of the hooks. Carefully, they laid Ian's body down, next to Captain Evans's corpse, on the marble slab used for butchering.

Teddy removed his hat. As Maggie covered Ian with a sheet, she murmured, "Rest in peace, Mr. Lansbury."

"Rest in peace indeed."

She looked to Teddy. "Two dead in two days. I'm sure it's not how they anticipated dying in this war—on some wretched Scottish island."

Teddy looked down at the two shrouded corpses. "When is the boat coming?"

"Should be any time now," Maggie replied. "I'll go back to the house to clean up and change—and get things in order for the new captain. Let's wait to tell the other inmates until we're assembled for cocktails."

"Yes." He sighed, then clapped his hat on. "This group of vagabonds needs a leader. Things fall apart, after all."

"Newton's second law of thermodynamics," Maggie murmured. "Works for people as well as objects."

The boat wasn't coming that day. Mrs. McNaughton had taken the message from Arisaig House: *Boat broken down. Needs new part. Will try tomorrow.*

No! Maggie reread the note, feeling helpless and frustrated. But they were on an island, there was nothing to be done—they'd just have to wait. *Stay calm. It's just one more day.*

"I'd like to reply to Arisaig," she told Mrs. McNaughton. "Would you mind unlocking Captain Evans's office for me again?" The housekeeper gave her a suspicious look. "It's important," Maggie assured her. "Please."

Sighing, Mrs. McNaughton reached for the key and then let the younger woman into the office. For a moment, Maggie stood on the threshold. She considered sending a message to someone— anyone—else. Her friend Chuck, or Sarah. David, at Number Ten. Detective Chief Inspector Durgin. *Help, I'm being held prisoner against my will!* she pictured herself signaling, *on some blasted Scottish island in the middle of nowhere. Rescue me!*

But she couldn't. Instead, she contacted SOE at Arisaig. "There's been another death. Ian Lansbury. Please send a boat ASAP. Over."

Another one? The woman's voice sounded gobsmacked. *Copy that, Scarra,* she amended. *We're doing our best. Arisaig out.*

Mrs. McNaughton was lingering in the doorway. As Maggie

turned from the wireless, the woman started. "I didn't mean to snoop, miss."

"No, of course not," Maggie replied, smiling, not believing her for a moment. "Thank you, Mrs. McNaughton. I'm finished."

"Are you all right, miss? You look quite done in. Would you care for a cup of tea?"

"No tea, but thank you." Maggie's wan smile flickered. "And you should know—Ian Lansbury's dead."

"No!"

"I'm afraid so. A terrible accident."

The housekeeper's scarred hand crept to the tiny cross at her throat. *"A Thighearna dean tròcair,"* she murmured. A faint color stained her cheeks. "It means, 'Lord have mercy on us.'"

"A Thighearna dean tròcair," Maggie agreed. Sighing, she left the office and climbed upstairs, through cold so thick it was almost visible, to take a bath, and then dress for dinner. Her room, one of many bedrooms off a long, chilly corridor, was a tortured mix of chintz and tartan, the centerpiece of which was a four-poster carved walnut bed bristling with ivy. *At least there's no taxidermy,* Maggie had thought when she first saw it.

On the nightstand was a lamp in the shape of the Roman goddess, the huntress Diana, topped with a long-fringed crimson shade. Next to the lamp were a broken bracket clock and a stack of books: Daphne du Maurier's *Rebecca,* Charlotte Brontë's *Jane Eyre,* and Richard Connell's short story "The Most Dangerous Game."

The only art in the room was a gold-framed reproduction of Landseer's work *Deer Stalkers Returning.* In it, a ghillie leads a pony through a hilly landscape, a dead stag tied to its back. Maggie hadn't paid much attention to it before, but now she was struck by how similar it was to the way she and Teddy had transported Ian Lansbury's body. She shuddered. Marching over to the etching, she took it down and turned it around to face the wall.

She allowed herself a grim moment of satisfaction before she went to the bathroom. She hated it—the toilet in the shape of a throne with an antler horn on the chain pull. But at least there was a claw-foot tub with a ready supply of brackish water, even if the tub's feet did look like they might start scrabbling across the room at any moment. But when she drew back the muslin curtain, she gasped.

A severed stag's head lay in the white enamel tub, dark red blood pooling and trickling down the drain. His eyes stared at her in accusation, tongue lolling at an angle. The smell was metallic and meaty.

She clapped her hands over her mouth and did her best not to scream.

McNaughton and Murdo were brought up to help dispose of the head and Maggie scrubbed the sticky blood from the tub, tears stinging her eyes. She felt surrounded by death—Captain Evans, Ian Lansbury, and now the stag . . .

But who would do such a thing? she wondered. *Could it be Leo?* She'd ruined his shot, so had he played a nasty prank on her by putting the deer head in her bath? She felt a strange detachment as she stood at the sink and scrubbed her fingernails in the brownish, freezing water, turning them scarlet with cold. She caught a glimpse of herself washing bloody hands in the mirror. *Well, you'd make a fine Lady Macbeth, now, wouldn't you?*

She dressed for dinner, again in her blue wool dress, pulling her hair back even more severely than usual. *You're a trained and experienced agent. There's nothing to be afraid of.*

As she descended the long staircase with its nicked serpent-head banister, she gazed at the oil painting of Lady Beatrix Killoch, Sir Marcus's wife. *Interesting it's not in the main room,* Maggie thought. *Why keep it hidden in the shadows?* Still, Lady Beatrix, at least in her portrait, had been beautiful—in a severe, uncompromising way. She was blond and slim, with skin like marble, and eyes full of secrets. *La Dame de Poisson-Tête,* Maggie remembered Helene saying. *Pish-posh, she looks nothing like a fish.*

Murdo was on a ladder, using a broom to clean spiderwebs from the corners of the first-floor corridor's ceiling. His shirtsleeves were rolled up, and she glimpsed a skull and crossbones tattoo on one forearm. She and the castle's caretaker hadn't had much interaction since she'd arrived at the castle almost six months ago. Murdo kept to himself, for the most part. But Maggie had watched him from her window, a gun over his shoulder, heading off into the woods daily to hunt.

"Hello, Murdo. Is that gum you have?" Chewing gum was an unheard-of luxury.

"What we on the island call 'gum,'" he replied, not meeting her gaze. "Codfish eyes. You can chew 'em all day if you want. Never dry out."

First a stag's head and now a fish's eyeball. Maggie felt queasy. "Thanks, I'll keep that in mind."

"Might not be good enough for you fancy folk," he muttered.

"I tried my hand at fishing today, actually. Much harder than it looks."

"Well, not all of us can relax all day. Some of us have to work. Not to mention fight the war—would if I could."

The words stung. Of course, she couldn't explain to him why she was being kept there, against her will. *Could Murdo have left the head in the bathtub?* She sighed again and continued to the great room. Maggie didn't know exactly what time it was—she didn't think any of the clocks in the castle had worked in decades—but the sun had already set and she guessed it was around six by the growl of her stomach.

The western windows of the great room already had their blackout curtains in place and the electric lights were on. The mounted stags appeared to gaze down over Quentin, elegant in evening dress, fixing cocktails, Monsieur Reynard posed at his feet. "Don't Sit

Under the Apple Tree" was playing on the wireless, its relentlessly cheery refrain echoing through the chamber.

"Is that song *always* on?" Maggie asked as she entered the room. She was trying hard to smile and appear normal. Or at least not reveal how gutted she felt by the day's events and how unmoored her conversation with Murdo had left her.

"Last night we listened to the Glenn Miller Orchestra version, Miss Hope. *This* is the Andrews Sisters. I absolutely adore this song—in all of its iterations," Quentin explained. "And how was your day?"

As Maggie walked toward him, sidestepping the lion-skin rug, she imagined how Mr. Churchill might answer the question. "Er, challenging, Mr. Asquith. A challenging day."

"What happened to the arrival of our new fearless leader?"

"Alas, he—or she—hasn't arrived yet. Arisaig sent us a message that the boat needs a new part."

"Ah, probably not easy to procure this far north. Do you think they will arrive tomorrow?"

"Let's hope so." Maggie approached the globe on its stand; it was outdated now, of course, with Germany conquering huge swaths of territory. As Quentin poured liquids from various bottles into a tarnished shaker, she spun the globe, contemplating how much the world had transformed, remembering the horrors she'd witnessed in Berlin and Paris. From the wireless and the newspapers they were given once a month, she realized the tide of the war seemed to be changing—the Allies had broken the Axis lines at El Alamein in Egypt; Operation Torch, the U.S. invasion of French North Africa, was ongoing; the Germans and Italians had invaded Vichy France; and they'd just received word about the Soviet counteroffensive at Stalingrad. And, still, she and the rest of them were being held prisoner on a remote island. Absolutely useless. Unable to fight. *And now dying.*

"First one's on me," Quentin joked, handing Maggie a cut-glass coupe full of amber liquid. With so much darkness and not enough to do, he'd taken to making cocktails earlier and earlier in the evenings.

She gave a tentative sniff. "What is it?"

"'The Forbidden Island,'" he declared with a flourish of one hand. "It's rum, cognac, and Maraschino. I was talking to Mrs. McNaughton today, and she informed me this cocktail was a favorite of Killoch's."

She sat on an overstuffed sofa and waited to take a sip until Quentin had finished making his own drink. "Do you know why this place is called the Forbidden Island?"

"Yes, Murdo explained that, too. It's because no outsiders were allowed to land on Scarra without express permission from Sir Marcus. It was quite the private kingdom." He eyed Maggie. "By the way, and speaking of private kingdoms—have you been in the ballroom?"

The castle's ballroom was closed up; there was no reason to go there. "No, I haven't."

"Well, *we* have," Quentin said, pointing down to Monsieur Reynard. "And it's . . . odd."

"This whole place is odd."

"No, I mean truly and extremely *odd*. Up in the orchestra gallery, there's a thick velvet curtain."

"What? Why? It would only muffle the orchestra's sound."

"So no one playing could witness what was happening down below is my guess." He arched an eyebrow. "And there are dumbwaiters."

"Dumbwaiters?"

"To pass food and drink into the ballroom without anyone entering. No waitstaff was allowed inside. Everything happening in there was kept utterly and absolutely private."

It took Maggie a moment, but then she understood what he meant. "Are you sure?"

"I asked McNaughton, and he confirmed it." Maggie's face must have registered disbelief. "It's true!" Quentin assured her. "The musicians and the staff never witnessed what went on during those balls—although of course they had their speculations. And, if you notice, all the windows are quite high up—there's no way anyone could see in."

"Goodness," Maggie responded. He'd finished making his drink, and they clinked glasses.

"Enjoy!"

Maggie took a tentative sip and grimaced. "Oh my stars, it's—strong."

"Well, this is a house party, after all. Although a house party where all the guests are walking weapons, of course. Would you like something different?"

"No—no." Maggie took another sip. "Tonight I think I need it."

"We all do." He settled in next to her.

You have no idea. "So, what did you and Monsieur Reynard do today?"

"We spent most of it reading—Scott's *Last Arctic Expedition*—about living off the land and all that. Captain Sykes recommended it, back at Arisaig House. Not my thing, but there's little else to do around here. And Monsieur Reynard seemed to enjoy it."

"So you'll read about living off the land, but not actually do it yourself?" She permitted herself a smile.

"Exactly!"

"I went fishing with Mr. Crane today—" Maggie took yet another sip of her drink. "I'm beginning to think you might have the right notion. Not my idea of fun."

"Catch anything?"

"No fish, alas." *Only a dead body.* "Just—cold feet."

"Miss Hope, I can't help but notice you're looking rather pale. What happened to you today that has you on edge?"

I can't talk about it, at least not until everyone's assembled. Best to wait. "Well, Mr. Kingsley very nearly shot me with his bow when he and Dr. Khan were out stalking deer this morning. And then someone left a bloody stag's head in my bathtub for me to find. Both incidents were upsetting, to say the least."

"A stag's head in your bath?" Quentin's jaw dropped. "Who would do such an execrable thing?"

"Who indeed?"

Quentin clutched Monsieur Reynard up to his chest. "I *loathe* hunting. *Abhor* it. My father adored it, though. In the thirties, he went stalking with Hermann Goering at Carinhall—Daddy nicknamed him Der Dick. Anyhoo, Daddy remembers Goering was always wondering what it would be like to hunt man."

"No!" Maggie felt queasy again. She set down her drink.

"I believed him. Back then, old fatty Goering was definitely breeding a menagerie of forest creatures by mating moose and elk with European beasts—he wanted wilder, more aggressive animals for his hunts in the primeval forests of Białowieża. He had a zoologist named Lutz Hecht 'back breeding' the animals, trying to resurrect wild beasts we now think of as extinct. Lord only knows where they are with the program now. . . ." Quentin shivered.

Hunting man? Maggie thought. *What is the world coming to? And yet, isn't that exactly what war is?*

"Hello!" Anna was the next to arrive, a cairngorm brooch at her throat relieving the severity of her dress.

"Welcome, Miss O'Malley," Maggie called, relieved to change the subject from Goering's stomach-turning pursuits. "Come, sit and have a drink with us."

"Thank you," Anna said, choosing a moth-nibbled velvet-covered chair.

"And what do you have there?" Quentin asked.

"Nothing . . . Well, my sketchbook. I did do a few little drawings today. Not anything grand. Just a couple of hats I might want to make, when I return to the real world, that is."

"May I see?"

Anna handed over the notebook for Maggie to take a look. She turned the pages, admiring the delicate pencil sketches and beautiful designs featuring feathers, flowers, and ribbons. "Gorgeous!" she exclaimed. Anna had real talent. "I'll be your first customer!"

Quentin peeked over Maggie's shoulder. "These aren't bad, really." He sounded surprised. "You know, we were just talking about my father—he's a bit of a bigwig at Harrods. I might be able to convince him to take a few of these to sell. When we're all back in that land we call 'civilization,' of course."

"*Harrods?*" Anna whispered the name reverently.

"I'm not promising anything, mind you, Miss O'Malley—but I'll see what I can do. I'll at least endeavor to get your designs into the hands of the right people."

"Oh, thank you, *thank* you, Mr. Asquith!" Impulsively, Anna jumped up and kissed him on the cheek.

"Well, no need for that," Quentin muttered, although he seemed pleased. "Cocktail? I'm serving up Forbidden Islands. Allegedly Marcus Killoch's own concoction."

"They're potent," Maggie warned the younger woman.

Anna was still beaming. "I usually don't drink, but tonight I'll take one." She looked to Maggie. "And what did *you* do today?"

Maggie wasn't ready to relay the whole story, at least until all the prisoners were present. "I tried fly-fishing. With Mr. Crane."

"Mr. Crane! Why, he's a hundred and three at least."

"Hardly," rebuked Maggie. She had Teddy Crane pegged as somewhere in his forties. "And I like him, I really do."

"Really." Quentin waggled his eyebrows.

"No, not like that, you horrible man. I find him interesting. And I always wanted to try fly-fishing. Alas, today I learned I'm not very good."

"Actually," Anna ventured, "I thought maybe you and Dr. Khan . . . ?"

"No."

"No? Because he's Indian?"

"He's British," Maggie corrected. "His father is from Vadodara, Gujarat, and moved to London decades ago. His mother's family is also from Vadodara, but she was born and raised in Bloomsbury. Dr. Khan was born in London, so he's British—not English, but British. And he's already engaged—to a young woman from India his parents have chosen for him. So Dr. Khan and I are friends."

"Ah," said Anna. "I'm relieved to hear it, Miss Hope. A fine Christian woman such as yourself should find an equally upstanding Christian man."

If only Anna knew how long it's been since I stepped foot in a church . . .

"Someone at home then, Miss Hope?" Quentin asked, handing Anna her drink. "Anyone waiting for you there?"

As far as DCI Durgin went . . . No, even if there had been something between them, the Chief Inspector had undoubtedly moved on by now. She'd been gone much too long, over eight months with no word, no call, no letter between them. *Life is passing me by, and it's not just the war.*

"I don't kiss and tell," Maggie replied lightly.

Teddy Crane entered the great room, chewing on his pipe and limping. "I'm telling you—a storm's coming," he was saying to Ramsey, silent at his side.

At that instant, a plump black cat darted across the carpet, ducking low. They could see the tail of a dead rodent hanging from its jaws before it disappeared down the hall.

"Ugh!" Anna pressed one hand to her heart, grimacing.

"It's Mrs. McNaughton's cat," Maggie explained. She couldn't help but smile. "Sooty. Usually he's kept belowstairs, but he seems to have escaped."

"With a rat!" Anna shrilled.

"Looked more like a mouse," Maggie suggested.

"Mice are horrible! They spread plague!" Anna took an unwise gulp of her cocktail and spluttered.

"They probably came to the island on a pirate ship in the time of Mary, Queen of Scots," Quentin offered. "They're rodents with a pedigree!"

"It doesn't help," Anna sniffed.

"I have a cat at home," Maggie offered. "Named K, for kitty— although I like how it makes him sound like the head of a secret intelligence agency. He used to bring me the occasional mouse and I always had to remind myself that, for cats, it's the ultimate compliment to their human, really. They're just trying to add to the house's food supply."

"Dead mice left for you? How creepy." Quentin stroked the stuffed fox in his arms.

For someone who carries around a stuffed fox, that's rich. "It's tribute," she tried to explain.

Teddy smiled. "I like cats."

"Good." Maggie was pleased. "I do, too."

"They're tasty," he said, with a wink.

"Ugh . . . that's terrible!"

"The moggie does more for the war effort than you lazy Sassenachs," Maggie heard Murdo mutter as he passed in the hall outside.

"Murdo," Maggie called to him, "would you please get your mother and father and then would you all come to the great room? There's something everyone needs to know." He colored, then ducked his head and continued on his way.

"Now?" Teddy asked Maggie.

"We might as well get it over with," she replied, steeling herself. "Mr. Asquith, would you be a dear and turn off the wireless, please? And Miss O'Malley, would you run and fetch the rest of the group? I'd like them to hear this, too."

Anna exited to the foyer, where she rang the gong. The balance of the prisoners trickled down to the great room—the new girl, Camilla; Helene on Leo's arm; then Sayid followed by Torvald. When all three McNaughtons had arrived from belowstairs, Maggie took a deep breath. Her eyes met Mrs. McNaughton's, who gave a small nod. "This morning, Mr. Crane and I were fishing in Loch Scresort. We found Mr. Lansbury."

"Well? Where is he?" Helene and Leo exchanged a look. "Is he all right?"

"No." Maggie bit her lip. Then she continued: "I'm sorry to say Mr. Lansbury was dead when we found him. It's likely he fell and hit his head on the shore, then ended up in the water. It appears he drowned."

Helene froze, then forced her lips to move. "No. I don't believe it. He's out hunting . . ."

"My condolences," Maggie said softly.

"No!"

"I'm afraid it's true, Mrs. Poole-Smythe," Teddy interposed. "I was there as well. We—Miss Hope and I—brought the body back to the house. He's in the game larder."

"No!" Helene repeated, but she didn't mean it anymore. She crumpled to one of the sofas, wrapping her arms around herself, moaning. Leo went to her, putting a hand on her shoulder. The rest of the group looked shocked, except for Camilla, who merely seemed curious, and Mrs. McNaughton who already knew. *Of course. Camilla's never met Ian,* Maggie remembered.

"I'll fetch you a cup of tea, ma'am," Mrs. McNaughton said and turned to leave the room.

"Jesus Christ!" Leo exploded. "Two deaths in less than twenty-four hours! First Evans and now Lansbury? Bloody hell!"

"Sir!" admonished Teddy. "This is not a bar in Marseille—there are ladies present!"

The ladies have no doubt heard worse. "Yes, two deaths—one heart attack and one accident," Maggie clarified.

Anna pulled at her brooch with trembling fingers, then picked up her drink. "People just don't die for no reason." She took a greedy gulp.

"Unfortunately," Maggie disagreed, "sometimes they do."

Torvald used a footstool to climb up onto a chair. "What are the odds of that?"

Maggie had studied probability theory. "The events aren't necessarily correlated, Mr. Hagan. For instance, when you roll one die, its outcome is independent of the roll of the second. The two dice rolls don't affect each other."

She could see everyone's confusion. *Well, at least it's taking their minds off things.* "A coincidence is something that's not planned or arranged—but seems as though it is. Technically, a coincidence is an occurrence of events happening at the same time, but by accident. From a purely statistical point of view, these events are random, not related. And they shouldn't be surprising because they happen all the time. Extremely improbable events are actually quite commonplace."

Sayid nodded. "True, true."

Leo remained unconvinced. "I'd say worse, but since we're in mixed company, I'll settle for—balderdash."

"No offense, Miss Hope," Torvald agreed, "but it seems unlikely."

Mrs. McNaughton had returned with a cup of tea, which she handed to Helene. The brunette put it to her lips, but couldn't manage to take a sip. Clumsily, she returned the cup to the saucer, wincing at the ensuing clatter.

Maggie didn't want them to panic. "Actually, coincidence—unfortunate and sad—is the most likely scenario here." Still, her mind raced. Captain Evans's death. Ian Lansbury's death. The stag head. All in less than twenty-four hours. *Are they really all just coincidences? Or are they somehow related? And if so, how?*

Then a thought popped into her mind: Camilla Oddell. *Camilla is the new variable in our equation. No one died until after she arrived.* She looked at Camilla, so petite and delicate, her face bright with curiosity. *She's new—she doesn't know anyone. And has no reason to murder her fellow agents. Don't be ridiculous.*

"Are you all right, Miss Hope?" Sayid stepped in front of her, frowning. "You look pale."

Maggie looked up at him and forced a laugh. "I'm a ginger—I'm always pale."

He put a protective hand on her shoulder. She said lightly, "I'm fine, Dr. Khan. Thank you, though, for your concern."

"I think it's a suspicious coincidence," Leo insisted, getting up to make a drink. "And coincidences may alert us to threats hiding in plain sight."

Camilla took a walk into the woods this morning. She could have killed Ian. And she had time before dinner yesterday, when we were all having cocktails, to put poison into one of the port glasses in the billiards room . . . Maggie thought. *But there's absolutely no proof it's even murder, let alone that Camilla had a role. . . .*

"When is the boat coming?" Torvald asked, his voice shrill. "Shouldn't it be here by now?"

"Arisaig told me the boat's been delayed. They need a replacement part before they can sail out. It should be here tomorrow." *Please, please let it be here by tomorrow. The worst of this situation is feeling so isolated on this island, cut off from civilization.*

"Well, better late than never," stated Quentin. "They'll investigate these deaths, bring in the police, and get the bodies to a coroner's."

"We must have a service . . ." Tears ran down Helene's cheeks. Anna frowned as Mrs. McNaughton touched her cross.

Maggie nodded. "I'll help you plan it, if you'd like. You can choose some readings. I can pick holly and evergreen boughs. We can have it here, or even open the chapel, if you'd like."

Helene nodded. "Thank you," she said, as if she were a windup doll. She suddenly appeared smaller, older, and broken.

Anna shook her head. "I have a very bad feeling about all of this."

As do I. "The boat will be here by tomorrow." Maggie forced a smile. "I'm sure of it. We just need to hold on one more night."

Chapter Seven

Breakfast at Killoch Castle was typically a simple affair, with oatmeal and circles of fried blood pudding, greasy and dark, plus dried fruit and tea, all laid out on a carved buffet table in the dining room. The next morning, the prisoners helped themselves to food and drink, reaching for toast in stag's head racks.

As she entered the room, Maggie heard Anna saying, "My father's words of wisdom were 'While it's fine to eat cold buttered toast, you shouldn't butter cold toast.'"

"A wise man," said Teddy, raising a teacup.

Anna sniffed. "About toast perhaps."

Ramsey started at Maggie's approach, dropping his slice mid-butter. Teddy bent to pick it up for him. "Why does it always land butter-side down?" he asked rhetorically, handing it back to the younger man.

Anna shuddered. "They say it happens when the devil is near."

"Thanks ever so much." Maggie, wearing tweed trousers, a white blouse, and a thick blue cardigan sweater, took her seat. She looked over to Helene, who was silent and very pale, the food on her plate untouched. "Good morning, Mrs. Poole-Smythe," she said. Helene flicked her eyes in Maggie's direction, nodded, then reached for her tea. "And to whoever left me the gift in my room yesterday, I'd like to say thank you."

Those at the table—Teddy, Helene, Leo, Sayid, Anna, Torvald, and Quentin—looked over. At the sideboard, Camilla didn't glance up, while Ramsey, silent as always, focused on pouring his tea. "What gift is that?" asked Anna.

"A bloody stag's head," Maggie answered. She found it was easier to be angry than scared, as she had been all night. "And I'm not blaspheming—it literally was bloody."

"What?" exclaimed Teddy, aghast. The others stared. Only Quentin appeared unsurprised by Maggie's announcement.

"Yes, someone left it in my bathtub. After all that happened yesterday, I didn't mention it—it seemed inconsequential compared to the truly serious events of the past two days. But I want whoever left it to know I didn't appreciate it. It would be less than amusing under the best of circumstances, but now, considering everything . . ."

Sayid glared around the table and saw that Leo was smirking. "This isn't funny."

"No one's laughing," Camilla pointed out. "Miss Hope, that's absolutely horrible!"

You say that. . . . But did you have time to do it and still get changed for dinner? "Well, will anyone admit to it?" Maggie pressed. "Mr. Kingsley? I interrupted your hunt yesterday—perhaps you wanted to pay me back?" Leo glared at her. But he said nothing.

"What about Murdo?" Torvald suggested. "He's an odd one, to be sure."

"I doubt it," Maggie replied. "Especially since I asked him to help me clean it up last night and he seemed as shocked and horrified as I."

Anna began to cry. She pulled a handkerchief from the sleeve of her dark dress and wiped at her nose. "The poor deer! And Captain Evans! And Ian!"

"Hush," Maggie said, laying a comforting hand on the young woman's back.

"I—I have no words," Helene said. "Why . . ." She gave up. "So much death," she moaned.

"It was inexcusably rude," Quentin stated, patting Mr. Reynard's head. "I like a good prank as much as the next chap, but given everything going on here—"

"As Hemingway said, 'Everyone behaves badly—given the chance.'" Leo waved his napkin in mock surrender. "All right, you found me out, Miss Hope. I was annoyed with you for getting in the way of my shot—and then being so high and mighty about it. It was meant to be funny, is all. And done before I'd learned about our fallen comrade."

Sayid shoved back his chair and stood, his face murderous. "Apologize to the lady. Now." Those around the table looked shocked that the usually charming doctor was so enraged.

Leo recoiled from Sayid's glare, then turned to Maggie, placing a hand over his heart. "I apologize, Miss Hope."

All right then, the culprit was Leo, not Camilla or Murdo. Maggie felt a sense of relief.

"Leonard!" Helene exclaimed, as Sayid sat. "That's dreadful. And in poor taste." The two exchanged glances.

"Thank you for owning up to your actions, Mr. Kingsley," Maggie said. "I'm glad we could resolve this matter. From now on, I'd like you to stay out of my room, if you please."

He dropped his gaze and everyone pushed food around their plates, silver scraping against china.

It was Quentin, seated facing the windows with a view of the bay, who saw it first. He jumped up and ran to the glass. "Look!" he called. "The boat! It's here!"

The inmates all rushed to see. There was a fishing boat in the bay, yes, but it didn't seem to be moving very fast. In fact, it appeared to be quite at the mercy of the tide.

Maggie ran through the castle and out, over the dry winter grass to the stones of the craggy inlet, overlaid with bladder wrack, a bright orange lichen. The shallow water of the bay was a silken blue-green, growing darker as it grew deeper. It was so clear, Maggie could see every pebble and strand of seaweed as if under glass.

She saw the vessel clearly, too—a small fishing boat, the hull painted scarlet and white. It was about sixty feet long, with an inboard motor and the name THE BONNIE CLAIRE painted in black on the wheelhouse. The cabin was large enough to hold two men, standing, plus the dashboard and controls; an aerial indicated a powerful long-range radio.

The boat was being carried by the tide as it flooded the shore in a silent, almost menacing arrival. The shearwaters and seagulls screamed as they swooped overhead, *The Bonnie Claire* continuing to drift in a desultory way, even as Maggie ran to the dock, waving her arms. But she couldn't see anyone on deck or through the windows of the crew cabin.

One by one, the other prisoners joined her, watching and waiting with excitement. And then in silence. For something was wrong. Dreadfully wrong.

When the boat was finally close enough to shore, Maggie stripped down to her blouse and trousers, kicked off her boots, and dove into the cold water. She reached the vessel, then climbed aboard. She bent down behind the red gunwales for a moment. When she rose, her face was stricken. She threw out ropes so Sayid, Leo, Ramsey, and Quentin could pull the vessel to the dock.

"This is the craft that left the island two days ago," she called to the rest, through chattering teeth. "Captain MacLean's boat. Not the one we're expecting from SOE.

"Captain MacLean and Dr. Jaeger—" She shouted over the rising wind. "They're—they're both dead!"

———

Drenched and shuddering with the cold, Maggie returned to her room to dry off and change into fresh clothes, then made her way to the game larder, nodding to Sayid, who was already there. Two more had been added to the slabs. Maggie approached one. *Oh my God.* It was Dr. Jaeger, his always pale face even whiter and more stone-like in death.

"Oh, poor, poor Dr. Jaeger," she murmured. She hadn't liked the island's mandatory psychoanalysis, but she had no issue with the man himself and, in fact, always thought the doctor a wry and witty gentleman. Under normal circumstances, they might even have been friends.

Then she glanced to the second dead man. His countenance wore the lines of someone who smiled more often than he frowned. On his left ring finger was a plain and well-worn gold band. "And Captain MacLean." *Four dead in thirty-six hours . . .*

When Sayid was done looking for visible signs of injury, rigor mortis, and lividity, he straightened, his forehead creased in concern.

"What do you think killed them?" Maggie asked.

"It's unclear," he replied. "I'd need to do a proper autopsy to know for certain, of course. But with both men from the boat, the arch in their backs . . . Well, let's just say it's odd."

"What would cause a symptom like that?"

"We'd need to run tests to be sure. But without laboratory equipment . . ."

"But what would you test *for?*" she pressed.

He hesitated, then answered, "Strychnine poisoning." The words echoed in the chilly, tiled chamber.

I want to go home. The thought came unbidden to Maggie's mind. But it was true. *All I want, in all the world, is to go home. But that's impossible.* Instead, she said, "You think they . . . were—?" She faltered.

"As I said, I don't know—I'd have to do a blood test, to be absolutely sure. Miss Hope, I'm sorry—but—"

To control her fear, she focused on the practical. "Where would anyone obtain strychnine?"

"Any household pest control," the young doctor replied. "I'd guess McNaughton has rat poison around."

"And what does it do, exactly—strychnine?"

"Strychnine works as an antagonist of glycine. It blocks motor neuron postsynaptic receptors in the spinal cord. The result is uncontrollable muscle contractions." Sayid looked down at Dr. Jaeger, then replaced the sheet. "Death occurs about two to three hours after exposure, most commonly from respiratory failure."

"My God," she said, remembering. "There were two mugs of tea on the boat's dashboard . . ."

"Now, now—we need evidence, not conjecture, Miss Hope."

"Yes, yes indeed." He was impressive in his adherence to scientific method. "I appreciate your not jumping to conclusions, Dr. Khan," Maggie said, taking the information in, trying to sort it into some kind of order that made sense. "I agree we must be careful when discussing these deaths with the others." *I'm barely holding it together myself.* . . .

"My thoughts exactly, Miss Hope."

Reverting to her beloved math to quell her rising fear, Maggie continued, "Statistics tell us when the pattern is likely to be apparent and when it's likely to be causal. The term is *P value*—really statistician-speak for 'how much tolerance for coincidence do you have?' "

"And what would you say about the P value here?" Sayid pulled the sheet back over Captain MacLean.

Math, math will never fail you. "Statistically speaking, our sample size is too small to have any significance." She took one last, long gaze at the draped bodies. "Although the reality of so many dead men, amassed so suddenly . . ."

Something locked in her throat as she realized she was grasping at straws, attempting to quell the growing uneasiness that threatened panic. *It could just be a tragic accident,* she thought. Yet the details surrounding the deaths nagged at her. *But four deaths? In such a brief period of time?*

Her thoughts went back to Camilla. *She's the new variable. She came with Captain MacLean and Dr. Jaeger on the fishing boat. Could she have done something to them? But why? What could possibly be her motive?*

"And how much tolerance for coincidence do *you* have?"

"Usually, a fair amount," she replied, looking up into his dark eyes. "But, just between us, it's beginning to wear a bit thin," she admitted.

"Wait—" Sayid turned back to the bodies and uncovered their faces. "There's one test I can do without any equipment. . . ." He bent to sniff their mouths.

"Anything?" Maggie asked.

"No." But at Captain Evans's body he stopped, then bowed to sniff again.

"What is it?"

"Bitter almonds."

"What does that tell us?"

"The scent of almonds, plus the color of his face . . . could mean cyanide poisoning."

She tried to neutralize her expression as she took in the information. "Cyanide?" *Like the suicide pill in the bottom of the lipstick tube I took to Berlin.* "How can you tell?"

"Cyanide is a mitochondrial toxin," he explained. "It prevents cells from using oxygen, essentially causing asphyxiation on the molecular level. In high concentrations, ingestion of cyanide leads to death in minutes. The cyanide-hemoglobin complex can cause the skin to remain flushed . . . and it has the smell of almonds, since it's derived from the seeds of the *Prunus* genus—cherries, apricots, almonds, and the like."

"Where else is cyanide found?"

"Household cleaners. Rust remover."

"You examined Captain Evans before and you didn't notice the smell?"

"I never thought to check," Sayid replied, reddening. "Heart attack seemed so obvious. As they told us at medical school, 'Think of Occam's razor when making a diagnosis.'" Maggie was familiar with William of Ockham's principle: *Among competing hypotheses, the one with the fewest assumptions should be selected.* "I'm rather embarrassed to have missed it."

"So, Captain Evans possibly dead from cyanide, Ian Lansbury dead from a blow to the head, Dr. Jaeger and Captain MacLean dead from strychnine poisoning? Could it be—" Once again, she had trouble saying the word.

"Murder?" Sayid took in her expression and his voice softened. "I'm sure there's a perfectly rational explanation for it. Maybe Captain Evans really did die of a heart attack. Mr. Lansbury could have fallen and struck his head."

"And the doctor and Captain MacLean?"

"Well, that's harder to rationalize. But that doesn't mean there's *not* a rational explanation."

"Of course," she murmured, lost in thought. But she kept thinking of the boat. *Why wouldn't it just keep going, to the coast of the mainland, even if both passengers were dead? Newton's law—a body in motion* . . . "When we found *The Bonnie Claire*," she said, thinking out loud, "the motor was off and it had been caught by the tide and washed into shore."

"You know with the tide, currents, and the whirlpools, everything washes back into the bay."

"Not with the motor on. What if something happened to the motor? What if it had been damaged somehow? What if there's evidence onboard?"

———

Together, they boarded the craft and investigated. Everything appeared normal. *No signs of a struggle . . .* "Let's check the fuel," Maggie suggested. The tank was empty. "Captain MacLean was an experienced sailor," she told Sayid. "There's no way he would have taken off without checking the petrol level."

They walked on the pitching deck to the crew cabin. Here, too, everything seemed to be as it should. Sayid gestured to the radio. "Should we ring someone?"

"The boat's coming. They promised. Still . . ." She turned on the transmitter and flipped some switches. "Mayday, Mayday," she said. "This is Scarra. Anyone copy?"

There was only the hiss of static.

"Mayday, Mayday," she repeated.

Nothing.

"We can try later," she said. "Sometimes the weather throws it off." Sayid nodded. Maggie went to the mugs of tea still on the dashboard. Sayid came up behind her, picked up one mug, and sniffed. "Strychnine," he confirmed.

Something wicked this way comes. Maggie looked out the window to the rolling waves. *Or, rather, something wicked is already here.* "So, it's quite possible the two men were poisoned. And then the fuel was deliberately compromised, so the boat would wash back into the bay."

"But who would do such a thing?" Sayid's face was stricken.

Camilla? But there's no evidence. No motive. Maggie gazed out the sea-splattered windows; a seagull was carrying a thrashing fish in its black beak as it flew low over the water. *But there* was *opportunity.*

"It's all right," Sayid said in a soothing voice, noting her pallor. He put one arm around her and pulled her close. For a brief moment, she allowed herself to lean her head against his chest, relishing the human contact. "It's all right," he repeated.

But it wasn't all right. Four people were dead. Most likely murdered. She pulled away. *Nothing is ever going to be all right ever again.*

Chapter Eight

The New Scotland Yard on the Victoria Embankment was a cluster of redbrick Romanesque-style buildings slashed by thick horizontal bands of white Portland stone.

It was chilly inside. In the office, DCI Durgin kept his coat on at his desk, which was surrounded by stacks of cardboard boxes, each marked EVIDENCE in thick black letters. Behind him, a grimy window overlooked the Thames, which curved like a gray-green snake through London.

Durgin's desk was spartan. There were no family photographs, no books, nothing personal at all, except for his nameplate and, tucked in one corner, a worn postcard of Hugo Simberg's *Wounded Angel*.

"I heard about what happened at the sentencing," said his office mate, George Staunton, a broad man with carroty hair streaked with white. "Must have been chaos in the courtroom."

"Indeed." Durgin flipped through the stack of phone messages his secretary had left for him, crumpling each and tossing them into the trash can.

"So he'll be going to trial. We know how much you *love* that!"

"Sarcasm doesn't become you, Detective Staunton." Durgin rummaged through his desk drawers.

"Maggie Hope will be a witness?"

"If we can find her."

"What do you mean?" George raised fuzzy orange eyebrows. "Where the hell is she?"

"No one seems to know." Durgin's head was bent low as he pawed through one of the boxes underneath the desk. "But we'll need her in order to make our case."

"Without her—" George left the words hanging. *Without her testimony, the Blackout Beast could go free.*

"Exactly." Durgin straightened, a black leather address book in hand.

"So, she's a missing person, is she?"

Durgin didn't look up from the address he was copying out. "Yes."

"And you're a big-deal cover-making detective." George pointed to the wall, where a framed magazine cover hung. The headline blared HIS MAJESTY'S GOVERNMENT'S REAL-LIFE SHERLOCK HOLMES, accompanying a photograph of a younger Durgin holding a magnifying glass. *Detective James Durgin is far more human than the great fictional sleuth, and the cases he handles are of a bloodier nature,* teased the caption.

"You know I loathe that picture," he said, ripping off the piece of paper and sticking it in his coat pocket.

"That's why we put it up," George said. "And that's why we keep it up."

"You need a hobby. I understand knitting is popular these days."

George's grin revealed widely spaced teeth. "So, the game is afoot, Detective Durgin! Unless you're too fancy to put the shoe leather to the pavement these days?"

Durgin dropped the address book in his top desk drawer. "Sod off, Staunton."

George was undeterred. "Plus, Hope's the first woman I've seen you look at in—well, let's just say, a long, long—"

Durgin stood, patting the pocket holding the slip of paper with the address. "Really, George," he said, not without affection. *"Sod. Off."*

Using the ship's radio, Maggie once again reached Arisaig House.

Yes, Scarra, came the woman's warm tones over their airwaves. *We know you're waiting on our boat. But a storm warning's reported now, and we don't want to take the risk. Colonel Rogers advises you to sit tight. Over.*

We have four dead men here! Maggie wanted to scream. Instead, she said, "Sit tight?" Her voice sounded high and strained. "Over?"

A storm's on the mainland. It's possible it will blow out to sea and we'll be able to get someone out tomorrow. At any rate, you'll just have to wait one more night. Over.

Maggie looked to Sayid, who was frowning. "Arisaig, there's something else. Over."

Yes, Scarra? Then, *Over.*

"I have news about the boat—the one taking Dr. Jaeger back to Mallaig. Over."

We know. There was a strained pause. *It's been reported missing. Over.*

"Well, it washed ashore on Scarra this morning," Maggie said. "Over."

What? What are you saying? Over.

"I'm sorry to tell you, the tide carried the boat back into our bay." She swallowed. "Captain MacLean and Dr. Jaeger are both dead. And we found the petrol tank empty. Over."

There was an explosion of static, then, *What? Over?*

"We on the island are now up to four dead in thirty-six hours. Four. Dead. We suspect foul play. Please tell *that* to Colonel Rogers. Scarra *out.*"

Anna and Camilla met up with Maggie in the kitchen, their faces accusing. "What were you doing?" Anna asked.

"Using the radio to contact the mainland," Maggie replied, keeping her voice level. "As I said I would."

"So, *you're* allowed to use the radio?" Camilla shrilled.

"To contact Arisaig," Maggie replied. "That's all."

The two younger women exchanged a glance. Maggie realized they'd been talking about her. Anna accused, "You could be using that radio for anything."

"Well, I'm not, I assure you," Maggie snapped, in no mood to engage in their paranoia.

"Next time you use the radio, I'll come with you," Anna told Maggie.

Camilla cocked her head and frowned. "No, *I* will. It's only appropriate, given my . . . background."

"Because you talk like a toff?" Anna rejoined, her working-class accent more pronounced. "Because you're some kind of *lady*? Not here you're not—you're just the new girl. We were fine until you arrived. No one died until you appeared. *You* should be the last person allowed near the radio."

"At least they'll understand me—how anyone can comprehend what you're saying through that burr of an accent is beyond me—"

"Ladies!" Maggie had had enough. "Let me remind you—four of us are dead. I'm only using the radio to communicate that fact with SOE in Arisaig. You're welcome to accompany me if and when I use the radio again. And both of you must know that any and all radio communication is being monitored by British Intelligence, so even if I wanted to send some sort of secret message—which I assuredly do *not*—it would be impossible."

There was an uncomfortable moment as the three women appraised one another with suspicion. Then Maggie sighed. "Look, it's been a hard morning," she said, attempting to ease the tension. "Why don't we make tea and take it up to the rest? We can all use it."

"I don't want tea!" Anna cried. "I want to go home!"

I do, too. But it's impossible now. Maggie clenched her teeth and walked to the stove, turning on the gas underneath the kettle. As the burner sprang to life with flickering, bright blue flames, she said, "Tea will have to do. Anna, would you please fetch the pot? And Camilla, would you get the cups?"

DCI Durgin knocked at the front door on Portland Place.

After a long wait, Chuck, really Charlotte Ludlow née McCaffrey, opened it. "Why, Detective Durgin!" she exclaimed in her lilting Irish brogue. "What are you doing here?" She shook her head. "Never mind, it's cold as last night's porridge—come in, won't you?" She wrapped her cardigan around her. "Hurry! It's a day for the fire!"

"Thank you," Durgin said, wiping his feet before entering. He was carrying a small paper bag with the name POLLOCK'S TOY SHOP printed on one side. He handed it over to Chuck. "For the young master," he told her, referring to Chuck's baby, Griffin.

"Oh my goodness!" Inside was blue tissue paper wrapping a puzzle piece matching game with nursery rhyme characters. "How lovely. And thoughtful." Durgin turned bright pink. "Griffin's just over a year now—he'd probably only chew on the pieces at this point. But I'll put it away for him for when he's older."

"I—don't know a lot about babies," Durgin confessed.

"May I get you a cup of tea, Detective?"

"James, please. And yes, that would be ideal if it's not too much trouble."

"I was just about to make a cuppa for myself, so your timing's perfect." Chuck guided him downstairs. "I'd serve in the library, but it's cold as a brass monkey—slightly warmer in the kitchen."

"Where's the little one now?" Durgin asked.

"Napping, thank heavens. Babies aren't hard exactly, but they're *often,* if you see what I mean. Not much rest for the weary." She gestured to the scarred wooden table. "Sit down! Sit!"

Durgin did as he was told, crossing his long legs at the ankles and stretching them out. "And your husband? I trust he's well?" Durgin recalled her husband was serving somewhere in the Middle East.

"As far as I know." Chuck busied herself with the tea things.

"Glad to hear—" Before Durgin could finish his thought, he noticed two green eyes staring at him from the floor. Unblinking, the marmalade cat climbed onto his ankles, then imperiously strode up his legs. The creature then proceeded to saunter up his torso, plunking his front paws on Durgin's chest and leaning in for a closer stare. Durgin inched his head back from the wet nose. He'd experienced any number of things on the job after all his years, but this inspection by cat was a first.

The kettle started to boil as Chuck pulled out teacups and a plate of carrot cookies. Durgin cleared his throat. "I—I suppose you're wondering why I'm here?" The cat began to knead his chest and purr.

"Well, I expect it has something to do with Maggie?" The kettle screeched; Chuck turned off the gas.

"I left a few messages . . ."

Chuck poured the boiling water into the teapot. "And I kept them for her. Although she hasn't been around for a while to pick any messages up."

The ginger tabby settled himself in Durgin's lap, purring enthusiastically.

Taking in the sight of the DCI's terrified face, Chuck smothered a laugh. "And I see you've met His Nibs, Maggie's cat. She calls him K—or Mr. K when he's particularly dignified."

"It felt like more of an interrogation than an introduction." He accepted a teacup. "May I ask when you saw Maggie last?"

Chuck poured his tea. "Sorry there's no sugar. Or milk."

"I take mine black."

"Like your clothing? Why am I not surprised." Her smile flashed. "Let's see . . . the last time I saw Maggie was an evening in late June. And she was only here for a moment or two."

"The last time you saw her was in *June*?" He'd last seen Maggie boarding a plane in April. Chuck's encounter was five months ago. He'd had no idea she'd been back to London.

"Yes, it was the strangest thing. She and Sarah—you remember Sarah, right? The ballet dancer?"

"Of course." Durgin blew on his tea, then took a sip. Mr. K looked up and observed him through slit eyes.

"Well, Maggie and Sarah returned from goodness-knows-where in late June. They came home together. Sarah went straight up to her room and didn't speak for days. Now Maggie, on the other hand, left that evening—never came back."

Durgin set down his cup. "You weren't . . . concerned?"

"Of *course* I was concerned! Still am! But you know Maggie does all kinds of government work. Won't tell the likes of me anything." She whispered, sotto voce: "No mummies allowed in the Hush-Hush Top-Secret Cloak-and-Dagger Club."

"And you haven't heard from her since? No telephone calls? No letters?"

Chuck blew on her tea. "Nothing."

"And Miss Sanderson? Is she here now?"

"Sarah's in Liverpool. Been there since the end of June. It's been just the baby and me—and Maggie's ridiculous moggie, of course." The cat looked to Chuck and favored her with a benevolent blink.

"Liverpool?" Durgin asked, frowning. "What's there?"

"Sarah's mother. She went home for a bit."

"Why did Sarah leave London?"

"Well," Chuck said, nibbling on a carrot cookie, "wherever they were and whatever happened there, Sarah had a rough time of it. Couldn't stop crying. I brought her trays of food up to her room, but she scarcely ate. Never wanted to talk. Next thing I know, she's left me a note saying she's gone to see her mother. No word on when she's planning on coming back. Or even *if* she's coming back."

"Do you have an address for Sarah's mother in Liverpool?"

"I do," Chuck managed through her mouthful of cookie. "And I'd be much obliged to you if you'd let her know I've been terribly worried about her. I've written her a few times at her mum's and haven't received any answer. And let me know about Maggie, too—please? You will, won't you?"

"Of course, Mrs. Ludlow," Durgin assured her, wondering how to rise without antagonizing the cat. "I'll let you know as soon as I can."

Dinner at the castle was a somber affair. No one said much during the soup course, cullen skink, smoked cod in milk with long strands of green seaweed. As a sour-looking Murdo cleared the dishes, McNaughton brought out the main course. It was haggis, a savory pudding of sheep heart, liver, and lungs, minced with onion and oatmeal, cooked encased in the animal's stomach, and plated with tatties and neeps—mashed potatoes and turnips.

As they were served, Sayid quoted:

> Ye Pow'rs, wha mak mankind your care,
> And dish them out their bill o' fare,
> Auld Scotland wants nae skinking ware
> That jaups in luggies

Maggie's voice joined with his:

> But, if ye wish her gratefu' prayer,
> Gie her a Haggis! . . .

"Robert Burns?" Leo drawled. "Now, of all times?"

"Poetry," Maggie rejoined, "is the best salve." Sayid looked to her.

A cold wind rattled at one of the windows; McNaughton locked it. "Storm's coming," he muttered.

"You see?" Teddy said, taking a bite of neeps. "My arthritis never lies."

"Of course Burns," Sayid told Leo. "Since we've had this . . . extended holiday here in Scotland, I decided to commit a few favorite poems to memory. Seemed only right to start with Robbie Burns, given our location. Miss Hope and I decided to learn verse together, as a way to pass the days. We're competing to see who can memorize the most in the shortest amount of time. Ian would come by and listen sometimes—" He stopped short, remembering. "I'm not sure if I'll have the heart to go on, now that . . ." He left the sentence unfinished, but in her mind, Maggie completed it. *Now that he's dead.*

Torvald, sitting on a chair boosted by a stack of dusty pillows, was pushing haggis around his plate with a tarnished silver fork. "What if someone wanted both Captain Evans and Ian Lansbury dead? As well as Dr. Jaeger and the ship's captain?"

Sayid's eyebrows knit together. As he and Maggie exchanged a look, she remembered the arched backs, the almond scent, the empty fuel tank. She looked to Camilla; the younger woman seemed unconcerned by the news of the two new deaths. Maggie shivered.

Anna looked up. "That many people just don't die for no reason. They die because someone wants them dead."

"Well, then who?" Helene's voice was sharp with fear. She pushed her untouched plate away.

"There's no need to overreact," Maggie said, terrified herself, but fearing mass hysteria. "It's a horrible, awful—"

"—coincidence," Sayid finished.

"Ah yes, Miss Hope and her *coincidences*," Leo sneered. He took a bite of the haggis, chewing on a tough bit of sheep heart. Anna grimaced.

"Well, who do you think would have done it?" Quentin ventured. "None of us, certainly." He laughed nervously.

"Why not?" Leo replied. "After all, we're all trained to kill—and I do believe we're all capable."

Anna blinked. "What if there's someone on this island? I mean, someone *else*?"

"Scarra's a small island," Teddy posited. "Surely if we were sharing it with anyone else, we'd have seen him—or her—by now."

"Not necessarily," Camilla interjected, dabbing at her lips with her napkin. Tonight she was dressed in a gray silk gown, not her FANY uniform, a strand of creamy pearls around her neck. "Not if they know the island well—and don't want to be found."

"How would such a person live?" Helene asked.

"We've all been trained to live off the land, even in winter," Camilla replied. "It wouldn't be easy, but it's certainly possible someone could do it, and do it secretly."

Trying to throw us off the scent, Miss Oddell? Maggie thought.

"I think it's Marcus Killoch," Anna stated.

"Killoch?" Torvald scoffed. "He's long gone. Dead since—when was it? Nineteen twenty-two. Twenty years."

"I've been seeing him," the girl insisted earnestly. "I've been seeing things in the woods—shadows, figures—this has the hand of Killoch all over it—"

"Marcus Killoch is dead, Miss O'Malley," Quentin interrupted. "The old bastard is dead and buried. There's a crypt, you know."

"I've seen him," Anna repeated. Her eyes glittered.

"The island's making her batty," Leo murmured to Sayid behind a raised hand, although they all heard him clearly.

"Living as we do here, isolated, without meaningful work, is enough to make anyone mentally ill," the doctor retorted. "Sanity would be odd in these circumstances."

"But how do we *know* Marcus Killoch isn't here?" Anna persisted. "We don't actually know he's dead. We didn't see him shoot himself. We didn't see the body."

"He murdered his houseguests, hunted them like animals before turning the gun on himself . . ." Helene said. She glanced uneasily around the table. "His tomb is on the eastern point of the island, isn't it?"

"And how do we know he's in it?" Anna shrilled. "And even if his body's there—it could be his *ghost!*"

"Jung would say ghosts are nothing but projections of our own unconscious thoughts and fears on the outside world," Maggie countered.

"I believe in ghosts. And spirits!" the young woman contended.

"Oh please, Miss O'Malley," Leo snapped. "Do stop being so emotional and superstitious. Someone might mistake you for a Sicilian."

"Miss O'Malley," Maggie intervened, reaching for the younger woman's hand. "There are no such things as ghosts."

"I don't believe in ghosts either," declared Torvald. "And, if you think about it, the deaths began the day someone new came to our little island home." He trained his glance on Camilla.

So I'm not the only one here who's had that thought, Maggie realized.

"What?" the pretty blonde exclaimed, reaching for her pearls and twisting them. "Me? I did nothing! I didn't!"

"We've all been here for months, some of us years," Helene stated. "And no one's ever died. Yet, since *you've* arrived, Miss Oddell, four people are dead."

"I've done nothing!" Camilla cried, her eyes shining with tears. "I've done nothing! Why would I kill anyone? I don't even know you people!"

Torvald turned to Leo. "Although *you're* the one with the motive, old thing."

Leo was refilling his glass; wine sloshed over the brim and onto the tablecloth, the red stain spreading. "Me?"

"Mrs. Poole-Smythe and Mr. Lansbury were obviously . . . friends." Torvald gestured to Helene. "You've mentioned you wanted her to be your 'friend' instead. Perhaps you conveniently herded your competition out of the way?"

"That's absurd," stated Leo. His forehead began to perspire.

The dwarf raised one eyebrow. "Is it, though? 'Women love to be hunted.' I've heard you say it on numerous occasions—not in mixed company, of course."

"Well, what about the other deaths then?" Leo protested. "Poor old Evans? And Jaeger? And some random boat captain?"

"It could be a cover," Torvald offered. "To get us off the scent." His attention went back to Helene. "Or perhaps you were tired of old Mr. Lansbury? Wanted him out of the way for a new lover? That could be motive . . ."

Helene rose, one hand raised as if to slap him. "You—you—*goblin*!" she spat.

"People." Torvald took a large bite of tatties, then continued, "Let's not name-call like children in the school yard. Because I assure you that not only have I already heard every insult about my appearance but I can dish them out as well." Helene sat and took a gulp of wine.

"Now, now!" Teddy looked aghast. "Come—let's not make accusations."

"Yes," Sayid agreed, "we must remain calm—"

Helene gazed at Torvald with tears flooding her eyes. "I loved Ian. Loved him. How can you possibly even insinuate—"

"I'm merely speculating—"

"Shut up, you little monkey," Leo snapped at the dwarf. "Maybe it was *you*!"

Torvald had finished the potatoes and turned to the turnips. "What motive could I possibly have?" he returned.

Anna narrowed her eyes. "Does evil need a motive?"

As the table descended into chaos, Maggie decided she'd had enough. "Ladies and gentlemen!" she called, rapping her spoon on her wineglass until everyone quieted. "Idle speculation and finger-pointing aren't helping. I've contacted the mainland several times now. They know what's happened. As soon as the storm's passed through, they'll send someone—with any luck, tomorrow. The SOE and, I presume, the police will sort this all out. In the meantime, we must all stay calm. We are trained agents, taught to perform dangerous missions in occupied territories, to withstand Gestapo torture. Surely we can behave like the professionals we are for another twenty-four hours, until the boat arrives."

"We should leave right now," Camilla said. "We could take that fishing boat—make it to Mallaig, or at least one of the other islands . . ."

"We're not going anywhere in this weather, with that tide and those whirlpools," Maggie stated. "It would be suicide."

"Better than just sitting here. *Waiting*," Anna muttered.

Maggie looked to Camilla. The blonde had dried her eyes and was tucking into her haggis. *Death doesn't seem to affect her appetite.*

A bolt of lightning zigzagged across the sky, followed by the ominous rumble of thunder. "I *told* you a storm was coming," murmured Teddy as he pushed tatties and neeps around his plate. "Arthritis never lies."

Chapter Nine

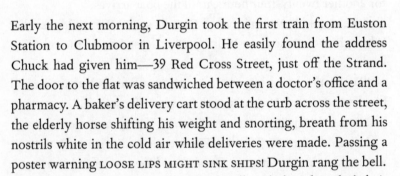

Early the next morning, Durgin took the first train from Euston Station to Clubmoor in Liverpool. He easily found the address Chuck had given him—39 Red Cross Street, just off the Strand. The door to the flat was sandwiched between a doctor's office and a pharmacy. A baker's delivery cart stood at the curb across the street, the elderly horse shifting his weight and snorting, breath from his nostrils white in the cold air while deliveries were made. Passing a poster warning LOOSE LIPS MIGHT SINK SHIPS! Durgin rang the bell.

A woman in her fifties answered, tall and slim, her dark hair flecked with silver. Seeing him, she hesitated. "Good morning," she offered, smiling.

"Hello—are you Mrs. Mary Sanderson? I'm DCI James Durgin, with Scotland Yard."

The smile faded from her lips. "What's all this?"

"I'd like to speak to your daughter, Sarah Sanderson, if I may."

"Sarah? How do I know you're really a detective?"

He pulled out his identification and let her examine it. She did at length, squinting. "Is my Sarah in any trouble?" she asked as she passed it back. Her eyes swept the street to make sure no one was watching.

"No, no," he replied. "Not at all. But one of her friends is missing, and she might have been one of the last people to see her."

Mrs. Sanderson studied his face a moment, then nodded. "All right, then. Please come in." She led the way upstairs. Durgin removed his hat and followed.

The flat above the pharmacy was spacious and bright, with two bay windows overlooking the street. The furniture was plain, but in good repair and well polished. There were Bakelite-framed photographs everywhere of Sarah with the Vic-Wells Ballet in costumes from various ballets—*Swan Lake*, *La Sylphide*, and *Sleeping Beauty*. "Please have a seat, Detective Chief Inspector. Would you like tea?"

"No, thank you."

"I'll just get my Sarah, then." Durgin perched on the edge of a buttoned chair, hat in his hands.

Mary Sanderson left him. There was a knock down the hall, then a flurry of exchanged whispers. Finally, she returned, alone. Durgin stood.

"Sarah will be with you shortly," she told him. "Are you sure about tea?"

"No, no thank you, ma'am." Then, "Yes, I'm sure. I mean, no thank you to the tea."

"All right then. I'm on my way to work." She went to a small closet near the stairway and shimmied into a coat, pinned on her hat, slipped on gloves, and picked up her purse.

"It was a pleasure to meet you, Detective." She stabbed a few extra pins into her hat to secure it against the frigid wind. "I do hope you find the young lady you're searching for."

When Sarah's mother had left, Durgin rose and walked to one wall, to scrutinize a framed newspaper clipping. It was from the *Daily Herald*, May 15, 1940. The headline blared: BRITISH BALLET GIRLS WERE IN 24 RAIDS IN DAY: *They Watched Nazi Parachutists Land*. Durgin read the article, about the Vic-Wells's tour to the

Netherlands, which coincided with the Nazi invasion. At the time, the ballet company was close to the German border and forced to evacuate, leaving behind all its scenery, costumes, and music scores.

A sound at the threshold interrupted his reading. The slim brunette was standing there, dressed from head to toe in black, her face drawn and without makeup. There were dark circles under her eyes.

"Hello, Miss Sanderson. I don't know if you remember me—"

"Of course I remember you, Detective Durgin," Sarah interrupted. "You were all over the papers after that bit of business with the Blackout Beast. And you're a friend of Maggie's." She made a graceful motion with one hand. "Please, sit."

They both did. "Go ahead and smoke if you'd like—I'm sure I can find an ashtray around here somewhere . . ."

"Thank you, but I don't smoke. And I'm here to ask you about Maggie, er, Miss Hope."

"Maggie?" Sarah looked up. "Is she all right?"

"Well, the thing is, no one's been able to contact her. When was the last time you saw her?"

"We returned from a . . . trip . . . in June. We arrived in London on June twenty-second, to be exact."

"So June twenty-second was the last time you saw her?"

"Yes, we were dropped off at her house on Portland Place." Sarah seemed lost in sadness. "I went upstairs, to my room, and stayed in that night, but she left for drinks with someone—and never came back."

"Who did she go out with?"

"Someone from SOE—Special Operations Executive."

"Do you know who?"

"No, I'm afraid I don't remember his name."

"Could you describe him?"

She closed her eyes, as though to conjure the man. "I'm sorry . . . I never actually saw him."

Durgin leaned forward. "But Miss Hope never returned home that night? You didn't see her after that?"

"No. I don't think she came home at all, not even to change her clothes. I would have heard her."

"And you weren't . . . alarmed?"

Sarah considered. "Maggie has had some *interesting* jobs. Since the war's started she, well—let's just say she comes and goes." The dancer turned her dark eyes to his. "And quite frankly, I've my own issues to deal with. I lost someone recently. My fiancé. He was killed." She began to pick at the hem of her skirt.

"I'm sorry for your loss, Miss Sanderson."

"Thank you." Sarah blinked away tears. Then, "Maggie—she's all right though, yes?"

"I'm trying to locate her. You may have heard that Nicholas Reitter has pleaded not guilty to multiple homicides. And so we need Miss Hope to appear in court, as a witness."

Sarah's eyes widened. "The Blackout Beast?"

"Yes. Without Miss Hope's testimony, it's possible he could go free."

Sarah took a soft breath and then shook her head. "I wish I could help you, Detective. I'm afraid I've been lost in my own world for the past several months."

"Do you know who she reported to at SOE?"

"Yes, Colonel Harry Gaskell. His office's at Sixty-four Baker Street. If Maggie's still working for SOE, he'd know where she is."

Durgin stood. "Thank you, Miss Sanderson. I'll let myself out."

Sarah's brow furrowed as she rose. "You don't really believe anything's happened to Maggie, do you?"

"I'm not jumping to conclusions, Miss Sanderson," he replied. "You shouldn't, either."

She studied his face, but said nothing.

"Thank you for your help." Hat in hand, he walked to the door, then stopped. "By the way, your other flatmate, Mrs. Ludlow, wanted me to convey her regards."

"Oh, good old Chuck . . ."

"She's quite worried about you. If you could see your way to writing her a note or giving her a ring—"

"I will, Detective Chief Inspector. Thank you. And please let me know when you find Maggie."

In the grudging wintry morning light, the island was a brooding, lonely place. A knife-edged wind carried the sweet smell of decay as Maggie finished her run, clutching her side and breathing heavily, finding a seat on a flat stone that looked out over the bay. Above, a peregrine swooped by, something small and dark clutched in his talons, as the shearwaters and seagulls screeched.

She was soon joined by a black and white osprey, gazing over a rock like a helmeted guard peering over a rampart. In the gloom behind her, the castle was a fever dream of paving bricks playing at being battlements, candle-snuffer turrets, and bow windows—ugly and yet still somehow eerily powerful.

Maggie turned back to the sea, her eyes on the whalebones and driftwood among the strands of seaweed tangled in the rocks. At her feet lay a white bird skull, an almost sculptural form with sightless sockets and a great piercing bill, the bones transformed by death and weather. She picked it up; in her hand, it felt impossibly fragile. Gazing out at the water, she thought for an instant she spotted a selkie—but it was a gray seal, who'd shuffled up onto a large flat rock and commenced to bark his sad song. The wind rose, ruffling Maggie's hair, but she ignored it. The air, although cold, was fresh and preferable to the castle's moldering interior.

Four dead in three days. She breathed out white clouds. *If there's a murderer on this island, who could it be?*

Then she remembered Torvald's calling out the new girl, Camilla Oddell, as a possible suspect at dinner the night before. *Camilla's the variable,* she mused, *the only new element in the equation. And yet, she's so petite, so young—and moreover has no motive. . . . Still, like the rest of us, she's trained to kill. Could it be Camilla? But* why? *What could she possibly hope to gain? And why was she sent here?*

"Miss Hope!"

She started, then turned. It was Sayid, approaching from the direction of the castle. She knew from his grim expression he came bearing bad news.

"Miss Hope—if you don't mind—"

"What is it?"

He shook his head. "Please. Come with me."

Her heart froze. *Could it be five?* She stood to accompany him, then threw the bird's skull into the sea. It sank, disappearing into the water without a trace.

"She's—?" Maggie asked, gazing at the figure lying on the bed. Without makeup, Helene's face appeared younger, vulnerable, almost childlike. Her skin was white and her eyes were lifeless.

"There's no pulse and rigor mortis has begun to set in," Sayid said. "She died sometime during the night."

Oh, God. Helene. All Maggie longed to do was to weep. Instead, she forced herself to breathe slowly, in and out.

Leo was also in the room, pacing the mottled carpet by the fireplace with its basket of damp wood, wearing striped pajamas mostly concealed by a long paisley silk dressing gown. His jaw was covered in dark stubble, his eyes red and swollen.

"How—?" Maggie asked, blinking back tears.

"When I woke up, she was—" Leo was unable to continue.

"She must have died in her sleep," Sayid answered for him. "The surrounding covers were undisturbed. I assume it was peaceful."

The room was much like Maggie's, full of mismatched tartan and dark wood furniture. A painted still life of a brace of pheasants hung above the dresser. On the bedside table was Helene's ivory cigarette holder, along with a crumpled pack of Craven "A," and a stag-horn ashtray filled with lipstick-covered filters.

There was also a glass. It was empty, but at the bottom was a white, powdery substance. Next to it was a small bottle labeled VERONAL. Maggie bent over to sniff, careful not to touch it. "Sleeping powder residue."

"Yes, I saw," Sayid replied. "She likely overdosed."

Leo stopped pacing to turn and address them. "She had insomnia," he explained. "Dr. Jaeger gave it to her. Said it would help."

Maggie nodded. "He recommended it to me, as well. Still, don't touch the glass—when the police arrive, they'll undoubtedly want to lift prints."

Gently, Sayid covered Helene's face with the embroidered linen sheet. "She must have taken too much."

Something's rotten, Maggie thought. *Five dead in four days. Still, it could be suicide, not murder.* "Was she particularly distraught over Mr. Lansbury's death? I realize the two of them were . . . close."

"Of course she was distraught! Didn't you see her? She was grieving!"

"I mean, Mr. Kingsley," Maggie said, "distraught enough over Mr. Lansbury's death—and the deaths of the others—enough to do something rash." The idea of suicide, of being so full of despair you didn't want to live anymore, was horrifying, yet not completely incomprehensible to Maggie.

"Do you mean, do I think she killed herself over that man?" Leo spat. "No! They'd broken things off some time ago, although that wasn't public knowledge. She merely wanted to sleep, is all."

"Were you with her last night?" Before he could object to the question, Maggie said, "Mr. Kingsley, I offer no judgment—just trying to piece together what happened."

"You were at dinner. You witnessed her. She was upset, yes. But in proportion to everything that's occurred. You must admit it's been a, well, upsetting few days."

That's an understatement. "What did she do after dinner?"

"We were together. I was . . . comforting her."

Maggie refrained from comment. "And then what?"

"And then she wanted to sleep."

"Did you see her mix the powder and drink it?"

"No," he replied. "Yes." Then, "I don't remember." He sat in a button-back chair and put his head in his hands. "She used the glass she always did. It had a powdery film in it, but I didn't think anything of it."

Could someone have preset sleeping powder in the glass, so that when Helene added hers, it became a lethal dose? While Maggie had never particularly liked Leo, she felt a stab of pity. "Mr. Kingsley," she urged. "Please think—it could be important."

Leo lifted his head. "She went to the bathroom to get water from the tap. Then she brought the glass out here and mixed the powder in. She drank it in bed."

"Did she seem agitated? Upset?" Maggie pressed.

"She was sad. Melancholy. Wistful, even. But I don't believe she was thinking about killing herself, if that's what you're implying."

"I'm very sorry for your loss, Mr. Kingsley," Maggie offered, walking to him and placing a hand on his shoulder. "Mrs. Poole-Smythe was a vivacious and spirited woman. She will be missed."

He looked up to her. "Five deaths now! *Five!* What do your damn mathematical theories say about that, Miss Hope?"

She withdrew her hand. "I—I don't know," she admitted. *I'm scared,* she wanted to say. *I'm scared and all I want right now in the entire world is to go home—or at least lock myself in my room.* But saying such things aloud would do no good to her or anyone else.

"We'll need to move her," Sayid said.

Leo rose. Moving to the bed, he pulled back the sheet and bent to kiss Helene's cheek. Then he took her long ivory cigarette holder from the table and slipped it into his robe's breast pocket.

Sayid replaced the sheet. "Steady on, old man," he urged as Leo walked around to Helene's feet. "Come now—on the count of three—"

MI-5 was officially known as the Imperial Security Intelligence Service, but no one actually called it that. It was located in a small, anonymous office building at 58 St. James's Street, but while it looked innocuous, important work happened there, labor crucial to Britain's wartime safety. MI-5's mission was to protect Britain against enemy agents, foreign and domestic. And, with the Prime Minister's blessing, doing so at any cost and by whatever means necessary.

Despite the massive roundup of German spies at the beginning of the war by MI-5 and Scotland Yard, Peter Frain was sure there must be a few still in place. He believed they were sleeper spies, just waiting for that one message from Berlin to tell them their mission.

And now he had proof. Three listening stations had triangulated a transmission coming from the United Kingdom to the German U-boat *U-159* in the Atlantic. Radio direction finding, a key tool of signals intelligence, wasn't magic but seemed like it: by combining information from three receivers, the source of a transmission could be triangulated. The intelligence had been sent to him via motorcycle courier from Hanslope Park, home to His Majesty's Government Communications Centre, which monitored the Abwehr, the German military intelligence service, around the clock. While the transmission's location couldn't be exactly pinpointed, Frain could see it was coming from somewhere on the western coast of Scotland.

The location of the transmission confirmed Frain's worst fear: a

German agent was operating inside the United Kingdom without MI-5's knowledge. He reread the messages with a sinking heart, then telephoned the senior officers involved in the Double Cross System, a counterespionage and deception operation run by MI-5. Since 1939, when a number of German agents in Britain had been captured, those who could be turned were used by British Intelligence to broadcast disinformation to their Nazi controllers. This campaign was overseen by the Twenty Committee, under the stewardship of John Cecil Masterman. The name of the committee came from the number twenty in Roman numerals: XX for "double-cross." To the best of the committee's knowledge, the German agents in the United Kingdom had all been captured and were controlled by the British.

Except for one, now broadcasting from somewhere in western Scotland.

Frain sat at his large oak desk, a reproduction of Goya's *Lord Nelson* hanging on the wall behind him next to an official photograph of King George VI. In front of him was a manila folder, thick with papers, all stamped TOP SECRET in heavy red ink.

Frain rubbed at his temples, realizing he also had to tell the Prime Minister. "God damn it," he muttered. He packed the documents into his leather briefcase, reached for his coat and hat, and barked at his secretary as he left, "Tell our Former Naval Officer"—Winston Churchill's code name—"that I'm coming to see him at the Annexe. It's urgent."

In the taxi, Frain was the picture of composure, except for one muscle, twitching underneath his left eye. The No. 10 Annexe was a flat in the New Public Offices, directly above the underground Cabinet War Rooms, where the Churchills now lived, as Number 10 was considered unsafe due to the Blitz. Frain found Prime Minister Churchill upstairs, in his large Victorian bath.

The P.M. was naked, immersed in steaming water and iridescent bubbles, chewing on an unlit cigar, a crystal tumbler of brandy and soda on a small table within reach, along with a box of wooden matches and an ashtray. Churchill was not the same man Frain had met in 1940—he looked tired and overworked. His once plump face had fallen, and his body sagged with fat.

Frain cleared his throat. "Prime Minister."

"Sit! Sit!" Churchill growled, splashing with his prune-shriveled hands. Then he bellowed to his typist, Mrs. Tinsley, who was seated outside the bathroom door with her noiseless typewriter propped on her lap. "Go away, Mrs. T! Off with you! *Shoo!*"

"Yes, sir." The long-suffering secretary rose and then made her way down the stairs.

The butler pulled out a wooden chair placed in Churchill's bath specifically for meetings. Frain removed his coat and hat, hung them on a hook, then sat. "Sir," he began.

"What's all this now?" the P.M. growled, gnawing on his Romeo y Julieta. "Mr. Greene told me you have urgent news. Be a good man and run some more hot water for me, won't you? I believe the temperature of my bath has dropped below one hundred and four degrees. Quickly, now, quickly!"

Frain turned on the tap marked HOT. When it was apparently enough, the P.M. jabbed his cigar at him. "Now sit!"

"Yes, sir." Frain twisted off the tap and retook his seat.

When Churchill turned to him, blue eyes rimmed with red, Frain took a deep breath and began. "Sir. I'll cut to the chase. We've intercepted a message from somewhere on the western coast of Scotland. It was transmitted to a Nazi U-boat."

"Damn!" The Prime Minister hit the bath's surface with his palms, causing water to splash everywhere, including on Frain's Jermyn Street suit and handmade Italian leather shoes. "I thought you and your boys caught all those Nazzi buggers!" The P.M. had his own idiosyncratic way of saying the word *Nazi*.

"Apparently not." Frain backed his chair away from the tub.

"What's the rat bastard been transmitting?"

"The weather's been too unpredictable for us to get a clear message or a precise location."

"And what do you intend to do?" It was not meant as an opening to a prolonged discussion.

"We're working on the assumption that if a German spy is signaling a U-boat, it's for a pickup."

"You needed a degree from Cambridge for that?" the P.M. grumbled. He slurped from the tumbler. "And why would a German spy be signaling for a pickup *now*?"

"He may have found something of import, something he needs to bring to Canaris's attention at Abwehr."

"It means he's completed his mission!" Another splash of frustration.

"Yes, sir. Most likely, sir." Frain moved his now-damp shoes away from the swelling puddle.

"And how are you handling our ghost?"

"We'll be monitoring the situation closely, moving more RDF trucks to the smaller towns on the Scottish coast. With luck, we'll be able to pick up a more specific message and pinpoint the location. Once we do that, we can head the spy off before a pickup can take place."

"God damn it!" Churchill swore, reaching for his glass again. He took a greedy drink, then kicked and splashed with hairy toes. "Do you remember when I asked you to come to work for MI-Five?"

"Yes, sir."

"You've done well."

"Thank you, sir."

The P.M. rose from the water and stepped out of the tub, dripping over the tiles. Frain looked away from the naked body and reached to hand him a towel.

Churchill wrapped it around himself. "But it will all mean nothing if a single German spy is able to leave Britain with any of our secrets."

"I understand, sir."

"Do you?" The P.M. sighed.

Frain grabbed the Prime Minister's robe from a hook and held it out for him. "I understand the stakes involved, sir."

Churchill slipped into the green silk robe embroidered with dragons and cinched the belt around his protruding midsection. "This Nazzi bugger must be stopped. He must be captured and then either turned or executed. Do you understand?"

"I do, sir."

The Prime Minister shoved his damp feet into velvet slippers. "And what about our other German spy? Hitler's Nightingale? Our little opera diva?" He was referring to Clara Hess, a high-level Abwehr spy who had been captured by the British but was rumored to have escaped from her prison during a fire. Clara Hess was also Maggie Hope's mother.

"We have every reason to assume she's dead, sir."

"I don't believe that for a minute." Churchill shuffled to the bathroom door, then gazed at his spy chief. "And neither do you. But that's for another day. Right now, this spy on the Scottish coast is your number one priority. Understand?"

Frain opened the door for him. "Yes, sir," he called as Churchill's slippered feet padded down the hall.

Chapter Ten

Everyone gathered around the leaping fire in the castle's great room. Maggie was the exception. Standing alone at the mullioned windows, she stared out at the darkening sky. She leaned on the window, her forehead hot against the cool glass pane. Her nerves were jangled, her stomach a roiling mix of fear and dread. And her mind raced, struggling to make sense of it all. Had Helene accidentally overdosed on the sleeping powder? Had she committed suicide? *Or was she murdered?*

Beside her was a bronzed brass telescope on a tripod; she put her eye to the glass, looking out to the horizon. The waves were churning and the sky a greenish purple bruise. *Here are the facts: five people are dead in four days. One might be an accident, but five? In such a short period of time? No, Helene's death couldn't have been an accident. Could Camilla—* She heard Leo's voice calling. "Miss Hope? Care to join us?"

A harsh gust of wind battered the windows, and the velvet curtains ballooned toward her as though they wanted to wrap around her and keep her imprisoned in the castle forever. Maggie shook off their damp touch, then strode across the great room, to the inglenook fireplace and the other prisoners.

"Another death," Quentin breathed, holding Monsieur Reynard close. "Ever get the feeling you're being hunted?"

"We're being killed off," Anna announced in a monotone. "One by one. And because we're trapped on this island, we're sitting ducks."

"Fish in a barrel," Teddy agreed.

"Please." Torvald hopped down from his chair to stab at the flaming logs with the poker. "No more clichéd metaphors."

Ramsey, mute as always, was standing slightly apart from the group, gazing up at the shark and harpoon.

"Marcus Killoch's back," Anna insisted. "If he ever left at all."

"Nonsense," snapped Leo. His face was stone.

Anna was undeterred. "It has to be Killoch. Or his ghost."

"Marcus Killoch's dead," Sayid reminded her. "And there are no such things as ghosts."

"Maybe it's his twin," Camilla suggested.

"It's *never* a twin," declared Quentin. "Don't you ever read mysteries? There are rules, you know."

"Not here, apparently," Camilla retorted.

"Besides," Maggie interposed, "if Marcus Killoch had a brother, the newspaper clipping Quentin showed us would surely have mentioned it."

"Is he dead, really? How do you know? He could still be here—living off the land—" Anna broke off. "Like she said, we've all trained to do it."

Maggie took another hard look at Camilla. She appeared pale and scared, true, but that could be feigned. *She* could *be the murderer. She could have added extra Veronal to Helene's glass by the bed while the room was empty. But* why? *Again, what's the motive?*

Mrs. McNaughton entered and began clearing teacups and saucers. "Is it at all possible?" Anna asked the housekeeper. "Could Marcus Killoch still be alive?"

Mrs. McNaughton blanched, but before she could answer, her

husband shouted from the hallway, "You have no business with things that don't concern you, Sassenach!"

Mrs. McNaughton straightened and whirled, eyes flashing. "Angus!"

The Scotsman glared at her. "It's true—what happened here is none of their damn business. And what are they all doing here any-way? Waiting out the war with their gin and whiskey and their din-ners and their books, being waited on hand and foot while the real soldiers are putting their lives on the line?"

Mrs. McNaughton flinched. "Hush, *an duine agam,*" she said to her husband. It was clearly an argument they'd had many times be-fore. He grunted, then thumped down the hallway to the stairs to the kitchen. She followed, carrying the tray.

There was an uncomfortable silence, then Leo stood and walked to Torvald, towering over the dwarf. "Last night you had the audac-ity to accuse me—and then Helene—of having motive for killing Ian Lansbury! Well, now *she's* dead. What's your little theory now?" He sneered, a cruel smile twisting his lips.

Torvald stood his ground. "I'm sorry for your loss, Mr. Kingsley. We were all terribly upset—*I* was upset. I meant no disrespect—"

For a moment, Maggie feared Leo might strike the small man. He lifted his hand—then lowered it abruptly, stalking away from the group to the piano. He sat, rubbing cold hands together, then hold-ing his fingers over the keys.

"Well." Sayid looked up. "There's only one way to be sure it isn't Marcus Killoch, isn't there? To prove the null hypothesis?"

Anna and Torvald looked at him, clearly bewildered. Maggie sighed inwardly. *If that's what we've been reduced to . . . well, I suppose some action is better than sitting around fretting ourselves into a frenzy.* She sank into a worn-velvet chair and explained, "To disprove all theories until the one left must be true," she explained. "We could do that—we could go to the tomb."

Camilla blanched.

"You surely aren't suggesting—" Anna, too, appeared horrified.

"Yes. To rule out Marcus Killoch as the murderer, we must prove he's dead and buried."

At the piano, Leo struck a series of ominous chords. Sayid ignored him. "Exactly, Miss Hope. Let's go now—before the rain begins."

"I won't be joining you," Torvald declared, settling into a chair. "Short legs and all—I'll just hold you up."

"How did you ever manage to get through SOE training, old thing?" asked Leo.

Torvald gave an enigmatic smile but did not reply.

"While you lot are gone, Monsieur Reynard and I will search the house," offered Quentin.

"Our rooms?" Leo rejoined acidly.

"I'm thinking the cellar. The attic. The library. Maybe there are some clues there. It's where I found the newspaper article, after all."

Maggie looked around the room, noting one absence. "Where's Ramsey?"

"He was just here, wasn't he?" Teddy checked the shadows. "It's probable all of this upheaval has upset him. He most likely went upstairs."

"Why don't you make sure he's all right?" Maggie told the older man. "You shouldn't go out in this wind, especially with your arthritis." She faced the remainder of the group—Sayid, Leo, Anna, and Camilla. "As for the rest of us—let's go."

"The storm will probably hit sometime after sundown," Leo observed, sniffing the air like a hound as the group left the castle. *He's right,* Maggie thought. It was clear something was coming and soon. The winds were cold and damp, and ashen clouds massed above a greenish sea. Gannets dive-bombed fish in the bay, and in the distance, Maggie thought she spotted a school of porpoises breaking the churning waves.

As they turned onto a narrow path that kinked and twisted, Anna shivered in her oversize oilskin. "Is this really a good idea—"

"Look, you're the one insisting whoever's doing this is Marcus Killoch. We're doing this for you." Leo didn't bother to conceal his annoyance.

"We'll make better time if we don't speak," Maggie suggested. In silence, the five prisoners made their way through the woods, then over a soggy field.

"*Fair is foul, and foul is fair; hover through the fog and filthy air,*" Sayid mumbled.

Camilla wrapped her arms around herself and shuddered. "I don't think quotes from the so-called Scottish Play will help."

"We're trained agents," Maggie said. "Let's just consider this a mission."

They passed the crofters' gardens, called "lazy beds"—at one time, the residents had grown hay, oats, barley, and potatoes. "These wretched people." Sayid gazed at the empty cottages, abandoned and in disrepair. "Lordism is what killed them off."

Leo cleared his throat. "I don't want to get into the rights and wrongs of big estates, but in his heyday, Killoch and his like employed hundreds of people. Those who worked for Killoch and his ilk were better off here than they would have been almost anywhere else."

Sayid's eyes flashed. "You think so, do you?" He passed the crowbar he was carrying from one hand to the other.

"It wasn't ideal, but a tyrannical society was most likely better than the Glasgow slums."

"No lectures from you, please." There was an edge to Sayid's voice.

"Gentlemen," Maggie interrupted. "The argument over hunting

estates is pointless now—very few, if any, will be left after the war. It's an era that's passed and will never come again. And maybe it's a good thing."

The little group climbed the steep path to the headland, cutting over dry stone walls, skirting scrambles of windblown pine. On the cliffs, the wind felt raw. Maggie checked her watch, then held it to her ear. There was no tick; it was dead. *Probably due to the damp.* She gazed up to the leaden sky. "We only have a few hours of daylight left. I don't know how long it will take at the tomb, so we need to hurry."

"We're almost there," said Camilla.

It was true. They had reached the westernmost point of the island, with its rocky promontory, the sea below pounding the chasms on each side. On the outcrop rose a polished sandstone, Doric-inspired temple; the name KILLOCH was carved on the top lintel in English Gothic letters. Maggie, Sayid, and Leo stopped to stare. Behind them trailed Anna and Camilla.

Camilla clapped her gloved hands together for warmth. "We just need to know if there's a body in there."

"I understand," Maggie said. "I don't think Marcus Killoch is alive, let alone murdering anyone—still, for Anna's peace of mind, we can rule it out."

"Even if there's a body, there still could be a ghost," Anna murmured.

"No such thing as ghosts," Maggie proclaimed, but her face looked troubled.

There was a padlock on Marcus Killoch's tomb. They didn't have a key, but that was hardly a problem.

"Remember the lock picker at Arisaig House?" Maggie laughed nervously as she jammed at the lock with an awl she'd brought. "What was his name? I swear he came directly from prison."

"The one from Aberdeen?" Leo responded. "Billy Donovan?" Donovan was a career criminal retained by SOE to teach recruits safecracking, lock picking, and detonation. "Vividly. Especially his foul whiskey breath first thing in the morning."

Maggie jiggled the barrel of the lock. "Billy would be so proud of us now—breaking and entering." She struggled; there was some initial resistance, but she persisted until the tumblers clicked.

The group appraised one another. "It's do or die now," Anna declared. "No pun intended." Leo rolled his eyes.

But Sayid had already put his shoulder against the door. It began to move, slowly at first. Then it swung on rusty hinges, the loud screech making them all flinch.

Leo pulled a flashlight from his coat pocket, illuminating the polished granite interior. "At least we're not digging up a grave," Sayid joked, his voice echoing against the stone walls. "Think of all the work that would take, especially in this cold."

"It's just as horrible, though." Anna crossed herself. She was pale.

"Yes, but just think of all the shoveling we're spared . . ." Sayid deadpanned.

"That's completely inappropriate, Dr. Khan!" she cried.

Maggie put her arm around Anna's shoulders. "We crossed the borders of inappropriate quite a while ago, my dear."

Inside, the space was cramped and the air thick with the unmistakable stench of death. Leo and Sayid approached the elaborately carved marble coffin. Leo held the flashlight, while Sayid pried open the lid with the crowbar. Groaning at its weight, they slid it halfway aside. The emerging odor was foul; they all gasped and recoiled. Maggie clapped her hand over her mouth and nose.

Sayid paused, then opened the lid the rest of the way. Leo shone the flashlight in for a better look.

From between her fingers held up to her eyes, Maggie glimpsed the remains of a man dressed in a black wool suit, his bone-thin hands crossed on his chest. Strands of black hair clung to the skull, while dark, vacant sockets gazed up from a face of leathery yellow skin stretched taut over the bones. Still, despite the decomposition, it was unmistakably the Marcus Killoch of the castle's painting.

"Well," Leo said, trying for a light tone despite the greenish tinge of his face, "unless Sir Marcus is a vampire, he's definitely not doing any killing." He turned and left the tomb.

Maggie couldn't bear it anymore. She bolted out, doubling over and gulping in the sweet, cold air. As Anna joined her, a slight movement to the side made Maggie straighten. There, at the edge of a field, she glimpsed a figure slipping away, vanishing into the darkness.

"Did you see that?" she asked Anna.

Leo was retching into the grass. "See what?" he gasped.

"Someone was watching us."

He looked around. "Are you sure?"

It was twilight. Her brain had been deprived of oxygen from the stale tomb. What had she really seen? A stag? A tree branch? A shadow? "No," Maggie admitted. "Or maybe it was a deer. Either way, let's get out of here." She squinted up at the sky. "I'd like to get back before sundown. And the storm."

Sayid replaced the lid of the coffin, then exited and pulled on the heavy door of the tomb. It closed with the same unholy bird-shriek as when it had been opened and then a resounding *bang*. "There's not enough whiskey in all of Scotland to make me forget that stench," he panted.

Leo turned to Anna. "Are you happy now?" he demanded.

Anna was trembling. "She's not *happy*," Maggie snapped, wrapping her arm around the younger woman. "There's nothing happy about any of this."

"Well," Leo amended, keeping his sarcastic gaze locked on Anna, "are you now convinced Marcus Killoch is dead and entombed?"

"Yes," she replied. "But that makes it even worse, doesn't it?"

"How so?" Leo asked as the group began the long trek back across the island. There was a hissing sound above them, and then the rain began pelting down, drenching them in moments. As a pack, they moved quickly, their breathing ragged. Maggie could hear the drops hitting the leaves; the rain mixed with the sweat on her face.

"Because," she said, "if it's not Killoch"—the wind gusted through the syrupy-smelling pine trees—"then it means the killer must be one of us."

Chapter Eleven

At the castle's great doorway, flanked by two bronze eagles with beaks like daggers, Maggie stopped. "I need some air," she said by way of explanation as the others pushed inside, turning instead to walk the covered pathway surrounding the castle. It had ostensibly been built so ladies could stroll outside even during the rain.

She paused at the low wall directly opposite the bay and leaned over to see the colors of the island draining to yellow, sepia, and gray as the light faded. The shore was furry with tall, dead grasses, and the waters swelled with large white-capped waves. In the lengthening shadows, the surrounding trees seemed almost human, like the gnarled apple-throwing ones in *The Wizard of Oz*. The air had a salty, ozone-charged scent. A few deer had the tenacity to graze, backlit by the dim light like Balinese shadow puppets. *I'm terrified*, Maggie admitted to herself.

Knowing she'd soon be cooped up inside by the storm, and craving a last breath of fresh air, Maggie walked from the castle down the path to the sallow grasses and hairy, lichen-covered rocks until she reached the wooden dock. A black shearwater flexed on a rock, wings outstretched, eyeing her warily. The wind was picking up, and the breaking waves looked like white horses on the green sea, tossing *The Bonnie Claire* like a toy. She half-expected to see a mythical sea creature with three loops, as drawn in the oceans on the castle's great globe, break the surface. *There's something both seductive and terrifying about an island,* Maggie realized. *Just as you lose touch with the troubles and worries of the mainland, you also lose touch with real life. On an island, anything can happen.* As she shivered and turned back toward the castle, she spotted rabbits crouched frozen in the grass, still as stones. They hopped away as a figure approached her.

Even before she could make out Sayid's face, she recognized his height, the muscular heft of his shoulders, the jut of his jaw. Nearer, she saw him smile, a dazzling transformation of his countenance from a scowl into something much warmer and more inviting. Once he reached her, she realized he carried the scent of fresh sweat and laundry soap. *No, this is not the man for you,* she told herself.

"I know you're a good swimmer," he joked, gesturing at the roiling water, "but you'll never make it to the mainland, not with this weather rolling in."

Maggie smiled. "I respect the current, tides, and whirlpools—that's why I always keep to the bay."

"I've seen you, you know. You wear a blue hat with pom-poms."

"I realize my cap's ridiculous," she admitted. "But it keeps my ears warm. Everything feels fine once you're submerged. It's just your head that gets cold."

He looked to the churning breakers and shivered. "I don't understand how you do it. Or why you do it, for that matter." He had to speak up over the roar of the sea.

"It reminds me I'm still alive," Maggie said. "That I'm still fighting. Even trapped in this wild and magnificent place."

He nodded. *"Subhanallah."*

"Subhanallah," she repeated slowly. "What does that mean?"

"If you're British and Muslim, it's a word you hear grandparents use. It's a bit old-fashioned—means 'glory to Allah.' But I think it translates to the U.S. southeastern vernacular *Bless your heart.*"

Maggie laughed then, loud and genuine. She'd known a few southern belles back in the States who could twist that expression easily.

The sea's surface was streaked with white, like fatty meat, and sounded like a hostile crowd. Sayid frowned. "It's as if the rest of the world's been cut off by a knife. I know Anna's superstitious, and of course I'm a doctor and a scientist—and agnostic at that—but in this atmosphere, in this light . . . well, I'd have a hard time *not* believing in ghosts."

"You've heard of the *Sruth nam Fear Gorm*? 'The Stream of the Blue Men'?"

He shook his head. "Can't say I have."

"The Blue Men are supposed to look like humans and be very strong. Allegedly, everything about them—their skin, their eyes, even their hair—is blue. They swim the waters looking for boats to sink and sailors to drown."

"Are you making this up?"

"Not at all! Anyway, according to Mrs. McNaughton, the channel through the islands of the Hebrides is called the Stream of the Blue Men. It's also known as the Current of Destruction."

"That's what I love about the Scots. Always so cheerful."

Maggie remembered Mrs. McNaughton's words. "They say the Blue Men swim near the water's surface, like porpoises. They can surface to speak, and when a group approaches a ship, the Chief will shout out two lines of poetry to the captain, who must finish the verse. If he fails, the Blue Men will capsize the ship and drown the crew. But if the captain succeeds, the Blue Men will let them go unharmed.

"After talking to Mrs. McNaughton, I found a book by a man named Donald Mackenzie in the library. It's called *Wonder Tales from Scottish Myth and Legend*. In it, he records an exchange between a sailor and the Blue Men." Maggie quoted:

*"Man of the black cap what do you say
As your proud ship cleaves the brine?*

"And then the Captain answers:

*"My speedy ship takes the shortest way
And I'll follow you line by line."*

Sayid grinned. "You'd have to be quick on your feet with these blue fellows!"

Maggie nodded. "So the Blue Chief says:

*"My men are eager, my men are ready
To drag you below the waves*

"And the captain responds:

*"My ship is speedy, my ship is steady
If it sank, it would wreck your caves.*

"And apparently the captain's wit saved them."

"Is that why you wear your blue hat when you swim in the bay? To fool the Blue Men?"

"I was trained to be an undercover agent—I know how to blend in," Maggie replied. "Mrs. McNaughton says she knows a fisherman who saw a blue man with a green beard and a crown of seaweed, floating from the waist out of the water, following his boat."

"Do you believe it?"

Maggie smiled. "I'm too old now to believe in fairy tales. Although," she amended, "on stormy nights like this, you can imagine how the stories came to be."

They stared down at the rollers hurling themselves to destruction against the rocky beach. The strong currents had uprooted vegetation from the depths and were flinging it in heaps on the sand and rocks. The movement of the sea was hypnotizing.

"These Blue Men—do you think they're relatives of some Celtic sea god?" Sayid asked, after a moment. "Or Neptune? Poseidon maybe?"

"A cloud of ancient fears and memories collected in the Jungian unconsciousness is my suspicion. There's an old Gaelic proverb that says the sea wants to be visited—but then tends to murder its guests." Maggie shrugged. "Mrs. McNaughton says that a fallen angel split into three races of magical creatures—the ground-dwelling fairies, the 'Merry Dancers' of the Northern Lights, and the Blue Men of the Sea.

"My best guess is the story originated with Scots who saw the Picts, painted blue. If the Picts were sailing in low boats, they may have given the impression of blue men raising themselves out of the water. Or maybe the Scottish sailors saw the Vikings' North African slaves and mistook their dark brown skin for blue."

"The sea gives life and it takes it away." The gusts stiffened, as jagged lines of lightning threaded the horizon. Sayid turned to her. "We should probably go back inside."

The air between them was as charged as the wind of the incoming storm. Maggie took one last glance out to sea. "We probably should."

They walked together back up the slope of lawn, gloved hands swinging close together as they approached the gloomy castle. Maggie tried to sneak a sidelong glance at his profile but was diverted by a flash of light from the highest ivy-strangled tower. She gasped. "Did you see that?" But it was already gone.

"The light? Yes! But it was lightning, wasn't it? Reflected off the glass?"

"Maybe. I've never been up there, in the tower, have you?"

"No, I've tried, but it's locked off." Sayid linked his arm through hers. Despite everything, Maggie felt a sudden frisson of what at another time might have been called happiness. "Mrs. McNaughton says there's too much water damage to the stone and it's not safe."

"So who do you think could be up there? Sleeping Beauty? Bluebeard's wife? Mrs. Rochester?"

Sayid smiled wanly. "On a night like tonight, I'd believe anything. I'm not proud to admit it, but I'm scared," he said, voice low.

Maggie looked up at him. "I'm absolutely terrified."

Maggie and Sayid closed the oversize heavy oak front doors, and bolted them against the increasingly violent winds. The air inside the castle was clammy and smelled even more strongly of mold and mildew.

Maggie felt like a sleepwalker as she entered the castle, the enormity of what was happening to them all registering anew. She noticed everything clearly, but at the same time it was as if she were looking at it all from the wrong end of a telescope. She felt calm, but also detached. *Is this what Freud would call "denial"?* Inside, the electric lights blazed, but cloudy dark pressed against the wavy glass. There was no visible moon, no glowing dot of a plane, nothing that might prove they weren't sealed off under the dome of their own world.

Teddy had lit his pipe, perfuming the room with sweet tobacco smoke. He and the other fellow prisoners had grouped again in front of the great room's fireplace, drinking whiskey, listening to the wireless, while McNaughton moved from window to taped window, making sure each was closed and pulling the blackout curtains. Maggie could hear him singing, under his breath:

The whorled dun whelk that was down on the floor of the ocean
Will snag on a boat's gunwales and give a crack to her floor . . .

Meanwhile, a man on the wireless proclaimed, *Hebrides, Storm Force Nine, rain, sleet, possible hail, visibility two hundred yards.*

We're completely cut off from civilization now, Maggie thought.

There was a crack and a lingering roll of thunder. Anna cried out, startled, and rain began tapping at the windows. Torvald rolled his eyes and climbed up onto a chair, sitting with a huff.

"So much for the calm before the storm. I'm assuming you're also having a no-good, very bad, terribly damp day. So I suggest whiskey," Quentin said, pointing to the bar. "Monsieur Reynard found a bottle of eighteen-year-old Macallan."

"Never drink a whiskey that isn't as old as a girl you'd want to—" Leo began.

"Mr. Kingsley!" chided Teddy, speaking clearly despite his pipe. "There are ladies present!"

"—kiss," Leo amended, raising his nearly empty glass. Maggie guessed it wasn't his first drink. "Relax, old thing."

All the inmates were in attendance—Sayid, Camilla, Quentin, Anna, Leo, and Teddy were sitting closest to the fireplace, while Ramsey sat in a nearby window seat, staring up at the antler chandelier. Torvald got up and began to pace in front of the wireless, his short legs spread wide, a cigarette dangling from his mouth. Maggie noted none of them had changed their clothing. All were still wearing the damp coveralls and muddy boots from their tomb expedition. Camilla's hair was uncombed, and there was a streak of dirt across Leo's left cheek.

"Well, that was an afternoon wasted," Leo complained to Anna. "I hope now you're assured Killoch isn't roaming the island."

"It still could be his ghost," Anna replied, buttoning her heavy sweater.

"McNaughton," Teddy called to the man making his way out of the great room, "is there any possibility of ghosts on this island?"

"Ghosts everywhere on the island," the Scotsman muttered.

"Have you ever seen one? A ghost?" Anna asked in a quavering voice.

McNaughton stopped and nodded in her direction, his eyes cold. "No, miss. No ghosts. Humans are bad enough, I'd say." As he stomped out, the group tittered in nervous laughter.

"Well then, shall we dress for dinner?" Teddy suggested. While Camilla nodded and rose, the others seemed almost startled at the idea. Reluctantly, they stood to comply.

"Five are dead, the world may be going to hell in a handcart, a murderer may be among us, and a storm may wash us all away to sea, but We. Are. British. Come, Monsieur Reynard," Quentin said, picking up the fox. "There are standards to be maintained."

The table seemed much larger with two of their usual party absent, the empty mahogany chairs grim reminders of those lost.

Gazing around the room, Maggie realized Leo hadn't quite washed off all the dirt from his cheek, Camilla's golden hair was frizzing in the humidity, Sayid was unshaven, Torvald's bow tie was askew, Teddy's jacket was wearing at the elbows, and Anna's dress had frayed cuffs. Quentin appeared as elegant as usual, but there were purple smudges of weariness under his eyes. Maggie realized her own bun was slipping out of place and tried to pin it back up.

Outside the blacked-out windows, they could hear the thunder rumble. As the chandelier lights flickered, McNaughton began serving cock-a-leekie soup from a steaming tureen and Murdo poured wine. "Where's Mr. Novak?" Anna's eyes were on the empty place next to hers. Her voice was high-pitched and nervous.

Where is *Mr. Novak?* Maggie thought. *Surely not another . . .*

"Novak's probably dead." Leo examined his fingernails. "No reason to let the soup get cold." He picked up his spoon and tucked in.

"That's horrible!" Anna protested.

"When was the last time anyone saw him?" Maggie asked. "Teddy?"

"We went upstairs together to change. But he went to his room and I went to mine. I came down alone."

"Do you want to head the search party?" Leo challenged Maggie. "Go ahead—no one's stopping you."

Camilla unfolded her napkin in her lap. "I think we should wait for Mr. Novak."

"Suit yourself," Torvald replied. He, too, began to eat. "I'm starving," he managed through a mouthful. "Besides, any one of us might be stabbed by a fish fork at any moment. No reason to go hungry."

"A fish fork—how dreadfully middle class," drawled Leo.

"Champagne bottle over the head then," Quentin offered.

"What's a fish fork?" Anna asked.

"Unnecessary cutlery," Maggie responded.

"Traditionally, one uses small pinchers for the snake course," Leo joked. Anna looked as though she didn't know whether to believe him.

"Well, it sounds as if your little adventure wasn't fruitful," Quentin said. He hadn't touched his food, Maggie noticed. Maybe, like Anna, he was waiting for the tardy inmate.

"Waste of time," declared Leo through a mouthful of soup. "As I knew it would be."

"I suspect there's someone *else* here," Quentin said. "A man smarter and more elusive than we're giving him credit for."

"Why do you assume this person's a man?" Camilla wanted to know. Maggie looked at her sharply. But the blonde's countenance remained placid.

"Touché. But, think about it—we usually stay on the paths. There are the woods, the mountain. Even the bothies could be inhabited. We'd never know."

Teddy started in on his soup, a drop staining his lapel. "If there *is* someone out there, he—or she—is getting very wet."

"Unless it's a ghost," Anna repeated.

"There are no ghosts!" Maggie exclaimed, as the lights flickered again. "Please! Let's not let our imaginations run away with us," she amended in gentler tones. "We must keep our heads. We're trained agents of the SOE."

"Perhaps we're being punished for not doing our duty," Torvald posited. "After all, the rest of Britain and now America are fighting or supporting the war—and here we are, locked away like animals in a cage."

Maggie had a sudden and horrible thought—what if SOE was having them killed off one by one? No, they might imprison rogue agents, but they would never kill them. Would they? She thought back to Colonel Henrik Martens, Mr. Churchill's so-called Master of Deception, and the lengths to which he was willing to go to protect information.

Yes, of course they'd kill us, she realized. *Without a second thought. And make it look like an accident.* Then she stopped herself. *Paranoia. That's what you're experiencing. Stick to the facts, Hope.*

"It's not safe here," Camilla said, "for any of us. SOE should know that."

"If there's someone else on this island, I'm going to find him." Leo looked at Camilla. "Or her," he declared. "As soon as this blasted rain stops."

"Besides," Quentin added, "when the tempest ends, the authorities will come for us. Then we can have a real hunting party. Catch whoever's doing this."

"We're completely cut off now, you know," Teddy observed, as drops from leaks from the ceiling plinked in the standing buckets. "There you are, old thing! We were about to call out the guards!"

Ramsey had ducked into the room, avoiding all eye contact. He was silent as usual, taking his seat and immediately lifting his soup spoon. Those who'd been waiting for him began to eat, too.

When they were finished, the soup course was cleared and the main—salmon, its skin seared and blackened, inner flesh the color of coral—was served.

"All right," said Teddy, picking up his fork and looking around at the eight remaining faces. "I think we should all go around and say why we're here."

Anna was aghast. "That's private!"

"Perhaps at one point," Teddy countered. "But now that five of us are dead, it may shed some light on motive."

Leo took a huge bite. "I don't believe it's one of us," he mumbled.

"I'll start," Teddy decided, ignoring him. "As many of you probably noticed, I'm a tad older than the rest of you and not quite as spry. Truth is, I'm not SOE. I was working at what we called 'Churchill's Toy Shop.'"

"'Toy Shop'?" echoed Sayid, frowning.

"Where do you think those secret agent gadgets you all so love to use came from? Well, someone has to dream them up—and then produce them. I was one of those people. Used to be an engineer— and read a lot of spy novels. Actually, many of those skills translate to the secret agent trade."

"So, what happened?" There was a bit of orange fish stuck between Torvald's upper front teeth.

Teddy smiled. "I became a little too friendly with a certain widow in the village, Mrs. Ethel Magowen, who ran the bakery. Tried to impress her by showing off a bit. Well, turns out she was sent by the Top Brass to weed out the talkers—and I was banished here as a result."

"Ah, the infamous honeytrap," Leo murmured.

"What were you working on?" Quentin asked Teddy.

"Ha!" Teddy exclaimed, his face flushing. "My claim to fame at the Toy Shop was 'Bad Odor as a Weapon of Offense.' I created a liquid with an absolutely foul smell to be sprayed on German great-coats hung up in restaurants, or when an agent bumped into a Nazi on the street. The coat's owner would become a pariah—and the affected coat would have to be destroyed and replaced."

Maggie smiled. "And did you use a squirt flower in a button-hole?" she asked, picturing circus clowns.

"It was a brilliant invention!" he protested. "Absolutely bril-liant."

"Not sure it will win us the war, but it's amusing, I'll give you that," said Leo.

Torvald glanced up from his plate. "What about you, Mr. Kings-ley?"

Leo cleared his throat. "I don't care to discuss it."

"Come now," admonished Teddy. "Fair's fair."

"All right, if you're insisting—I—" The rest was unintelligible.

"What was that?" Sayid asked.

"I said—" Leo exhaled. "I said, I spoke English in my sleep."

"You talked in your sleep!" Quentin barked out a chortle. "I've heard of it as a disqualifier, but never met anyone who actually did it!"

"Well, it was at a late stage and I'd already been briefed on the mission. And by that time I knew too much about the cell I was sup-posed to be joining. And so . . ." He waved his hands. "Voilà. I was brought to the island." He turned to Anna. "Miss O'Malley, why are *you* here?"

Anna's sharp intake of breath was audible. "I'd rather not say."

"You must," Leo insisted.

"It's not a matter for gentlemen to know."

Torvald's eyes glittered. "Let me guess—you got preggers."

"Mr. Hagan!" Camilla scolded.

"*With child,* then," he amended, sounding unrepentant.

"Yes. I—I found myself . . . with child . . . when I was at Beaulieu, about to leave for France," Anna confessed in a breathless rush. "And so they wouldn't let me go. They thought I was loose, had no morals, no discipline . . ." She glared at Leo. "Are you happy now?"

Leo wasn't done. "Doctor? What about you?"

Sayid touched his napkin to the corner of his mouth before replying. "As I've mentioned, while I'm British, my father is from India. But I was born in London, and before I studied medicine, I was a Reader in Classical Archaeology and Fellow of All Souls College, specializing in Greek colonization in southern Italy, specifically in Sicily and Calabria. SOE found my knowledge helpful. They were planning on sending me to Italy, but then the higher-ups decided I was too dark to pass for Italian. Maybe it was that, or possibly it was because they didn't like my ethnicity." He shrugged. "So they pulled me, and, well—the rest you all know."

"I didn't make the physical," offered Quentin, stroking Monsieur Reynard. "I did well at a lot of the requirements—perfect French and German, superb shot, excellent radio skills—they just didn't feel I could get over the Pyrenees if push came to shove. I was heartbroken, let me tell you. I might not look like your usual patriot, but I'm a Briton through and through."

"But that wouldn't be enough to have you sent here," Anna pointed out.

Leo's eyes narrowed. "She's right. So what are you not telling us?"

"Well, the truth is . . ." Quentin took a deep breath. "If you must know . . . I'm 'like that.' You know—the opposite of NSIT."

"NSIT?" Anna asked, bewildered. "What does that even mean?"

"*Not safe in taxis,* meaning 'real taxi tiger.' As opposed to VVSTPQ, which means, 'very, very safe in taxis, probably queer.'" He took a long slug of his drink, then sighed. "They found out I'm a homosexual, my dear Miss O'Malley. And instead of letting a well-trained patriot do his job for his country, they pulled me. And banished me as punishment."

There was a moment of silence as everyone digested his revelation. "Mr. Hagan, what's your story?" Leo asked, unruffled by Quentin's admission. "I must say, I've been keen to know ever since we met."

"Well," the dwarf stated, "obviously I'm not the ideal SOE candidate, at least in terms of physical capabilities." He laughed. "However, there was a particular mission where a person of my . . . stature . . . was deemed useful. To reach a certain part of a factory in enemy territory."

"What happened?" Maggie asked, intrigued.

"Mission was scrubbed," he replied. "And at that point, I knew too much."

"That's my situation," Maggie said. "Knowing too much."

"Well, do tell!" urged Leo.

"I can't." Maggie had information on the place of the D-Day invasion, information still in play, as far as she knew. Information crucial enough that SOE was willing to send their own agents to probable death at the hands of the Gestapo to keep the Nazis from learning it.

"It's not like we'll talk to anyone," argued Leo. "I mean, really." He glanced around. "Who could we possibly tell? A taxidermied stag? A stuffed and mounted fish?" Quentin reached down to the fox, as if to comfort it.

"No," Maggie said. "There are some things I won't discuss."

Torvald shrugged, then eyed Ramsey. "Mr. Novak, what about you?"

Ramsey's curious gray-blue eyes were expressive, but he did not reply.

"From what I understand," Teddy interjected, "our friend Mr. Novak witnessed something so horrible he lost his power of speech. Of course, an agent that traumatized can't be on active duty. So he was discharged here." He added, "I think he might have been chosen as part of the Czech and Slovak team for the mission to assassinate Reinhard Heydrich in Prague, but was cut from the team before they left." The rest glanced at Ramsey, who remained expression-less.

Quentin picked at his fish. "Miss Oddell, what's your story?"

"Nothing," she replied. "I didn't do anything."

"Come now—tell us," Leo coaxed. His voice was soft, but it contained a threat.

"I didn't do anything!" she insisted.

Leo held up his wineglass to the light. "That means you did do something—and it was *quite* naughty."

Camilla, realizing she was cornered, took a deep breath. "I— I killed a man. During training." They all looked at her blankly. "One of us," she explained. "A fellow trainee."

Around the table, people's expressions turned to shock, then horror.

"It was an accident, on our last preparation mission." Her words tumbled out one over the other. "And now he's dead and it's all my fault!" Camilla began to weep, burying her head in her hands. "And now I'm trapped here . . ."

"So you were deemed to have violent tendencies?" Leo asked after a moment. His voice was almost tender. *It's unlike him,* Maggie realized, *to be so gentle.*

"I'm a nice girl, a good girl—a debutante!" Camilla protested, looking up with wet eyes. "It was an accident!"

"Of course it was," Torvald agreed, finishing the wine in his glass. He reached for the decanter and saw that it was empty. "Just as all the deaths that have happened since you've arrived have been accidents?"

Camilla's the variable, Maggie remembered as a chill went through her. *The Blackout Beast—Reitter—killed female SOE agents sequentially. Could Camilla be the same breed of murderer? Have some sort of violent compulsion?*

"I did nothing!" the girl cried. She stood, knocking over her chair, and bolted from the room. They heard the pounding of her heels as she ran down the hall. The sound of her voice trailed away. "Nothing!"

When the diners had sufficiently recovered, Torvald hopped down from his chair, then dragged it to the sideboard. "Obviously it's Miss Oddell." He scrambled up to reach another bottle of wine. "She's the murderer," he murmured, refilling his glass.

"We don't know that for sure," Maggie countered, even as she considered the possibility. *Facts, though. We need facts.* "Even if she had opportunity, what's her motive?"

"Who the hell cares what her 'motive' is? Mr. Hagan's onto something," Leo mused. "Look, it all fits together—her predilection for violence, the timing of the deaths, all since she's arrived . . ."

"I hear what you're saying." Maggie took a sip of wine. "It does look bad, but there's no actual *proof*."

Leo rose and walked to the sideboard, grabbing the bottle just out of Torvald's reach and bringing it back to the table. He refilled his glass. "Perhaps we should lock her up, just to be sure. I know *I'd* sleep better."

"There's a dungeon here," Quentin offered.

Anna gasped, and everyone turned to look at her. "What?"

"I'm presuming Marcus Killoch had it built," Quentin continued. "It's in the cellar next to all the wine."

"This 'castle' isn't even a real medieval one." Anna seemed confused. "Why would there be a dungeon?"

"Some people," Leo remarked with a cryptic smile, "find them entertaining."

"Entertaining?" Anna didn't understand. "Entertaining how?"

"*Some* people," Leo continued, seeming to enjoy piercing the younger woman's innocence, "enjoy certain sexual practices. Including flogging, whipping, chains, and the like . . ."

"Mr. Kingsley!" Teddy snarled. "Let me remind you, yet *again*, we are not only at the dinner table, but also in the company of ladies!"

"Oh, it's all in good fun," Leo declared, but he sounded annoyed. He turned back to Quentin. "But you say there's one here? A genuine dungeon? Are there shackles? Maybe we should keep Miss Oddell strapped in there until the boat arrives."

Quentin quirked an eyebrow. "There *is* a Saint Andrew's cross—"

Leo roared with laughter. "That sadistic old bastard . . ."

"We are *not* shackling anyone," Maggie declared, standing.

Sayid stood, too. "No one's getting locked up. If we all stay together, we'll be safe."

Leo glowered, gulping his wine. "Sorry, old man, but I vote to lock up the murderous blond bitch. Who's with me? Show of hands?"

He and Anna raised their arms.

"And all opposed?" asked Maggie. She, Quentin, Teddy, and Ramsey raised theirs.

"Two against four—not enough, Mr. Kingsley," Maggie said, pushing back a stray lock of hair. "Democracy—and civility—still hold sway over more primitive impulses here. Nevertheless," she amended, "we should all lock our bedroom doors tonight. And perhaps put a chair up against them." Sleep would not come easily, she knew.

"As you wish, Miss Hope," retorted Leo. "But when we find the next dead body tomorrow morning, perhaps you'll reconsider. That is . . . if said body isn't yours."

Chapter Twelve

Dawn broke in London with a red sky, but DCI Durgin had long been up and dressed, and was already at the door to the main office of SOE, at 64 Baker Street. It was an unremarkable limestone building, not far from Sherlock Holmes's fictional address and Regent's Park, only one of the many SOE offices scattered around the Marylebone neighborhood. Due to lack of space in Whitehall, the Baker Street area had become home for SOE, and several buildings in the neighborhood bore discreet plaques indicating its code name, Inter-Services Research Bureau.

Upstairs, on the building's third floor, it was dim and intensely cold. The icy reception room was small and narrow, with a single window and a low ceiling. There was a fire extinguisher mounted on one wall and a notice pointing out the direction of the air-raid shelter on another. Two women walked by speaking rapid French, while a man in a European-cut suit smoked a stubby, harsh-smelling Gauloise.

"Detective Chief Inspector Durgin for Colonel Gaskell," the detective said to the freckled young woman at the front desk. A postcard of the Eiffel Tower was tacked up on the peeling wall behind her.

"Of course—one moment, sir." She picked up the telephone

receiver, exchanged a few words, then looked back to Durgin.
"Through that door, please."

Colonel Harry Gaskell sat behind an ornate mahogany desk facing a somewhat grimy window. "Detective Chief Inspector Durgin!" he exclaimed, rising to shake his hand. The Colonel was in his
late forties, a short, rotund man with yellow hair, a double chin, and
a fleshy, shining face reddened by rosacea. "What can I do for you?"
The Colonel resettled in his leather desk chair as he gestured for
Durgin to sit.

"I'm here about one of your agents, a Miss Margaret Hope. She's
missing—and I was wondering if you could shed any light on where
she could be."

Gaskell fixed his pale eyes on the detective; his genial expression
didn't change. "Is she in some sort of trouble?"

"Not at all," Durgin explained. "She's called to be a witness in
the Blackout Beast trial. It's imperative we find her, and quickly."

Gaskell scowled. "Nasty bit of business, that Blackout Beast. Followed it in the papers."

"The murdered girls were your agents, weren't they? All
F-Section?"

"I didn't know them, of course, poor souls. So many people coming and going these days . . ."

"Sir, do you know where Margaret Hope is?"

Gaskell gazed out the window. "A bit flighty, that one," he declared, turning back to rearrange a few items on his desk. "Never
had any proper military training—and it shows, unfortunately."

Durgin was doing his best not to lose patience. "Do you know
where she is?"

"I can't possibly comment, you know, old thing. We do top-
secret work here!"

"Is she working for your organization at the moment? Surely
you can answer without revealing any Crown confidences?"

"I can tell you Miss Hope is not working for me anymore," Gaskell admitted.

Durgin often consulted his "gut" when on a case, and his gut was screaming at him that there was more to this story. "Do you know who she's working for now?"

Gaskell gave a guilty smile, as if he'd been caught red-handed. "I couldn't possibly comment, Detective Chief Inspector. However, you might want to talk to Colonel Henrik Martens. He's also with MI-Six, I believe. Oh, who the hell knows these days? So many people with cryptic titles. 'Master of Deception,' I think the P.M. calls him."

"Colonel Henrik Martens," Durgin repeated, committing the name to memory. He rose. "And where would I find him?"

"His office is in the Cabinet War Rooms. I'll have my girl set up an appointment for you."

Ironically, Neville Chamberlain had ordered construction to begin on the bombproof War Rooms the very day in 1938 he had returned from Munich declaring "peace in our time." But Winston Churchill had taken the rooms over, and they now served as the labyrinthine underground bunker where the Prime Minister and his staff sought shelter during bombing raids. It was located beneath the streets and buildings of Westminster, in walking distance of Number 10 Downing Street. Only an armed Royal Marine at the sandbagged doorway of No. 2 Great George Street betrayed the address's importance.

After showing his papers to the security guard, DCI Durgin was led by yet another guard through winding corridors of worn brown linoleum, with treacherously low-hanging red drainage pipes and men in uniform walking and carrying folders and memos. Even though the air was filtered, it was stale and smoky. A sign on one side of the hallway warned, THERE IS TO BE NO WHISTLING OR

UNNECESSARY NOISE IN THIS PASSAGE, while another admonished, MIND YOUR HEAD. As he followed the guard, Durgin could hear the clatter of typewriters from the secretaries' room and the shrill ring of telephones.

At last they reached an office door marked with the sign MASTER OF DECEPTION. The guard knocked.

"Yes?" came a low male voice.

"DCI Durgin to see you, Colonel Martens."

"Come in." Colonel Henrik Rafaelsen Martens, a lanky white-blond man, looked up from the numerous piles of papers on his desk. He had done clandestine SOE work in Norway and had been injured in Operation Archery—the British raid against German positions on the island of Vågsøy—before being promoted to Winston Churchill's Master of Deception, a liaison between SOE and MI-6, who were both running cells of agents in France, sometimes at cross-purposes.

"Welcome, Detective Chief Inspector. Please, have a seat." Martens's office was cramped, the white walls smoke-stained. A black fan circulated stale air. "May my secretary fetch you some tea?"

"No, no thank you. I'm sure you're busy, Colonel Martens, and I won't take up more of your time than I have to."

"Well, I do hope I'm not under arrest!"

"No, sir. You see, I need to find a young woman who's been working with Special Operations Executive. It's imperative. She's needed as a witness for the trial of Nicholas Reitter." Martens's expression remained blank. "The Blackout Beast," the DCI clarified.

"Ah, yes—that." The Colonel shook his head. "Terrible, just terrible. A dreadful business."

"Yes," Durgin agreed. "I've spoken with Colonel Gaskell in F-Section. He referred me to you."

"What's this agent's name?"

"Miss Margaret Hope."

Martens, still stone-faced, pulled a dented cigarette case from his breast pocket. He opened it and offered Durgin a Player's. "Smoke?"

"No, thank you."

"Good—it's a filthy habit, especially down here." Martens lit one for himself and puffed until the tip glowed red.

Durgin tried to conceal his impatience. "Reitter rather unexpectedly pleaded not guilty. And so the case is going to trial. Margaret Hope is one of our most important witnesses. It's imperative she testify against him."

Martens tapped ash into a chipped mug. "Why do you think I can help?"

"Colonel Gaskell told me that Miss Hope worked for him at one point, but doesn't anymore. And then he indicated you'd know where she is now."

Martens took a long puff, then exhaled blue smoke, studying it as it spiraled to the grimy ceiling. "Miss Hope," he said, as if reading a memo, "is on active service in the field."

"Surely, though, you can get a message through to her?"

"Sorry, Detective." Martens stood, indicating the meeting was at an end. "I know your work is important, but I'm afraid I can't help you. Now, if you'll excuse me—we have a war to win."

Moments after Durgin left, Martens picked up the rotary telephone receiver and dialed the number for MI-6. "Colonel Martens for Colonel Bishop. Yes, I'll hold."

As he waited, Martens reached for a slip of paper and doodled a castle, complete with turrets. Finally, Bishop answered. "What?" he barked.

"I just had a most interesting visit from a Scotland Yard detective."

There was a pause. "What about?"

"The DCI in question is looking for Margaret Hope, sir."

"Why?"

"It turns out Miss Hope was working with the police on the case of Nicholas Reitter—you know, the Blackout Beast. And now she's apparently needed to testify as a witness. The detective insists her testimony is imperative to putting the bastard away."

Bishop cursed. Then: "What did you tell him?"

"I told him she was 'on active service in the field.'" Martens tapped more ash into the mug, then took another drag.

"Good, good."

"But can't we let her out to testify—and then return her straightaway? It rather seems like this trial depends on it."

"You know the answer's no," Bishop replied. "Our talking birds must be kept in cages, Martens. Just remember our eye must always be on the big picture: winning this war. While it's unfortunate, the people on that island know too much. And pose too high a security risk to be set free, even for a murderer's trial."

"Yes, sir," Martens replied.

"You don't think this fellow will keep asking questions, do you? Those Scotland Yard buggers are trained to investigate."

"I can assure you, sir, the detective has reached a dead end."

"Well, security is more vital than ever. Still," Bishop continued, "I've just received a report showing illicit radio signals coming from inside Britain to a U-boat."

"*What?*" Martens nearly dropped his cigarette. "How many transmissions?"

"Two so far," Bishop replied. "We're keeping an eye on them."

"Have you been able to pinpoint a location?"

"The western coast of Scotland, nothing more specific than that. I've copied you on the memos—you should be getting a packet today."

Martens crushed out the cigarette. "Western coast of Scotland— that's where most of the SOE training camps are."

"And the Isle of Scarra."

"Christ." Martens reached for a pencil. "Does anyone else know?" He added a few towers to the castle.

"Frain, of course, and he's already informed the P.M. And Gaskell at SOE. But I'm not worried about Gaskell. He's too stupid to put anything together if there's a fox in the henhouse," Bishop replied.

Martens continued to doodle, this time adding a hooded figure with a bow and arrow to the top of the castle's battlements. "What's Frain doing?"

"Adding more RDFs—manned by amateur radio enthusiasts and volunteers, God help us." Bishop's voice dripped with disdain.

"Any one of them being sent to the island?"

"No, according to Frain."

"If there's a German spy in one of the SOE training camps, he won't be able to pick up much information," Martens noted. "Missions and specific information are revealed only at Beaulieu, after all of the paramilitary training is completed."

"True. A Nazi agent couldn't get much of anything from them."

"But the prisoners on Scarra know things, especially Hope. That's our weak spot."

"Too true." Bishop sighed. "If there's a spy in Scotland trying to call for a ride home, he'll be stymied by the weather, though—there's a bad storm bearing down on Scotland's west coast now."

Martens sketched knights with lances charging the castle. "That will buy us some time."

"Yes, but not much."

Martens added a princess in one of the towers, her arms stretched out as if calling for help. "We haven't given the prisoners on Scarra cyanide pills, have we? Just for this sort of emergency?"

"No, we have not."

Martens drew a heavy black X over the princess's face. "Pity."

Chapter Thirteen

Maggie was dreaming of Blue Men—reaching, grasping, pushing her underwater—when she heard the pounding on her bedroom door. "Get up! Get up!" It was unmistakably Leo's voice coming through the thick wood.

She opened her eyes and remembered everything—the five deaths, the boat not coming. *Oh, God. What now?* Still, she called, "Coming!"

As she rose from bed, shoved her feet in slippers, and pulled on her old flannel robe, he was pounding and shouting down the line of doors. Everyone convened in the long carpeted passageway in various states of dishabille—the men in pajamas, the women in nightgowns, all unwashed and unbrushed. Teddy was putting on his eyeglasses as Ramsey came up behind him. *This is very, very bad . . .*

Leo was by Camilla's open door, panting. "I just wanted to check on her—make sure she was all right. It didn't sit well—how we'd left things . . ."

Maggie sidestepped the throng. On the bed lay Camilla—impaled by a harpoon, the one from over the inglenook fireplace in the great room. The barbed spear had been thrust into her abdomen, bayoneting her. Her nightgown and the bedclothes were soaked with drying, rust-colored blood, her mouth open.

Maggie felt sick. She forced herself to take big gulps of air so she wouldn't faint. *Six*, she thought. *Six dead. Now there are only eight of us left.*

Anna shrieked, then pressed her hands over her mouth as Ramsey eyed her with worry.

Leo glared at her with undisguised contempt. "You are a trained agent of His Majesty's Government, Miss O'Malley!" he cried. "Keep your dignity."

"Jesus, Mary, and Joseph," Anna whispered, crossing herself. She ran to the hall bathroom and slammed the door; they could hear her retching.

"Well, I think this definitely rules out Miss Oddell as a suspect," Torvald offered.

"Shut up!" cried Quentin from the doorway, holding Monsieur Reynard close. "This is no time for jokes!"

"Sorry," Torvald muttered, looking almost ashamed. "I make bad jokes when things are dark. Viking humor, I suppose."

Maggie forced herself to take one more look at Camilla. *I'm sorry. I'm so sorry I ever suspected you.*

"I need to examine her," Sayid told the group as he entered the room and approached the body. "It appears as though she was killed in her sleep," he said, closing her eyelids with his fingertips. "I don't see signs of a struggle. The whole thing was probably over before she knew what was happening."

Maggie saw Anna emerge from the bathroom and gazed over with concern. The younger woman didn't meet her questioning look.

"She's been dead for a while." Sayid picked up Camilla's arm and tested the rigidity. "I'd say at least six hours."

"She couldn't have done it to herself," Leo murmured.

Torvald shot him a look. "You found her—perhaps *you* did it!"

Leo swung to face the small man. "And why would I do that?"

"*You* suspected her. You even accused her. Perhaps you wanted to kill her before she killed *you*!"

"Balderdash! Why are all the others dead, then?" Leo grabbed the smaller man by the shirt. "I'm well and truly sick of your allegations!"

"That's enough!" Maggie warned. Begrudgingly, Leo released Torvald.

"It's the ghost," Anna moaned. "Punishing us for our sins. Six dead . . ." She began to sob.

"Do shut up about your damn ghost!" snapped Leo. "This is not Cawdor Castle—Banquo isn't roaming about!"

"Mr. Kingsley," Maggie warned, putting a protective arm around Anna, "shouting isn't helping."

He took a moment, then shrugged. "Sorry," he offered.

Anna sniffed. "Quite all right."

Quentin stepped into the dead woman's room. Approaching the window, he pulled aside the curtains and blackout shades. "Where's the damn boat?" he barked, eyes searching the bay.

But the morning's weather remained unforgiving. The winds were still blowing fiercely, the rain pelting the windowpanes, the waves twisting into white froth.

"I can radio again," Maggie offered, "but I doubt they're sending a boat in this storm. And I wouldn't recommend taking out the one that washed to shore, either. We'd never make it past those whirlpools."

Everyone seemed stunned with disbelief and horror. Maggie glanced at the small body on the bed, and then back to the group. "Leo and Sayid," she said, "please carry Miss Oddell to the game larder."

Leo crossed his arms, scowling. "I'm afraid there's no more room."

"Well, to the ballroom, then. I'll help you."

"No," the doctor replied, looking to Leo. "We can manage."

"We will all get dressed," Maggie continued. It took every bit of her willpower to keep her voice from wobbling. "And then we will go downstairs for breakfast."

"Breakfast?" Quentin croaked. "Miss Hope, I don't think anyone will be able to keep anything down. I know Monsieur Reynard and I won't."

"Well then tea, coffee," Maggie amended curtly, in no mood for his nonsense. "Water. I don't give a flying fig. We need to keep to a schedule, to hold on to a sense of normalcy."

"Someone has to come for us soon," Anna muttered, as though convincing herself, as she padded back to her room to change. "They *have* to."

The group assembled in the dining room, silent, pushing uneaten food around their plates, the rumble of thunder and the rain driving hard against the windows a constant background noise. All were dressed but still looked disheveled. Leo's hair was greasy, while Anna's was limp and uncurled. The men were unshaven, and Ramsey's tie was coming undone. Quentin's cardigan sweater had a small moth hole. Even Monsieur Reynard's fur looked mangy. Maggie realized her own hair rolls were slipping out. She tried to fix them, then gave up, pulling out the pins and shaking her hair so it fell loose to her shoulders.

"What about McNaughton?" Leo queried. "He could be the murderer. Have you ever seen his hands? They're huge—"

"What about Mrs. McNaughton?" Sayid posited. "They say women are more likely to use poison. We have several dead bodies that look to have been drugged."

"Poison?" Anna said, splattering tea on her blouse. "Oh, dear." Ramsey handed her his handkerchief. She seized it with trembling hands. "Thank you." Their eyes met before Ramsey turned away.

Maggie was aghast. "Sayid!"

His look to her was both sad and resolute. "I didn't say anything earlier because I did not want to cause a panic, but I'm afraid panic has arrived regardless. We may as well have all the facts out on the table." He folded his hands around his teacup. "Perhaps someone will have an idea which will lead us to uncovering the murderer in our midst."

"What kind of poison?" Quentin asked.

"Cyanide," Sayid replied. "Possibly." He and Maggie locked eyes and he shrugged in apology. "And strychnine."

"Cyanide and strychnine?" Leo exclaimed. "Why the devil do you think that?"

"I don't know for sure," Sayid responded. "I don't know anything for sure anymore. I'd need to carry out tests to make a definitive diagnosis. Which is why I wasn't going to mention it. But now . . ."

"But what makes you think poison was involved?" Teddy's forehead was puckered with concern.

"Captain Evans's face was red and his corpse smelled of almonds," the doctor answered. "Two of the hallmarks of cyanide. And Dr. Jaeger's and Captain MacLean's bodies were twisted in a way consistent with strychnine poisoning."

"It could be the young one—Murdo," considered Torvald. "Wouldn't that be perfect? A murderer named Murdo. . . . He has a motive, too—thinks we're all scrimshankers for not doing our bit for the war effort. While he rides things out here in comfort, I must add."

"You know no army would take him," Leo declared. "With that clubfoot."

Maggie picked at an oatcake, breaking off tiny pieces, which she forced herself to eat. The rest of the prisoners around the dining room table weren't doing much better, though the tragic events didn't seem to affect Torvald's appetite. He devoured toast slathered with orange marmalade. "Still," he remarked through a mouthful, "Murdo could be doing *something*. Work in a factory, farm—"

Sayid stood to pour more tea. "As could we."

"Stop," Anna whispered. "They might hear us!"

"Who cares?" thundered Leo. "They're affected by this, too. They're probably laying bets on which one of us is guilty even as we speak."

"There's more." Sayid put down the teapot. "We also discovered that the boat's tank had no fuel."

In for a penny, in for a pound, Maggie thought. "The whole operation must have been calibrated so that the petrol would run out at the same time the two men died," she explained, "ensuring the boat would wash back into the bay."

"Look at you two," Leo jeered. "You've become quite the detective duo. But maybe it's you who are pulling it off, killing us as a team. . . ." He leaned back, folding his arms across his chest. "Wouldn't it take someone good at maths to formulate the timing?" he said to Maggie. Then he looked to Sayid. "And you know all about poisons and dosages."

"And our motive would be what?" Maggie challenged. "Boredom?"

"Camilla did mention it's not safe for us and that's reason for SOE to come," Torvald speculated. "Perhaps this is a way to get their attention and end our little holiday here."

The thought that SOE could be behind it all—a way to get rid of them for good—troubled Maggie's brain once again. But she brushed the suspicion aside.

"It's also odd no one in the McNaughton family has been affected," Torvald mused. He alone seemed impervious to the latest murder and the morning's terrible revelations. "Just us prisoners . . ."

Maggie pushed back her chair, rose, and walked to one of the windows. The rain had turned to sleet, tapping at the glass and blowing sideways, making it nearly impossible to see outside the castle. The bay faded in and out of view, as though from another dimension, as the panes rattled in their casings. "We should turn on the wireless," she said. "See if we can get any word on how long this storm's supposed to last."

"It's not as if anyone's eating anyway." Torvald threw his napkin on the table and climbed down from his chair.

In the great room, the eight prisoners clustered around the fireplace, the air humid and smelling of stale pipe and cigarette smoke, the water from leaks hitting the tin buckets in a maddening drip. Ramsey was poking at the damp logs, the flames struggling to take hold. On the wall, the space where the harpoon had been displayed was ominously empty. Maggie fiddled with the dials of the wireless, trying to find a station. The only one coming in, over a wave of static, was playing "Don't Sit Under the Apple Tree."

Maggie switched the wireless off. *I'm starting to loathe that song.*

"Look, we must be rational," Teddy was saying, picking up the fishing fly he was working on and wrapping in more silver tinsel and feathers. "Six people have been murdered. We must find a connection. There must be one."

Quentin frowned and set his fox down near the grate. "We've already been through why we're here."

"What about Dr. Jaeger's notes?" Leo asked. "They might shed some insight."

"We can't read them," Anna cautioned. "They're private."

Thank goodness I never told him anything, Maggie thought.

Leo snorted. "Who gives a damn at this point? I'd say all bets on civilized behavior are off now."

"And they're locked in his desk," Anna amended.

Leo flashed a devilish grin. "Since when does anyone trained by SOE let a lock stop us?" He stood. "Who's with me?" A nervous laugh escaped him. "I'd, er, feel better going to the library as a group."

Leaning heavily on his walking stick, Teddy approached Maggie. "Miss Hope, may I have a word with you?"

She stopped and smiled at him. "Of course, Mr. Crane." They both waited for the rest of the group to disappear.

"Miss Hope," Teddy began. "I am not—I am not a young man. The rest of you—you're young, well trained, probably in the best physical condition of your lives. And I'm . . . not."

With a pang, Maggie realized what he was saying. "I'll keep an eye out for you, Mr. Crane," she assured him. "Not to worry."

"Thank you, Miss Hope." His face creased in a relieved smile. "And I'll do the same for you."

Maggie was grateful for his concern. "Why, thank you," she said, holding out her hand. They shook firmly.

Durgin had one last card to play. He knew that in addition to Chuck and Sarah, one of Maggie's best friends was a man named David Greene, who worked as the head private secretary to the Prime Minister.

He was able to arrange to meet with David that morning. Maggie and David had worked together in Mr. Churchill's office at Number 10 during the summer of '40.

"It's about Maggie Hope," Durgin began without preamble, as the two men shook hands at the Marlborough Gate to St. James's Park. Although the ornate ironwork had been removed to be melted down for munitions, the stone columns remained. The air was chilly and frost coated the grass. They trod the paths, finding themselves by the curving green lake, its surface ruffling in the wind as white pelicans, introduced to the park in 1664 as a gift from the Russian Ambassador to King Charles II, preened their feathers on the bank.

"Maggie?" David's breath made white clouds. He was just past thirty, elegantly slender and fair, eyes framed by round silver spectacles. A bowler hat and university scarf lent him gravitas, but nothing could suppress his innate vivacity. "Merciful Minerva—what's wrong? Is she in some sort of trouble?"

"When was the last time you saw her?"

"Oh, let's see . . . the last time I literally laid eyes on her was almost a year ago. But I heard from Chuck—that is, Charlotte Ludlow—that Mags swung through town this past spring."

"Do you know where she is now?"

"Couldn't say."

"Can't—or won't?"

"What's this about?" David demanded, brows knitting together in concern. "Is Maggie all right?"

"She's needed as a witness in the trial of Nicholas Reitter. We can't find her and no one seems to know where she is. I'm concerned."

They turned to walk over John Nash's graceful suspension bridge. Through the branches on one side was a view of Buckingham Palace and on the other, the Horse Guards Parade and the red-brick Old Admiralty.

"Miss Hope's testimony is of utmost importance," Durgin continued. "And no one seems to know where she is or how to find her. I spoke with the man I believe to be her current supervisor, Colonel Henrik Martens, and he says she's on active service in the field."

"I know Martens. He was with SOE in Norway for a while. He suffered an injury and Mr. Churchill named him Master of Deception or some such title recently. If Maggie's working for him and that's what he says—well, that's it, then, yes? Not much we can do about it." He shrugged. "There are secrets in war, DCI Durgin. And while I appreciate the fact Maggie's absence might be inconvenient to your trial, the war's the bigger picture here."

Durgin stopped. "I didn't like the way he said it."

David stopped as well, pushing the frames of his glasses up his nose. He nodded. "Go on."

"I don't trust Martens. My gut tells me something's off. Something's not right."

"Your 'gut'?" David frowned.

"It's never steered me wrong."

David's eyes followed one of the pelicans as it waddled to the water and splashed in. Then he inhaled. "Let me see what I can do, Detective Chief Inspector."

"I know you must be busy," Durgin said, "but time really is of the essence."

"This is about Mags," David reassured him. "You can believe I'll move heaven and earth to find her." He smiled. "Then give her a good what-for for worrying us."

The prisoners had pried open the drawers of Dr. Jaeger's desk with his letter opener and pulled out a pile of folders, bringing them back to Maggie and Teddy in the great room. "Perhaps to no one's surprise, some of us were telling half-truths at dinner," Leo began, slamming the paperwork down on a low table in front of the fireplace. "I'll start with Miss Hope—what brings you here?"

"Remember?" Maggie looked up from her knitting as the lights flickered. "I decline to say."

Leo pressed. "And apparently you wouldn't talk about it with Jaeger, either."

"No." Maggie continued to knit, mangling the heel of the soldier's sock. "And if I didn't feel I needed to discuss it with Dr. Jaeger, why should I tell you?"

"Because we're all being hunted by a murderer," Anna offered with a furious gesture. "We all know why we're here—all of us, except for *you*."

"Miss O'Malley, you're a trained SOE agent. You've also signed the Official Secrets Act. Why on earth would you press me on this?"

"But why won't you tell us?" Leo insisted, his face reddening in frustration. "It's not as if we can reveal any huge war secrets from this back of beyond!"

"It's the principle," Maggie stated, finishing her row.

Leo glared. "You. Will. Tell. Us."

"No. I. Won't." *I've resisted questioning from more dangerous men than you,* Maggie thought. *Kept my mouth shut in front of the SS, the Abwehr, and Hermann bloody Goering. You've never even been on an assignment, you stupid novice.*

As Leo stepped forward to confront Maggie, Sayid stood, blocking the way. "Be careful," he warned. "No one likes a bully."

Leo faced the doctor, a muscle in his jaw twitching. "Don't test me, old thing."

The lights went out. The room was left deep in shadows, illuminated only by the flames in the fireplace and the sickly greenish light of the storm raging outside. Ramsey gasped. "What's happening?" Quentin cried.

"The storm," Sayid explained. "It's blown out the power."

"Or the McNaughtons have cut it," Torvald suggested. "To make it easier to finish the rest of us off."

Maggie set down her knitting. "Everyone needs to remain calm."

"I'll fetch more candles," Anna offered.

"We'll need oil lamps, with these drafts!" Torvald called after her.

Sayid turned his back on Leo. "I'm going to take the files upstairs to read."

"I don't need light," said Teddy by the fireplace. "I can make flies by sense of touch at this point."

Maggie's gaze went to Quentin. "Shall we get a candle and explore the castle?" she suggested. "You seem to know all its secrets, but maybe we can learn something new—find a piece of evidence we've overlooked." Leo threw up his hands in resignation and turned away.

Quentin acquiesced. "Lead on, Macduff."

"Would anyone like tea?" Teddy queried. "I can ask Mrs. McNaughton."

"Damn the tea," Leo growled, heading for the bar. "I'm getting some bloody whiskey."

As the Prime Minister's head private secretary, David had access to top-secret files, kept in a vault in the basement of Number 10. He took his bristling key ring and walked down narrow stairs, let himself through multiple doors with various locks, and eventually found a small metal room with drawers upon drawers of files. He looked through those Colonel Martens's office had sent over since he'd been promoted to coordinate the work of SOE and MI-6 in the spring. But going through file after file stamped TOP SECRET in heavy red ink, David saw nothing mentioning Maggie.

Finally, he found a single piece of paper, wrinkled and folded, at the end of a file on SOE training camps. It referred to "The ISRB Operation at Isle of Scarra." There was a list of names and at the bottom, *Margaret Rose Hope*. In loopy handwriting in pencil was the cryptic instruction *If relatives or friends ask about agents interred at ISRB Scarra, have them told, verbatim, that the agent is 'on active service in the field.' Agents at ISRB Scarra are allowed no communication whatsoever.*

"Great Odin, what's ISRB Scarra? And what the devil's happening there?" David muttered. "Why are communications cut off? And why is there no paperwork explaining the nature of this camp?"

But he'd worked for the P.M. long enough to know the answer: plausible deniability. Whatever was happening on the Isle of Scarra, Colonel Martens didn't want Mr. Churchill to know the specifics.

Which did not bode well for Maggie. "Maybe Durgin's right . . ." he said aloud, putting the file back in perfect order, replacing all the folders, then locking the drawer. "Maybe Maggie *is* in danger."

Chapter Fourteen

"I've never been much for reading," Quentin admitted as they searched through books in the dark mahogany library, taking each one out and flipping through it to make sure the pages didn't contain any secrets. The scent of ink, vanilla, and decay prickled Maggie's nose.

"Well, most of these aren't very good books," she pointed out as she flipped through the gold-tooled leather tomes that looked as though they'd never once been cracked open, let alone read. She'd heard of decorators buying volumes by the yard, for ornamental purposes.

She sighed, wiping dusty hands on her trousers. They'd been at it all morning and afternoon and had found nothing. "I'm sure if you had the *right* book, you'd fall in love with reading." She stepped back from the floor-to-ceiling shelves, gazing up. "We'll need the steps for the high ones." She looked at the library steps, a curved wooden staircase with a carved twisted snake as the railing.

"Are you certain?" Quentin gave the staircase a push in her direction; as it rolled, it squealed a noisy protest. "It doesn't seem very safe."

"Fiddlesticks." Maggie scrambled up the creaking stairs to reach the top shelves, on level with the room's chandelier. The dust seemed thicker there, mixed with dead insects and cobwebs. The volumes on these higher shelves differed from the rest, as if they hadn't been bought as part of the set. They were narrower, darker, and looked well worn. When she paged through, she realized to her astonishment that they were appointment books. She picked one up and opened it, sneezing. "What year did the Killoch murders take place?" she called down to Quentin.

"Nineteen twenty-two. Seventeen November, I think."

Maggie rifled through until she found the book for that year and plucked it from the shelf. Climbing down the stairs, she brought the volume to the desk and opened its heavy tooled-leather cover, revealing exquisite Florentine endpapers. She flipped through the pages. "It's Marcus Killoch's diary," she said, as Quentin came to stand behind her, peering over her shoulder at page after page of cramped Victorian-era script.

"So many names of women," she realized. Every evening had names, written in the same heavy, controlled script, the male friends and business associates who'd died. But also: *Fflur, Aideen, Nesta. Oona, Aela, Ertha.* And *Shona, Valma, Fiona.*

Her eyes returned to one name. *Fiona.* It appeared quite a number of times through the month. In fact, it appeared in the last entry, for the evening of November 17, 1922—the date of the murders. Maggie felt a chill.

"Are you all right?" Quentin asked. "You look as if you'd seen a ghost."

"Maybe I have." Maggie's mind whirled. Mrs. McNaughton, she knew, had been a maid at Killoch Castle before she married. And Fiona was Mrs. McNaughton's first name. All the women's names listed, at least for the last month, were Scottish Gaelic, names the island girls would have had. Not upper-class names. Not names of Killoch's guests' wives.

The names of his female servants.

"What? Tell me!"

Maggie pointed. "Fiona is Mrs. McNaughton's first name."

Quentin digested the information. "Why would she be in his appointment book? She was only a maid."

"Think, Mr. Asquith."

"Oh." Realization dawned on his face. "You suspect Mrs. McNaughton had an affair with Killoch?"

Maggie bit her lip. It was twenty years since Killoch's murder. "How old is Murdo?"

"Wait—" His eyebrows shot up. "You think Murdo's the son of Mrs. McNaughton and Marcus Killoch?"

"Well, Fiona may not have been Mrs. McNaughton then, but the dates seem to coincide."

"I know his birthday—it's August nineteenth, nineteen twenty-three. He just turned nineteen."

"How do you know his birthday?" Maggie asked, puzzled.

"It's awfully boring here," Quentin admitted, color flooding his face. "Men need to get their exercise somehow." He glanced at her, to gauge her reaction. "You're not shocked, are you?"

He was not the first man—or woman—she'd met who was "like that." Maggie tilted her head. "Hardly."

"I hoped you wouldn't be. Of course now I'm shaken. He's always been a wee bit off, if you know what I mean, but . . ." Quentin rubbed at his chin. "So Murdo could be old Marcus's son—do you suspect he could be our murderer? That it runs in the blood?" He shuddered. "To think I've been . . . intimate . . . with him." He grabbed at his fox, wrapping his arms around the dead creature for comfort.

Maggie closed her eyes as she did the sums in her head. "November nineteen 'twenty-two is nine months before August nineteen 'twenty-three. And Murdo doesn't take after McNaughton—he's dark and fine-boned. Just like Marcus Killoch."

Quentin smacked himself on the head. "Why didn't I see it before?"

Maggie felt stupid as well. "We can't be sure."

"Oh—oh—" Quentin went to one of the bottom shelves and pulled out a box, covered in marbled paper. "I saw these when I first arrived." He brought it over to the desk and opened the lid. Inside, there were photographs, hundreds of them. Photographs of women in various states of undress, in different positions, most often tied up, some with bruises and other dark marks on their flesh. "Didn't do much for me," he admitted. "Not my thing, if you know what I mean. Killoch must have taken the pictures of the girls in his dungeon in the cellar. I never would have dreamed that . . ." His voice faltered.

Maggie sorted through them, battling revulsion, until she noticed a girl who looked like a younger version of Mrs. McNaughton, bound and gagged. She looked closer. The woman's flesh was bruised, but the eyes were the same. "Oh, God."

"So Murdo really could be Marcus Killoch's son."

"We need to burn these—" Maggie said.

"No, we need to show the others—"

"No!" Her instinct was to destroy them immediately, but deep in her heart, she realized that they were all evidence.

"It *must* be Murdo—" Quentin began pacing, cradling Monsieur Reynard. "He likes things a bit rough. I should have guessed . . ."

"We don't know Murdo did *anything*. The date book and the photograph prove nothing."

"It all happened before, and it's all happening again—this time with us as the victims."

Maggie was trying to think it through logically. "But even if Murdo *is* Marcus Killoch's son—and I'm not saying he is—it doesn't mean he's done anything wrong. You can't visit the sins of the father on the son and label him a killer just because—"

"He hates you—" Quentin cut in. "Us, I mean. The English.

The toffs. Especially those of us on the island—he thinks we're lazy and shirking our duties. Believe me, I know. We've talked about it.

"He's said, on multiple occasions, he'd love to kill every last one of us."

David was very nearly late to the security meeting Churchill was presiding over at Number 10. "What will you have?" General Hastings Ismay, Churchill's personal Chief of Staff, asked the assembled men, as he stood by the bar cart in the Cabinet Room.

"Gimme whiskey and soda," the P.M. answered. "Light on the whiskey." He was already seated at the head of the oak table, scowling at the papers spread before him.

"Brandy and soda for me," General Stewart Menzies stated. "Heavy on the brandy." He walked to the window, lifted the blackout shade, and peered out. The sky was gray and overcast.

"Take those blasted shades off!" growled Churchill. "If I wanted to meet in the dark, I would have held this meeting down in the War Rooms."

Even though the Blitz had paused, the Prime Minister's staff preferred him to work underground, in the protected Cabinet War Rooms. But the P.M. loathed working in the basement offices, "like a troglodyte." He favored either the Annexe, the Churchills' private wartime residence, or Number 10. Which made his team nearly apoplectic in their concern for his safety—the two-hundred-year-old building had been bombed by the Luftwaffe on October 14, 1940, with damage to the kitchen and state rooms. The bombing had taken place while Churchill dined mere yards away in the Garden Room.

But the Prime Minister insisted on light and air. And so the day's security meeting was being held in Number 10's rectangular Cabinet Room, though the windows were taped over, the portrait of Sir Robert Walpole by Jean-Baptiste van Loo was in storage, and the mahogany chairs replaced by gray metal folding ones.

The men gathering around the green-baize-covered table with their drinks included General Ismay; General Sir Alan Brooke, Chief of the Imperial General Staff; Menzies, chief of MI-6; Colonel Lord Roger Leycock, the director of SOE; and Martens. David was there to take notes for the P.M., and at the last minute Frain joined the group.

David waited, his back ramrod straight, until there was an opening in the conversation on activities by various cells in France. When Martens paused, David held up one hand.

"What, Mr. Greene?" growled Churchill, through a cloud of blue smoke.

"I have a question for Colonel Martens," David said.

The Master of Deception frowned.

"The ISRB operation on the Isle of Scarra, in Scotland. What exactly goes on there? What sort of a venture is it?"

"That's—that's top-secret!" Then, "How did *you* hear about it?"

"Something crossed my desk."

"We're not here to talk about that operation," Martens snapped. "It's an entirely different conversation."

"If it's in Scotland," David pressed, "it must be some sort of training operation, yes? SOE? But it would be coordinated with MI-Six by your department, wouldn't it, Colonel Martens?"

David glanced at the other men. Their faces were stone, except for Frain's. The Major General looked intrigued.

"Yes," answered Martens reluctantly.

"Well, what sort of special training goes on there?"

"Mr. Greene," Martens countered, "I will not discuss specifics with a . . . a . . . private secretary."

"With all due respect, sir," David persisted. "The agents there are unreachable. Which is unfortunate, because one of them is Miss Margaret Hope—who, Colonel Martens, used to work for the P.M. Miss Hope is rather desperately needed right now by Scotland Yard to testify in the Blackout Beast trial. So why can't anyone communicate with her?"

"Ah, Miss Hope!" boomed the P.M. "What's she doing there?" He turned to Leycock and narrowed his eyes. "Isn't she one of yours in SOE?"

"She was in Paris and returned safely to London in June." Leycock shrugged. "I'm not sure why she'd need any additional training, though." He turned to Martens with a raised eyebrow.

Martens glared.

"Colonel Martens." Frain leaned forward. "Perhaps you could answer Mr. Greene's question in vague terms?"

When the P.M. nodded, Martens spoke, not bothering to conceal his reluctance. "The facility on Scarra is a special training ground for advanced operational needs," he said, as though reciting from a textbook. "Individuals are sent there to prepare for different situations. We use our setup on the Isle of Scarra to give highly sensitive training to those who are going on important missions. That's all I can say."

"And why can't we get through to the agents there?" David asked him. "Why is no communication allowed?"

"For security reasons," Martens replied stiffly. "But I wouldn't say no to more tea, if you'd tell the girl now. Who else would like tea?"

"One more thing," Frain interposed, holding up a hand. "Where exactly is this Scarra?"

"It's an island off the western coast of Scotland," Martens admitted.

"MI-Five has picked up a few rogue transmissions from the west coast of Scotland to a German U-boat," Frain said. Churchill nodded. "We're concerned they may be coming from one of the camps."

"If there's a German in SOE, have at him," Martens spat.

"SOE trainees at the paramilitary training camps in Scotland don't receive any information a German spy would want," Leycock pointed out. "We do it on purpose. They'd be useless. The agents-in-training obtain specialized information only at Beaulieu."

"But this camp on the Isle of Scarra—if it's as advanced as you say," Frain went on, "would an enemy agent be able to glean anything important there? Who are these agents? And what are they working on?"

Martens replied, "Of course we keep everything top-secret."

But David saw the panic flare in Martens's eyes. He looked to Frain, who gave an almost imperceptible nod in return. And then he knew—Maggie was in real trouble.

Chapter Fifteen

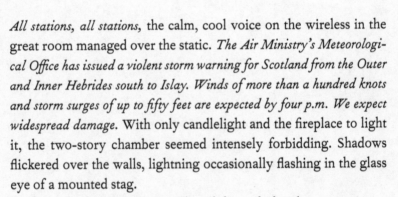

All stations, all stations, the calm, cool voice on the wireless in the great room managed over the static. *The Air Ministry's Meteorological Office has issued a violent storm warning for Scotland from the Outer and Inner Hebrides south to Islay. Winds of more than a hundred knots and storm surges of up to fifty feet are expected by four p.m. We expect widespread damage.* With only candlelight and the fireplace to light it, the two-story chamber seemed intensely forbidding. Shadows flickered over the walls, lightning occasionally flashing in the glass eye of a mounted stag.

Maggie and Quentin entered, and through the gloom saw Anna, Teddy, Leo, and Ramsey, huddled in the nook by the fireplace. Outside, the winds moaned. *The madness of living in darkness,* Maggie thought and repressed a shiver.

"Where's Torvald?" Quentin asked.

"Torvald is dead," Leo said.

Quentin clutched his fox tighter. "What?" Maggie's jaw dropped. *No. No, it can't be . . .*

"While you were off exploring," Leo explained.

Maggie's heart was thundering. Still, she walked closer. "How?"

"Garroted with a wire," Leo answered. Anna began to sob; he

ignored her. "One of the favorite SOE murder techniques. On the toilet, of all places. Poor little bugger—what a way to go."

"Was everyone here—when Torvald went up to use the loo?" Maggie asked.

"Well, *you* weren't," Anna snapped. "Mr. Asquith wasn't. Dr. Khan was in his room. Teddy left to ask Mrs. McNaughton to make tea . . ."

"We all left at various points," Teddy explained. "Including Mr. Novak." Maggie saw he was huddled in his usual chair in the corner.

Seven dead. In five days. This is true insanity. All Maggie longed to do was curl up in the fetal position, squeeze her eyes shut, and pray she'd stay that way until she woke from this terrible nightmare.

"What's all this?" Sayid asked, entering the room and sensing the group's anxiety.

"Torvald is dead," Maggie stated. Her voice was flat.

"No!"

"And what were *you* up to all afternoon?" asked Leo.

Sayid held up a book, *The Strange Case of Dr. Jekyll and Mr. Hyde.* "I was reading."

"He's not even a Christian," Anna muttered.

"What does that mean?" Sayid asked.

"You and your people worship *cows,*" she continued, not bothering to hide her disdain. "And God knows what else."

Sayid studied the distraught girl a moment before saying, "The people who worship cows—or, rather, think cows are sacred—are Hindu. I'm a Sufi Muslim. There *is* a difference."

"Then you know all about *Jihad,*" Leo said. "The so-called Holy War."

"*Jihad,*" Sayid explained, setting down the book, "means *struggle* or *striving*—for self-control and betterment. It doesn't literally mean war. Or any kind of violence, for that matter."

"To spread Islam, you need to fight a war," Leo argued, walking closer. "Against the infidel. Which we all are. That's your motive right there."

"Mr. Kingsley!" Sayid's voice held an edge of warning. "Please consider what you're saying."

"You were gone all afternoon." Anna's voice was shrill with threat. "Out of all of us, you had the most time to kill Mr. Hagan."

"I'm a doctor who has taken the Hippocratic oath, a loyal British citizen, and one raised as a Sufi Muslim," Sayid countered evenly. "Which might not mean much to you, but I was brought up in a both mystic and ascetic tradition, focused on purifying the inner self. I don't believe in violence. As you may recall, I take photographs of deer rather than shoot them."

"You're from India. A mussie. A hajji." Leo pursed his lips as though he'd tasted something foul. "A Mohammedan."

"I'm from *London*, and moreover, I'm an honorable man. A gentleman." Anger crept at last into Sayid's voice. "A Briton who was just as willing as you to join up and risk my life in SOE against the Nazis."

But you were unaccounted for during the time the murder took place, Maggie thought. *I hate to doubt you, Sayid, and yet . . .* The gong for dinner stopped any more conversation.

"We're not dressed," Quentin stated. Maggie realized she was still covered in dust from their search of the library.

"Well, it hardly matters at this point," said Anna. "Surely you must realize most Britons think what they're wearing during the day is just fine for tea?"

"Philistine!" cried Leo in mock horror.

"It's *dinner*—not *supper* or *tea*," muttered Quentin into Monsieur Reynard's ear.

"We might be from different religions and traditions. And we may come from different social backgrounds. But we're *Britons*," Teddy snapped. He stood. "Ladies and gentlemen—please conduct yourselves accordingly."

Maggie's mouth twitched at his stiff upper lip. It was completely inappropriate to giggle, and yet finding grim humor somehow bolstered her courage. *Seven dead and we're squabbling over the rules of etiquette. But Torvald would have been the first to laugh,* she thought, remembering the little man's dark sense of humor.

"I'll need to examine the body first." Sayid turned to leave.

Maggie wasn't about to let him go alone. "Wait, I'm coming with you."

Maggie took a glass-covered oil lamp and they made their way down the seemingly endless dark corridor to the ballroom. She repressed a gasp as they entered. The vaulted high ceiling boasted an astonishing filigree of animal skulls and antlers, thousands of them. The sprung parquet floor, a geometric mosaic of rare woods, had warped from decades of leaks. Rows of water-stained scarlet silk chairs edged the room. In one corner sat the dusty shell of a grand piano. The chamber was lit from stained-glass windows set high in the walls. No one outside could possibly see in, Maggie realized.

She couldn't look away from the two bodies wrapped in sheets and laid in the center of the room. As if he read her thoughts, Sayid offered his hand as they approached. For an instant, she hesitated, then took it. She gazed at his face; in the lamp's glow, he seemed to have aged terribly in the last few days. There was a deep gash of a worry line between his eyebrows, and his lips were pressed together.

He pulled back the sheets and they looked down at Torvald. His neck was ripped and bloody. Maggie swallowed to keep from vomiting. Another dead. It didn't seem possible.

Sayid bent to examine Torvald. "Death by garrote. Just as we were taught at Arisaig House."

"That's the thing," Maggie murmured. "All of us know how to kill. We all have the potential to be murderers."

"Well, I know *you're* innocent." Sayid pulled the sheets back over the corpses. "I know *you*—there's no way you could kill any-one, Maggie. At least without a damn good reason."

She tried to smile, but inside she felt cold. Could she say the same about him? What did she know about him, really? They'd met only a few months ago. And he'd been charming, but always somewhat distant. Maggie wanted to say something reassuring back to him, but her voice felt paralyzed. She remembered how angry he'd been with Leo, how his eyes had glinted. *Could he be the killer? Or am I just being paranoid?*

"I'm sorry they said those horrible things to you," she offered instead. "They shouldn't have."

"It's not the first time I've heard any of that rot—and surely not the last."

As he spoke, Maggie walked over the warped parquet floor to below the orchestra gallery and peered up. *Quentin was right,* she realized. There was a black velvet curtain, pulled to one side, which could only have been used to prevent the orchestra from seeing what was happening on the dance floor below. She decided to inves-tigate further and found the dumbwaiters, designed to ensure the butler and servants could provide food and drinks while unable to observe what was happening inside the vast ballroom. She turned back to the room. *If these walls could talk* . . . Then she saw the two shrouded forms again, and felt as if the world were closing in.

Sayid noticed her stagger and went to her instantly, his arms cir-cling her waist and pulling her close. She listened to the steady, strong thump of his heart as he held her against his chest, and leaned in, enjoying the physical contact, a rare moment of not thinking. Maggie closed her eyes and pretended they were somewhere else. The Boston Common. A jazz club in London. A garden in Paris after the war. Her bedroom. She could almost imagine the horror away. Yet while it worked for a brief, fragile moment, reality would not be put off.

"The rest will be waiting for us for dinner," she said finally, pulling away.

Sayid exhaled. "I know. We must go back." He reached for her hand. "Whatever happens, I'm not leaving your side, until the boat gets here."

"Promise?"

He held her hand to his heart. "I promise. We will both live through this, I swear to you."

It was dim in the dining room, lit only by flickering candles and hurricane lamps, when Maggie and Sayid joined the others. The seven inmates sat, a small group at the long table, their number diminished. *Seven dead and now only seven prisoners alive*, Maggie thought. *The number of the dead now equal the number of the living.*

Most had made no attempt to dress for dinner, and their day clothes looked shockingly out of place. The men looked as if they needed to shave, and Anna's hair was uncombed. McNaughton arrived with a platter of sandwiches, oat-studded bread stuffed with cold salmon.

"No soup course?" asked Quentin, looking shocked. "No hot entrée?"

"Sandwiches tonight, sir," McNaughton replied gruffly, taking in the newly empty chairs.

As Maggie and Sayid took their seats, no one reacted; they merely continued to stare at the food with dull eyes. It was as if the shock of all the deaths had numbed their senses, slowed their reactions. There was no panic, no outburst of fear or anger, just a distancing, a numbing of emotion. Seven were dead: acceptance of horror and death was now the norm. Sayid grasped Maggie's hand under the table. His fingers felt warm and strong. She squeezed back.

Outside was absolute darkness; rain continued to hiss against the glass. "No blackout curtains tonight?" Teddy said. Ramsey glanced to the windows, then trained his eyes back on his plate.

"I doubt the Luftwaffe's flying overhead in this storm," replied Leo. "And even if they are, I refuse to believe they can see our candles."

"We should put up the blackout shades anyway," said Anna. "It's the rule, after all." But she made no move to do anything. *There are no rules anymore,* Maggie thought.

"At least there's wine!" Quentin indicated the bottles on the sideboard. He stood, filling his glass to the very top and taking a noisy gulp. "This is really quite good." He drained his glass, then refilled it. He turned back to McNaughton. "Where's Murdo?" He picked up the bottle to bring it to the table.

"Aren't you going to decant it, old thing?" asked Leo.

"We could be dead at any moment—I'm not going to waste time fussing over perfectly good wine," Quentin retorted.

"He's helping his mother," McNaughton told Quentin, who nodded.

Leo took out his cigarette case, and Teddy raised his eyebrows. "Smoking at dinner?"

Leo stuck a roll-up in his mouth and lit it with a silver monogrammed lighter. "We're not dressed, there's no soup, no entrée. I don't see why not. All bets are off, it seems. The animals are running the zoo." He exhaled, blowing smoke in Teddy's direction. The older man coughed, but said nothing.

"Then I'd like a cigarette, too, please," said Anna. Ramsey looked up, as if he were disappointed in her.

"Well, well, well . . ." Leo regarded her appraisingly. "Good for you, Miss O'Malley." He handed one over, then lit it for her. She held it in a trembling hand for a moment before inhaling. The tip glowed red in the gloom.

McNaughton hadn't forgotten Quentin's question about his son. "Why do you need to see Murdo?"

"It's not your place to ask, McNaughton," Quentin replied, reaching for his wine.

"Mr. Asquith—" Maggie began. Lightning illuminated even the darkest corners of the room, followed by a roar of thunder. Everyone at the table jumped, then laughed nervously.

Quentin contemplated the wine bottle. "We know he can't be killing any of us now, as we're all in here."

"Mr. Asquith!"

"What, Miss Hope? You were there. You saw what we found."

"What did you find?" Teddy asked, taking a bite of his sandwich.

"Nothing," Maggie said, wanting to respect Mrs. McNaughton's privacy. She felt protective of the woman who had endured so much. No one had to know of her humiliations at Killoch's hands. No one needed to see those pictures. "Nothing of any importance."

Murdo arrived bearing a bowl of pickled onions. Quentin looked up from his wine. "Ah, here we are! Ladies and gentlemen, may I present—our murderer!"

The glassy-eyed prisoners looked up. "What the devil?" exclaimed Teddy.

"Mr. Asquith—" Maggie said again.

"Are you mad?" retorted Murdo, thumping the bowl down on the table. "I'm no killer."

"Well, of course he'd *say* that," Quentin told the table.

"Wait—you think it's *Murdo*?" Anna looked at Sayid, then to Murdo, then back again, not convinced.

"Why would I kill anyone?" bristled Murdo, even as his father put a warning hand on his shoulder.

Quentin tipped back his glass, finishing it with a gulp. "You hate them all. Isn't that what you told me?" He studied his empty goblet with feverish eyes. "And now we know who your father really is."

"Aye," said McNaughton, warning in his voice. "We all know who his father is—me."

"I mean," continued Quentin, undeterred, "his *real* father."

Around the table, everyone's face except Maggie's and Quentin's registered shock.

"What?" Murdo's face flushed with anger. "What are you talking about? Are you daft?"

"Sir Marcus, of course." Quentin poured more wine. "Marcus Killoch is your biological father."

"No! You're mad!" Murdo spun to look imploringly at McNaughton. "He's mad! Isn't he?"

"The dates fit," Quentin stated. Ramsey's face registered disbelief, then dismay.

"What the devil?" Leo muttered, bewildered.

Teddy was quicker to do the sums in his head. "Good God."

"What dates? What the hell are you talking about?" Murdo asked.

Quentin spoke slowly, as if to a small child. "You're nineteen years old. You were born in August, nineteen twenty-three. You were conceived just before Marcus Killoch killed himself in November, nineteen twenty-two."

Anna swayed in her damask-covered chair. Her cigarette continued to burn, the column of ash glowing heavier and heavier, until it dropped to the carpeted floor. "Oh!" she yelped, startled.

Leo made a dismissive gesture. "Leave it. Rome is burning, my dear. A few more ashes here and there won't make a difference." Anna settled back, but crushed out the glowing cigarette on her plate. It made an ugly black stain on the antique china.

"What?" The sound Murdo made was halfway between a snort and a laugh. "My mother would rather die than sleep with Killoch or the likes of him."

"And yet," Quentin persisted, "she did." He gulped more wine.

"Quentin," Teddy warned. "These are serious accusations—"

Murdo yanked free from McNaughton's grip. "I don't believe it!"

Quentin glared at Teddy. "I know it's serious. Deadly serious."

Before Maggie could stop him, Quentin pulled something from his pocket. It was a yellowed and curling photograph. In it Fiona McNaughton's eyes were black holes of terror and defeat.

"Mr. Asquith!" Maggie exclaimed, horrified. "No!"

Unrepentant, he looked to her. "I'm sorry, Miss Hope—but I'm not about to die just to spare anyone's delicacy." He held up the photo for everyone else to see.

"Jesus Christ," breathed Leo as the rest stared in mute shock. A vein began to throb in Angus McNaughton's forehead. But the big caretaker didn't move.

"That's—that's Mrs. McNaughton?" Anna stammered. "Let me see." Quentin handed her the photograph, and she gazed at it in horror, struggling to find a connection between the respectable housekeeper she knew and the bound and terrified young woman in the picture.

"Stop it!" Murdo cried, seeing her expression. "Give that to me!" He grabbed the photo and squinted at it. Before Quentin could stop him, he touched the picture to one of the candles' flames, watching with tears in his eyes as it disintegrated into ash.

"You can destroy the photo, but you can't dismiss the truth," Quentin pressed. "Your mother slept with him, conceived you, bore you, raised you as McNaughton's son. Look in the mirror, my friend. You're the murderous old bastard's spitting image."

They stared. It was true: Murdo was slim and dark, with the same aquiline nose as Killoch's in his portrait. "Why didn't I see the resemblance before?" Teddy muttered.

Leo crushed out his cigarette in his uneaten sandwich. "Sweet Christ."

"My God," Anna whispered, looking up to Murdo. Even Ramsey's eyes widened.

"Your father was a killer and now you're ours. The apple doesn't fall far from the tree," Quentin concluded. "Except now we found you out—and you won't be able to kill anyone else."

"Why would I kill anyone?" Murdo repeated, staggering. "I'm not a . . . killer!"

"You're a hunter, we know." Quentin shrugged. "It runs in the blood. Your father did it—committed murders en masse. And now, apparently, it's your turn. Well, we've found you out, you sick little bastard! You're not going to get away with it!"

"No," Murdo whispered hoarsely. Then, "No!" He ran from the room. McNaughton whirled and followed him.

Leo poured more wine, then held up the glass to examine the dark red in the candlelight. *I have supped full with horrors.* He looked to Anna. "Maybe Murdo is your ghost?"

Anna's eyes were glassy. She didn't seem to hear him at all.

"You shouldn't have done that," Maggie said to Quentin.

"With all due respect, Miss Hope, I'm not about to die on this godforsaken island just because you're afraid to hurt young Murdo's feelings."

"I'm thinking of Mrs. McNaughton's as well," Maggie countered. "And the dates and that photograph don't prove anything. You're just causing people unnecessary pain."

"You knew, Miss Hope?" Anna frowned at her.

"We found the pictures and an appointment book in the library this afternoon," Maggie admitted. "But even if Murdo is Marcus Killoch's son, it doesn't mean he himself has killed anyone."

"Poor young man." Teddy wiped his lips with a napkin. "His whole world's been turned upside down."

Quentin's head snapped up. He stared Maggie straight in the eye. "If not Murdo, then who is doing this?" He stared at them all, one by one—Teddy, Ramsey, Anna, Leo, Sayid, and then Maggie. "One of you?"

"No," Anna protested. "I can't believe one of us is a murderer. There must be someone else in the castle. Not Murdo. Someone else, hiding. Or out there on the island. There has to be." She had gone so pale, Maggie feared she might faint.

"If there's anyone else on the island, they're doing a good job of getting in here without anybody seeing," Teddy remarked, reaching for his pipe.

"There's no one else here," Leo insisted. "Don't you understand? It might be Murdo and it might not. And if not, it must be one of us." He finished his wine and poured more. "I daresay the scene down in the kitchen tonight won't be pretty." He drained his glass again. "And I doubt there will be pudding. However, I do have a little something that might help . . ."

He reached into his jacket and pulled out a cloisonné pillbox. When he opened it, Maggie could see it was filled with white powder.

Sayid tilted his head. "Cocaine?"

"It was Helene's," admitted Leo. "But she's not needing it now, is she?"

"I'm not sure that's a good idea," Sayid countered. "It's dangerous to start, then mixing it with wine?"

"Well, then, it's a good thing I'm not asking for your permission, now, isn't it, Doctor?" Leo rose, frowning, then turned back to pick up the wine bottle by the neck. "I say we move this party into the billiards room and forget our troubles for a while. What do you say?"

"Should Miss Hope and I come, too?" asked Anna. "Aren't the ladies and gentlemen supposed to separate after dinner?"

"Separate and die," Leo said bluntly. "Life is short, after all." He raised the wine bottle high into the air. *"Carpe vinum!"*

Chapter Sixteen

The rumbling of thunder was masked by the sentimental strains of Charles Harrison's "I'll Be with You in Apple Blossom Time" playing on the gramophone in the billiards room. Maggie looked around; she hadn't spent much time in this room, as it was considered the men's territory. It was, improbably, even uglier than the rest of the castle, the furniture covered in fur pelts, the mounted heads, horns, and antlers of both American and African animals staring down from the walls. Kenyan carved wooden poles to commemorate the dead, ivory figurines in what looked to be the shapes of phalluses, and a golden Ethiopian crown adorned the walls and tables, while Masai shields and spears framed the gigantic fireplace.

The last time she'd been in the room was when she'd gone to Captain Evans's dead body . . . She closed her eyes, as if that would get rid of the memory, but she only saw his face more clearly.

"Maggie, have a drink!" she heard Quentin say, as he pressed a brandy snifter into her hand. "We *can* call you Maggie now, can't we?" he asked, indicating the stuffed fox, its beady eyes glinting in the candlelight. The air was filled with a desperate hilarity.

"Of course . . ." She tried out his first name. "Quentin."

"And Reynard."

"Yes, and . . . Reynard."

The room was wood-paneled, with a gold and green leopard-print wallpaper above the wainscoting. The floor was covered with an immense red Persian rug. There was a dais in the center, and on that was the green-baize-covered billiards table. An enormous bar lined one wall. Maggie noted the vents behind the paneling to remove cigar and cigarette smoke, while clean air was pumped in from underneath the pool table. Still, the room retained the stink of stale tobacco. She felt sick.

Quentin changed the record, and male voices sang in three-part harmony:

> I found a rose, in the devil's garden,
> Wandering alone, little lonesome rose,
> For her the sun is never shining,
> For her the clouds have no silver lining . . .

"This song"—he told the other prisoners, leaning back on a brocade wing chair, swigging from his bottle of port—"came out before the year of the murders. Might have been the last thing those poor souls ever heard."

"My, you're feeling ghoulish," Leo retorted. He took a scoop of cocaine under the nail of his pinkie and snorted like a pig searching for truffles.

He offered the pillbox to Quentin, who declined. "I prefer port, old thing. Any port in a storm, yes?" No one laughed.

"At least it's not 'Don't Sit Under the Apple Tree,'" Maggie remarked, putting a hand to her head. She was feeling the tightening behind her eyes that always led to a headache. "I'll never be able to listen to that song again." She sat in a daze, paralyzed by shock. The high ceiling caused the voices and music to reverberate in a ghostly echo, and for a moment she felt as if she were on a sinking ship. *Really, the first-class salon of the* Titanic *must have looked similar after hitting the iceberg—the mahogany paneling, the thick carpets, the brocade-covered chairs—the desperate gaiety.* She closed her eyes and rubbed at her temples, unable to escape the image of icy seawater lapping at the feet of the great ship's passengers as they sang out a final brave chorus of "Nearer My God to Thee."

"May I have another cigarette?" Anna asked Leo.

"Of course," he responded, taking a pack from his jacket pocket and handing it to her. She shook one out and leaned over to light it from a candle in a twisting ormolu candelabra, her blouse falling away from her collarbones, revealing a lacy slip. Leo stared.

"Cigarette, Maggie?" Anna asked, offering the pack. Maggie noted the use of her Christian name but didn't correct the younger woman.

"No, thank you." Maggie watched as Anna leaned back, crossing her legs, the edge of her stocking and garter belt clearly visible. Leo appeared mesmerized.

Quentin wandered the outskirts of the room, drawn to a long sofa topped with a zebra hide. He pulled the skin over himself, peeping through the cut-out eyeholes.

"Oh, wait!" Leo scrambled to his feet. "Let me play the lion!"

He returned with the lion-skin rug from the floor of the great room thrown over him and growled. *"I will roar that I will do any man's heart good to hear me. I will roar that I will make the duke say 'Let him roar again, let him roar again!' "*

The lion chased the zebra around the room, almost knocking over the lit candles. Maggie ran to get them out of their way. *The last thing we need is a fire.*

"I feel we're on safari, watching the beasts hunt on the Serengeti," Teddy remarked.

"War certainly does make strange bedfellows," Maggie said to him in disbelief, as she watched the pelt-covered men attack and feint, jumping over furniture, the revelation about Murdo seemingly forgotten. Anna clapped her hands, laughing. Ramsey sat next to her, eyeing her shyly. "And this is the first time I've seen Ramsey interact with any of us besides you."

Teddy watched, looking displeased. *Is he jealous Ramsey's coming out of his shell, making new friends? But why?* He tore his eyes away from the group. "Miss Hope," he said in a low voice, "would you come with me?"

Maggie nodded, and together they walked past the billiards table to the shadows at the far end of the room, Teddy leaning on his bear-topped walking stick. "Things are not going well here," he said.

"Rather an understatement."

"With the possible exception of Dr. Khan, I feel as though this is a squirrelly lot. I don't trust any of them."

"Not even Mr. Novak?"

"I feel great affection for the boy, but he obviously suffers from shell shock. I saw it with veterans returning from the Great War—their minds were turned somehow. Twisted," Teddy replied. "I don't know how stable Ramsey is, really, when it comes down to it. What I suggest, Miss Hope, is that, as two of the more stable personalities of the group, you and I go even further than friendship—and make an alliance."

"An alliance? What kind of an alliance?"

"We have come to be friends, you and I. And, I think by sticking together, we'll get through this mess. What do you think?"

Is Teddy frightened, too? Of course he's older, less spry, and therefore more vulnerable. "Of course, Mr. Crane," Maggie said, feeling a rush of protectiveness toward the older man, one of the few prisoners she could talk to. "We shall stick together, you and I—never fear."

"Thank you, Miss Hope." She thought she might have seen his eyes shine with tears, but perhaps it was a trick of the light.

Sayid made his way over to them. "It's a good sign," he said as he watched Anna try to talk to Ramsey while Quentin in the zebra skin dodged Leo the lion. "Maybe the only good thing to have happened these past few days." He cleared his throat. "Please call me Sayid, by the way, since it seems we're using first names now."

"And I'm Maggie."

They smiled at each other. *His eyes are so trustworthy,* she decided. *He couldn't possibly be him—could he?* Maggie shook off her doubts. She was being foolish. He was a doctor. He had taken the Hippocratic oath. He was no killer, he couldn't be. The impossible stress of their situation was making her paranoid.

Quentin and Leo left off chasing and passed a bottle of whiskey between them, still wrapped in their animal skins.

The record had reached the end, and Teddy went over to change it. "Here's another one from before the murders—Marion Harris's 'I'm a Jazz Vampire.'"

Take a tip, take a tip, take a tip from me
For I am all the evil music has.
I stood by the ocean, no one around,
Shook my shoulders and the sun went down . . .

To her astonishment, Sayid offered his hand. "Would you care to dance, Maggie?"

"Why, thank you, Sayid—I would."

They started a one-step at the edge of the room. Soon Leo dropped the lion pelt and he and Quentin pushed furniture out of the way and began dancing, too—unsteady, port and brandy sloshing in their glasses, spilling over and staining the rug. Quentin kept the zebra skin on. Ramsey rose and offered his hand to Anna. Looking surprised, she accepted, and they began a tentative dance.

When the record ended, all the dancers but Quentin sank back into chairs and the sofa, out of breath. "Helene would have loved this," Leo remarked, gazing at the flickering candles as he changed the record to something more upbeat. "The dancing, the drinking, the decadence . . ."

"To Helene!" Quentin called from under the pelt, holding up a brown bottle of port. "Tell us," he asked Leo. "Were you fucking her?"

Teddy glared. "Mr. Asquith! May I remind you there are ladies present? Mind your language, if you please!"

"I assumed you were—you know," Anna slurred to Leo. "With Helene. Which was why I was always so annoyed with you two. Because I wanted to"—she giggled—"you-know Ian." Leo threw back his head and roared. She glared at him. "Why are you laughing?"

"What a mess we've all made." Leo chuckled, tilting back a bottle of rare cognac.

Quentin, still covered in the zebra skin, was dancing the Charleston in an alarmingly vigorous fashion. Anna stumbled over to Maggie and giggled. She whispered, "Do you think he'd be good or bad in bed?"

Maggie watched for a moment, then dismissed the idea. "I don't want to know."

"The inmates are running the asylum," Sayid murmured.

The music changed again, louder and faster. A loose windowpane rattled in time to the beat. Sayid unbuttoned his jacket. "One thing this tragic mess has done is put my own life into perspective."

"How's that?" asked Maggie. They were sitting so close, she realized if she moved her leg just the slightest bit it would touch his.

"I've realized I don't like my life back home very much, when it comes down to it. I don't want to marry some girl I don't even know, one my parents have chosen for me. It's not what I want. And life is too short to waste."

"Now's probably not the time to make a decision like that," Maggie offered. "Why don't you wait until you get off the island? Then decide. This isn't the time to do anything rash—"

"This is the *only* time." Sayid watched as Anna pulled Ramsey out of his chair and onto the makeshift dance floor. Ramsey held her like a captured wild bird. Sayid's eyes turned to Maggie's, intense and warm. "I can't live my life pleasing other people."

"This isn't real," Maggie protested gently, even as her heart beat faster. "You know it's not. It's fear and adrenaline . . ."

"I don't care . . ." He tucked a stray curl of her hair back. "You are a dazzling woman, Maggie Hope. Getting to know you has been the only good thing to come from this nightmare." He bent and whispered, "Don't go back to your room tonight. Come to mine instead." Maggie swallowed.

"Good night, all," the doctor declared, rising. "I'm going to bed."

A long bar of light seeped from beneath Sayid's door, shining in the dark corridor. Maggie hesitated, trying to make a decision. Finally, she knocked. "It's me. Maggie."

The bolt snapped and the door swung open. Sayid had taken off his jacket and tie, and a fire glowed behind the grate.

"Well, aren't you going to invite me in?" she tried to joke. "There's an insane killer out there somewhere."

"Oh yes, of course, please come in—" His eyes were so dark they seemed almost black. "Are you cold?"

She realized she was shivering. "It's freezing."

"Would you like a sweater? Or a blanket?"

He walked the few steps to a wingback chair and picked up a crocheted afghan. When he'd wrapped the cover around Maggie, he pulled her close. She rested her head on his shoulder.

Outside, the rain had turned to hail, pelting as if it might shatter the windows.

"I love your hair," he murmured, wrapping a loose strand around his fingers. The tips were cold as they brushed her cheek.

Maggie raised her head. "I just want to feel normal. Just two people who fancy each other, sharing a kiss. I want to forget where we are and everything that's happened . . . that's happening. I want to escape." His body was warm; she could smell the lingering trace of his aftershave.

"You're so beautiful. I've wanted to kiss you from the moment I first laid eyes on you. I'd move mountains, cross rivers . . . I'd even kill Blue Men for you."

She smiled. "No talk of killing tonight. Please."

Sayid leaned closer. Maggie closed her eyes, but before the inevitable kiss, there was the distinct sound of a meow outside the door.

She opened her eyes. "Is that Sooty?"

"Ignore him." Sayid leaned in again.

But Sooty didn't stop, his meows turning into a frantic wail. Maggie broke away from Sayid's embrace and went to the door. She opened it. "Sooty? Sooty?"

She saw the shadow of the black cat at a tapestry of a lady and a unicorn. He was pawing at it, his yowls growing in intensity.

"Sooty, what on earth are you doing?" Maggie asked, walking toward him. Sayid followed behind her, holding a candle.

"What's above us?" she asked him.

"The tallest turret."

"Maybe there's a—" She pulled away the tapestry to reveal a wooden door.

Sooty looked up at her, as if to say, *Open the damn door, you silly human!*

Maggie whispered, "Sayid—someone might be up there—in trouble. We should go and see."

"Should we get the others?"

"No, they're too drunk—"

"True, true."

"We saw the light up there last night . . ."

"I thought it was the reflection of lightning in the window." Sooty yowled again and pawed at the door. "Maybe it wasn't."

She was frightened, to be sure, but also angry. Seven were dead; she wanted to find the murderer before any more lives were lost. "Let's go up."

"It's locked." Sayid twisted the door handle back and forth.

"Wait." Maggie stood on her tiptoes and reached above the door frame as Sooty rubbed at her ankles, purring. A hunch led her fingers along the dusty wood until they touched something. "There's a key."

When the key scraped the lock, the door creaked open, revealing a steep winding stairway, drenched in shadows. Sooty scrambled up the steps, as if he'd been there many times before. Maggie and Sayid exchanged a look. At the top they found another door. A tiny paring of light was just visible underneath.

Sooty was pawing at it and Sayid reached out to open it, but Maggie's hand stopped his. Heart pounding, she knocked, instead. Sayid gave her a puzzled look, then a low voice responded, "Come in." Then, "Goodness gracious! I won't eat you."

Maggie gnawed her lip, biting back a high, nervous laugh. She swung the door open, and the cat darted inside. She forced herself to step over the threshold. Sayid followed close on her heels. Her eyes adjusted to the light from candles and a few hurricane lamps.

The room was dim, and it held a peculiar smell: tea, lavender, dust, and things from the past kept too long. The ceiling was quite low, and the walls were covered with floral wallpaper—enormous, blowsy cabbage roses and bluebells. The lack of taxidermy was a relief.

Sooty shot straight to Mrs. McNaughton, seated on a faded chair in the tower's rounded chamber, and leapt up on her lap. At that moment, Maggie realized another figure stood in the shadows, by a narrow window.

The figure turned; it was a woman. "It took you two long enough to find me." Her voice was definitely human, low and warm. She stepped toward them, her outline tall and graceful. A fine shawl was draped over her shoulders, worn velvet slippers on her feet. Closer, there was no mistaking her patrician features or her white-blond hair.

"We had a bit of help from the cat," Sayid offered.

"Well, come in," the woman told them. "I must be better than I thought at playing hide-and-seek—I was certain a house full of secret agents would have found me before now. Come, sit down. Quite the evening you've had downstairs, I hear." She gestured to two worn silk-covered chairs across from the housekeeper.

Maggie turned her attention to Mrs. McNaughton. "Are—are you all right? I know Mr. Asquith told Murdo certain . . . things he'd discovered."

"I'm fine," the housekeeper answered, her hands stroking the cat's midnight-black fur. But the tightness of her lips belied her assurance.

"It's kind of you to be concerned for her," the silver-haired woman offered. "But secrets are often like unwanted guests—and they always come at the worst possible time. It's all right—you're safe here," she said to Maggie and Sayid. "I won't hurt you. You both look as though you've seen a ghost!" She laughed. "Please, please sit down."

"We thought you might be one," Maggie admitted as she and Sayid sat on faded blue silk armchairs. "We noticed a light from the tower—we thought at the time it was a reflection, but it must have been yours. Have you been locked up here? And I could have sworn I've seen a figure out of the corner of my eye any number of times . . ."

"Well, I'm not much to look at anymore." The woman grimaced as she moved closer. The scars were more evident in the light. "But I'm still spry. And I haven't been locked up. I come and go as I please—taking walks around the island. And I *have* been watching all of you. But you're all too self-involved to have noticed me."

Maggie thought back to Anna's insistence she felt watched, convinced she'd seen a figure the day of the fishing lessons, suspecting she'd glimpsed someone at the tomb. "We *have* seen you. We just didn't believe our eyes."

Sayid finally found his voice. "You're Lady Beatrix. Lady Beatrix Killoch."

"Yes." The woman nodded. "However, I go by my maiden name now—Beatrix Granville."

"We—we thought you'd died," Maggie managed.

"Reports of my death have been greatly exaggerated." Beatrix laughed, then stopped abruptly, as if it were still too painful.

"But it was in the papers," pressed Sayid.

Lightning flashed, illuminating the room. Beatrix turned to the tower's long, thin window. Rain was drumming against it like skeleton fingers, and she waited for the answering growl of thunder. "Never believe everything you read in the papers, Doctor."

"How do you know who I am?"

"Mrs. McNaughton has kept me informed of all of you," the silver-haired woman replied. "She's told me you and Miss Hope are the only two she trusts."

"But what happened?" Maggie asked Beatrix, thoroughly confused. "Why did you let people think you were dead? Why are you living here in the tower? And, Mrs. McNaughton—you knew this the whole time?"

"When everything . . . happened," Beatrix answered. "The murders . . . I was injured . . ." She glanced to the housekeeper; the cat had fallen asleep in her lap. "Fiona nursed me back to health." The candlelight flickered over her face, pain undeniable.

Maggie leaned forward. "But why let everyone believe you'd died?"

"For a time, Miss Hope, I wished I had died with the rest of them—with all my heart. But then I realized I had no desire to return to my previous life. I'd be known as a monster. I couldn't go back into society—I'd be forever branded the widow of a mass murderer. And so I decided to stay here on the island instead. Fiona and her husband have graciously allowed me to live with them. When the British government took over the island, in nineteen forty, I went into hiding up here."

"In light of your continued existence, I just have to ask." Maggie's brain whirled, as she tried to absorb all she'd just learned. "Is Marcus Killoch really dead? That's not a fake body in the coffin?"

"Oh, he's dead and gone, to be sure," Mrs. McNaughton assured her. Beatrix and Mrs. McNaughton exchanged a significant look. "*That* part the papers reported correctly."

The raindrops continued to ding against the window. "Lady Beatrix—" Maggie began.

"Miss Granville is fine."

"Surely there's no reason for you to hide."

"I've become used to the solitude, the seasons, the sea. I didn't want to change things." She took a ragged breath. "I didn't want to answer questions. People can be so cruel . . ."

I know. "Please," Maggie urged. "Come downstairs with us."

"No, I like it up here. I have my books, my tea, a splendid view of the ocean . . . Besides, Fiona tells me things are getting a bit messy downstairs. Yet more murders—you're up to seven dead now? I'll stay up here where it's safe, thank you!" Beatrix shuddered, then sighed. "We probably should have burned the whole place down when we had the chance. I always loathed it—it's a monstrosity, isn't it? Still, when you're inside, you don't have to look at it. And I can't complain about the view."

"What happened that night?" Maggie asked. "Did it happen the way the newspaper accounts said? Your husband killed the guests and then shot himself?"

"There were ten men, plus Marcus, who died. We don't speak of it," said Beatrix, sitting beside Mrs. McNaughton. The two women grasped hands.

"Bea," Mrs. McNaughton offered. "You know I've always thought sunlight is the best disinfectant."

"Some things can't be made clean, Fiona. And what could possibly come of talking about it?"

"Part of it—well, it's my secret to tell," Mrs. McNaughton insisted. After a long moment, the silver-haired woman pulled her shawl tighter around her and nodded.

"Marcus and Bea had an arranged marriage," Mrs. McNaughton told them. "He was a terrible man, Marcus Killoch. And he had terrible friends. They did just as they pleased. No one ever stopped them. They . . . did things. You saw the pictures."

"Did you know what was going on?" Maggie asked Beatrix.

"As Fiona said, we had a sham marriage, for appearances' sake only," she answered. "Marcus always had quite . . . unusual tastes. But as long as he went elsewhere for his fun and didn't bother me, I ignored what he did. After the Great War, however, his appetites became more . . . voracious. The usual ladies from London he invited here to the castle didn't satisfy. He took to paying girls from Mallaig to come to the island. Unspeakable things happened in that ballroom. Usually staff was barred—"

"The dumbwaiters." Maggie nodded. "And the orchestra gallery's curtain."

"Fiona was working for us then—and she was so young and pretty." Beatrix glanced to the housekeeper with a soft smile. "Eventually, Marcus stalked her and brought her into his fold. But Angus and Fiona were engaged to be married, you see—she a maid and he the ghillie."

Mrs. McNaughton lifted her eyes. "When I went missing that

night, Angus came looking for me—opened up the door to the ballroom and saw what Sir Marcus and his friends were doing to us girls—"

There was a peal of thunder. Maggie had to remind herself to keep breathing. "And—" Once again Beatrix and Mrs. McNaughton exchanged looks, their faces clouded. "Angus—he found a rifle and killed them all. He saved us." Mrs. McNaughton's fingers crept to the cross at her throat, and her eyes looked lost in the labyrinth of memories. "Saved me." Maggie blinked as she struggled to absorb this new revelation.

Mrs. McNaughton took a handkerchief from the sleeve of her dress and wiped at her nose. "I keep asking myself, Why didn't *I* ever do anything?"

Beatrix put a comforting arm around the housekeeper's shoulder. "Shhhhh . . . There was nothing you could do, Fi." Then she turned to Maggie and Sayid. "You can't tell anyone. You mustn't. You need to keep our secret. Please."

"No one dared say no," Mrs. McNaughton said, lifting her eyes. They burned into Maggie's. "No one dared stop them. He was *Sir Marcus,* and they were all powerful men. With a lot of money and influence. Here on the island, they just ran wild, like animals, killing and rutting . . ."

Sayid leaned forward. "What about the police?"

"The police in Mallaig were paid off handsomely to turn a blind eye. That's what money gets you—a different set of rules. They knew what was happening to the girls from Mallaig and Fort William—to us servant girls. And they didn't give a damn, as long as they got their payout. We did what we had to, to survive. You couldn't think about it. During the day, when it wasn't happening, I'd make myself forget. When it was happening, it was like I floated out of myself, like I was looking down from some high point on the ceiling. And then, when it's all over, you put it away, in a box. So there was normal life and then there was—that."

Mrs. McNaughton covered her face with her fingers. "Oh my God, the ballroom . . . I'd lift up and out of my body, not part of it at all. I cut off a portion of myself and I left it in that cursed ballroom. Or so I prayed." She dropped her hands and looked to Maggie. "Murdo said . . . there was a picture?"

"It's burned," Maggie assured her. "Destroyed. And I can burn all the photographs of all the other girls, too."

"Yes, bless you, please do that. That chapter of my life needs to be closed." She sighed in relief. "Angus saved me." She laughed, a bitter chortle. "I didn't think I was good enough for him. He saved me that night. And then he saved my life when he stayed with me, married me. Raised Murdo as his own—never held it against me or the child. We never spoke of it again." She swayed, clutching her cross. "I pray. I pray . . . When the memories return, I pray."

"I'm so sorry," Maggie offered. But seeing the agony etched on the woman's face, she realized how useless her words were.

"When the police finally came," Beatrix added, "there was no one alive—at least no male aristocrats—to dispute our story. All ten of the men and my husband were dead. Angus had shot them all. The girls kept quiet. And Fiona hid me and tended to me and kept my secret." She choked back a sob. "Marcus was an evil man. He deserved to die. I can think of no death more appropriate for him and his lot—being hunted down like the prey he used to shoot and kill."

There was sadness in her voice, the echoes of terror, but also, Maggie realized, a small but unmistakable glow of pride.

"So *our* murderer then—it's not Murdo and it's not Marcus." Bewildered, Sayid rubbed at the back of his neck. "Who is it, then? Have you seen anything? Do you know anything?"

"How could I know anything, up here in this tower?"

"You said you love the view," Maggie pointed out, looking to the window. "Have you seen any unidentified people on the grounds? Anything unusual at all?"

Beatrix frowned. "Well, someone's been going to the boat. Not openly. At night, with a flashlight. I don't know who it is—or if it's a man or woman. But I've seen a figure coming and going."

"The boat Dr. Jaeger was on," Maggie said, realizing, remembering the long antenna. "The boat in the bay—it has a radio."

We're in touch with SOE already. So who would need to use it? Oh, God . . . "A German agent could be using the radio," Maggie posited, "for a pickup. So it's possible we don't have only a murderer here." More pieces clicked into place with sickening clarity. "We might have a Nazi spy on the island." Sayid's mouth opened, and Beatrix and Mrs. McNaughton looked at her in shock.

Maggie jumped to her feet. "We need to destroy the radio! *Now!*"

Chapter Seventeen

❖

"Wish we had a baseball bat," Maggie said, eyeing the radio on Captain Evans's desk. They'd done away with the formality of asking Mrs. McNaughton for the key and simply broke in.

"I don't know what that is." Sayid looked around for something, anything, to smash the machinery. "And whatever it may be, I doubt anybody in Scotland has one."

"It's like a cricket bat," Maggie said, picking up one of Evans's walking sticks and testing it. "Maybe McNaughton has a tool in the shed we can use?" Sayid nodded and left.

But first . . . Maggie flipped on several switches and the set buzzed to life, red and yellow lights blinking as the device warmed up. She experimented with the dials, trying to pick up a signal. The radio hummed, then crackled. She gave a sigh of relief—the set was still working, despite the severe weather conditions. She could send one last message to SOE before she destroyed it.

She flipped a switch to Transmit and called over the noise of the storm, *"Mayday!"* The weather was blocking the radio waves, making it nearly impossible for a signal to penetrate. And yet, she couldn't give up . . .

Once again, she flipped the switch back to Transmit. "Mayday! Mayday!" Nothing. She flipped the switch over again. "This is

Scarra Island. We have six—no, now *seven*—dead. We believe there's a German agent on the island, one who's killing us off one by one and who I suspect will try to arrange a pickup off the island once the storm's over. You need to get here ASAP . . . *over!*"

There was only the hiss of radio waves.

She hit Transmit once again. "Mayday, Mayday. We're destroying the radios now."

Nothing but static.

"Mayday," she called again desperately. Then, "Scarra out."

Sayid stood in the doorway, carrying two axes. Maggie drew in her breath; but he merely handed one to her. "You take care of this radio," he told her, swinging the other over his shoulder. "And I'll take care of the one on the boat."

Under cover of rain and darkness, a figure wearing a mackintosh and carrying a flashlight made its way down the dock. It jumped onto the fishing boat, lashed by icy rain. Dripping water, the shadow slipped inside the wheelhouse, moving to the instrument panels and controls, finding the vessel's radio. The figure swayed. Even though the boat was moored, the water was turbulent, making balance difficult. Hail struck the windows like thrown pebbles. The gloved hand flipped on several switches and the device hummed to life, the lights blinking on. The hand experimented with the dials, trying to pick up a signal. The set buzzed with static, then crackled.

There were charts rolled into tubes stored below the navigation table. Using the flashlight, the person took the maps out, seeking precise coordinates. Letting the maps fall to the floor, the figure grabbed hold of the wooden steering wheel with one hand for balance, while the other switched on the radio, twisting the dials and turning the volume all the way up.

The individual continued to explore the airwaves, picking up a few faint messages, trying to tune to the frequency of the German U-boat that was patrolling the Irish Sea and listening in. A sigh of relief—the set was in working order. Once again, the fingers flipped the switch back to Transmit. "Come in, Ulster Lady. Come in. Over," a voice said. Nothing. Another try. "Come in, Ulster Lady. This is Petrus."

Nothing. Then a crackle of static and a faint *Come in, Petrus. This is Ulster Lady, over.*

"I need a pickup. Coordinates are latitude 57° 00' 50" north and longitude minus 6° 13' 20" west. Over."

Copy that. You're asking for a pickup at latitude 57° 00' 50" north and longitude minus 6° 13' 20" west. There was a long hiss and more static. *When? Over.*

"As soon as the storm breaks. Based on a trip of nine kilometers to the pickup point and a speed of eight to twelve knots, I will leave an hour prior to pickup. Estimated window, between seventeen and nineteen hundred hours. Over."

Estimated pickup window between seventeen and nineteen hundred hours. Over.

"Correct. Over."

Copy, Petrus. Out.

Smiling, the figure picked up the ax from the floor and smashed the radio.

Oberleutnant zur See Haupt Alaric Weber, *U-135*'s intelligence officer, put the microphone down. He was on the bridge of the submarine, a claustrophobic, dank metal tube bristling with pipes, dials, and glowing red buttons. A sign above his head warned, HEISS! BITTE NICHT BERÜHREN! *Hot! Do Not Touch!*

A faint haze had settled within the boat, causing his face to shine; at periscope depth, everything was slick with condensation. The air was low in oxygen, causing mental slowness, making it hard for cuts to heal and difficult to light cigarettes.

And then there was the smell. There was little water available for bathing, and most of the crew showered only every ten days or so. Laundry was out of the question. The result was a unique odor, a stew of sweat, diesel fuel, cigarette smoke, hydraulic fluid, cooking oil, and sewage. The constant humidity allowed mold and mildew to fester throughout the boat, as well as large cockroaches the crew could never quite seem to eradicate.

Weber looked up and caught the captain's eye as he walked into the control room. "It's our ghost, Herr Kaleu," the intelligence officer said, using the diminutive form of *Kapitänleutnant,* as tradition dictated. "Has something important. Wants a pickup."

Weber was one of Admiral Canaris's Abwehr agents, working for the German military intelligence service. He was bald, with a fringe of dark hair over his ears, and angled eyebrows that always conveyed an expression of surprise. He was a Berliner, but a surprisingly silent one, preferring to read Thomas Mann rather than play cards with the others. Worse, he seemed to have no bad habits, not smoking, drinking, or using profanity, unusual on a submarine. Underneath those comically slanted eyebrows, Weber's actual expression rarely changed from guarded.

"And where is our ghost, Herr Weber?" Kapitänleutnant Ferdinand von Siemens was short, golden-haired, aristocratic in accent and bearing, and sported a signet pinkie ring. He was also short-tempered, foulmouthed, and feared by his crew. He had once been handsome, but now modeled the same sunken eyes, gray pallor, and unkempt beard as his fellow submariners.

"Off the west coast of Scotland, sir." Weber rattled off the coordinates. "Wants a pickup between seventeen hundred hours and nineteen hundred hours."

"Weather?"

"There's a bad storm there now. It's expected to blow over just around the time of the requested pickup."

"All right, let's head in closer to shore in preparation, Schäffler," the Kapitänleutnant ordered.

"Aye, sir." First Officer Kurt Schäffler was a round-faced, green-eyed Bavarian, with an easygoing manner that made him a favorite among the crew.

"We'll come fifteen kilometers from the pickup point and circle, Schäffler."

"Yes, sir." There was disappointment in the first officer's voice. Schäffler found their assignment, waiting for one of Admiral Canaris's spies, uninteresting and would rather have been hunting down Allied ships in wolf packs with his fellow submariners. Still, there was an upside to coming in so close to the Scottish islands. "Sir . . ."

"What is it?" The Kapitänleutnant picked up the weather report.

"There are sheep on those islands, sir."

He continued reading. "Mmm?"

"Sheep are good to eat," Schäffler continued. "Perhaps while we're waiting for our spy, we could go to one of the deserted islands and pick up a sheep or two? Roast mutton—now that would make a nice change from all the canned rations . . ."

"Schäffler, the weather's execrable. Far too rough for a rubber raft to get to shore," the Kapitänleutnant barked. "I will not jeopardize the safety of my crew, not even for mutton. No. Sheep."

The first officer's eyes registered deep disappointment. "Aye, sir."

Weber turned back to the transmitter. "I'm sending a message to Canaris." He composed the message, encoded it on the Enigma machine, then sent it via Morse code, using special Abwehr settings. The message would go first through BdU, the Kriegsmarine headquarters in northern France, then to the Abwehr radio center near Hamburg, then to Canaris's office in Berlin. "Telling him we'll pick up his agent tomorrow. I'll leave out the bit about the sheep."

———

"You look like Mickey Mouse," Malcolm Miller told his partner, Howard Grant. Miller was a retired engineer from Edinburgh. The two men hunched over a receiver and radio direction finder in the back of an unmarked truck with four tall vertical antennae. They were pulled over on the shoulder of a deserted dirt road on the west coast of Scotland, not far from Fort William. The mobile voluntary interceptor was just one of many requested by Frain to augment the specificity of the directional finding stations and locate the transmission to the U-boat.

"Mickey what?" grumbled Grant. He, too, was retired, a former surgeon from Aberdeen. He was also an amateur radio enthusiast, in addition to being a breeder of lavender point Siamese cats. He had a beaky, prominent nose, and his neck was wrapped in a chunky hand-knit scarf. "What do you mean?"

Miller, the green lights of the control panel shining on his bald and sun-spotted head, spun the dial to scan through target frequencies. "You mean *who*—and I'm saying you do. Look like Mickey Mouse, that is. The cartoon," he explained. "Your headphones are like mouse ears."

Grant was not amused. "I'm doing serious work here!"

"Right, right. Of course you are."

"Wait!" Grant put his hands to the offending earphones.

Miller raised his shaggy eyebrows. "What is it?"

"Just a plane." Grant took off the headset. "Oi, my ears hurt. I have cauliflower ears."

"Mouse ears." Miller rubbed his eyes and yawned. "Cauliflower brains, more likely."

"Well, you, my friend, have something else for brains, something I won't say," Grant said, taking a swig from his mug of cold tea. Then, in milder tones: "Not bad work, really. Though I'd rather be a young man on the front lines."

"I was in the Great War, in the trenches. I've already done my duty," Miller countered. "Happy with this little operation to do my bit. Even though I doubt we'll ever hear anything."

"Well, they must suspect *something*, don't you think? Otherwise, why are we here?"

Miller rummaged through a rucksack and found a knit cap, slipping it over his bald head. "At least it gets me away from the missus for a night or two."

As the pair slumped to wait in silence, a rapid beeping began, indicating the signal was active. "Yes!" Grant exclaimed. He put the headphones on again and listened intently, dictating numbers to Miller. They already had information from two other stations. With three geographically dispersed stations receiving the same signal call, they could chart the location.

Miller whistled through his teeth. "It triangulates perfectly."

Grant pulled at the map. "Let me see." The pencil marks indicated the source of the radio transmission somewhere in the inner Hebrides. "Where the hell is that?"

Miller squinted down. "Says 'Isle of Scarra.'" He looked up and grinned at his partner. "Guess that those mouse ears are good for something after all."

From the windows of the train from Euston Station, David watched the dark slate sky change to pale gray as dawn broke and the orange sun rose. His destination was Watts Park, about half a mile southeast of the village of Hanslope in the Borough of Milton Keynes in Buckinghamshire. Once a great house built by a textile fortune heir, Watts Park was now commandeered by the British government and used for the storage of war-related documents.

From the train station, he walked the half mile to the house, his brogues crunching on the gravel of the sweeping front drive. After signing in at the front office and showing his identification, David was driven in a jeep down a dirt road to a wooded area. There, in the high-security compound, stood the warehouse SOE shared with MI-5 and MI-6 to house top-secret documents.

David was admitted through a set of double doors by a frowning Coldstream Guard; the corridor beyond led to a dim, cavernous warehouse. "Thanks," he told the guard, flipping on the light switches. "I'll take it from here." In the frigid air were rows upon rows of metal file cabinets, each neatly labeled TOP SECRET in red ink.

He walked aisle after musty aisle, sidestepping puddles from the leaking ceiling, his footsteps loud on the cement floors. At last he found the cabinets he was looking for, from the "Inter-Services Research Bureau." He searched in vain through file upon file, page after page.

As the minutes turned to an hour, and then two, David's fingers grew stiff with cold. He blew on them, then shifted his weight from one frozen foot to the other. He didn't know exactly what he was looking for—he just had a grim suspicion that if Maggie couldn't be found, there was something shifty going on. People, even people in SOE, didn't just vanish. "Hammering Hephaestus . . ." he grumbled, continuing to rifle through paper-stuffed files.

"Are you still there, sir?" called the guard.

"Yes, indeed—and I'd dearly love a cup of hot tea if you can spare one!" David called back.

"No food or drink allowed in the file areas, sir."

"Of course not," David muttered, flipping up his coat's collar against the cold.

"Do you know how long you'll be, sir?"

"As long as I need!" David shouted. Finally, he pulled out two pages stapled together and headed *RE: The ISRB Operation at Isle of Scarra.* "Now we're getting somewhere," he murmured.

At the top was the usual stamp TOP SECRET, but this one, interestingly enough, had *Copy No. 3 of 3* written under the stamp. Only three copies of something—well, that wasn't very many. It appeared to be from Colonel Martens to Colonel Bishop, with a carbon copy sent to a name David didn't recognize. As far as David could tell, the document was, as Martens had said, about a secret SOE training camp on the Isle of Scarra, a small island off the western coast of Scotland.

But as he read further, his brow furrowed:

The prison will be jointly operated by MI-6 and SOE, and called a training camp. It will be operated from Killoch Castle on the Isle of Scarra. Unsafe agents are not to be given the real reason for their imprisonment until they arrive. As far as they must know, when they leave SOE, they are merely receiving more specialized training before undertaking their next mission. The families of the prisoners will be informed only that they are on active duty. Prisoners will continue to be paid and have their salaries deposited in their accounts, as they would on active duty. Prisoners are allowed no outside contact. Prisoners are allowed no telephone calls, no letters, and no radio transmissions. The Isle of Scarra is declared a prohibited zone under the Defense Regulations. The local police and coast guard will be informed only that it is a secret government training facility. If any civilians should discover the existence of the prison, they will be silenced under orders from the Ministry of Information. Likewise, journalists. When the war is over, a committee will report on which, if any, of the agents will be admitted back into society.

"What the devil?" David muttered, returning the file to its proper place. "'Which, if any, agents will be admitted back into society'? What the hell is going on up there in the hinterland? And, Mags, what in God's name have they done to you?"

Chapter Eighteen

Icy rain, driven by furious winds, hit the castle's windows in a relentless tattoo. Even with her bedroom door locked and a chair pushed up against the knob, Maggie had managed to doze only fitfully. In her dreams, Quentin's fox was alive and being pursued through the woods by a pack of rabid dogs. Then she was the fox and the dogs had cornered her, barking, fangs bared, bloodlust blazing in their eyes. Maggie jerked awake, coated in metallic sweat, the bedclothes in a tangle around her feet.

And now, a new problem: a potential German spy in their midst. But he—or she—would never find out what she knew. *The war won't be lost on my watch.*

To calm herself, Maggie thought about numbers. She deeply missed math, its logic, its order, the peculiar joy of working a problem to its conclusion. How simple math was, even the most sophisticated equations, compared to the horrors humans created. In reality, there was no order. When humans entered the calculation, the center never held.

She deliberately slowed her breathing as she turned on the bedside lamp and focused on a brown water stain on the ceiling. But her thoughts were still terrifying. *Seven dead in five days. And now, day six. Who will die today?*

And will it be me?

She couldn't lie still any longer. As her thoughts spun and churned, she slipped out of bed and opened the blackout curtain. The storm raged on, causing enormous white-capped rollers in the bay. Torn branches and downed trees littered the lawn. *There will be no boat today. No rescue.*

Adrenaline surged through her, clearing the fog of exhaustion and fear. *All I have to do is survive.* The insanity of it all caused her lips to twitch with the shadow of a smile. *Survive,* she decided. *Outfox and endure. I survived Berlin. I survived Wannsee. I survived Windsor and Paris, the Blitz and the Blackout Beast. No craven, two-bit Nazi stool pigeon is going to kill me—or anyone else on this island.*

There was nothing to do but wash up and get dressed. After a cold splashing from the bath's shower hose, she threw on training coveralls, thick socks, and boots. Her first order of business was to check on Lady Beatrix and try to convince her to come downstairs.

At the top of the tower's stairs, Maggie knocked. "Lady Beatrix?"

"I told you, it's Bea Granville now," rang a voice, and then the door opened. "Your friend's already here."

Maggie looked past the woman to see Sayid on one of the chairs, a white bandage around his head. "My word," she said, walking to him. "What happened to you?"

"I went out to destroy the boat's radio," he said slowly, as if in great pain. "But someone must have come up behind me—cracked me on the back of the head. Whoever did it probably left me for dead on the lawn, but I regained consciousness a few hours later."

"Any recognizable features?" Maggie asked.

"Nothing. Couldn't even tell if it was a man or woman."

Lady Beatrix walked over to both of them. "You poor dear," she said to Sayid, taking the seat beside him.

"What happened to the radio?" Maggie asked.

"When I came to, I went to the boat. The radio was already destroyed and the ax I borrowed from McNaughton was on the floor."

"So, the spy could have made one last transmission."

"Yes."

She searched his face, looking for any trace of deception, and found none. "Well, I'm glad you're all right," she said, smiling down at him. "Thank goodness." She turned to Beatrix. "I think you should come downstairs with us this morning."

"Oh no—I couldn't possibly—"

"I think it's the safest way to proceed. If one of the others finds you, let's just say I'm not convinced they won't kill first. You have no idea how tense things are down there."

Beatrix looked to Sayid. "What do you think?"

"I think Miss Hope has a point. If we could find you, it's only a matter of time before someone else does. Might as well get it over with."

Beatrix smoothed her flowered day dress and pulled her cardigan around her. "I haven't been downstairs in so long . . ."

"I'll go and prepare everyone over breakfast," Maggie said. "Please wait for my signal and then come into the dining room for introductions." She smiled into the older woman's troubled eyes. "We're getting used to losing people—it's a blessing to gain one." She turned to leave.

"Be careful," warned Sayid.

"I always am."

In the dining room, the other prisoners—Quentin, Teddy, Ramsey, Anna, and Leo—were already assembled and seated. "Last night—" Quentin began.

"Let's not speak of it," cautioned Anna. Maggie slipped into the room and took her accustomed seat; the table hadn't been cleaned from last night's dinner. Burned-out candles and hardened wax drips punctuated the crumb-strewn cloth.

The group looked equally untended. Buttons were undone, ties askew, clothes were wrinkled as though they'd been slept in. Everyone's shoulders were hunched with tension, and Quentin seemed to have developed a nervous tremor in his hands, apparent as he stroked Monsieur Reynard. Maggie realized she hadn't put up her hair. "Last night—" she echoed.

"—after last night, we couldn't possibly expect Mrs. McNaughton to prepare breakfast," Anna interrupted, rubbing at her temples to try to keep the hangover at bay.

"Bugger that. I feel barely human. Dreadful headache." Leo held one hand to his temple. "I need tea—that bloody woman needs to keep a stiff upper lip and do her duty and feed us." Teddy was too tired even to object to Leo's swearing.

"I'll go see where she is," Anna offered, standing.

"No, stay a moment, Anna, please," said Maggie. Anna blinked and sank back down into her chair without protest. The rest of the prisoners glanced around in a daze. There were so many empty places at the table. Five empty places. Seven people murdered in total. The inmates appeared hungover, yes, Maggie thought, but also frightened. There was no idle conversation, just tense, exhausted silence.

"Last night," Maggie began again, "Sayid and I heard a noise—and went up to the tower."

Despite his headache, Leo leered. "Is *that* what you two are calling it?"

Maggie ignored his taunt. "We found Mrs. McNaughton, who was, understandably, quite upset from the evening's revelations. We also found someone else."

The eyes of the remaining prisoners focused and snapped to her. Even Ramsey stared her way. "Who?" Quentin breathed.

"Lady Beatrix Killoch. She is very much alive."

"Jesus, Mary, and Joseph," Anna whispered.

"She's been killing us off?" Leo thundered. "A *woman*?"

Maggie shook her head. "No. We don't believe she's killed anyone."

Leo's color heightened. "What the devil is she doing here?"

"Language," Teddy cautioned, but it sounded perfunctory. Leo pulled a face.

"We all thought she was dead!" Quentin cried. "The newspapers said so!"

"According to Lady Beatrix, the events at Killoch Castle twenty years ago didn't happen quite the way the official accounts described," Maggie told them. "Lady Beatrix and Mrs. McNaughton told us that Marcus Killoch had abused young women from the island and the mainland."

"The pictures . . ." Anna began, then faltered.

"Yes," Maggie replied. "What happened to the women was nonconsensual and violent. It was rape. Fiona Morrison was one of Marcus Killoch's victims. When her then-fiancé, Angus McNaughton, heard a rumor of what was happening, he shot the men in the ballroom, then told the girls to leave. In the confusion that night, Lady Beatrix was injured. Mrs. McNaughton nursed Lady Beatrix back to health in secret," Maggie continued. "McNaughton made up a story for the police, so they would be convinced it was a murder-suicide. There were no witnesses except the girls—and they certainly weren't going to say anything." Around the table, the prisoners' faces were blank with shock.

Maggie rose and walked to the door of the dining room. "Lady Beatrix? Mrs. McNaughton? Would you please come in now?"

Sayid led the two women in, with Murdo a few steps behind. Maggie heard Quentin's sharp intake of breath. Anna crossed herself.

"I must apologize if I've frightened any of you in any way," Beatrix began. She was pale but composed. "After the events Miss Hope just told you of, I had no wish to return to so-called society. I decided to stay here, on Scarra.

"Of course, when the British government established their camp here, it made things a bit more . . . difficult. But I have to thank Fiona, Angus, and Murdo. They protected me and nursed me to health and kept my secrets—as I have kept theirs. Until now. And now I'm asking you to keep mine, too."

Those around the table stared in shock at Beatrix, Anna raising one hand to cover her mouth.

"Who exactly would we tell?" Leo shot back, scowling. "The damn taxidermy?"

"Speaking of McNaughton," Teddy said, looking around. "Has anyone seen him this morning?"

Frain had been in his office since before dawn, but he was still crisp and impeccable. He put on gold-rimmed glasses to go through the latest dispatches from various Y-stations. As he read one document from the Yorkshire station stamped URGENT, his eyebrows raised when he noted the estimated point of transmission: Y-service's best guess was somewhere in the inner Hebrides, most likely the Isle of Scarra.

"Sweet Jesus—someone's expecting a U-boat pickup off that blasted island!" Frain stood, then kicked the wastepaper basket. It flew across the room, spilling crumpled paper. "God *damn* it!" he thundered.

His secretary, a stout woman used to such explosions, poked her head in the door. "Yes, Mr. Frain?"

"Get me Henrik Martens on the line!" he barked. *"Now!"*

"Yes, sir," she said, ducking out.

Frain stormed around his office; finally, Martens was put through.

"I know you receive the same decrypts I do," Frain began without preamble. "Tell me you've read what I've read."

"Someone from Scarra is signaling for a Nazi U-boat pickup."

"He—or she—has asked them to be ready after the storm abates. What's the weather like up there right now?"

"It's bad," Martens replied. "One of the prisoners on Scarra has also been in touch with the nearest SOE camp—in Arisaig. Something odd's going on."

"Odder than a German spy asking for a ride home?"

"Scarra and Arisaig have had limited contact, but from what I understand, four of the prisoners are dead, as well as their commanding officer, a doctor, and a ship's captain. Seven victims in all. The last transmission was spotty, but it indicated they suspect one of them is a Nazi agent."

"Jesus *Christ*," spluttered Frain.

"I suspect the spy is one of the prisoners, but we don't know who yet."

"Let's cut directly to the chase—what's the worst thing a Nazi spy could learn from that group?"

Martens pursed his lips. "A lot of things we don't want the enemy to know. But the worst is the secret of Overlord." For once in his life, Frain was speechless. "One of the agents has knowledge of it— Margaret Hope."

"Miss Hope? The agent Scotland Yard is trying to find to testify at the Blackout Beast's trial?"

"*Yes,*" answered Martens, his frustration apparent. "Now you *understand*—we thought protecting that information was worth keeping her from testifying."

Frain's sudden calm was more terrifying than his temper. "You see the irony, Martens, yes?"

"It's not lost on me."

"Well, we need to call the cavalry."

"It's a matter of the weather. It's not safe—"

"If we can't get to them, our German spy can't leave either. I guess that's cold comfort. When's the storm scheduled to break?"

"We expect the weather to let up shortly before dawn tomorrow. That will make it easier to conduct search operations."

"It will also make it easier for our German friend to reach the U-boat." Frain cursed, softly. "All right. In the meantime, get everyone into position to stop this spy from making it off that island. I want every ship, sub, and plane we have."

"Already on it. I've spoken with both the Royal Navy and the local coast guard in Mallaig and Fort William. The Navy at HMNB Clyde is moving a pair of corvettes into the area as we speak, as well as a submarine. They'll get as close as they can and commence search operations immediately. The coast guard is handling things closer to shore. And the RAF will put up planes as soon as it's safe."

"And when do we expect that to be?"

"Tomorrow at around seven A.M." Frain could hear a match scrape.

"No time for smoking, Colonel. You will meet me at RAF Northolt at noon."

"Sir?"

"I have a few things to wrap up. And then, you and I are flying to Scotland."

The winds picked up once more as Frain hurried across Parliament Square toward the Annexe. As he strode over the green, he glanced up at the statues of former prime ministers: Lord Palmerston, Edward Smith-Stanley, Benjamin Disraeli. All looked impervious to the damp and cold. All stared down on him in judgment at Britain having reached such a perilous juncture. Frain flipped up the collar of his raincoat and walked faster.

In his bedroom at the Annexe, Churchill was still in bed, wrapped in his favorite dragon-embroidered green silk robe, the first cigar of the day between his fingers. His precious Box, filled with the day's top-secret documents, was to one side, and his black cat, Nelson, was curled by his sock-covered feet.

He made no move to cover himself as Frain entered. The MI-5 head pulled up an armchair and regarded the figure before him. The P.M.'s complexion was tinged with gray. He did not look well. "Would you like anything more, sir?" Inces asked, taking away the P.M.'s breakfast tray. "Tea? Coffee?"

Churchill waved the butler away as Frain began. "Sir, we've intercepted another message from the German agent operating inside Britain to a U-boat. This time, we were able to triangulate the signal. It's coming from the Isle of Scarra."

"Scarra," the P.M. muttered. "Why do I keep hearing about this damn Isle of Scarra?"

"There's an SOE camp there, sir," Frain replied. "It was mentioned in our last meeting. Mr. Greene seemed particularly interested in it, as his friend and your former secretary, Maggie Hope, has been stationed there."

"Well, if you've triangulated the signal, man, get the agent! Shoot him! Drop a bomb on him! Take the bugger out!"

"We're trying. The west coast of Scotland is in the middle of a nasty storm. We can't get there. But that means the agent can't get out, either. We have everything and everyone ready for when the weather breaks. But if that agent is able to reach the sub with any information, that's it—it's over."

Churchill growled.

"The good news," Frain continued, "is that the message from the island said they were aware of the agent and were destroying the radios. In order for our German agent to get any secrets to Abwehr, he or she will have to be picked up by the U-boat. And we have ships, a sub, and planes getting into position right now."

"Damn it!" Churchill pounded his fists on the bed, disturbing

Nelson, who jumped down to the carpet and began grooming. "What's going on there, on this Scarra?" The P.M.'s cigar had gone dead. He relit it, then puffed on it furiously, until the tip glowed orange. "What a name—Scarra. Like *scar*. Or *scare*."

"Martens won't say, but I'd hazard a guess it's a camp for agents who've washed out of the SOE program. For spies who know too much, who need to be taken out of the equation, to keep our secrets safe."

"The SOE's version of a cooler," the Prime Minister muttered thoughtfully. "Then how did a German spy end up there, pray tell, Mr. Frain?"

"That we don't know, sir. We're poring over the files of everyone assigned there. No one raises any red flags."

"That's the unfortunate truth about war, Frain," he growled, jabbing his cigar into a smoke ring. "While no man alone can win a war, it is entirely possible for a single man to lose one." He took another long puff. "Or a single woman, in this case."

"You don't think Miss Hope—"

The Prime Minister waved dismissively. "Miss Hope's experienced. She's done multiple missions abroad. She won't talk."

Frain raised an eyebrow. "I certainly pray not."

Churchill harrumphed again. "Frain, you've worked with her. I believe if she's interrogated about something that important, that imperative to winning the war, she'll realize what's going on and . . . take care of things." The words hung in the air; both men understood the stakes.

"There's another factor, sir."

"Damn it, man, now what?"

"We received a message from Scarra last night. Seven on the island are dead. It looks as if the agent's picking them off one by one in order to make an easier escape."

The Prime Minister appeared exhausted, his face chalky and drained. He patted the bedclothes next to him, and Nelson jumped up, purring triumphantly, rubbing against Churchill's offered hand. "That's a good boy," he murmured. "Those on the island must channel the bravery of your namesake, Lord Nelson, and keep bloody buggering on."

"I'm on my way to Scotland, sir, to oversee the assault on the island when the storm lifts," Frain continued, rising. "I'll send word the moment I know anything. Right now, it all depends on the weather and Miss Hope."

"Miss Hope, I believe, we can trust. The weather, alas, is in God's hands." As Frain gathered up his things and showed himself to the door, he heard the P.M. growl behind him, "KBO, Mr. Frain, KBO. That's what we all must do, including our Miss Hope—Keep Buggering On."

Chapter Nineteen

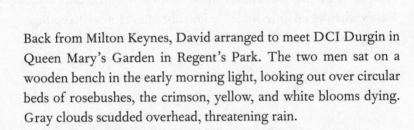

Back from Milton Keynes, David arranged to meet DCI Durgin in Queen Mary's Garden in Regent's Park. The two men sat on a wooden bench in the early morning light, looking out over circular beds of rosebushes, the crimson, yellow, and white blooms dying. Gray clouds scudded overhead, threatening rain.

"You were right," David told the DCI. "Or your gut was, anyway. Maggie isn't on a mission—she's at some sort of SOE 'training camp' in Scotland." He ground his teeth. "Look, Durgin, I know you've signed the Official Secrets Act, so I can tell you—it doesn't seem to be a training camp. It's a prison for agents who've learned too many secrets. It's a way to isolate them. To keep them quiet."

"For how long?"

"Until the end of the war, I imagine." David grimaced. "Although there was verbiage on the document I saw to indicate they may be imprisoned indefinitely."

Durgin gave a bitter laugh. "Sounds to me like no one's getting out alive."

"What do you mean?"

"They're being held prisoner by their own government. Whoever set that situation up isn't going to want it to get out—"

"The Official Secrets Act—"

"Official Secrets Act be damned! That's huge. *Enormous*. They won't want a syllable of this coming out after the war. And while patriots will keep wartime secrets for the government they fight for, if they feel they've been treated unfairly by said government . . ."

"And so you think they'll—kill them?"

"Maybe imprison them there indefinitely," Durgin amended. "Who knows? But it doesn't look good for Maggie—or any of them."

"So," David said, after a moment. "How do you feel about taking a wee trip to the Scotland Highlands?"

"Yes! I'm ready to leave when you are—don't feel right with her in there."

"I thought you'd say that. Already procured us tickets for the Caledonian Deerstalker to Fort William. It leaves this morning from King's Cross. From there, we'll transfer trains and go on to Beasdale; it's the private stop for Arisaig House. We'll get in late, but they'll be expecting me and I'll talk you in."

"Good, good. We need to get Maggie out of there." Durgin gave David a sharp glance. "Are you sure the Prime Minister can do without you for a few days?"

"Since the war started I haven't taken a single day off. I deserve this. Actually"—he grinned—"I deserve a beach holiday on a warm tropical island with a fruity drink and a tiny paper umbrella, but Scotland in November will have to do." David handed Durgin a slip of paper. "So it's not just about the trial?"

"Of course it's about the trial," Durgin insisted, standing and pocketing the ticket. "Of course."

David stood as well. "If you say so."

"I do."

"See you in an hour." He called back over his shoulder, "Don't forget your Sherlock Holmes hat."

———

The group ran downstairs, calling out for McNaughton. There was no reply.

As they headed along the servants' corridor, Anna glanced at a window protected from the worst of the pounding rain by an overhang. "There's something out there," she shrilled. The others peered out and saw McNaughton, lying on his side. His leg was pinned in a steel animal trap, the rusty teeth biting through his shin and calf. A puddle of blood mingled with the rain.

Sayid was the first of the group to run outside, Maggie at his heels. He knelt by the injured man, then gazed up to Maggie's white face. "He's still alive!" he yelled into the wind. "We need to get him inside!"

Don't you dare be number eight!

"Don't we need to remove the trap?" Leo asked.

"No! Leave it—otherwise he could bleed to death."

They carried the injured man to the scarred wooden kitchen table. He was slipping in and out of consciousness, moaning and breathing hard. Sayid bent to examine the wound.

"Oh, God in heaven!" Mrs. McNaughton rushed over. "Angus!"

"He's lost a lot of blood. Please find some clean sheets, Mrs. McNaughton," Sayid said. "We'll cut them up and use them for bandages. And a leather belt—we'll use it as a tourniquet." She nodded, her eyes wide with terror, and flew off.

Maggie pulled him aside. "The McNaughtons and Lady Beatrix aren't part of this," she said. "What if you went with them to the ghillie's cottage? You could treat McNaughton there and Murdo could keep watch. Mrs. McNaughton and Lady Beatrix could assist you." She lowered her voice. "It would be easier to protect them from there."

"Good idea." He nodded. "I can transport him using one of the ponies. Just promise me one thing." He put a hand to her cheek. "Promise me you'll stay safe."

"Of course." Maggie smiled grimly.

She turned to the rest of the group—now just Leo, Anna, Quentin, Teddy, and Ramsey. "Let's go around and lock all the doors. We'll do it in pairs. We must all stay together. This storm isn't going to last forever." She looked to Teddy and nodded, remembering their pact. He dipped his head in return. "And I intend for all of us to be alive to greet the rescue boat."

David and Durgin caught the train at King's Cross Station, cold and smelling of coal smoke, crowded with businessmen, soldiers, and a noisy group of rosy-cheeked Land Girls. They settled in the first-class passenger car for the long ride on the green train nicknamed the Deerstalker Express. In first class, the seats were dark velvet, and over the compartment door was a framed painting of a golden eagle on a tree branch. The engines rumbled, and David sat next to the window and pulled up the shade to watch as women embraced their husbands, lovers, and sons, tears streaming down their faces.

Durgin picked up a freshly ironed *Daily Mirror*. The headlines declared: ROMMEL ROUTED! HUNS FLEEING IN DISORDER! *9,000 Men Captured, 260 Tanks Destroyed, 600 Planes Knocked Out*. He sat across from David. "Things seem to be going well in the desert, at least," he remarked.

David nodded, the shouts of the conductors echoing faintly from the corridor. "All aboard! All aboard!"

"Old Monty has them on the run," Durgin continued, gazing out the open window at the steam.

"All aboard!" The engines rumbled and a high-pitched whistle sounded, and the train began to move. The two men listened to the soldiers in some of the other cars singing lustily over the *chug-chug-chug* of the wheels:

If I catch you bending
I'll saw your legs right off

Knees up, knees up
Don't get the breeze up
Knees up, Mother Brown!

"We're late," David remarked, checking his watch as the train gained speed and they slipped away from London.

"The trains in Italy allegedly run on time," Durgin retorted.

"Point. I'd rather have our politics and late trains."

Durgin inclined his head. "Cheers." A man in uniform came by to punch their tickets.

"So . . ." David ventured. "You're Scottish, then."

"Aye, Mr. Greene," Durgin replied, making his Glaswegian accent even broader. "And a nod's as guid as a wink tae a blind horse."

"Sorry—no idea what that means." A police officer entered the compartment, checking identity cards. They both proffered their documents; after examining them, the officer shuffled off. Outside, the pastures were shrouded by a mist of fine rain.

"It means," Durgin continued, "both actions are pointless."

"Ah," said David. "How insightful."

Durgin grinned. "In Glasgow, if you say your father's died, they'll ask you, 'What size was his shoes?' We have a black sense of humor."

David laughed, delighted. "So, you think Scotland will ever declare independence?"

"Not until the war's over, certainly, but I do anticipate its coming." Durgin closed the window against the damp and chill.

"It will be the end of Britain as we know it," David intoned.

"The end of 'Britain as we know it' is already happening, my friend. It's starting in India. And in Scotland, too. I'm certain the push for Scottish independence will begin with Glasgow. No offense meant, but in the corridors of power in London, and even in Edinburgh, they just don't give a brass farthing about the rest of Scotland." The midland mist coated the windows, condensing and falling in rivulets.

"I've heard Glasgow's pretty rough," David said. "Is that how you became a policeman?"

Durgin shook his head. "I eventually left Glasgow for Oxford with dreams of the ivory towers of academia, but I had what the doctors call a 'cervical rib.'" He pointed to the right side of his chest. "A protrusion of bone, which caused a spot of pain. I went to hospital for surgery and my roommate happened to be a former officer of the Metropolitan Police Department. He'd been shot in the face, poor man, while trying to apprehend a suspect. So I was bored, and he was bored, and soon I had him talking about all of his adventures on the Force. It brought back the memory of all the Sherlock Holmes and Sexton Blake stories I'd loved as a young lad."

"But police work, detective work—it's much different from the stories, yes?"

"A universe away—the reality is that working a case is slow and often tedious. But murder detectives, well, we've seen it all—the worst human beings can do to each other. And I have a theory: we all have a capacity for violence, every last one of us. It's our primal animal instinct: fight or run. Hunt or be hunted. So we must learn *not* to be violent. And then teach others not to be. Because no matter how good the police are, we can only contain the violence, not diminish it. Not end it."

"So we should embrace the murderers?" David asked. "Make them feel loved and wanted? Give them chocolate bars and teddy bears?"

Durgin didn't smile. "We're all born with animal instincts, Mr. Greene, but people can be taught to use reason and logic. We need to teach alternatives to violence. That we're not beasts, and don't have to act like them. That we can stop, and take a moment. Think. And then talk things out. Because, let's face it, what we're doing now—it isn't working. Certainly not in the long run. So my thought is—let's try something different. Can't make things much worse. And we just might make them better."

Durgin once again picked up the newspaper. "May I have the crossword?" David asked, and the Scotsman handed it to him as the fields turned into a tangle of brown woods, blurred by the rain.

"You know, we could be too late," Durgin said softly.

"You don't know Maggie the way I do," David assured him. "I've seen her work in some tight situations. Nothing's carved in stone." He removed the fountain pen from his jacket pocket to start the crossword.

"At least not yet."

Chapter Twenty

With Sayid and the McNaughtons gone, Anna turned her attention to scrubbing blood off the kitchen table with rags and a bucket. "This is a nightmare," the younger woman said. "Who do you think set the animal trap?"

"The same person who's trying to kill us all, obviously," Quentin said.

Leo leaned against the sink, watching them without offering to help. "With Mrs. McNaughton at the cottage, I don't suppose you or Miss Hope could do something about breakfast?"

"Breakfast?" Anna held up hands bloody from scrubbing. "How can you look at—at all this—and still think about *breakfast*?"

"I'll take a peek in the pantry," Teddy volunteered. "See what we have."

"Relax, Lady Macbeth. I'm hungry is all," Leo reassured Anna. "Doesn't mean I'm a monster, just means I'm alive." Lips pressed together, Anna dumped the contents of her cleaning bucket in the sink and ignored him.

"I radioed Arisaig last night," Maggie told them, "but I'm not sure they received the message. The weather's affecting reception."

"Oh, they'll come," Quentin predicted. "Eventually. All we need to do is stay alive until then."

Teddy returned with apples, oatcakes, and slabs of dried venison. "This all right?"

Leo curled his lip in distaste. "It will have to do."

Anna nodded. "I'll finish up, then make the tea."

"So," Quentin said, looking around at the four other faces surrounding the kitchen table—Maggie, Teddy, Anna, Ramsey. Leo alone remained standing. "It's one of us six, then."

"Still could be Dr. Khan." An ugly expression flickered across Anna's face. "I don't trust him."

"You don't trust anyone," Quentin pointed out. "The thing is"—he gnawed at dried venison—"everyone here's capable of it. Murder, that is. We all know how to do it."

"But only one of us is a possible German spy," Maggie reasoned. "Quentin, you told me your father hunted with Reichsmarschall Goering. What's your connection to the family?"

He scowled. "Well, *Maggie*—as long as we're on a first-name basis now—the connection with Goering, and my command of German, is exactly what helped me into SOE. Because I'm British through and through, a patriot. And although I wasn't cut out to be a soldier, I wanted to do my bit for King and country."

Their eyes locked. Quentin looked away first.

Leo said, "I don't like him much, either, Maggie, but I don't think he's a murderer."

"Who do you think is, then?" Teddy asked, gnawing at an apple.

"Could be you, old man. Although, come to think of it, you don't have the same training and skill set we all do. I'd especially like to hear what our man Ramsey has to say about all this. But wait—he doesn't talk," he said, glaring at the younger man. "What secrets are you conveniently hiding behind your silence, *Ramsey*?"

Ramsey remained mute, his eyes on a water-splashed window. "It's like some awful dream," Anna complained. The kettle whistled, and she poured its contents into the pot. "Sit down." She handed a brown Denby mug to Leo. "You look like an animal, eating standing up."

"I *won't* sit down!" He flung the mug against the wall, where it shattered in an explosion of pottery and steaming water. "We're about to die and I won't *sit around* drinking bloody *tea*!" He stalked to the door, grabbing McNaughton's oilskin from a hook.

"Where are you going?" Maggie called.

"Out. Away from all of you."

"Leo, don't," Teddy cautioned. "It's not safe."

"I'm getting the devil out of here before I'm the next dead body."

"It's dangerous out there," Anna said.

Leo laughed, a hard edge to it. "It's dangerous *in here*."

"The storm hasn't let up," said Teddy.

"Your touching concern is duly noted."

Teddy stared at him. "They'll find you, you know. SOE. The police. You won't get away with this."

Leo pawed through the coat's pockets. "I always suspected the old man carried one," he said, pulling out a pistol, then checking the barrel to make sure it was loaded. "Get *away* with this?" Leo reached for the doorknob. "You think *I'm* doing this? You're mad, absolutely barking. I'll take my chances with the deer."

"Leo, wait!" Maggie cried. The door slammed behind him, the panes rattling in their frames, a gust of wind chilling them all.

Teddy grabbed Maggie's arm before she could leap up. "Let him go."

"But the killer could still be out there." Anna was on the verge of tears again.

"How do we know *he's* not the killer?" Teddy countered. "But he can't get the boat out in these winds—he'll end up smashed on the rocks."

"Or the killer could still be in here, hiding like Lady Beatrix,"

Anna insisted. "I can't believe it could be one of us. I mean, the *Nazis* are the real enemy, not a bunch of washed-up agents. . . ."

And then there were five.

The ghillie's cottage was built of the same blood-red sandstone as the castle, but unlike the castle, it was human in scale, a two-story building surrounded by still-blooming rosebushes.

Sayid, Mrs. McNaughton, Lady Beatrix, and Murdo were bunched around the bed in the master chamber. McNaughton's leg was bandaged and propped up on pillows and his eyes were closed. His breathing was erratic.

"Do you think he'll make it?" Murdo's face was boyish with fear.

"We will pray," Mrs. McNaughton murmured, smoothing a lock of her son's dark hair.

"He's lost a lot of blood," Sayid told them. "The sooner we can get him to the mainland and get him a transfusion, the better."

Mrs. McNaughton felt for the cross around her neck. "What if we can't?"

"We must."

"But the storm . . . How much time does he have?"

"I'd like to see him in a proper hospital by this time tomorrow. In the meantime, I'll do my best." Sayid glanced at Murdo. "Why don't you take your mother downstairs and fix some tea and broth for Mr. McNaughton? We need to keep pushing fluids—there's still one more night of this storm to weather.

"And, please," he added. "Please double-check the locks on every door and window."

Maggie was frowning, trying to work the case out on the sheet of paper spread before her on the kitchen table. Sooty was curled up in the warmth of her lap, sleeping. The cat twitched and extended a paw, as if hunting. The rest of the group were smoking and drinking cold tea. Quentin had a grease stain from the dried venison on his shirtfront, and Teddy was eating from a tin of baked beans.

"Here's a list of all the dead, in order, and with probable cause," Maggie said, showing them her notes:

NOVEMBER 12

Captain Bernard Evans—poison, cyanide?

NOVEMBER 13

Ian Lansbury—head injury, drowning (discovered—death could have been November 12)

NOVEMBER 15

Dr. Jaeger—poison (discovered—death could have been November 14)
Captain MacLean—poison, strychnine? (Ibid.)

NOVEMBER 15

Helene Poole-Smythe—poison, Veronal?

NOVEMBER 17

Camilla Oddell—harpoon (discovered—death could have been November 16)
Torvald Hagan—garrote

Beneath these names, she added:

NOVEMBER 18

Angus McNaughton, steel trap—STILL ALIVE

"This is hell," Anna murmured. "We're all in hell."

"More like the fifth circle," said Quentin, trying for humor and failing.

"The boat's not coming." Anna was close to hysterics. "We're all going to die here."

"It's going to be all right," Maggie said, trying to be reassuring.

"It's not all right! It's never going to be all right! Ian is dead! Helene is dead! The rest of them are dead! And we're next!" She drew in a raw, shaky breath. "I just want to go home."

Don't we all. "Anna!" Maggie snapped. "Pull yourself together! We are agents of His Majesty's government. We will survive! You're a trained agent—start acting like one." While Anna's eyes filled with tears, Maggie continued in a softer tone, "All we need to do is stay together until the storm ends." She reached down to stroke the cat in her lap, taking comfort in his warmth.

Anna was unconvinced. "If we make it that long . . ."

Maggie always depended on logic in times of trouble. This was no different. "The first person dead, although not the first one found, was Ian Lansbury. Five days ago . . . Who was doing what on that day?"

"I was inside, of course," answered Quentin. "Poking around in the attic."

"Yes, but can anyone vouch for your whereabouts?"

"There were no *people* with me," he replied, stroking Monsieur Reynard.

"Does anybody recall what Leo was up to?" Maggie asked.

"He was out with Sayid," Quentin said. "He told me he'd been hunting and Sayid had taken photographs."

"And neither of them are here now, to give their account," Anna reminded them.

"Actually, I ran into Leo and Sayid in the forest that day," Maggie said. "They really were out there."

"But, let's remember, four of the deaths were likely caused by poison—as a doctor, Sayid would know how to use that sort of thing, wouldn't he?" There was no denying the accusation in Anna's voice.

"The poisons used were those found in any household, for wasps and rodents," Teddy pointed out, lighting his pipe. "It doesn't take a doctor's license to slip something into someone's food or drink."

"Noted," Maggie replied. "And where were you, Anna?"

"I was in the great room, drawing hat designs. I can show you my sketchbook . . ." The younger woman locked eyes with Maggie. "And where were *you*?"

Maggie tried to remember. "I met Leo and Sayid on my way to go fishing with Mr. Crane."

Teddy cleared his throat. "And I was fishing, of course. First alone, and then with Miss Hope. Afterward, I spent time with Mr. Novak."

Quentin appraised Teddy with narrowed eyes. "So you say . . ."

"Where were you, Ramsey? Before you met up with Mr. Crane?" Quentin walked over and waved a hand in front of the man's eyes. "Come now, speak up. Don't be shy."

"Stop it," Maggie ordered.

"Well, if he won't speak, why doesn't he *write* for us?" Quentin went to Mrs. McNaughton's sitting room and returned with pen and paper. "Here," he said, shoving both in front of Ramsey.

Ramsey took both and threw them in the fireplace.

"So much for that idea." Quentin watched the paper burn. "So, really, any of us could have killed Ian. And it's probably the same for all the victims. We all tend to go off on our own . . ."

There was a pause in the wind, and the group heard the distant clang of church bells from the abandoned village. "What the—" In all her time on the island, Maggie had never heard the bells ring before. "It could be Leo," she offered. "He could be in some kind of trouble."

"Or it could be a trap," Teddy warned.

"This is why we need to stick together! We can't leave a man down." Maggie gazed out the window, gauging the rain and wind. The church bells stopped. And then began to toll again. Maggie gently moved the cat from her lap, then stood. He gave a *meow* of disgust, then slunk away. "I'm going."

"If you are, I am, too," said Teddy. Maggie looked to the older man, grateful for his steadfast friendship.

"I'll go with you," Quentin volunteered. "But not without a gun."

Anna nodded. "We'll need weapons."

"There's a gun room near the back door," Quentin said. "But everything's locked."

Maggie smiled, she felt as if for the first time in days. "And your point?"

The grounds of the castle were a muddy quagmire that sucked at Maggie's Wellingtons like quicksand as she stumbled to the path, followed by the four others. It seemed to take twice as much strength as usual to put one foot in front of the other, and she struggled to stay upright.

The wind was still gusting across the island. Towering firs bent before the tempest, and though Maggie should have been able to hear the shuddering branches and the waves crashing against the rocks, the wind drowned everything else out. She no longer heard the church bells. *Have they really stopped? And who was ringing them?*

As they blundered forward under the huge and ancient oaks, Maggie felt small and alone. The crackling twigs, the rustling of leaves as the wind tore through the branches, the screams of the Manx shearwaters filled her ears. Maggie pushed the feelings away. *This is a mission*, she reminded herself. *Leo is at the church, he rang the bells—we need to find and help him.* She looked back to make sure

Teddy was all right. But he was fine, not even leaning on his walking stick.

The Free Presbyterian Church of Scotland wasn't far from the crofters' cottages. It was a small gabled rectangle, constructed from rough-hewn whitewashed stone. The prisoners, armed with rifles taken from the gun room, approached through the rain, which had slowed to a drizzle. The bell in the tower was ominously still.

The weathered blue door was ajar. Ramsey opened it, the resulting creak echoing within. The group entered, one by one, rifles raised, lining up shoulder to shoulder. Inside, it looked as expected for a structure unused for twenty years, but the plain wooden pews were intact, most of the leaded-glass windows miraculously unbroken. Once in, Anna lowered her gun, bent to one knee, crossed herself, and bowed her head.

"*Now?*" Quentin asked.

"I don't care what sort of church it is," Anna replied, her eyes closed, "I think we could all use a prayer."

"Leo?" Maggie called as she made her way through the shadows and down the center aisle. "Leo?" Rain pattering at the glass was the only sound. The rest followed, wary. "Leo? Are you all right?"

They approached the altar. There was a noise from the choir loft, and Maggie whirled to face the open door.

It was Leo, gun trained on her. "Think about it," he said, voice thick with anger. "One of you has to be the Nazi."

"The bastard lured us here." Quentin shook his head, not taking his gaze or his rifle from Leo. "Lured us here deliberately." He clicked off the safety.

"Leo, put down your gun," Maggie called.

It was as if he didn't hear her. "If I kill all of you, I'll kill the Nazi among us, too. I'll stay alive."

"But you'll kill innocent people, Leo," she said. "People on your side. People who've trained with you. Your fellow agents."

"In war, sacrifices must be made."

"But, Leo, we're not at the point of sacrifice. Look, the rain is letting up and the winds are dying—help is coming," she said in what she hoped was a soothing voice. "There's no need to kill innocent—"

Leo's gun exploded. Maggie and the other agents scattered, ducking behind the pews and shooting back. The small structure reverberated with the sound of gunfire.

Maggie spotted two shadowy figures on their hands and knees at the wall end of a pew. "Maggie," Teddy called, gesturing to her. "Come!"

She did. She and Ramsey and Teddy scrabbled with their heads down toward the church door, as Quentin and Anna shot up into the loft, covering for them.

Once outside, they paused. "Run!" Teddy cried.

Maggie hesitated. Then she ran.

Chapter Twenty-one

Under interlocking branches of pines, protected from the rain and wind, they stopped to catch their breath. Teddy was wheezing; Ramsey had forgotten a hat and was drenched. "If Leo is coming after us," Maggie told the others, "we'll need to be smart."

"He's just one man," Teddy countered, clutching his side. His face was ashen, and Maggie felt a pang of concern for him. "And this is a relatively big island."

"He's an experienced hunter," Maggie countered, "and it's not really so big."

"We can hide," Teddy insisted. "We can go to the boat in the bay. That way we'll see anyone coming and have a good shot." Ramsey nodded.

"Or we can split up," Maggie suggested.

"No, I think we should stay together," Teddy replied. "The storm's passing."

Maggie gazed up at the sky. He was right: the gray was brightening. The winds were dying down. She nodded. "To the boat, then."

A branch broke in the underbrush, and Maggie started. The three of them froze like deer, sniffing at the air, eyes alert. Slowly, Maggie turned her head.

Leo had her in his crosshairs. "It's you. I knew it was you from the beginning."

"No, Leo." She was eerily calm as she stared down the barrel of his pistol. A song ran through her mind, one of Mr. Churchill's favorites: "Run, Rabbit, Run."

She shook her head to clear it. "Leo, the rain's letting up. It's over. The boats will be here any time now. There's no reason to shoot anyone." She needed to buy time. "Where are Anna and Quentin? Are they all right?"

"Don't worry your little head about them." *What did that mean?*

In an instant, to Maggie's astonishment, Ramsey popped off the safety on his gun and shot. Leo flinched, swore, and tried to return fire. But he staggered back, a bloodstain blossoming on the outside of his thigh. His bullets flew up into the tree branches, startling a raven, who flapped away with deep, throaty cries of *kwaa*. Leo dropped the pistol. He fell to his knees, gripping at his leg.

Maggie stepped in and grabbed his gun. "Ramsey, take care of Leo. Use pressure to stop the bleeding. Just keep him alive until we can get off this island." *I don't particularly like you, Leo, but you won't be number eight. At least, not if I can help it.* She turned to Teddy. "We need to make sure Quentin and Anna aren't hurt. Come on!"

The storm that had shrouded Scarra was sweeping inland; Arisaig House was now bearing the brunt. Outdoor training had been suspended and calisthenics had been moved indoors. Martens and Frain sat in front of a blazing orange fire in Colonel Rogers's office in the former library. The colonel was at his massive desk. Captain Lewis was there as well, pacing by the windows.

"We'd only just sent Agent Oddell to Scarra," Rogers said, putting on tortoiseshell-framed glasses as rain splattered against the windows. "Four days ago, to be precise." He frowned; the fire's valiant best was doing little to cut the chill.

"*Why* was she sent to the island?" Frain took out a cigarette from a silver case. "What exactly did she do? It's not as if she was sent there for *specialized training*."

"She—" Lewis began. He and Rogers exchanged a look; Rogers dropped his gaze as Lewis lifted a brass ashtray from his desk and handed it to Frain. "That is, we didn't consider her mentally balanced enough to be safe to herself or others during the stress of missions."

"So this is a lunatic asylum, this Scarra? SOE's private Bedlam?"

"The people on Scarra—we've trained them, they've learned our secrets, but they're defective in some way," Martens replied. "We can't risk sending them abroad *or* keeping them here at home. They pose a danger to the war effort, and so they must be hidden away."

"And how are they 'defective,' exactly?" Frain challenged, lighting his cigarette.

"They're the agents who were too likely to talk when drunk, too violent and a danger to others, who speak English in their sleep . . . any number of reasons."

Frain narrowed his eyes. "And you didn't see fit to inform the other intelligence agencies of the existence of this prison island?"

"We need to protect our secrets," Martens insisted. "And Bishop at MI-Six knows. He's the one who set it up, actually."

"And you didn't see fit to inform *me*?" A muscle twitched in Frain's cheek. "Why exactly is Agent Hope there?"

Lewis looked to Frain. "To be honest, I wasn't aware Agent Hope had been sent to Scarra," he admitted. "I worked with her both as her instructor and as her colleague when she returned here to teach last year. I can vouch for the fact she was a hardworking trainee and then an excellent, if strict, instructor."

"Whose order put her on the island, then?" Frain's voice was dangerously even.

"She knows one of the biggest secrets of the war—about the invasion," Martens said. "I took it upon myself, with Colonel Bishop, to intern her there when we found her to be a security risk."

"Half of Whitehall knows the details about the invasion, you blithering fool!" Frain exploded, knocking over the ashtray. "And you've sent her straight into the clutches of a German undercover agent!"

"Let's focus now on the problem at hand," Martens asserted. "Which is the practical matter of rescuing those still alive on the island and capturing the German." He made a steeple of his hands. "Colonel, you say the last transmission from the prisoners said seven on the island are dead. And they're aware one of them is a sleeper agent."

"Yes," Rogers said.

Lewis turned back from the window. "Well, then, they know there's an agent among them. If we've trained them properly, they'll discover who he is and take him out. They'll just need to identify him before he can make his U-boat pickup."

"What's the weather like out there now?" Martens asked.

"Meteorologists say it's clearing a bit there," Lewis answered. He looked out the window and the other men followed his glance. The treetops were bending in the wind, dead leaves swirling down with the rain. "But the moving storm will make it hard to take a boat out."

"And Mallaig? Fort William?"

"Same weather as here."

"The Navy's corvettes, though, they're large—they can make it regardless of weather?" asked Martens, his voice hopeful.

Frain lit another cigarette with sharp, angry movements and retrieved the fallen ashtray. "We have a corvette approaching the island, listening for any radio signals."

"The message we received said the Scarra agents planned to destroy the radios," Rogers offered.

"Good. The island's harbor's not big enough for a corvette, of course, but when the storm clears, it can land a smaller boat. We've contacted Coastal Command aviation assets. They're sending six Spitfires to shoot at anything that surfaces. The local coast guard is ready to move, too—although they're most likely to be grounded by the weather."

Frain nodded. "It will depend on who arrives there first—us or the U-boat."

"You've covered all the bases," Rogers replied.

"The Spitfires won't be able to do much real damage," Martens pointed out.

"They can strafe the sub—drop a few grenades," Rogers told them. "Cause some trouble. Maybe buy us more time."

"You do understand the signal to the U-boat could be a distraction—he might really be trying to reach Ireland." Frain exhaled blue smoke. "We just don't know."

"What do you think he knows?" Martens took out his own dented cigarette case. "Do you think Hope's talked?"

Rogers shook his head. "The prisoners know the same rules apply on the island as on the mainland. They've all signed the Official Secrets Act."

"But she *could* have talked," Martens insisted, pulling out a cigarette, trying to hide his shaking hands. "The way I sent her to Scarra . . . wasn't exactly gentle." Frain glared at the man. "She could be resentful enough to throw the rules out the window. Or scared enough to talk. Especially with Captain Evans dead."

"Well, what chance do we have of catching the German bastard before he's picked up by the U-boat?" Lewis asked. It took Martens three tries for the lighter to catch. The tip of the cigarette glowed reddish orange in the gloom.

"It's anyone's guess," Rogers replied, reaching over to turn on his desk lamp. "The spy will try to escape the island as soon as the storm clears. We just need to beat him to it."

Frain regarded Martens. "I know Agent Hope. I've worked with her. And I don't believe she'll talk. However, *because* she won't talk,

I anticipate he'll try to take her with him." His gray eyes pinned Martens in his seat. "You never should have told her the information about the invasion. It was too much too soon. She'd literally just returned from occupied Paris—one of her friends died there."

The colonel realized Frain had pieced together what he and Bishop had done. "Fine. I overstepped. But if the Gestapo gets their hands on her, she could lose us the fucking war." He rose with some difficulty and walked to the photograph of Winston Churchill on the wall, gazing up at the growling countenance. "If it looks as though the kraut's taken her, either bringing her by boat to the pickup or at the U-boat itself, we'll need the RAF to shoot. Both of them." He turned. "Tell them, Colonel Rogers. They need to shoot to kill. Even if Agent Hope's on that boat, too. *Especially* if she is."

The room was silent. "Are we not all in agreement here?" Martens asked, voice rising. "I'm not a villain, but I am willing to do what it takes to keep information vital to the invasion from reaching the enemy." He paced on the worn carpet in front of the fireplace. "Wouldn't you kill Eve holding the apple before she handed it over to Adam? I would. We can't afford mercy at this point. Not even to our own."

Frain crossed his legs. "I set aside my own morals long ago in this war. And yet, I must say I *hope* we don't have to cross that bridge."

There was a knock at the door. "Colonel Rogers?" It was a fresh-faced young woman in a brown FANY uniform. "You have . . . guests, sir."

"Good God, what now?"

"Two men—a Mr. David Greene, from the P.M.'s office, and DCI Durgin, from Scotland Yard. They say they're here about an agent named Margaret Hope."

"Send them in." Colonel Rogers leaned an elbow on the desk and let his open palm catch his forehead. "And bring us all some bloody tea."

U-135 floated just below the turbulent waves on the water's surface. Kapitänleutnant von Siemens squinted through the periscope, looking for ships and aircraft, as well as rocks and shoals missing from German charts. First Officer Schäffler stood with him on the bridge; together, they listened for engine noises on sonar—either ships leaving harbor or the corvettes approaching. "The window opens in forty minutes, Herr Kaleu."

"I am aware, Schäffler."

"We have had no further communication from the Abwehr agent, Herr Kaleu. And our systems show two British corvettes approaching."

"We signaled our ghost we would meet him during the window and we will, Schäffler."

"Herr Kaleu, it's not safe for us to remain so close to the Scottish coast for much longer."

"I am aware of the complications, Schäffler. But I won't let a fellow German officer down. He'll most likely be coming in something small—a fishing boat or even a rowboat. A wooden raft, for Christ's sake. Who knows what condition it might be in? The agent himself might be injured. And then there's the wind, and the tide and the waves . . ."

"Herr Kaleu—"

Von Siemens smiled. Everyone on board knew a smile from the captain was a very bad sign. Schäffler swallowed and forced himself not to take a step backwards.

But the impending tirade never came. "Fetch me coffee, Schäffler," the Kapitänleutnant ordered. "For once, make sure it's hot."

"Yes, Herr Kaleu. Right away, sir!"

The Kapitänleutnant peered back through the periscope. "It's going to be a very long watch."

———

At the chapel, Maggie found Anna and Quentin lying on the stone floor. Quentin had a bullet wound in his shoulder—he'd managed to take off his jacket and was using it to put pressure on the injury. Blood had soaked through the wool, but when Maggie took a look, it was a through-and-through shot on the outside of the shoulder. "You'll be all right," she told him. "Just a little longer."

"Leo?" he asked.

"He's been . . . neutralized," she said. "Shot, but still alive. Ramsey's with him." He groaned, then nodded.

Then Maggie went to Anna. She'd been hit in the chest. There was blood everywhere and the young woman's face was ashen. Her eyes were closed. Maggie felt for a pulse at the base of her neck; it was thready.

"We can't move them," Teddy warned. "We need to go to the dock and meet the boat. Then we can direct them to the chapel."

"We'll be all right," Quentin assured them. "You go." He tried to smile. "Just remember to come back for us."

Maggie took a long look at Anna and bit her lip. *How long can she last?*

"There's nothing you can do," Quentin said, as if reading her mind. "And I'll be here for her. Now go! *Go!*"

Maggie nodded to Teddy. They both grabbed their rifles and left.

Chapter Twenty-two

Ramsey had used his woolen scarf as a tourniquet to stop Leo from bleeding out; his hands and feet were tied with rope and he was unconscious. As Maggie and Teddy approached, Ramsey raised then lowered his rifle when he recognized them through the drizzle. "Where did you get the rope?" Maggie asked, catching her breath.

"Brought it." Maggie started. She'd never heard Ramsey's voice before. It was disarmingly normal. "Just in case."

"You *can* talk."

"I can," he replied. "But I chose not to. Now it's safe. Enough of you lot are dead."

"What the hell does *that* mean?"

"I didn't want you people getting anything out of me. Anything your side can use."

"What side is that?"

"I know all about you—and your camp. This is a Nazi-run camp. You're Germans! You're trying to seduce us into letting our guard down. Telling our secrets."

"*What?*" Maggie felt her brain slam to an absolute halt at the absurd shock of the accusation. "No. No! No, we're all British subjects. Why on earth would you think we're Nazis?"

Ramsey shook his head. "You want me to tell my secrets."

"No. We're British," she insisted. "But there *is* a German agent somewhere on the island—a madman—and we need to escape."

"You're trying to convince me that's what's happening, so I'll tell you what I know. And then you can inform Abwehr. But I won't," he said, raising his rifle again. "I won't tell you anything!"

"I don't care what you know." Maggie's eyes blazed in frustration. "In fact, I'd rather *not* know!"

"That's what you say, but you're only trying to have me lower my guard." He added, "And I'm no madman. I've been surviving."

"What the devil are you talking about now?"

"I've been picking you all off, one by one. Fewer Nazis in the world."

Maggie felt as if she'd been kicked in the gut. "*You're* the murderer?"

"I'm not a murderer. I'm a *soldier*," he clarified. The rifle remained steady in his hand. "This island just happens to be the battlefield."

Oh, God. Maggie repressed a shudder. "We're not Nazis," she repeated. "Look—the war, and the isolation, and the darkness . . ." Her thoughts were spinning. "Why on earth would you think we're Nazis?" She'd heard of war veterans becoming delusional after missions—was that what had happened to Ramsey?

"You're a Nazi," he spat. "Of course you'd deny it."

"No!" *How to convince him?* "How could you possibly think I'm German? And Leo? He was trying to shoot everyone to ferret out the German spy among us—does that sound like something someone in a Nazi-run spy camp would do? No, that's what someone British would do."

"Nazis kill their own all the time."

"The British don't. Anna and Quentin are wounded, but they're not dead. Leo just wanted to incapacitate them. Nazis *don't* have any mercy. The British do."

Ramsey glared at her, daring her to betray herself. Then he shivered. "Oh, Christ." He exhaled, his entire posture deflating, his eyes forlorn. "Anna?" He lowered his rifle. "Leo shot her? How bad is it?"

"Anna's injured, but she's still alive, Ramsey. Now put the gun down, please. We can talk about this." The young man's eyes darted from Maggie to Teddy.

"Ramsey—" Teddy began, an edge in his voice.

"Oh, God! I killed all those people . . ." the young man cried.

"What about Anna?" Maggie asked him. "Do you really think someone like Anna could be a Nazi? We need to save her life, Ramsey."

Ramsey seemed as if he might pass out. "I killed all those people—and they were *British*?" His face crumpled in anguish, and he swayed. "Tell Anna . . . I'm sorry."

"Ramsey, *no!*" Maggie cried, lunging forward to stop him, but it was too late. The shot echoed through the forest. *Eight*, she thought, looking away, her soul numb. *Eight dead.*

She barely registered the sound of startled birds taking wing before there was a stunning flash of pain, and she slumped to the ground.

All Maggie knew, as she surfaced from a deep, sparkling blackness, was that every bone in her body ached. Her stomach roiled and pitched; her senses swam with pain and nausea.

Eventually she realized it was the surface she was lying on that was pitching, not just her stomach. The air smelled of seaweed, and there were rhythmic splashing slaps somewhere below her. She cracked open blurry eyes to discover she was in the wheelhouse of the boat, lying against one wall, her hands tied behind her with coils of rope.

She struggled to sit up, grimacing in agony as a blinding pain radiated through her skull. Slowly, she struggled to piece things together, her thoughts sluggish and stunned. *Ramsey is dead,* she remembered. *He shot himself, when he realized . . . Leo, Anna, and Quentin are injured. The others—they're dead, too. . . . What about—?*

She looked around. "Where's Leo?" Maggie croaked, testing the ropes around her hands and feet. They were tied adroitly, as any expert fisherman would know how to do. "Is he all right?"

"Dead." Teddy's voice had lost its friendly warmth. It was lower now, harsh and tight. It was still raining, but not as hard, and behind the clouds, the red sun was sinking. Maggie realized she'd been unconscious for hours. "I shot him—put him out of his misery. It's too bad, really. But this is war. If it's any consolation, I didn't want it to end like this."

Leo, dead as well. Number nine. Dear God.

She looked back up at Teddy. Or whoever he was. Her friend had vanished, along with his twinkling eyes and easy camaraderie. This man was a stranger to her, she realized, unable to catch a breath for shock. It was this man, not Teddy, who'd convinced Ramsey, poor impressionable, vulnerable Ramsey, to kill the prisoners. It was this man who'd drained the petrol in the boat's tank, so it would wash back to shore and he'd have a way to escape. It was this man who'd snuck out at night to use the boat's radio to contact the Germans, not realizing he'd been seen by Lady Beatrix. *Teddy . . .*

Maggie realized Teddy wasn't using his walking stick. She appraised him critically. Did he seem surer in his movements, his back straight, his stomach pulled in? He appeared decades younger. "Your arthritis seems a lot better."

He turned to her and winked. "The storm's passing." She had a sudden vision of how easily he moved through the storm on their way to the church. He'd been lying all along. He'd played her.

Pain turned to panic, which then unexpectedly morphed into rage. Captain Evans, Ian, Dr. Jaeger, Captain MacLean, Helene, Camilla, Torvald, Ramsey, Leo. All dead—because of him. McNaughton,

Anna, and Quentin injured, perhaps dying, because of *him*. And Sayid—he almost killed Sayid. It was too much to bear.

She struggled against her bonds. *Stop it, Hope. If you want to make it out of this alive, you must be smart. Smarter than he is.*

"We will rendezvous with a U-boat a few miles from here," the man told her, moving the shift. "They'll surface to pick us up tonight, in the darkness."

She was tired. So tired. And in so much pain. *If I close my eyes, just for a minute . . .* Someone surely had to be coming. SOE, the Navy, the coast guard . . . She had to hold on, to stop him from meeting up with the U-boat. *Do this and then it will be over*, she told herself. *Think, Hope.* The effort made her so dizzy she feared she'd faint.

He pulled out the choke. *Keep him talking*, Maggie thought, testing the ropes around her wrists. As long as he was still talking, she was still alive. And she wanted to stay alive more than anything. "You had Ramsey convinced we were all Germans," she began. "Convinced he was in a Nazi prison camp, where we were all trying to obtain information from him."

"They exist in England, you know," the man she knew as Teddy said coldly. "Camps like that. I've heard of them." He primed the engine and pulled the starter. The motor flared. Then it coughed and died. He scowled.

"So he was working with *you*—that's how you could kill so many of us without anyone suspecting. You were working together. But why?" He tried pulling the starter again. Nothing. He gave the starter another, harder pull. Again, it didn't catch. "*Scheisse,*" he muttered.

Good, she thought, even as she fought for consciousness. The boat pitched and juddered.

"You said something," he continued. "In one of our conversations this autumn—you said something about the needs of the few versus the needs of the many. Do you remember? I realized then you knew something, some sort of immense sacrifice your side was willing to make—and that's why you were imprisoned on the island. From my knowledge of your personality, I guessed you hadn't gone along with it."

The double agent continued to pull at the starter, muttering profanity in German. The engine made a few grumbling attempts to start before falling silent once again. "Whatever you know was big enough for you to go to prison over. Even here, in relative safety, you wouldn't reveal it. And I thought, What's the biggest secret of the war? Then I realized—the Allied invasion of Europe."

The most precious secret of the invasion—Normandy, not Calais. Maggie cursed the day she'd learned it.

He opened the switch panel to check the wiring. "I've spent almost three years in this stinking country with British idiots. I'm not about to die here. I'm going home, back to Germany, and I'm taking you with me. You're my golden goose, Miss Hope. With you I'll be welcomed as a hero, with the secret to the invasion. Without you, I'd be shot as a spy or else I'd have to live the rest of my life on some damp and cold island." He looked to her, his expression almost droll. "Honestly, both options sound terrible."

The agent had found a red wire. "So I planned to capture the boat and kidnap you, then rendezvous with a U-boat for a ride home."

"You work for Abwehr," Maggie stated, even as she felt her courage drain. *This is it. This is the end.* But she wasn't about to give him the satisfaction of seeing her fear. And, if she had to, she would take them both out. "How did you end up here?"

He yanked the red wire, disconnecting it. "I was hired to work at Churchill's Toy Shop. Unfortunately, it didn't lead to anything. I was making the weapons, but I didn't know where they were going or how they would be used—information kept from us, the day laborers. Then I heard a rumor. About a camp, a very special camp,

for people who knew too much. So I made sure I was sent there."
He glanced up from the wires, back to her. His grin made her want
to vomit. How could she ever have liked him? "It's been most edu-
cational."

"I thought we were friends, Teddy."

He tugged the starter again. "This whole operation was fishing
and hunting, *Maggie*. Fishing for information, then hunting the person with the best. Nothing personal, my dear. I actually quite like
you. I've enjoyed your company, and I hope you've enjoyed mine."

"This feels quite . . . *personal*. To me. And the arthritis, another
lie?"

He ignored her, renewing his attempts to start the engine. *"Küss
meinen Arsch,"* he muttered. "I'll make sure you're taken good care
of in Berlin. Just cooperate when we arrive. Tell them what you
know and I'll make sure you're treated well."

"I won't tell you—or anyone—anything!" Maggie spat. "If I'm
willing to go to prison to keep a secret, why would I tell the Nazis?"
She squirmed against the ropes.

The engine caught at last, rumbling to life. Maggie's heart sank.
"Look," he said reasonably. "I don't want to die here—and I don't
think you do, either. I took the *Fahneneid,* the German oath to country, the blood oath of a warrior. We are both soldiers, you and I.
And now, like a good soldier, you must surrender—there is no
shame in it." The agent took out a compass from his pocket and
checked the direction, then switched on all the boat's lights. "You
did your best. And you know what they'll do to you if you don't
cooperate."

Maggie flinched; she knew all too well what they could do.

"Just be a good girl. This is the choice I mentioned—that day we
went fishing. Your choice to cooperate. Just do it, and I'll make sure
you have a pleasant life in Germany. A wonderful life." He smiled.
"We can go fishing! The Schlachtensee, in the Green Forest just
outside Berlin, is my favorite lake."

"You're quite the fisherman."

"And you are my beautiful mermaid." He opened the throttle and pulled the boat away from the dock.

Von Siemens, wanting a better view, decided to take a chance and gave the order to surface. *U-135* broke through the waves as the sun set behind the clouds, the 20-millimeter deck guns manned and ready as an anti-aircraft measure or in case the pickup was some kind of a trap. Soon he and his first officer were standing in the conning tower, splashed by waves, breathing in the cold, fresh, salty air. The Kapitänleutnant gazed toward Scarra through Zeiss glasses. In the distance, he spotted the lights from the fishing boat. "It must be our man," he muttered. "No other fishing boat would risk using lights in the blackout." Then, louder, "Schäffler! Take us forward toward the craft. Prepare to board."

"Yes, Herr Kaleu!"

"Then we must leave, as soon as possible. The damn Brits are finally learning how to sail."

Three miles due west of *U-135*, the Royal Navy's Corvette 548 plowed through tempestuous seas. On its bridge wing, the captain and officer of the deck stood, binoculars raised to their eyes, peering into the darkness. They could see nothing in the rain. The German agent could come as close as a hundred yards and they could still miss him. "Wait!" the captain snapped. "Look to the port bow. There's a light!"

"I don't see anything, sir."

"You're decades younger than I am, with better eyes—how can you not see it? It has to be our German friend's boat. Must have turned on the lights so they would see him approach. Go back to the bridge," the captain commanded. "Turn and head for that light. Tell our men to prepare to fire. First the boat, then the sub. Take them both out."

"Sir, there's supposed to be one of ours on that boat. . . ."

"I said, take them out! That's an order, Lieutenant!"

"Yes, sir. Right away, sir!"

The water in the bay was rough, lifting the boat high and then dipping it down, like a child's rocking horse. "Deceiving an enemy in wartime is similar to fly-fishing, isn't it, Maggie? You cast patiently. You change your venue and your flies. There are many ways the trout—the enemy—may be lured in," the agent mused, his back to her.

Maggie was so tired, and yet she forced herself to listen. She braced her bound hands behind her back, forcing her body upright.

The huge waves were rendering it difficult for him to make headway through the water, crashing over the boat's gunwales. "And then, if you're patient enough, the fish swallows the hook, line, and sinker."

Finally standing, Maggie worked the knot of the ropes around her hands against the hook of a life preserver ring. She felt almost preternaturally calm, as if she were in a dream. *Nothing seems real except the pain in my head.* . . . Despite her exhaustion, she prodded: "So morals mean nothing to you?" The life preserver hook gashed her wrist; she ignored the pain.

"We're at war, my dear," he replied, almost apologetically, as he wrestled with the wooden steering wheel. "And it seems to have come down to the two of us." He glanced back at her. "But, as I told you, it isn't personal."

"And yet it is." Her hands were slippery from rainwater and the blood trickling from her wrist.

"We're both trying to stay alive. To help our country win."

"Some of us are trying to *deserve* to stay alive."

"Then you won't last long." He said it with regret.

"Germany isn't what you remember, you must realize that. Americans and Brits are bombing the factories and cities." Maggie had loosened the ropes around her wrists enough to work her hands free.

"We can rebuild. These long, painful years are over for me—I'll arrive home a hero! My wife will be so proud of me." The agent glanced down at an open map, then to the dials on the instrument panel.

Maggie bent over to tackle the knots at her ankles while Teddy was distracted. And then she was free. She lurched for the door of the wheelhouse. If she could reach the deck and dive overboard, she could swim back to shore. *Or at least evade capture.* That would be enough. He had nothing without her.

The deck was awash in icy water, and she slipped on the wet wood, falling painfully on her hands and knees. Her vision swam. The boat climbed and plunged. It skidded over another enormous wave. Standing was impossible. She grabbed for the rail and held on.

The boat rolled and the wheelhouse door slammed shut; the noise startled Teddy. In the reflection of the windshield, he caught a glimpse of her. *"Gottverdammt!"* he shouted. He leapt from the wheelhouse as she flung a leg over the rail. Seconds before she could dive off, he caught her from behind in a crushing bear hug.

"No!" he cried as they grappled. She twisted in his grip to face him, kicking hard. The agent grimaced in pain but held on. "You're my only chance!"

As the waves threatened to upend the boat, Maggie's eerie calm returned. She was keenly aware of the smallest of details: the brine of salt water on her lips, the crash of the waves, the dark stubble on Teddy's determined face. There was no questioning, no thinking, only action.

Maggie heard an animalistic howl, a roar both primal and terrifying. There was a long moment before she realized it had come from her. She pulled her head back and slammed it forward, smashing into the man's nose as she kneed him in the groin.

He wailed in agony. His grip loosened; she shoved him away. He grabbed for her again, and somehow her fingers closed around his pinkie. Her fury fortified her as he wrapped his free arm around her in a sickening parody of a dance. He snarled at her in German, his face a rictus of fear and anger. Maggie snapped the finger back and heard the bone crack. He screamed.

She tried to push him away far enough to throw herself over the gunwale, but he wouldn't let her go. Then, in a moment of clarity, she knew what she had to do.

Maggie pushed at him, forcing the German to bear down. Then, she abruptly wilted. His weight and effort, plus the erratic movements of the boat, flung them both against the rail. Gasping from the unexpected agony of the blow, she leaned back, letting momentum take them both over the side of the boat into the wild waves.

They both gasped as they hit the frigid water. *"Scheisse!"* he screeched. Maggie maneuvered her feet up into his stomach, then pushed. He let go, too stunned to hang on. She swam away.

"No," he gasped, reaching for her. *"No!"* The fury in his voice changed to panic. He flailed, choking as the waves slammed over his head.

Maggie easily stayed out of his reach. Treading water, she rode each powerful wave the best she could. He wasn't a swimmer, as she was; he wasn't acclimated to the cold. He fought for breath, dipping up and down with the white-tipped waves, hyperventilating and swallowing seawater. *"Hilf mir . . ."* he spluttered. "Maggie . . ."

As Maggie watched, he sank, embraced by the cold and uncaring sea.

She heard the whistle of a bomb, and even as she glanced up, the boat exploded into a brilliant conflagration, dazzling in the darkening sky, shooting off sparks of red, orange, and gold. It was so close, she could feel the heat from the flames scorch her face.

They must be here, she thought, as her ears rang from the blast. *SOE, the Navy, the coast guard . . .* Then, *I could have been on that boat. . . . It could have been me. . . .* There was a second explosion that set the entire craft aflame, a popping, crackling, raging red inferno. Waves slammed into her. Surfacing, she watched as the boat listed, sliding into the sea like a Viking's funeral.

And mine will be next if I don't move. She swam away from the burning boat, in the direction she hoped was the shore, not looking back. Around her, waves heaved in green mountains of seawater, glittering in the light of the soaring flames. Dark shapes rippled under the water, rose into the air behind a wave. Blue Men? Selkies diving? A mermaid playing a melody on a flute? Or maybe it was all a hallucination.

Her lungs were burning and her arms and legs ached. She gasped for air and choked on a wave. She felt the arms of the Blue Men, grabbing her, holding her down—or maybe it was seaweed.

Under the water, she opened her eyes. There was still light from the blazing boat, light enough to see. And then she saw a blurry figure—their chief, all blue, wearing a crown of seaweed. She thought she heard him say:

Lass with the red hair, what do you say
As your body sinks in brine?

And then she remembered what Mrs. McNaughton had told her about the Blue Men. And that legends told of how they would quote two lines of poetry to the sailors, and if they couldn't say two lines to complete the verse, the Blue Men would overturn the boat, drowning the humans. Maggie thought quickly:

My body and spirit fight the waves
To reach the rocky shore's line

The Blue Chief replied:

My men are eager, my men are ready
To drag you below the waves

This can't be real. She was drowning, she knew she was. It was lack of oxygen that was causing her to imagine the Blue Men who floated about her in a taunting ring, reaching for her, grabbing at her hair and clothes. But still she managed one last reply:

My stroke is strong, my stroke is steady
This water will not be my grave.

Chapter Twenty-three

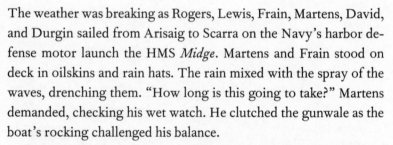

The weather was breaking as Rogers, Lewis, Frain, Martens, David, and Durgin sailed from Arisaig to Scarra on the Navy's harbor defense motor launch the HMS *Midge*. Martens and Frain stood on deck in oilskins and rain hats. The rain mixed with the spray of the waves, drenching them. "How long is this going to take?" Martens demanded, checking his wet watch. He clutched the gunwale as the boat's rocking challenged his balance.

"I heard the captain say it's an eighty-minute journey," Frain told him. "But with the wind and waves, maybe a little longer."

In the distance, they saw three RAF Spitfires. Circling at low altitude, the planes looked like seagulls watching for fish. A second formation was flying by overhead to join them.

David was out of breath when he made it up to the deck to give Martens and Frain the latest update. "The U-boat's surfaced," he reported. "Corvette 548 can see the conning towers. The Spitfires are taking shots, but they don't seem to be doing much." He put both hands on the rail, looking green.

"Seasick?" Frain asked, not unkindly.

"No," replied David. "Terrified my best friend will be shot by one of our own en route to a submarine pickup."

Martens gazed at the horizon. "That's the worst-case scenario."

At that, there was a reddish orange explosion in the distance, black smoke billowing. "The boat," David said, realizing. "The boat Maggie's probably on. She could be dead now, for all we know."

"And our German spy dead, as well."

"All thanks to *you*, Colonel Martens," David spat. Martens's jaw dropped. "It's easier to play these games when you don't know and love the people involved, isn't it? Well, if Maggie's dead, I will hold you personally responsible!"

Martens replied, "I can only tell you what Churchill told me. 'We don't have time for feelings—none of us, not now.'" He walked unsteadily toward David on the slippery deck. "I've learned to set aside whatever qualms I may once have had, whatever human sympathy and empathy, and do everything and anything it takes to win. The secret of the invasion is at stake, the fate of the entire war. Civilization as we know it, all of humanity. Thousands have died for this, and by the end, perhaps millions will have, Greene. With those numbers in play, isn't it worth taking one life?"

David was silent.

"We will do what we must to protect humanity's future—no matter how painful, no matter how repugnant. Is that clear, Mr. Greene?"

David nodded. "Yes, sir."

Maggie lay on the rocky shore, hair plastered against her skull, skimming consciousness. She was achingly cold. Her lungs felt as though they had burst, her bones shattered, her face slapped. All she could smell was the fresh seaweed, torn up from the bottom of the sea and flung onto the beach by the storm, and all she could hear was the hiss of the waves breaking.

She opened her eyes reluctantly; even that small movement was painful. *They're here*, she realized. *They finally made it—SOE, Navy, coast guard . . . They took the boat out. They're here. Maybe there's hope for Anna and Quentin and McNaughton. And maybe even for me.*

Maggie wanted nothing more than to lie still, but she knew the longer she lay there, the more likely she'd never move again. *Newton's first law of motion,* she thought in a daze. *Newton . . . Apple, don't sit under the apple tree. Devil, snake.* Her mouth tasted of brine, and she shivered. The image of Teddy's eyes, just before he drowned, haunted her.

She swallowed, then attempted to move, starting gingerly with her fingertips and toes. Astonishingly, nothing seemed broken. She tried her legs and arms; they, too, appeared to work. With immense effort, she raised herself to a sitting position. Pain vibrated through every cell of her being. She coughed, bringing up seawater. She didn't remember how she'd got to shore, only something about Blue Men? *But how could that be?*

All right, Hope, on the plus side, you're not dead. Also, it's finally stopped raining. She tried to focus on the two positives, even as she flashed back to the horror of what had happened. *Are Anna and Quentin still alive? McNaughton?* She had to be optimistic. *If you don't know, it's like Schrödinger's cat, though—they're both alive and dead at the same time,* her brain taunted her. *Stop it!*

She checked the horizon. Was the sky turning lighter? Just a hint of gray at the edge? She couldn't be sure. *Maybe. No, wishful thinking. But . . . ?* But the utter blackness of the sky surely seemed to have a violet hue where the water met the horizon. As she watched, the line grew lavender, brightening into a pearly pink.

In the distance she thought she heard a voice—or was it the cry of a Manx shearwater? She looked up to the castle, eyes stinging from salt, and glimpsed what she thought was a mirage—a group of men, heading her way. All were in uniform—coast guard, police, and Royal Navy. Then she saw one figure, one unmistakable figure, leading them. Her heart lurched.

"Maggie!" she heard him say, as he fell to his knees and enveloped her in a hug.

David, oh, David. But "Ow" was all she could manage.

"Sorry." He dropped his embrace but kept one arm around her protectively.

Men in uniform swarmed about her. She felt hands under her shoulders, assisting her to her feet, swaddling her in wool blankets. "I'm fine, I'm fine," she kept protesting in a croak, though she wasn't at all sure that was true. The lump on the back of her skull felt huge and throbbing. She put a hand to it, and it came away sticky with blood.

Durgin and Frain stepped forward. "I see the gang's all here . . ." she tried to joke, but her knees buckled.

"Miss Hope!" It was Henrik Martens. "Let me through!"

When he arrived in front of her, he had the grace to clear his throat uncomfortably. "The Abwehr agent—"

"—was Teddy Crane," she finished. "He was manipulating Ramsey Novak, making him think this was a German prisoner of war camp and that you—*we*—were trying to make him spill." Despite the blankets, she was shivering. She gathered her strength and straightened to her full height. "Ramsey killed himself when he realized what he had done."

"And Crane? Was he on the boat? The one that sailed from here at sunset?"

"No. Well, yes, and no."

"*Yes and no?* Was he or wasn't he?"

Maggie would have laughed at the panic in Martens's face, but it would have hurt too much. "He was. He's dead." The words came with great effort. "He had me tied up. But I was able to get free. My plan was to dive overboard and swim back to shore."

She shuddered, remembering. "But he wouldn't let me go. We were fighting, and I took both of us over, into the water. He drowned." Her stomach turned as she realized how close he had been to taking her and meeting the submarine.

Martens was shouting something at her, sounding far away. "Did you tell him? Miss Hope, did you tell him anything?"

"No." Without warning, Maggie doubled over and vomited sea-water. She saw Martens's shoes moving out of the way of the spew. She dimly hoped she'd hit him anyway.

"You're sure?"

She wiped her mouth with the edge of a blanket. "Of course." She looked up at him with disgust. "You put me on this island so I wouldn't talk—and I didn't. Not to any of the other prisoners, not to Dr. Jaeger, either—and he kept asking me to reveal what I knew in our sessions. Crane read all of Jaeger's notes. If I'd trusted your Dr. Jaeger, Crane would have learned everything I know."

"You kept your secret, Miss Hope?" Martens repeated it, quieter now, as though to make sure.

"Yes. I kept *your* secret. *Our* secret."

"Thank God." His face sagged with relief. "We thank you."

"Tell the Prime Minister you're welcome. If he even knows about this place," she said, her teeth starting to chatter. Her clothes were soaked, cold, and muddy. The blankets weren't helping. She managed, "You need to go to the church . . ."

"The church?" David asked. "What church?"

"About a half mile inland. There are two injured agents there—Anna O'Malley and Quentin Asquith. Angus McNaughton's hurt and at the ghillie's cottage with Dr. Khan. Mrs. McNaughton and Murdo are there, too."

A man in a police captain's uniform barked orders, and men swiftly dispersed.

"Is anyone else still alive?" Martens asked, his voice incredulous.

"No," Maggie said flatly. "Everyone else is dead. Ten are dead." Ramsey was dead. Leo was dead. Camilla, Torvald, Helene, Dr.

Jaeger, Captain MacLean, Captain Evans, Ian . . . And now Teddy was dead, as well.

"Come on," David insisted, holding her tight. "Let's bring you inside, warm you up. Do you want to be carried?"

"I can walk," she rasped. She felt hot, so very hot, yet she couldn't stop shivering, her muscles wracked with spasms. "I—I—"

David caught her before she fell.

The Kapitänleutnant was on the U-boat's bridge, drinking cold coffee. He'd seen the fishing boat holed and sunk by the British corvette. His U-boat had taken damage before they'd submerged. Although they were safe for the moment, the Brits were on their trail. His head hurt from the strain and he couldn't remember the last time he'd slept.

"The corvette is pinging for us, Herr Kaleu."

"I am aware, Schäffler."

"The Abwehr agent died in the explosion."

"Indeed." It was over. The spy was dead. And even if he'd seen the danger and had been able to swim back to the island before the fishing boat exploded, there was nothing they could do now.

"They will send aircraft with radar—"

"Yes. We have limited mobility so close to the Scottish coast. It's too easy for the *wabos*," the Kapitänleutnant said, using slang for depth charges. "Engines full, best speed. Take us out beyond the twenty-fathom line and make a course for the North Irish Sea. Passing the forty-fathom line, make your depth one hundred and eighty feet. Is that clear?"

"Yes, Herr Kaleu." As Schäffler strode away, the first depth charge made a direct hit.

———

Maggie's window rattled as a deafening explosion detonated. In the distance, beyond the bay, there was a fountain of flame. It continued to smoke.

"I think that was the U-boat," David said. Maggie managed a small nod from the bed.

"This damn place is like an icebox," Frain groused, laying wood on the bracken kindling and then topping it with coal. Maggie almost smiled, seeing the head of MI-5 on his knees, waving a newspaper to help the flames catch hold.

There was a knock and Sayid entered, carrying a tray. "I have brandy and tea," he told them. "And some of those oatcakes." He set a tray down on the bedside table. "There are also some supplies."

Maggie caught a glimpse of cotton gauze, tape, and scissors. "It's a bit crowded in here. . . ." she murmured.

"I'm a doctor," Sayid explained, seeing David's scowl. "I'd like to make sure Mag—Miss Hope is all right." He patted the tartan-covered chair in front of the fire. "Why don't you come sit here, Miss Hope?" David gently helped her upright, and she managed the few steps before collapsing onto the chair.

David roamed about, examining the Victorian artwork, the grotesque finials on the bed, the antler pull in the bath. "Jumping Jupiter, what a hideous room. Whoever designed this should be shot."

"Actually . . ." Maggie tried to joke, then began coughing.

The fire in the hearth had caught and was burning brightly. Frain went to wash his hands as Sayid cleaned the wound on Maggie's head, then bandaged it.

"I can tell you're a good doctor," she said.

"You're worse for wear, but you'll be fine. Just a few scrapes and bruises. The swelling on your head should go down in a few days."

"Come on, out of those wet clothes," David ordered. "You'll catch your death of cold."

Maggie pressed her lips together. "I'd prefer not to have an audience."

"I think you need help," Sayid said. "As a physician—"

"No!" Maggie responded. Then, "David can stay."

Sayid gave them an odd look, but both he and Frain left. "Come now, don't brood," David admonished, undressing her as though she were a small child.

"I wasn't brooding."

"You were. Or sulking. Yes, sulking. And you're still shaking. Sulking and shaking."

"Not as much as before." She lifted her arms to let him pull the shirt over her head. "So many people . . ." she said in a hesitant voice. "Dead."

"But some of your friends are still alive—Anna, Quentin, and Angus McNaughton. They're being transported to the mainland. An ambulance will take them to hospital in Glasgow."

"Did Sayid—Dr. Khan—say anything? Do you think they'll make it?"

"He seemed confident in all of their recoveries," David reassured her.

"Thank heavens."

David was rummaging through her dresser. He pulled out a worn flannel nightgown. "Merciful Minerva, what is this *schmatta*?" he said, examining it with distaste.

"What does that even mean?"

"It's Yiddish for 'rag.' No wonder you don't have any lovers— your nighttime attire would scare off anyone. Speaking of lovers—" David's familiar grin flashed.

"Quiet, you," she ordered with affection.

"I think Durgin has it bad for you, Miss Hope. Stand up." He lifted the flannel over her head.

"Who knows? It's been a long time," she answered through fabric.

"Still . . . And this Dr. Khan? You're using first names?"

Her head poked through. "Nothing happened. Well, not really. He has to marry a woman of his own faith." She pushed her arms through the sleeves too quickly and winced.

David quirked an eyebrow. "I didn't say anything about marriage."

"David!" Maggie, now enveloped in dry, heavy fabric, sank back onto the wingback chair. "You should meet Quentin. He hates the castle too—called the décor 'Sir Walter Scott Vomited,' I think— I can't remember. . . ."

"I come from new money," he reminded her. "Doesn't mean you don't have taste. Or can't hire someone with taste . . ." He found her quilted slippers under the bed.

Slippers in hand, he turned. "Right, Mags? Maggie?"

But she had fallen asleep.

Chapter Twenty-four

Maggie floated up from the thick blackness of sleep, where she'd been dreaming of Blue Men, selkies, and U-boats.

Wait—the U-boat was real. Groaning, she pulled the blanket over her head, hiding. *And ten people dead.* At some point someone must have moved her to the bed, she realized. The fire had burned out; the room was cold. Then she threw off the covers and sat up, every fiber of her being screaming in protest. Her hand crept around to the bandages at the back of her head. It still hurt, but less.

She limped to the blackout curtains and pushed them aside. It was late; the sun was past dawn and the sky had a surreal bluish tinge. She peered out over the bay. The dinghies the men had used to come ashore were now tied to the dock. She could just make out the silhouette of a Royal Navy corvette on the horizon. For some bizarre reason, she remembered Mr. Churchill, who had been First Lord of the Admiralty, had had a hand in reviving the name *corvette* for the relatively small ships, and they all had flower names, such as the HMS *Alyssum* and the HMS *Chrysanthemum*. She almost smiled. It was easier to think of such things than of what had actually happened.

Biting her lip as various aches announced themselves, she changed into underthings, trousers, a blouse, and sweater. She leaned over to tie her shoes, and the memories of all the deaths surfaced. She felt tears prick behind her eyes, and then let them flow.

She cried until she had no more hot tears left, then went into the bathroom and scrubbed her salty, puffy face with harsh soap and cold water. Resolutely, she brushed her teeth and combed her hair, fixing it in low, tight rolls, checking them in the cracked mirror and adding extra pins for good measure. *Pull it together, Hope,* she told herself, even as she noticed her hands were shaking.

In the castle's kitchen, men in uniforms collected about the fireplace, smoking and drinking mugs of tea as they listened to the wireless. Mrs. McNaughton was the first to spot Maggie. She called, "Would you like some porridge, dear?" It was the first time she'd ever used a term of affection, and Maggie was suddenly unsure whether to laugh or start weeping again.

Maggie went to her. "How's your husband?"

"He's in Glasgow," the older woman responded, reaching for a mug. "And Murdo is with his *father*." Her emphasis was unmistakable. "We just received word—it might be slow going for a while, but my Angus is expected to keep his leg and make a full recovery." She laid a gentle hand on Maggie's arm. "We all will."

"Oh, that's wonderful news," Maggie said, with a genuine smile as she accepted the cup.

"Here." Mrs. McNaughton ladled salted porridge into a pottery bowl. "Have something to eat. You'll feel better."

Maggie took the offered dish and spoon. She sat down at the table as men in coast guard uniforms made room for her and passed buttered toast. The warm bread smelled heavenly. She heard the newscaster say: *The Allied forces of the Eighth Army, led by General Bernard Montgomery, have routed the Axis forces led by Field Marshal Erwin Rommel. The Huns are bolting in chaos as the Nazis panic after the Second Battle of El Alamein . . .*

The uniformed men cheered. But she saw in their eyes they knew all too well the cost in blood such a victory demanded.

"Any word on Miss O'Malley and Mr. Asquith?" she asked, taking a sip of steaming tea.

"The two from the chapel?" one guardsman, his skin the color and texture of leather, asked. She nodded. "Looks like they'll both pull through, lassie."

Maggie's throat unlocked. "Thank goodness." She realized she was ravenous.

A man in a police officer's uniform asked, "You're Miss Hope, yes?" Maggie nodded as she swallowed an enormous spoonful of salted porridge. "The police are examining the bodies now. They'll want your statement. Er, after you've eaten, of course."

So many dead. Tears stung her eyes and her stomach cramped. "Of course."

Colonel Martens appeared in the doorway. He caught Maggie's eye and she nodded, touching a napkin to her mouth and rising. "Colonel Martens," she said stiffly.

"Miss Hope," he replied in kind. "Would you mind coming with me? I'm using Captain Evans's office for the moment and I'd like to go over a few things with you. Tie up the loose ends."

As long as you don't have a hypodermic needle in your pocket, she thought as she followed him at a decided distance. "How long will you be here?" she inquired as she took a seat across from him in the castle's former library.

"Not long. Back to London tonight on the sleeper train."

Not me? She swallowed hard, trying to contain her disappointment. She was doomed to stay behind on the island, seeing ghosts of her fallen comrades around every corner, sitting out the war, doing nothing to help. . . .

Damn it, she had kept their precious secret. She didn't deserve to be here. She lifted her chin and looked Martens in the eye. "And me?"

Before Martens could answer, Frain entered the room without knocking. "Ah, there you are, Maggie," he said, dapper as ever, as if he'd just come from his club. "I was searching for you." He appraised her with cool admiration. Martens's eyebrows raised at the major general's use of her Christian name.

Both gave Maggie a small glow of satisfaction. "And I wanted to speak with you, Peter." They had used first names ever since her work for MI-5 at Windsor Castle.

"You'll be coming back with us, of course," he told her. "DCI Durgin, Mr. Greene, and me. We'll travel by train to Fort William. From there, we'll take the train down to London."

"I'm—I'm coming with you? I don't have to stay here?"

"That's correct," Frain answered, staring down Martens, who slowly nodded his agreement.

"I can go? Leave? I'm free?"

"Of course. If you can keep your secrets when confronted with a murderous Nazi spy on a deserted island, you can surely hold your tongue in London. And I want to offer you a new assignment—a job with the Double Cross Committee. Frankly, we need your help. This war's not half over yet. As Mr. Churchill said recently, 'It is not even the beginning of the end. But it is, perhaps, the end of the beginning.'"

Home. She felt as if she couldn't quite catch her breath for the amazement of it. And then she smiled.

Frain nodded to Martens. "Turn the radio to the Royal Observer Corps frequency, would you?"

A new radio had been brought in to replace the one Maggie had destroyed. Martens did as he was told. "Scarra calling," Frain said. "Patch me through to the Former Naval Officer in London, over."

Yes, sir. Hold on, sir.

There was a long pause, then a familiar voice inquired, *Frain. That you, Frain?* Maggie couldn't help herself—she gasped.

"Prime Minister," Frain replied, smiling at Maggie. "We caught our prey, sir. He's dead."

Good, good! Elation bubbled through the P.M.'s familiar rumble. *Did he chat with his friends before he was taken out?*

"Absolutely not."

Well done, then, well done!

"Don't congratulate me," Frain said. "By the time we arrived, it was all over. Agent Margaret Hope took down the quarry herself. The Spitfires destroyed the fishing boat. And then one of the corvettes took care of the U-boat."

Splendid. Told you we could rely on her. Where is she?

"Miss Hope is sitting right here with me, sir. She was injured, but we expect her to be back in fighting shape in no time."

Miss Hope!

Maggie beamed, hearing the imperious bellow. How many times, when she'd been his secretary, had he roared at her in exactly those cadences? "Yes, Mr. Churchill?"

Well done, Miss Hope.

"Thank you, sir." His words did a great deal to lift her battered heart.

The quarry . . . The P.M. paused and Maggie pictured him chewing on his cigar. . . . *Are his friends aware of his untimely demise?*

She knew what he was thinking. The U-boat had been destroyed. There were no witnesses to Teddy's death. She and Frain exchanged a look of understanding. "No, sir," she replied. Theodore Crane's identity could be used in the future by the XX Committee to send disinformation.

Excellent. Churchill chortled. *Make note of that, Frain! Out.*

Martens had risen and Frain turned to leave, when Maggie called, "Wait." She wanted to forget and yet she also wanted to know. "Who was Teddy—Theodore Crane—really?"

"I've done some investigating," Martens told her. "Theodore

Crane was a real Briton. He died under, shall we say, unusual circumstances and his identity was stolen by the German agent Adlar Geier. He was born on twenty-six May, nineteen hundred, in Berlin. His father and his father's family had been in the Army for generations. He graduated from Gross-Lichterfelde, married twice, had no children, and joined the National Socialist Party early on. He became friendly with Admiral Canaris and began a career in intelligence."

"Most of Wilhelm Canaris's spies have been, to be blunt, morons," Frain continued. "Poorly trained and unprepared for their missions. We caught most of them at the beginning of the war. But Geier was a different kind of agent, a sleeper—smart, superbly trained, patient. He faded into English life and waited to be activated. He was hired by Churchill's Toy Shop but couldn't pick up much. Then he somehow found out about this little camp Martens and Bishop established"—he didn't bother to hide the disdain in his tone—"and talked enough to have himself sent here. Thought it would be a terrific place to pick up secrets. And he wasn't wrong."

Maggie nodded.

"Crane—Geier—is another German spy who will be 'working' for us and the Double Cross Committee." Frain grinned wolfishly. "I say—let's deliver a message to his handlers, shall we? Would you like to do the honors?" He indicated the telegraph they had brought from the mainland.

"Me? Transmit to Abwehr?"

"I think you've earned it." He looked to the colonel. "Wouldn't you say, Martens." It was not a question.

"Er, yes."

"All right then."

"His code name is Petrus," Marcus said.

Peter, fisher of souls. "But my fist will differ."

Frain shrugged. "Tell them you're injured."

Maggie cracked her knuckles, then poised her index finger over the telegraph's black knob.

MISSION COMPROMISED. STOP. RENDEZVOUS INSECURE. STOP. INJURED. STOP. WILL MAKE CONTACT AGAIN ASAP. STOP. PETRUS. STOP. HEIL HITLER. END MESSAGE.

When she was finished, she leaned back in her chair, exhausted. Frain appraised Martens. "And we're shutting this place down."

Martens reddened. "We *need* a cooler. You know we do."

"Yes," agreed Frain, "but not here, and certainly with better rules in place. And you can't expect an SOE agent, just back from a mission, to turn on her fellow agents. No man left behind—*nemo resideo*—it's as old a concept as war itself. It's the spirit of Dunkirk!"

"Frain, you of all people should know: to win this war you must harden your heart. Christ, you need to rip the damn thing right out of your chest! We don't have time for honor—none of us. We must do whatever it takes to *win*."

"Yes," Frain replied, "but you've served in battle—you should understand that no soldier will turn on his—or her—fellow soldier. They are brothers—and sisters—in arms. And we shouldn't ask them to betray their own."

"They're spies, not soldiers."

"They're *soldiers*," Frain insisted. "Maybe not along traditional lines, Colonel Martens, but soldiers nonetheless."

"So it's all right to ask someone else to do it? Someone from the outside, then?" Martens's lip curled. "That will make it better? Neat and tidy?"

"I'll review it all when we return to London," Frain said. "Including the allegation that F-Section cells are compromised and no one's looking into what's happening."

"It's funny," Maggie mused, "how animals fight, and animals

kill. There's a dignity to what they do. That's not a judgment on humans, mind you," she added, "especially given our opponent—but an observation."

Frain nodded. He offered his hand to Maggie, who accepted it and rose. "As Dostoyevsky said, 'People speak sometimes about the animal cruelty of man, but that's terribly insulting and offensive to animals.'" He straightened his cuffs, their golden links gleaming. "Still, until we've won this war, I make no apologies."

Martens appeared flabbergasted. But Maggie knew Frain outranked him. With the confidence from her redemption, she asked Martens, "Are we done now? *Sir?*"

"I—I do believe we are, Miss Hope." Martens looked from her and the cat to Frain and then back again. "I do believe we are."

"*There* you are—" Durgin managed before Maggie leapt into his arms.

"James!" She buried her face in his shirt, her own arms reaching up and around his broad shoulders. After a long embrace, he pulled away, his eyes searching hers.

"Are you well?" The last time they had seen each other was on the tarmac before she'd gone to France, in April. *So many things have happened,* she thought, *and yet he's here.*

"Just a little worse for wear is all."

David cleared his throat. "I don't mean to interrupt, but Durgin here was trying to find you—"

"The Blackout Beast case—" The detective chief inspector nodded. "But I was also worried—"

"—we both were. No one knew where you were, not Chuck, not Sarah . . ."

"Sarah—is she well?" Maggie asked. "All things considered?"

"She's fine—living with her mother in Liverpool at the moment," Durgin assured her. "She even spoke of returning to London."

"And Chuck?"

"Doing well. Although I think her little boy and that feline of yours are quite demanding."

"And what about the Blackout Beast's case?"

"Reitter pleaded not guilty," Durgin said, frowning. "I'm afraid you're going to have to testify in court."

"So be it." Maggie blinked back happy tears. "I'm glad Chuck and Sarah are both all right. And I'm glad you noticed I was gone. Even if it was for a case." She tried to grin but her mouth didn't want to cooperate. "Was wondering exactly how long it might take."

"*Noticed!*" David spluttered. "We were worried sick about you, young lady!"

"Well, it's not as if I had any choice in the matter—" As Maggie looked at David and Durgin, she was filled with so many conflicting feelings—gratitude, resentment, joy, sadness . . . She inhaled, not wanting to cry. "Well, a lot's happened," she finished.

"I know," David replied. "And knowing you, that's an understatement." Durgin put his arm around her, and she leaned into his embrace.

"Ah, Maggie, er, Miss Hope, there you—" Sayid walked in, then stopped short at the sight of the three of them. "I, er, Major General Frain asked me to examine your head before you left." Sayid removed the cotton and adhesive tape.

"Yes, well, then," David said. "Perhaps we should leave you two. Right, Detective Chief Inspector?" Durgin made a noise of agreement, and they both left.

As Sayid examined the wound, Maggie asked, "How was it with Mr. and Mrs. McNaughton and Murdo?"

"Well, McNaughton will be fine—after a long recovery, of

course. And I do believe the family will be all right, too. They might not be overly demonstrative, but there's a great deal of love there. And with the father injured, they came to some sort of resolution."

"And Lady Beatrix?"

"She's coming forward to reclaim the island for all of them," he said. "For her and also the McNaughtons. Murdo is the heir, after all."

"Good, good," Maggie murmured as he layered on fresh bandages. "The island will be theirs—it seems only fitting."

"At first Lady Beatrix wanted to tear the castle down, burn it all, and salt the earth. But with the war on, she—and they—decided they'd keep it. They want to make it a home for convalescing veterans. Fresh air, good food, a change of scenery—"

"—and they'll be able to use the radio and *leave whenever they'd like,*" Maggie finished.

"Yes." Sayid added, "I think the castle, minus some taxidermy, will be a wonderful place for wounded soldiers to rest and recover. It will be a welcome change of purpose for the place. Instead of existing for the privileged few, it will serve the many who deserve our help."

"That's fantastic," Maggie told him, smiling. "The best possible ending."

"An ending and a new beginning. I'm staying on, actually," he said. "To help turn the castle into a hospital, and then to be a doctor on staff, to tend to the wounded."

"You're not coming back to London?" Maggie's heart sank.

"No," he replied. "I just feel—I feel they need me here. And as for me, after witnessing so much death, I want to tend to the living and help them recover. Nothing would make me feel more useful."

"They're lucky to have you," Maggie said, raising herself up on tiptoes to kiss his cheek.

Sayid pushed back a lock of hair from her face, tucking it behind her ear. "You've been through a lot."

"As have you."

"Are you all right? I mean your soul, not your body. It might take some time—"

"I'll be fine," Maggie assured him.

Sayid glanced down the hall. "DCI Durgin—"

"Yes?"

"Well . . ." There was an awkward pause and he gazed at her. "He seems to be a good man," Sayid said finally.

She thought of her detective and smiled. "He does, doesn't he?"

"You'll see him when you return to London?"

"I'm going to have to—I'll be testifying in a murder case he's involved with."

He shook his head. "You need to rest."

"I will."

"No you won't. I know you too well. . . . So you'll be spending time with him."

"Yes. . . . And you're still engaged."

"Yes." Then, "I wish—"

I wish we could be a normal couple, too. To go on dates—picnics in the park, ice skating, dancing. But it's just not to be. Maggie put her hand over his. "I know."

They heard footsteps approaching. It was the police officer who'd spoken with her earlier. "We need your statement now, Miss Hope, if you don't mind."

"I'll send you a copy of *Winnie-the-Pooh,*" she said as she left.

"Thank you," Sayid replied. "For everything."

When Maggie was finished with the police, she excused herself. There was one more thing she had to do. She went back to the library; using the ladder, she brought down all the boxes of photographs. One by one, she fed them into the greedy flames, burning all the evidence of Marcus Killoch's crimes. She didn't want to look at the pictures as they burst into flames, but couldn't help it. So many girls, their eyes haunted. She had to look away.

Lady Beatrix and Mrs. McNaughton entered the room and closed the thick wooden door behind them. "Is that all of them?" Lady Beatrix asked.

"Yes," Maggie replied as the final image caught the flames and flared. "All the pictures have been destroyed."

"Thank God," Mrs. McNaughton whispered, her hand clutching her crucifix.

As the last of the photographs crumbled into ash, Maggie just had to ask. "Lady Beatrix . . ."

"What is it, my dear?"

"Was it really Angus McNaughton who killed Sir Marcus and the men?"

Lady Beatrix quirked an eyebrow, then she and Mrs. McNaughton exchanged a look. "What would make you ask that, Miss Hope?"

Maggie couldn't explain, really. "A detective friend of mine calls it 'the gut.' It's just a feeling I have. That there may be just a bit more to the story."

"Angus McNaughton is a fine man," Lady Beatrix said. "And you're right, he's no killer. It was I," Lady Beatrix declared, as if relieved and even proud to tell her side of the story at long last. "I killed Marcus and his friends. They acted like animals, and I shot them like animals. Worse than animals. Animals might kill, but they're never cruel."

Maggie looked at both women with admiration, respect, and a tinge of fear. "Ladies," she said. "I swear—your secrets are safe with me."

Epilogue

In the slant of late afternoon sunlight, they reached the Fort William train station. The air was thick with coal smoke. At the end of the platform, an enormous green locomotive rumbled, building up power. Maggie, Frain, David, and Durgin made their way through the crowds: soldiers on leave, porters hauling baggage, and female conductors shouting. A shrill whistle blew. Maggie felt like a time traveler finally reaching the present after an arduous, perilous journey. Living at Killoch Castle had been not just isolating but lonely, heavy, and all-encompassing. Now, away from it all, she felt light, supported, perhaps even approaching a momentary contentment— even as she knew she would never forget the names and faces of all who were lost.

Through clouds of steam they boarded the train and presented their tickets. The Royal Scotsman pulled out from the station at exactly 4:30 P.M. by the hands of the enormous black clock. Maggie sat back in a plush chair in the first-class lounge car, lulled by the rocking of the car and the steady heartbeat of its engine. The sun shone in, making trapezoids on the carpet; she stretched to reach it, the warmth bathing her bruised hands.

Maggie glanced around her. It was the usual mix of gleaming

dark woods, polished brass, and tartan, but she was relieved to see there were no animal heads, only paintings of thistles. Outside, pine forests flashed by, punctuated by steep, snowcapped mountains, lochs, and fuzzy sheep grazing.

She sat next to David, with Durgin and Frain opposite; Frain was frowning at the newspaper in his lap, while Durgin made notes in a Moleskine journal. But David, as always, seemed to read her mind. "Everything all right, Mags?"

"Perfect," she replied.

A waiter in black tie approached. "Would you like anything?" he asked with a small bow. "Scotch, perhaps?"

No. It reminded her too much of endless tedious nights of cocktails in the great room in front of the inglenook fireplace. "Champagne, please."

David and Frain ordered single malt Scotches, Durgin asked for tea, and when everyone had something to drink, Maggie raised her flute. *"Sláinte,"* she toasted, the wine in her glass pink and sparkling.

"Cheers," the three men chorused.

"To you, Mags," David added. Then, "How does it feel to be off the island?"

"Indescribable. I feel reborn," Maggie answered. It was true, and yet the feeling was bittersweet. Nine people had been murdered, their lives cut deliberately and maliciously short. She could see them all: Evans, Ian, Dr. Jaeger, MacLean, Helene, Camilla, Torvald, Leo, and poor, misguided Ramsey. And Teddy—Adlar Geier—dead as well. Because of him, nine souls were gone, erased, voided. The nine would never see their families again, fall in love, smell a rose, read a book, kiss a child. And Sayid, Anna, Quentin, the McNaughton family, and Lady Beatrix—they had all barely escaped with their lives. So much violence in one week.

The train was passing over the graceful parapets of the Glenfinnan Viaduct, the longest railway bridge in Scotland. The viaduct overlooked the waters of Loch Shiel and the River Finnan, and also the Glenfinnan Monument, a tribute to those who fought in the bloody years of the Jacobite Risings. The lone kilted highlander at the monument's top was a poignant reminder of the seventeenth- and eighteenth-century clansmen who gave their lives to the cause.

The evening sun burned through the remaining clouds and split open a blue sky, making the waters glow. Before they pulled back into the woods, Maggie glimpsed the distinctive dark silhouette of an antlered stag at the top of a hill, backlit by bright gold.

She caught Durgin's eye and winked, which caused the detective to color and then beam with pleasure.

"So what will you do back in London?" Frain asked, reaching for his silver cigarette case. "We'll need someone as a handler for the newest recruit to the Twenty Committee, of course."

"Well, there's testifying in the trial of the Blackout Beast," Maggie replied. She glanced to Durgin. "Which I'm dreading. Still, it must be done. But other than that—I don't know, really. It might be time for something different."

"Different?" David asked. "Would you be willing to come back and work for the Boss?"

No! Never in a million years! "Perhaps something else."

"You don't need to decide today." David patted her hand and she smiled.

Frain narrowed his eyes. "You look well, all things considered."

"Thank you." *I owe it to the ten who'll never leave the island to never waste a precious moment. I owe them that.* Maggie realized that in just over twelve hours she'd be in London, with Chuck and K. And perhaps Sarah, soon enough. "I'm happy to be with all of you, right here and right now," she said, "and I'm happy to be traveling back to London. To home." She smiled. "I'm happy to be going home."

"By the way," said Durgin, reaching for a package he'd placed on the floor near his feet. "This is for you."

Maggie accepted the brown-paper-wrapped package. It was bulky and oddly shaped.

Frain nodded. "When we spoke to Mr. Asquith at the hospital, he made us promise, nay, *swear,* that we would give it to you."

Maggie got the knots undone and then opened the paper to reveal a coppery brown fox. "It's Monsieur Reynard!" she exclaimed, looking into the animal's beady black eyes.

"It's a what?" David asked.

"It's a *who,*" Maggie corrected, holding him close. "Monsieur Reynard—Reynard to his intimate acquaintances. It's Quentin's pet fox."

Seeing David's expression, she scolded, "No, don't judge—being trapped on a secluded island with all that taxidermy is enough to make anyone a bit daft. Monsieur Reynard helped him through." She petted the fur on the fox's head. Then something occurred to her and her lips began to twitch. The others noticed.

"Mags," David asked. "What's wrong?" Maggie burst into giddy laughter, hugging the fox to her.

"What is it?" Durgin leaned forward and Frain frowned.

"Mags?" David asked, concerned.

"Mr. K!" she answered finally, eyes sparkling with tears. "My cat. He's going to be so *mad* when I get home!"

Acknowledgments

Thank you, Kate Miciak, world's best (and certainly most patient) editor. Thank you also to the rest of "Team Maggie" at Penguin Random House, including Kim Hovey, Allison Schuster, Melissa Sanford, and Alyssa Matesic. Also, huge thanks to Vincent La Scala and the wonderful copy editors, as well as the talented production team, designers, and intrepid sales force. Thank you, too, to artist Mick Wiggins for yet another gorgeous cover painting.

Thanks to Victoria Skurnick, aka my beloved "Agent V," and the fantastic team at Levine Greenberg Rosten, including Jim Levine and Miek Coccia.

Thank you to Idria Barone Knecht. I truly don't know what I'd do without you—and I do know all of this would be a heck of a lot less fun. So thank you for your intelligence, your patience, and your humor.

Thanks to the warm and generous Sarah Winnington-Ingram, Kitty Winnington-Ingram, young Master Magnus, and the kind people of Arisaig House for letting me stay with them and helping me do research both in Arisaig and on the Isle of Rum. Not to mention sharing delicious Scottish food and drink!

Tapadh leat to Mary MacMaster from Arisaig House, who read over and corrected this Yank's Scottish Gaelic.

Thank you to Ronald Granieri, Director of Research, Lecturer in History at the Lauder Institute at the Wharton School at the University of Pennsylvania (as well as *paesan*) for checking over historical elements and being a terrific sounding board and font of knowledge.

Thanks to Dave Bermingham, another dear friend, for kind and patient assistance with military details (especially anything and everything to do with ships and submarines).

Thank you to Phyllis Brooks Schneider, British expat, London Blitz survivor, and friend, for reading for veracity and authenticity.

Thanks to Heidi Keefe, Wellesley College sister, for introducing me to British barrister Louise Delahunty, who made sure my British legal details were correct, for which I'm grateful.

Likewise, thank you to Meredith Norris, MD, Wellesley sister and dear friend who made sure all my medical details were correct (and bodies toppled over in the right position!).

Thanks to Scott Cameron for such great notes and constant enthusiastic support (and pretzels).

Last, but certainly not least, thank you to my husband, Noel MacNeal, and son, Matt MacNeal, who make everything possible (including a last-minute trip to Scotland).

Historical Notes

Yes, there really was a "cooler" for SOE agents who proved themselves unsuited for life in the field during World War II. It was run by the Security Section and located in Scotland, at Inverlair Lodge, in Invernesshire. According to my sources, there was a gorge around the property, which helped SOE keep prisoners from escaping. I thought an island would be more fun for my fictional inmates, and started to research isles in the Hebrides.

I found inspiration in visiting the very real Kinloch Castle, a Victorian hunting lodge on the Isle of Rum, just off Scotland's western coast. Kinloch Castle was built by Sir George Bullough, a textile tycoon from Lancashire who had inherited the island, which his father had purchased as a summer residence and shooting estate.

While the Bulloughs were in no way the inspiration for the fictional Killochs, salacious rumors and gossip about them abounded. One thing I *can* say for certain is that the ballroom of the castle really did have dumbwaiters so staff didn't enter and a curtain so the orchestra couldn't see the revelers down in the ballroom—make of that what you will. And although the Isle of Scarra is also fiction, it bears a strong resemblance to Rum in both its flora and fauna (those Manx shearwaters) and also its proximity to Mallaig and Arisaig.

I would like to thank the Isle of Rum Community Trust, "established in 2010 as a response to the need for a collective voice for community landowners in Scotland." I'd also like to thank the Kinloch Castle Friends Association, who provide public tours and are waging a campaign to save the deteriorating castle from demolition.

In addition to visiting Arisaig House (now a lovely bed and breakfast run by the Winnington-Ingrams) and Kinloch Castle on the Isle of Rum, I also consulted the books and documentaries listed below.

Books

Eccentric Wealth: The Bulloughs of Rum, by Alastair Scott

Castles in the Mist: The Victorian Transformation of the Highlands, by Robin Noble

Findings: Essays on the Natural and Unnatural World, by Kathleen Jamie

Bare Feet and Tackety Boots: A Boyhood on the Island of Rum, by Archie Cameron

Sea Room: An Island Life in the Hebrides, by Adam Nicolson

A Hunter's Heart: Honest Essays on Blood Sport, edited by David Petersen

MI5: British Security Service Operations, 1909–1945, by Nigel West

Kinloch Castle, Scotland's National Nature Reserves, Scottish Natural Heritage

Documentaries

History Rediscovered: Submarines at War

Secrets of War, season 4, episode 13, "Secret Submarines in World War II"

If you enjoyed *The Prisoner in the Castle*, you won't want to miss
the next suspenseful novel in the Maggie Hope series.
Read on for an exciting preview of

THE KING'S JUSTICE

by Susan Elia MacNeal

Coming soon from Bantam Books

Prologue

On the sand- and silt-covered banks of the Thames, the mudlarkers who patrolled the shores of the Thames paused their search for salable pieces of history to watch a fleet of German planes fly past. "Good riddance," Martha Biddle said to her young mudlarking partner, her twelve-year-old grandson Lewis.

Her grandson shook a pink fist at the sky. "And don't you come back!" he shouted, as the last aircraft disappeared back into the clouds, before returning his attention to the river's edge. These days the Thames was filled with ships of the British Navy, bristling with artillery, guided by tugs, as well as the Metropolitan Police's Marine unit boats and garbage scows, heaped with refuse and ashes, infested by rats. Each incoming tide of the Thames brought fresh debris, and when it receded, mysteries could be found in the silt. There was always trash, but there was always also the hope of treasure: the spiral necks of green wineglasses, small silver thimbles, naked white china dolls, gleaming coins from ancient times.

"Granny, look!" Lewis cried. "There's something down here—something big!"

"Careful now, love," Martha warned. A compact woman in her late fifties, Martha had iron-gray hair mostly covered by a floral scarf. She wore a shabby wool coat with buttons that strained at the holes; tall, black rubber waders protected her feet and legs.

The boy was using a sharp-edged trowel to scrape at something metal buried beneath the frozen sand, his small hands protected by oversized leather gloves. "Granny!" he called over, his voice carried by the chilly breeze. "I think it might be "—he poked at the object, making a metallic sound—"an anchor, maybe?"

"Careful, love," she said, picking her way over cautiously.

The boy brushed away more sand, broken shells, and bits of chipped red brick. "It's an old anchor by the looks of it—lots of rust." Lewis looked up to his grandmother, his eyes sparkling. "Most of it's still buried."

"Leave it be, pet—we aren't strong enough to carry it, anyway. And be careful—UXBs could be anywhere. 'Souvenirs' from the Blitz. Government hasn't dug them all up and disposed of them yet—probably never will." Martha fixed her gaze on the boy. "Don't mistake one for a buoy, lad."

"Yes, Granny." Lewis had heard his grandmother's warnings about unexploded bombs many times before. "I won't, Granny."

She caught his tone. "Don't 'Yes, Granny' me, young man!" she said, shaking her trowel at him. But she was smiling, and he grinned back before walking away from the anchor.

They were mudlarking on a stretch of the Thames near the Tower, the square Norman towers of the White Keep visible. Above, the sullen white sky had taken on a violet cast; it had been threatening snow all day and flakes were beginning to fall. The air on the riverbanks was cold, damp, and raw, and smelled of seaweed. To reach the banks, they had descended icy lurid-green moss-covered stone stairs, the remains of London's lost water-taxi service from Windsor to Greenwich, with its crumbling landing stations, river ways, and causeways. Victorian bronze verdigris lion heads, mooring rings clamped in their mouths, served as flood warnings.

When the lions drink, London will sink. When it's up to their manes, we'll go down the drains, the old saying went.

A seagull landed on a nearby boulder and eyed Martha and Lewis, letting out a harsh cry swallowed by the wind. "Nothing here for you!" Martha called, waving her arms at the bird. The gull ignored her and stayed where it was, preening. "Cheeky," she muttered.

An icy wind blew. She watched Lewis pull his hand-knit scarf tighter around his throat and look out over the Thames. The river was both ancient and ever-changing, broad and vast, murky and dangerous. Today the brackish water was a brownish-green color; a mixture of fresh from its estuarial inland origin and salt from its ultimate demise in the sea, mixed by the eddies of the current.

A small tugboat passed, causing waves to lap the pebbly shore. Above, seagulls circled, and higher up, a skein of geese flew by in a long, ragged V. There were people, small as ants, making their way back and forth across Tower Bridge. A dark-plumed cormorant dipped its yellow beak into the water and caught a wriggling eel; it twisted, trying to escape, as the bird carried it away through the air.

Lewis tore his eyes away from the sky and focused on the sand and stones in front of him. The best things to discover were the ancient love tokens—in the seventeenth century, it had been fashionable for young men to bend a silver sixpence in a circle to make a ring for their beloved. If she liked him, she'd keep it—but a good number had also ended up in the river. Even more modern rings were a fairly regular find. The Yanks loved them and bought them for their sweethearts back in the United States at inflated prices.

As grandmother and grandson worked in the fading afternoon light, they were aware of the tides, aware of the deep mud and silt that could suck them in. Still, something glinted in the muck. "Granny!" Lewis shouted.

Martha looked up, and seeing his joyful expression, made her way over. He was kneeling, digging away the cold sand with his gloved fingers. Finding the gloves too clumsy and awkward, he ripped them off and used his bare hands, finally uncovering a golden ring. He held it up reverently, like a priest with a consecrated host. "Here," he said, handing it to his grandmother.

She took out a pair of spectacles from her coat's breast pocket and put them on. Peering through the glass, she examined the details. "It's a poesy ring," she told him. "Probably from the time of Henry the Eighth." She squinted. "It says, 'I Live in Hope.'"

Lewis looked at her with wide eyes. "Is it good?"

"Oh, yes it's good, ducks—*marvelous,* even. It'll fetch a pretty penny from one of those loud gum-smacking Americans, to be sure. You did well, my love." She put a hand on his shoulder. "I always say mudlarking's twenty-five percent practice, twenty-five percent knowing where to look, twenty-five percent knowing what to look *for,* and twenty-five percent good luck. Today you had all four!"

Lewis grinned; he knew what a good find meant. "Tonight we'll have sausages?"

"And tonight we'll have sausages. Do you want to go home for tea now?" she asked, taking in his pink cheeks. The wind had picked up and snow stung their faces. "Or do you want to stay out longer?" She was experienced in gauging the tides and knew they still had some time left. "It's up to you, love."

Lewis was invigorated by his rare find. "Let's stay!"

Martha smiled. "All right, then." She looked up at the rising tide. "Just a half hour more, though, and then we'll go—"

"Hey, looky here—" he called, racing over to what he spied.

"Careful!"

"No, it's not a bomb, Granny—it's a suitcase." A brown leather valise, embossed with a rough crocodile pattern, poked up from a heap of seaweed.

"Lord have mercy." She'd read the papers. "Don't touch!" She shivered, not from the cold. "Let's go, Lewey. I baked some nice scones this morning and they're waiting for our tea. And we can pick up those sausages."

But Lewis was already dragging the suitcase from the shore to higher ground. He opened the lid. He looked up to his granny, face ashen. "Bones," he called over the wind.

"Jesus H. Christ," Martha muttered, making her way over. "Don't touch." Unheeding, Lewis began to search through the bones for any incriminating evidence. "I said, don't touch!" She grabbed his hands and smacked them.

He stopped and looked ashamed. "Sorry, Granny."

"Close that thing up and let's find us a copper," she told him in gentler tones. "Then he'll take care of the bones and take the case to the boys at Scotland Yard. They'll know what to do."

She grabbed at her head scarf, coming loose in the wind. "I hope."

PHOTO: © NOEL MACNEAL

SUSAN ELIA MACNEAL is the *New York Times, Washington Post,* and *USA Today* bestselling author of the Maggie Hope mystery series. She won the Barry Award and has been nominated for the Edgar, Macavity, Agatha, Left Coast Crime, Dilys, and ITW Thriller awards. She lives in Brooklyn, New York, with her husband and son.

susaneliamacneal.com
Facebook.com/maggiehopefans
Twitter: @susanmacneal
Instagram: @susaneliamacneal

ABOUT THE TYPE

This book was set in Fournier, a typeface named for Pierre-Simon Fournier (1712–68), the youngest son of a French printing family. He started out engraving woodblocks and large capitals, then moved on to fonts of type. In 1736 he began his own foundry and made several important contributions in the field of type design; he is said to have cut 147 alphabets of his own creation. Fournier is probably best remembered as the designer of St. Augustine Ordinaire, a face that served as the model for the Monotype Corporation's Fournier, which was released in 1925.